WHY DEAD GODS WEEP

Book Two *of* The Symphonic Masquerade

WHY DEAD GODS WEEP

Book Two *of*
The Symphonic Masquerade

EMERY BLAINE

First Published in the Republic of Ireland in 2025 by

Wild Door Publishing
77 Camden Street Lower,
Dublin City D02 XE80

An original CIP catalogue record of this title is available at the
British Library and Trinity College Dublin Library

How Strange the Son - Prequel Novella
Where the Silence Sings - Book One
Why Dead Gods Weep - Book Two

ISBN-13 978-1-0682824-6-1

Cover Illustration by SAPRO (@saproartist)

Typeset at Wild Door Publishing
Printed and bound by Ingram Content Group

www.wilddoorpublishing.com

To those who need to hear it:

you are not alone.

A Weathered Journal Entry, Written in Faded Ink

I met my partner today. She says she's sirin, but I'm not entirely sure what that is. Regardless, she's certainly not partial to the more common terms for her kind, so I'll simply stick with calling her by her given name; Amanastré.

I've heard stories about them, how they're perfectly adept in alkonostic arts, so precisely balanced that their eyes don't even weep with aether. So far, this rings true. Amanastré is so well attuned to alkonos that it seems to effortlessly bend to her will.

It's when I see feats like this that I feel for my poor Ca'ille. Her balance is so skewed towards creation that she couldn't manipulate alical manifestations even if it were through the purest, most potent ore in existence. It's not uncommon, not really, but most folks seem rather in the middle of the spectrum, dealing with elemental alica just fine.

I fear for those skewed towards destructive affinities. It must be daunting, living with knowledge that each manipulation could be your last. When they attune to it, their eyes seep crimson, same as when creation-skewed folks don't know how to filter it. It's truly a terrifying scene, this.

There must be something we can do to negate this through an external influence; perhaps a different kind of conduit? I have a few ideas. It just might work.

L-o-Y.

A Memory of Calamity

Sakaeri, witness to Seraeyu's bloody rise to power

The realm flipped sideways, frustration filtering from her heart, trickling down to her extremities. Sometimes, pacifism didn't cut it, and she didn't have time to deal with idealistic notions, especially not those which were doomed.

She saw the red splatted across woollen fibres, dusted with debris that could have been an arm, or perhaps it had once been a leg. Understanding and placation be damned.

Ever malevolent, the realms answered her with a crack of thunder, too loud to have been from the sky. All it took was a moment, and something in her tore as flesh split under pressure, claws ripping through, sparking with bloodlust. Someone screamed.

And then she was beside her father, the one who was always two steps away. And then he was lifting a calloused hand, eyes begging for exoneration; absolution. A treacherous part of her wished they said something else. An affirmation she longed to hear. But they did not, and now they never would. From this moment on, there wasn't a chance left. So, she took her dagger in hand, grasp stronger than her resolve, and she let tears shed freely, because she had to allow herself at least that.

She would not let his last thoughts be sullied with burden, so she told him, "I will watch them grow old in a peaceful realm, and I will love them as if they were my own."

His eyes closed then, grimacing mouth reflecting what could have been a smile.

She never thought metal so cruel until steel met skin.

CHAPTER ONE

It swam in her head as she watched his hand reach in vain. A possible future, promising and hopeful, slipped with callous circumstance through strained fingers. His tone of desperation didn't fit right around her name – not hers, definitely not her name – and it adhered to her soulsong, latching onto some buried dissect of her heart.

"Sakaeri!"

Too soon, the realm before her was made of miasmic lightning, swallowed whole as gravity again slung its weight upon them. Seraeyu crumbled beneath her and stilled, his eyes turning a terrifying shade of black before they wept crimson. His grip lost its strength as his chin dropped to his chest, as if threads snapped and recoiled. She scrambled to remove herself then, pushing Seraeyu away with a harsh shove, his form swaying like a rag-doll. Kaisa was quick to order her downed by way of two grunts – brutish figures she was unfamiliar with – while the Dracon of Orin looked on, displeased and gleaming in a swath of rich fabrics that had no place being worn at the likes of a Kaisan Pit.

Rust-metalled hands forced Sakaeri against the pavement. Intricate and shined mirrors of them caught Seraeyu in place, supporting him from collapse.

"And what shall we do with *you?*"

It was spat with a viperous smile, Kaisa's mouth full of scorn and sharp edges, the tightness of his grin giving away his disdain.

As Sakaeri mustered courage she wasn't sure she could follow through on, the Dracon tutted and sent a terse swat towards Seraeyu's shoulder. He was still hunched on his knees, his saviour Draconguard having stepped back. It could have been comical, in its own twisted way, that the father-killer himself seemed to regain his wits in artificial coordination with the Dracon's actions. It *would* have been if the situation weren't so dire. Sakaeri sneered at all their feet from her lowered vantage, her ear scraping the ground under some brainwashed worm's pressured hold atop her head.

"Praetor Thasian." The silken call from the Dracon had Seraeyu's attention darting to the side, both towards Orin's ruler and a small battalion of Draconguard dispersing the nearby crowd. "I'm afraid you have something on your face."

He didn't move yet, that much Sakaeri could still witness, and instead his head was bowed, his fists clenched and knuckles white. Sakaeri considered that if she were to do the same, she would surely draw blood. Her prediction rang true when his hands slowly unfurled, sharpened nails tinged painfully crimson at their tips.

Draconguard were filling up Sakaeri's periphery more and more with each passing second, the king who commanded them elegantly preening in her heightened position beside the toppled Praetor of Raenaru. Next to them, gaudily dressed, like he'd purposefully picked the most garish selection of attire simply because he could afford it, Pitmaster Kaisa was wearing an increasingly more petulant face. Sakaeri thought it a bit asinine, the way he glowered at Raenaru's greatest weapon. But Kaisa was nothing if not brazen.

"Praetor Thasian?" the Dracon questioned.

While smooth and refined, as diplomatic as it should sound when speaking to another of similar rank, Sakaeri picked up on the thinly veiled annoyance. It was a tone she'd often heard when a client was speaking to their mark while keeping clean appearances. Practising pleasantries while plotting assassinations. They all had the same ugly sneers beneath their carefully crafted smiles, minds full of dreadfully morbid machinations.

There was a passing beat where Seraeyu twitched, the movement barely catching the corner of Sakaeri's periphery. Her sight, strengthened by infusion, caught the frantic way his aethereal aura stuttered, as if it didn't know how to meld into something less volatile. When it did, it was taut. Like he'd forced something. Locked it away and held it at bay. When he stood, he did so slowly, stilted motions almost arthritic, as if each joint dragged against his body's demand.

Sakaeri stared at his shins. She wished it was his face instead. She wanted him to see the raging fire he'd kindled in her gaze. The one that promised him retribution.

"It's nothing," Seraeyu said, far too curt and casual, not at all matching the Dracon's address. He seemed to acknowledge this himself, continuing hoarsely, "Don't concern yourself with something so insignificant."

The Dracon offered a brief hum. "Is she not your problem, Praetor?"

"What an utter disappointment," said Kaisa. Sakaeri could feel his glare upon her even if she couldn't quite see it anymore, his stance having shifted towards the two regents. "Oh, pet, you do continue to disobey most ardently, don't you? Certainly, I'd be happy to relieve you of—"

Whatever Kaisa was spouting came to a halt as Seraeyu's energy pulsed violently. That wrangled aura lashed out in a silent burst, an oppressive wave washing over both them and their onlookers. The quiet that followed was long and crushing. Within it, Sakaeri attempted an odd angle to look up at them – the whole lot of their smarmy presences. All she managed was the sight of Seraeyu's feet taking a staggered step. Something about it struck discord in Sakaeri's soulsong. A distant whisper, warped in its delivery, communicated a shrouded insight she couldn't quite connect. Perhaps more odd, to his side, she recognised Kaisa's aborted retreat, followed by a quick reconsideration to stand his ground.

"You might be happy to do a good many things," Seraeyu said, his voice thick, calloused yet steady. It again pulled at something in Sakaeri's mind, something cloying for her memory to take note. "But taking her will not be one of them."

"What will you do about this? Either of you; Kaisa, Praetor? That masked daemon was clearly the perpetrator, and she—" the Dracon's accusatory finger manifested within Sakaeri's range of vision, "—is obviously a co-conspirator. She should be executed."

"No!" Seraeyu said, too fiercely, too quickly. He stilled as heavy attention rested on his shoulders. "No, I would like to deal with her myself."

"Oh?" Kaisa offered. There was something layered beneath it. "Why the change of heart, my most benevolent Praetor?" Sakaeri watched as Seraeyu stood still, that aura of his cascading around far too unstable. Especially compared to the Dracon's blanket of tempered faux-geniality and Kaisa's ridged binding of ill-formed patience. "I thought you enjoyed the shows. Hadn't you yourself said that any who stooped so low were nothing more than wretched, worthless vermin?"

"Do you question my authority?" Seraeyu asked, his posture screaming in defiance, a burgeoning crackle of Essence simmering loudly in his palms, escaping in smoky wisps. "Would you like to make an enemy of me, Kaisa?"

A strained bout followed, Kaisa finally relenting as he said, "Praetor Thasian, you and I have discussed certain terms." A reminder, Sakaeri considered, as much as it was a threat. And yet, Seraeyu stepped forward once more, a little surer. A little more menacing. Kaisa hesitated, then he carefully retreated with his palms lifted in surrender. "Of course not, Praetor. But if you have no particular use for her, I can—"

"I would rather die," Sakaeri croaked out, grunting against the Kaisan's hold against the back of her head, "than go anywhere with any of you."

With that, Sakaeri considered, she may have just signed her own death warrant.

Finally, Seraeyu said, "She is Raenaruan, and is therefore under my domain."

"Yet she is conscribed to me for offences of the past," Kaisa retorted.

Sakaeri wanted to crow at that, sing to all the realms about how ridiculous the statement was. Instead, she said, "You took your revenge, and all Raenaru owes its loss to your act." She spat, a globby pink splatter hitting the stone below. "If anything, you should be persecuted for that."

"What is she speaking of?" The Dracon demanded, circling enough that Sakaeri could side-eye her with what she hoped was a threatening look.

"Delusions of grandeur. She's convinced I wiped out the Sirin," said Kaisa. "I'm afraid she's painted me as quite the villain. In fact, it was her who was contracted with my death, a mission she failed. Thus, I have repaid her efforts in kind. Nothing less, nothing more. Her time in the arena has obviously twisted her perception, poor bird."

"I see," said the Dracon. "However, if the Praetor requests that this woman be handed over to him, it's well within his jurisdiction to do so. She is, as stated, Raenaruan, and now that her involvement with the suspected terrorist has come to light, he has every right to question her himself." The Dracon paused, impatient and pinch-mouthed. She turned to Seraeyu.

"Perhaps you intend to interrogate her? I only ask that, if you do, you share your findings with your alliances."

"I wouldn't consider doing anything less," Seraeyu offered, and if Sakaeri hadn't known the ghost of who Seraeyu once was, she wouldn't have picked up on the relief hidden under that surface-level obligation.

"This is most disappointing," Kaisa said, and Sakaeri would bet he looked about as sour as he sounded. "But who am I to question the Praetor?" He sighed obstinately. Sakaeri wished she had enough strength left in her body to shatter his cheekbone. "Though I do hope we can chat in the near future about other things."

Whatever *other things* might be, Sakaeri was already sure she didn't like them. It promised undesirable ripples; a nefarious implication, to be sure.

"You've managed to keep our presence hushed, but I'm not sure how you intend to keep two men disappearing through a self-made gate held under discretion."

Sakaeri noticed Seraeyu's sudden twitch at the Dracon's words, that strange unbound quality of his being wobbling erratically again, and she thought it odd. It didn't sit right. Someone who coldly mauled his own kin shouldn't seem nervous.

Nerves had no place in a monster like that. Sakaeri would know.

"Yes, well, I have precautions in place for attendees of higher distinction, such as yourselves. But this was a most unexpected event." She could *hear* Kaisa's sardonic smile, his chin just above her eyeline. "I'm afraid not much can be done about any rumours that start to swirl about our Bone Soldier. Rest assured, however, that your presence will remain under wraps with my helpful influence."

A reassurance and a threat; how very similar to the Dracon Kaisa sounded. It was something Sakaeri was familiar with among political rings, this tired game. It extended to crime lords as well, it seemed. Notorious syndicate heads who appeared to indeed be ingratiating themselves into the upper echelons of aristocracy.

"Well," the Dracon stated, absently motioning to her Draconguard. "Our efforts on Mhedoon are quite timely after all. Praetor Thasian, I will assist you with the transport of your prisoner."

"Lift your hand," Seraeyu told the Kaisan who forced Sakaeri's head down.

"Praetor Thasian, I do not think that's wise," Kaisa reasoned, but it met deaf ears.

Not a moment later, Sakaeri felt the pressure against her head abate and she was able to fully glare at her perpetrators. Her freedom was still locked behind heavy gauntlets that pressed down upon her shoulders, her position one of fealty as her knees dug into the ground below. But her eyes burned into them, unwavering.

In the distance, the crowd was being ushered by Kaisan, Draconguard acting as a barrier, the gap between spectators and regents widening. That left Sakaeri staring down a small party of the realms' most fearsome leaders. Her stomach twisted while her presumably broken rib screamed at the bodily shift from flattened to upright.

Seraeyu, however, was not looking back at her. Instead, his still-bloodied expression was fixed on Kaisa, who was looking back at him with barely obscured perplexity.

And Seraeyu read different, peculiar under Sakaeri's new perspective.

Something shifted, perhaps, but it was present in a way it hadn't been when he was in the stands above the raving crowds of onlookers. He flickered his gaze in her direction, his focus melancholic as it hit her face, then unreadable when it latched onto her blunted horns.

"I will handle my affairs internally. This one included, as it seems fit to do so now."

"There, done. Now, what do you intend to do, Kaisa?" the Dracon asked again, ignoring the narrowed look Kaisa levelled against Seraeyu.

In turn, Seraeyu ignored the Dracon's query.

"Our terms," Seraeyu began, and Sakaeri noticed his hands clasping in front of him. It made him appear diplomatic, despite the drying burgundy that painted his stoic expression. But she also recognised it as a way to hide anxious tremors; to provide comfort. "They can be discussed again. Soon. But, as I'm sure you'd agree, circumstances have changed."

"If he has gained strength, Praetor, then we must work as one."

Kaisa's statement landed an unease in the air as Seraeyu studied the surly pitmaster.

Sakaeri saw the puzzled furrow of Seraeyu's brow. *Sakaeri* saw the guarded lock of his shoulders. *Sakaeri*, in her tired, battle-weary state, wondered if she imagined the little nuances that reminded her of a younger boy she once knew.

"And we will," said Seraeyu. "But right now, you will relinquish Sakaeri Naen, hired hand of Oagyu Thasian, to me."

Naen. She hated that term. *Naen. Nothing. No one. Nameless.*

The signature of a bastard child, pariah, or hermit.

That seemed to have done what it needed to, and Kaisa offered a flourished bow as he stepped back and his Kaisan let go of her entirely. As Sakaeri stood, the Dracon motioned indistinctly towards Seraeyu's face, seemingly under duress even looking at his spoilt pristine persona. Seraeyu made the effort to scrub at his cheeks.

Sakaeri, upon unsteady feet, noticed the way he avoided looking at the scarlet smear left on his wrists. The *audacity* he had to be squeamish when he'd already committed such brutal acts. She snarled with what depleting energy she had left, forcing Seraeyu's attention.

His patricidal eyes slid over. His betrayal-heavy gaze met hers. His ruthless hand stretched out, and it almost looked like Aeyun's.

"It's time to return to Raenaru," he said, sombre.

"Why would I follow you anywhere?" Sakaeri asked, unable to keep the scorn from leeching through, even as she wheezed. "Why would you invite me like it's a favour, after all you've done?"

If there was surprise, it was quashed with precision. Seraeyu watched her, his hand lingering in the air for only a moment longer until it fell back to his side. He looked down, but she noticed the way his eyes flickered first towards Kaisa, then the Dracon.

"You worked for my father once—"

"And you ensured there was no piece of him left to employ me," Sakaeri was quick to spit back. But she wasn't quite prepared for the look he returned to her. Something wide-eyed and plagued with dissonant murmurs she couldn't hear.

It was buried just as quickly as the past cracks had been.

"Perhaps you will find that, despite it all, you and I share a similar vision," Seraeyu said, his gaze boring into her. He swallowed once, then added, "And if you do not, you're welcome to return to Raenaru's embrace, or to the dirt of the Pit, if you so choose."

Sakaeri paused. There was something she was not reading, something that was misaligned. And yet she couldn't help herself, so she asked, "You're offering me death?"

"I'm offering you an out," said Seraeyu.

"A gracious provision," the Dracon said, her impatience manifesting with the idle, rhythmic taps of her fingers against her arm. "I would accept the Praetor's offer if I were you. Though, I am not. Perhaps you prefer the violence of Kaisa's games."

Sakaeri said nothing. She instead took in Kaisa's wooden posture, as if he was actively reining himself in, and the Dracon's surly scrutiny. The armour-laden footmen around them dutifully remained impartial, standard infantry glaives held steady, knowing their opinion to be moot. Seraeyu looked back at her, and she saw something different in his amber gaze.

"I will tell you nothing," she warned, but Seraeyu smiled.

It was smug and suited him entirely, something well in character that she recognised, and so far from the cold visage she'd come to know. And yet, there was a hard edge to the corners of it. Something a bit guarded, a bit morose. A burden hung there.

"Yet to be seen," said Seraeyu. "Rosalyn," he addressed the Dracon, and the use of her given name seemed to startle her. "I expect you will not betray my trust if I leave you and Kaisa here to talk?"

"No." The Dracon smiled in that fake way those with too much power always did, full of saccharine lies. "Of course not. Would you like an escort back to Raenaru now? My Draconguard will be happy to assist an ally as valuable as yourself."

"Seeing as my Sentinels are not present, I would expect at least one of you to see to my safe return," Seraeyu countered, just as full of kindly aggression.

"My Kaisan are—" Kaisa looked up past them towards the arena doors, "—on damage control right now. So, if the Dracon would be so kind to spare a few Draconguard, I believe we would all find benefit in that."

14

"And you can fix this?" Seraeyu asked, his hands once again clasped before him.

"This?" Kaisa gestured towards where the crowds had been contained. "Oh yes, they will not speak of names. You need not waste one pretty little thought on that."

The Dracon smiled again, turning towards Seraeyu. "I will have a chat here. How about we arrange a meeting where you can discuss any findings gleaned? I will ensure that we are all on the same page." She gracefully spun back towards Kaisa. "As I'm sure we are."

"We surely are," Kaisa said, too mulish to be considered genuine.

"Kaisa," Seraeyu called. "I will not accept betrayal."

It left a sour note among the group of them, but Kaisa grinned as he said, "And you will have none."

Seraeyu was fully being led by the Draconguard, that much was clear to Sakaeri. To her, he nearly seemed like a young fowl teetering in a world anew, and it was so very jarring. Where was the derisive presence he'd lorded over the populace? Where was the icy glare he cast upon all who dare defy him? Who in all the void was this stilted, silent man with a shifting gaze that replaced the steel-hearted Praetor?

Sakaeri noticed, too. When she wheezed too loudly, her abdomen crying out to *please just stop*, Seraeyu would slow his pace for her, thus forcing the Draconguard to slow. He was accommodating for her, but that was also incorrect. Misaligned. In her mind's eye, she replayed the last time she'd been this close to him, when he'd pierced a hole through Jourae's chest and ripped Raeyu's muscles apart, cracking her bones without so much as a blink.

Seraeyu spared a glance in her direction, barely caught from the corner of her eye. It wasn't right, the way his gaze was softened. Wounded almost.

Sakaeri did not have time for cruel games.

"Tell me, *Praetor*," Sakaeri hissed, heaving in a breath as her chest constricted. "What twisted lie are you telling yourself? How have you rationalised your transgressions?"

This time, Seraeyu did not look at her as he murmured, "Which transgressions are you referring to?"

The gleaming, onyx-armoured Draconguard around them – only four, one flanking each corner – dutifully trekked on, but Sakaeri did not forget them. They may have their eyes trained forwards, but their ears were certainly leant inwards.

"You want to air your dirty, traitorous laundry here?"

There was no reason to protect him. She had no reason to protect him.

Even so, the accusations curled upon her tongue, refusing to slip past her lips.

"You're a fool. You've always been a damned fool," she said with a scoff. A pulse of pain caused her to wince, unsteady in her step. Seraeyu slowed further. "Do not mistake yourself for someone forgivable. I've made peace with my place among the realms. You should reconcile yours."

She grimaced, aching to hold her side, but unable with the Orinian shackles entrapping her wrists. They were a Paladian make. A unique manifestation of vulcan ore that was unfortunately capable of swallowing tunes before they manifest, perfect for suppression.

"You cannot hide your true form from the endless aether."

"That is, perhaps, my very worst fear," Seraeyu said with little mirth.

After a moment's reprieve and a few turns around sterile-looking corridors, Sakaeri asked, "What is the point of taking me alive, Seraeyu?" His steps faltered, but he held his head high. "You know I will not submit to you. You know I will not satisfy your demands. I know you know, because you have not forgotten me, even if you've forgotten yourself."

Seraeyu blinked too rapidly, purposefully aiming his gaze towards the ceiling. His hands clasped again, and he took a deep breath in through his nose. The blood was no longer marring his features, but there was a splotchy flush appearing on his cheeks, his nose crinkling in a purposeful effort to dissuade any remit of emotion.

"No, I have not forgotten you," is what he returned with, the octave of his voice slightly off, as if wrenched, lower than his natural tenor.

The rest of their walk was quiet. Sakaeri's vision started to swim at its corners. She took the occasional glance in Seraeyu's direction, but his eyes never flickered to her in return. Instead, his focus stayed resolutely ahead, pinned to the middle-distance between the front two Draconguard's shoulders. Sakaeri had half a mind to ask if Seraeyu would like another prisoner, doubling his prize. That wouldn't be any sort of liberation for Goeth, though. Surely, that would only be a path to further suffering.

She would miss him. Him and his beguiling humour.

"Praetor," one of the Draconguard prompted as they arrived at a sheltered parking bay, his arm stretched towards an idle land-skimmer. Another of his compatriots went about unlatching the heavy metal door, preparing the craft for their entry.

"Much obliged," Seraeyu responded. It came off despondent, lost in lethargy.

Sakaeri was herded in first, the Draconguard by the door urging her in none too kindly. She was followed first by Seraeyu, then by the remaining Draconguard. The pair left outside stared at her through helms made of metal and hardened ore, faceless and detached. The perfect shield for a king like the Dracon.

Sounds of movement, muffled through the reinforced exterior, reverberated until the craft shook with the slam of an egress near its bonnet. Muted conversation, quick and precise, slipped through the grated barrier between the driver's quarters and where the rest of them resided. Sakaeri took it upon herself to slump onto one of the leather-trimmed benches within, since no one seemed arsed to direct her otherwise.

One of the Draconguard, the one closest to Seraeyu, sat stiffly and outside arm's reach. He inhaled, as if preparing to say something. The direction of his helm indicated his intention to voice whatever thought directly to Seraeyu. After a moment, he seemed to rethink his actions. He instead shifted to face forward, his standard-issue infantry glaive grasped firmly before him like a grounding instrument.

Sakaeri regarded the Draconguard's behaviour with interest. She could almost sense the contention in the man's head as her exhaustion swept in.

Within moments, however, dreamless sleep beckoned.

CHAPTER TWO

Sakaeri sucked in a breath, twitching away from whatever had landed on her ankle. As it turned out, the *what* was Seraeyu's flighty poke.

Discombobulated, she blinked herself awake and took stock of the inside of the land-skimmer. Two Draconguard, tense but restraining themselves thanks to Seraeyu's placating, outfaced palm. Seraeyu himself looked shaken at her silent calculation, and there was that look in his eyes again that ate at her soulsong.

"We're arriving at Keou," he said.

Keou? Sakaeri frowned as she got her bearings.

We're on Raenaru? I missed the jump?

Seraeyu eyed her cautiously, saying, "You need medical attention."

Sakaeri scoffed. "Medical attention. Without—"

It hung there precariously, her bleary awareness nearly betraying her admission.

Without Aeyun, she considered, *my recovery will be poorly at best*. His secret practices, etched throughout his veins by a realm unknown, were the only she knew of that could repair as much as regenerate. Healing practices throughout the realms were limited to salves and balms and tinctures. His, though, they were small miracles that shouldn't be possible.

"Can you … can you stand?" Seraeyu asked. It had barely been a whisper. Behind him, the faceless Draconguard stared on.

Sakaeri considered her options. Be stubborn and stay put, likely causing hassle for the lot of them, but also for herself by undue consequence. Be compliant and stand, but risk setting a precedent. Or worse, *try* to stand and instead collapse entirely. All options led to an admission of weak positioning, and she didn't like it. Sakaeri had learnt many lifetimes ago that what she liked was not often what she got, however. In defiance of that, she had to work situations to the least of her detriment.

Right now, taking advantage of Seraeyu's befuddling hospitality was what would get her the furthest. It sounded like he had intentions of helping her recovery, for whatever gain that might lend him. If Sakaeri could just get a bit stronger, enough to toss a knife and sling a tune, she could manipulate his misplaced generosity and get the upper hand.

Eventually.

What it meant now was being vulnerable in reciprocity, as much as she perished the thought. But Sakaeri was practical. And Sakaeri was used to doing things she didn't like.

As such, she responded, "Probably not."

Seraeyu reached out again, then flinched back, his whole body teetering away. "Do you want—?"

Sakaeri was used to things she didn't like, but she loathed the idea of

Jourae's killer holding her – supporting her, lifting her with his fiendish grasp – so she said, "We'd better let the armoured suits do it."

"Right," Seraeyu said, and Sakaeri convinced herself she hadn't heard dejection.

As advised, one of the Draconguard came over – the same who'd nearly spoken out of place before – and he knelt down to offer Sakaeri a shoulder to grasp. She bit back a grimace and took the provided crutch, allowing him to lift them both to standing height. It took everything in her to not loudly bemoan her torn abdomen. With a strained sigh, Sakaeri tried not to imagine whatever transfer had occurred between the land and water on Lu-Ghan

There was a knock at the sea-skimmer's door. Seraeyu's attention snapped towards the noise, and he made to move in its direction. The other Draconguard slipped ahead and barred his access, her broad back operating as a wall.

"Speak," the Draconguard called.

"Transfer when ready; glory be to Orin's Majesty."

"Glory be to Orin," the Draconguard responded dutifully in that way one only could if the sentiment was iterated and reiterated many times over. She turned back around, saying, "At your word, Praetor."

"Please," Seraeyu said, not quite looking at her, but at the door she guarded. Anticipating.

The Draconguard gave a rap against the metal shell, warning of their exit.

Light flooded the opening, first by the slim line of its seal, then throughout the entire egress. It washed into the interior, soaking across the group of them, and Sakaeri watched as it filtered from Seraeyu's horns down to his boot-clad feet, his amber-brown eyes warming like honey as they glistened, dewy. From the abrupt change or something else entirely, Sakaeri couldn't be sure.

"If you would," the Draconguard by the door beckoned.

Seraeyu shook himself from his reverie. He sent a look in Sakaeri's direction – *apprehension, yearning, determination* – and then he gathered his hands together before him and set the pace, his boots landing with finality against the hull's metal grates.

Out in the daylight, Sakaeri could see the distant outline of Keou's main docks, their own mooring having taken place at a private wharf, reserved for more high-profile travellers. Sakaeri supposed that *Praetor* could fairly be considered of high profile. At the junction of the pier, two Sentinels stood, their bodies risen like pillars on either side of the slatted boards.

The procession was sluggish, led by the tall Draconguard with the broad back, followed by Seraeyu, Sakaeri, then finally the silently contentious Draconguard in the rear. As they walked, Sakaeri breathed in Raenaru, revelling in its seaweed-scented shores and rocky, cliffy profile that sprouted leafy growths, a chorus of chirps sounding like fanfare. It was a sight she'd not witnessed for what felt like millennia. For how much things had changed, it may as well have been that long.

Sakaeri focused on steady steps. She would not trip or falter here. Not now. She would hold her head high, greeting her homerealm with dignity.

When the Sentinels became more than distant impressions, she noted that they stood stern, rigid in a way the versions in her memory had not. Their visors were drawn, only showing the pull of their mirrored frowns, and their armoured, gloved hands remained near the hilts of sheathed nephrite swords, refined to sturdy perfection. Sakaeri wondered if they recognised her; she did not recognise them.

"We've anxiously awaited your return, Praetor," the Sentinel on the right stated as the group of them came to a halt. "There has been an incident in Narui." He paused, and Sakaeri thought she spotted a scowl. "The parties involved have been taken into custody for excessive force."

There was a tense expanse of bloated silence before the next words were spoken, and Sakaeri found herself staring at the back of Seraeyu's head.

"Thank you for informing me," said Seraeyu.

The realm ground to a halt again until the Sentinel on the left cleared her throat. "Perhaps we will first return to Haebal, and then the Praetor will decide his next action."

Seraeyu perked at her voice, a subtle lift of his shoulders, and he agreed with her suggestion. He seemed to first debate something, looking around the group of elite guards, then he shook off whatever hesitation he had and requested that they head on.

Sakaeri watched. No one said a word to her. In fact, it was almost like she were mere luggage. Not a captive at all, despite her fetters. The two Draconguard shifted position to the back, sandwiching her and Seraeyu between them and the Sentinels leading the pack. Behind them, back at the pier, Sakaeri heard the sea-skimmer rev up again, unmoored and ready to return to whatever post the final pair of Draconguard were meant to be stationed.

On the walk to the land-skimmer, its body a familiar shell of bulk and metal machinery over treaded wheels, Sakaeri roved her eyes across Keou's lush coastal expanses. The town was still too far to see clearly, a smattering of roofs and barges in the distance, but she strained her vision to narrow her field of focus, calling upon her alica-enhanced eyes for assistance.

There were dock workers milling about the piers, loading and unloading boats of all creeds. The market was still standing, hawkers calling out for their wares to be purchased, and the busker that always performed near the square played his instrument in daily routine, fingers plucking at vibrating strings.

It was odd to see so little changed, and it unsettled something in her chest.

Beyond the normalcy and monotony, she did spot subtle things, however. A woman crumpled in a doorjamb, a cup extended in her hand. A child slipping nimble fingers into a stranger's pocket, retrieving a purse that would be sorely missed. A group of haggard-looking youths mumbling and glaring by storage barrels, one of them twisting an alicant between their fingers. And then there was the hooded figure leant against a warehouse.

When her gaze trailed from cape-dusted feet to a shrouded face, hidden beneath a cowl, it was like a jolt of recognition speared through her body. The feeling of being watched in return sank in like an anchor to water. It was then that Sakaeri felt marked.

"Sakaeri." Seraeyu's voice drew her back. "It's time to go."

It wasn't a suggestion, nor was it an order. Nothing more or less than a simple statement.

Sakaeri once again found herself taking stock of Seraeyu, the fearsome, murderous Praetor of Raenaru. The merciless usurper who took a guardian from her that she'd never truly had the pleasure of knowing, but so wished she had. There he stood, fingers woven, holding tightly to opposite knuckles, gaze angled down, withdrawn.

He looked up at her then, without hesitance. "It's time."

She wasn't entirely sure he was speaking to her at all.

"You're not a face I expected to see again," the apothecary said, vowels tinged with a drawl not quite abandoned from Raenaru's mountainous lands of Yunae. "The Praetor wants you evaluated. Would you mind sitting up there?"

The spot the man indicated was a cot with fresh-laid linen, situated next to a local strain of flora that was meant to provide a calming aura. A bloom that was aptly named a serenity blossom, even its colouring a pleasant and powdery yellow. It, however, did nothing to quell the rising nerves firing throughout Sakaeri's system.

The windows of their transport had been eclipsed throughout the duration of the trip, not allowing her to glean any insight as to the state of the Raenaru's capital city. Instead, they'd been driven straight into the parking bay, and she could practically feel Seraeyu's frame growing more and more tense the longer the journey went. He broke rank with her when they'd reached the Thasian Tower, allowing himself to be swept away by his entourage of multi-realmal guards. But that was only after giving the directive to ensure that Sakaeri received medical attention, a task handed to the Sentinel he'd reacted to at the docks. He'd also told the Sentinel, after some thought, to bring Sakaeri to the Praetor's room after her evaluation. Sakaeri found this to be strange phrasing; was *he* not Praetor, after all?

That very same Sentinel stood watch by the door, arms folded and mouth turned down in a contemplative frown. She'd yet to raise her own visor, but Sakaeri could feel her staunch attention, nonetheless. The apothecary, though, wrinkled with age and mottled with sunspots, was instead very much focused on rifling through various bottles and jars.

"Something to do with your side, is it? And I can tell you're dehydrated. Probably deficient in iron as well." He paused, taking a glance at her, his half-moon glasses sliding down his sharp nose. "Muscle cramps? Dizziness?"

Sakaeri couldn't help the bitter snarl that rumbled from her throat. "What do you think, phys?"

"Adding irritable to the list," he mumbled, plucking a particularly gooey vial from the mix.

Sakaeri huffed a groan before shifting her weight from her less accommodating side. "It's my rib," she admitted. "I think it's broken."

"I'm afraid that's likely only the just of it," the apothecary murmured, reaching for a mortar and pestle, as well as a tray of several ore and herbs. "And whatever you've been doing has not been kind to your wellbeing."

Sakaeri bit back her scathing remark about *whatever she'd been doing* and instead asked, "Does Seraeyu bring all his prisoners in for treatment? Directing them to his chambers afterwards?"

That had the apothecary lingering, peeking over his shoulder, just once, before he went back to his shuffling. "You *do* have restraints on, don't you?" It was less of a question and more of an observance. "It is not my place to speak of Praetor Thasian's ongoings."

"Then what can you speak of?"

"That I provide medical treatment to those I'm asked to, as well as those in need."

"You should count yourself lucky, Sirin," the Sentinel groused, bringing Sakaeri's attention snapping over. "If what you're accused of rings true, it will be all of Raenaru that seeks vengeance."

That gave Sakaeri pause. "And what is it that I'm accused of, exactly?"

It must have held enough weight that the Sentinel wanted to pin Sakaeri where she sat with her own eyes, because she slipped her visor up and glared sternly. Something cold coiled around her pupils. "I would not play ignorant when the Praetor lends you an ear, as he's so graciously decided to do."

"What have I been accused of?" Sakaeri countered, undeterred.

"Treason."

Ludicrous. Sakaeri thought. *Absolute bollocks.*

"You and all Sirin."

"The Sirin …" Sakaeri gnawed on the scattered sentiment before continuing, "are accused of treason? Since when? By whom?"

The apothecary started crushing an ailment-curing mix, the scrape of stone on stone filling the room. Sakaeri stared down the Sentinel, just as the Sentinel did her. A strange gurgle of a laugh erupted from Sakaeri's diaphragm, and she punctuated it was a snort.

"What a truly *ridiculous* joke," she said. "This whole mess of a life is a *joke.*"

The apothecary returned to Sakaeri, a rolling cart teeming with jarred treatments in tow. He said, barely a murmur, "I didn't know you were a

Sirin."

Sakaeri looked at him as he uncorked a bottle, obediently focused on his task. He was not a new face within the Tower. She remembered his mug from when the Thasian siblings would need tending to for something or another. Or when a housemaid did.

Ah. Sakaeri *did* know him then. Surely, that was where he recognised her from, too.

Giving into her own curiosity, and wishing to derail the current line of conversation, Sakaeri asked, "How is Haebal? The realms have little knowledge of the state of things here, and I—" she grimaced at the recollection of her months in hazy-minded solitude. "I certainly don't."

"Haebal is as Haebal ever was," the apothecary stated. "Resilient."

Sakaeri sniffed and wrinkled her nose, looking down. She no longer wished to connect gazes with either of the room's other inhabitants.

"And hopeful," the Sentinel added. Sakaeri was sure it was meant as a poke to her pride. "We are a people whose will is not easily broken. And the Praetor is ensuring our strength only builds."

"I see," said Sakaeri.

"You will," the Sentinel responded, and Sakaeri gave a befuddled glower at the tone of it.

Do you have Raenaru entirely on your side, Seraeyu? Have you bled your ideals and your lies into their brains so easily? Have they dismissed Raeyu's absence so quickly?

"Here," the apothecary said, handing her a cup of something nauseating.

He listed brief directives she should follow for recovery of several conditions – from broken bones to a broken immune system – and she distantly tried to file the prescriptive list away. When he told her to drink the concoction in her hand, she did, because what did she have to lose? Drowsiness, swift and consuming, hit her like a brick wall.

As her realm spun, she watched the Sentinel's glare turned from resolute to inquisitive just as the dregs of awareness relinquished their hold.

CHAPTER THREE

Sakaeri awoke staring at a velvet canopy.

It was unfamiliar and unwelcomed, and it had her hinging up in a soon-to-be regretted sudden shift. The pain of the movement hit her first, an aggrieved groan pulling from her sternum, then she slammed back into luxurious bed dressings with a second jolt of discomfort. Grunting a heartily delivered curse, she took time to elevate herself on the second attempt. When she was finally sat upright, she saw Seraeyu situated in a chair beside the door, his hands cradling his head.

"I thought I could do this," Seraeyu said, but it was muffled by the downward tilt of his chin. "I'd hoped I could."

Sakaeri waited. And as she waited, she observed. Seraeyu, the room; they were both tearing at the seams, rife with shadows of lost prevalence and glory, sullied by time and turmoil. What struck her most, however, was that the room was not Seraeyu's own. She recognised nothing within it, and there was something else picking at her senses, telling her that the ransacked state of the place teased elusive clarity.

"I need to ask you." It was only a whisper, floating across debris and the remnants of some record of destruction. "Were you there?"

That question wasn't one Sakaeri expected, and she wasn't sure what it was referring to. Groggily considering the Paladian cuffs that still encircled her wrists, she dared to ask, "Where?"

Seraeyu winced, looking so unlike his holocaster persona. It was jarring, and it had her still-foggy mind spinning. *Who is this man wearing Seraeyu Thasian's face?*

"When Raeyu disappeared."

Sakaeri had to strain her ears to hear it.

"When Uruji-nee and my father died. When—"

The halt was followed by what may have been a whimper, she couldn't tell.

When Uruji died? Was I there? Wouldn't he know? Wouldn't he already know that?

"Are you ... playing games?" she asked, low and viperous. "Of course, I was there; you know as well as I do that—"

Wait, her sluggish mind told her. *Wait. Watch. Listen.*

Seraeyu had frozen. Slowly, so slowly, he removed his fingers from his dishevelled hair. Instead, he stared at his open palms, watching them shake.

He did not clasp them. Not this time.

"What did I ... What did I do, then?"

The question hung in the stagnant air, swirling with everything else that didn't make sense. Sakaeri was stumped, and every fibre of her being told her to tread carefully – no quick movements – because what Seraeyu asked did not align with the truths of her haze-plagued memory.

"What do you mean?" she asked, slow and wary.

Seraeyu didn't respond right away. He took long moments to twist his hands over, clenching them atop his knees before he looked up. Sakaeri wasn't sure she'd seen such a cratered expression on his face in all her memory, like a soldier whose mind hadn't left the battlefield. A certain depth layered atop something searing and dreadful, eroding a space that may have once been bright and optimistic.

"How did they die?"

The tension in Sakaeri's head wanted her to turn away. But she couldn't. Her attention was locked on his red-rimmed gaze, and it held her there in a vice, unwilling to allow her escape. Sakaeri swallowed once, a dry and grating thing. *What's his game?*

She remained silent, and Seraeyu finally looked down again with a defeated sort of huff.

"Yes, well, I suppose that makes sense," he mumbled.

Sakaeri very much thought the opposite.

With a sniff, Seraeyu rose but did not approach her. Instead, he walked towards the window, peering at the realm and city beyond. From her vantage, Sakaeri could see the bright, sun-dyed sky and some of the tallest rooflines. She could also see the tight pull of Seraeyu's frown splitting his profile, his fingers interwoven, his posture again rigid.

"These are my father's quarters," said Seraeyu. "I couldn't bear to see his face, so I took his picture down."

Sakaeri didn't dare move. She didn't dare even flinch. She hung on each word, each minute statement, all in the hopes of peeling back whatever varnish Seraeyu had cloaked himself in. It was falling, disintegrating in a lacklustre display, and she so very much wanted to see what horrors it would reveal once vanished.

"I didn't want you thrown into a prison, but I know better than anyone that this room isn't very far from that." Seraeyu placed a hand on the glass barrier before him, the press of his fingers as soft as the words that followed. "I didn't know what else to do."

"What do you want, Seraeyu?"

"Freedom," he said, punctuating it with a bitter little laugh.

"You're more free now than you have ever been," Sakaeri said, tiredly turning her bound wrists this and that way, testing her sluggish reactions.

"I'm terrified that you may be right."

"Had you always planned it?" Sakaeri asked. "Or was it more opportunistic than that?"

"Planned what?"

"Don't be coy."

" … Is this about Raeyu?"

Sakaeri snarled, straightening up, ignoring the sting that dug into her side as a consequence of her rash repositioning. "Of course, it's about Raeyu! And everything! How long had you planned to seize praetorship?

How long had you pretended to be Untuned?"

Seraeyu did not turn to her. Instead, he angled himself further from view, his figure silhouetted by the glare of the window, his frame only a darkened shadow among the bleeding light.

"What changed at the Kaisan Pit? What happened to Aeyun?"

He knows it was Aeyun. Sakaeri's thoughts unravelled, an unfamiliar fear creeping in. *Oh stars, he knows it was Aeyun who fought; who created a rift to somewhere else.*

"What do you mean?"

"He could have killed me. Ended it." There was an unfitting blandness to the words. "But maybe he wasn't …"

Seraeyu finally turned towards her once more, a thoughtful expression sketched across his features. He regarded Sakaeri where she sat, a gnarled impression of the woman she was the last time her presence haunted the halls of the Thasian Tower. Woozy in her recovery, broken in bone, but still stubborn to a fault. Seraeyu looked like he wanted to ask something more, like it was teetering just between his teeth and his tongue. But instead his hand drifted towards his chest. It hovered there momentarily before dropping completely.

"I …" he said, then stopped. His brows furrowed and his mouth flattened, a debate passing behind his eyes. Then his gaze hardened with a steely determination. "It was not something I'd considered. I saw a chance—"

It was stilted. Like Seraeyu was forcing himself not to waver. To aim his words right at Sakaeri's soulsong, shattering and almighty.

"—and I took it."

Later, Sakaeri would reprimand herself for staying frozen. Later, she would berate herself for not responding, or not driving some sort of weaponised object into his heart or throat then and there. But, in that moment, she processed the revelation – his callous admission – in petrified silence, barely taking note as he fled the room and the door locked shut on his departure.

As it turned out, there wasn't much to do in a fallen patriarch's chambers. Sakaeri had already rifled through what was readily available, finding the room suspiciously barren of anything she might consider useful. That said, there was something strangely gratifying about adorning robes meant for diplomats, luxurious fabrics that held history itself within their fibres.

The fun of that didn't last long, though, as too soon her reflection looked unrecognisable, covered in furs and silks and velvets. When she gazed in the mirror, she began seeing sneered grimaces stitching over her mild consideration, twisting her image into that of an imposing presence. Something too like the late Praetor Oagyu himself.

Red smattered across a fine-woven rug. A fleshy chunk, bits scattered—

She shrugged off the robe and hung it away, out of sight. The next hours were spent quietly moaning and grumbling about her aching side as she picked up indiscernible ceramic shards – a lamp, perhaps? – and remnants of regalia strewn across the floor. Not once did she let her mind stray from her simple tasks. Not once did she allow her thoughts to wonder into the ropy, treacherous malaise of *why*.

When the moon graced the skies with its ambient glow, hung over the city like a beacon, a knock resounded on the door that barricaded her from the rest of the Tower.

At first, Sakaeri didn't bother retreating from her spot by the window. The new arrival would enter, or they would not. And that was that. But it was the raised voices that had her attention flitting towards the barrier, curiosity clawing its way into her brain.

"I've told you that you may leave," Seraeyu's voice grated, irritated. "Dismissed."

"With all due respect, Praetor—" It was a masculine timbre, one Sakaeri didn't recognise. "—I cannot, in good faith, allow you to face this woman alone. I cannot understand how you are so keen to place yourself in a room, one on one, with someone who did what *she'd* done at those wretched games—" The pause was so abrupt, Sakaeri could almost picture the faceless man's jaw snapping shut. Only those allowed to have opinions could share them, so maybe this was a grunt who'd gulped down too much bravado for his own good. "I speak out of turn, Praetor."

"You do. And you are meddling in affairs outside your dominion."

There was a bout filled with what Sakaeri imagined was a loaded stare-down, and she found herself folding her arms across her body, intrigued. Was this a Draconguard? Which one? She'd bet coin that it's the same who'd been weighted down in a cloud of contention.

"For fuck's sake – I'm just bringing her dinner," Seraeyu lamented, breaking his noble persona, sounding addled with both exhaustion and annoyance.

"And I offered to do it in your stead."

"And I said no."

"So, I accompanied you."

"Directly against my request for you to kindly leave me be."

"It's for your own safety, Praetor. You are not only important to Raenaru, but all of Orin."

There was a loud groan, then the door was swinging open to reveal a very sulky Seraeyu Thasian, hands gripping a dining tray far too tightly, and one hulking Draconguard behind his shoulder, like a mollusc combating the raging ocean.

Sakaeri peered towards them, her expression entirely nonplussed, but her mind spinning across frantic leaps and hurdles. As her gaze latched onto Seraeyu's face, she saw his consternation dissipate into something less volatile, less fiery, settling instead into a melancholic appraisal of the now-tidied quarters. This was the third facet of Seraeyu Thasian that

Sakaeri found herself cataloguing; the version that didn't quite exist in the mists of the past or the dust of holocaster projections. This one, this forlorn, sombre one.

Seraeyu's tray contents rattled as his steps carried him into the room. The Draconguard loomed behind him, closing the door and situating himself in front of it. His eyes bore holes into Sakaeri even through his helmet. As the presumed dinner was set aside, placed upon a clutter-free dresser, Seraeyu took a second, just a moment's pause.

"I asked the chefs to make Yisnugaru," he said, still with his back turned.

A surprised, dark chortle erupted from Sakaeri's throat. Wasn't it just disgustingly humorous that he'd had that *stupid* celebratory soup concocted for her. It wasn't her birthday, and there wasn't any festival. Was this meant to be a homecoming olive branch of sorts?

"Is this *funny* to you?" Sakaeri growled, acutely aware of the Draconguard's attention. "Some sort of cruel 'welcome home' gag?"

"I didn't think about it like that," said Seraeyu.

"Really," she drawled the word out, rolling it sourly across her tongue.

Seraeyu didn't clarify. Instead, he stayed where he was, head bowed towards the wall. Sakaeri didn't drop her gaze, staring at him from the other side of the room. The moon's light beamed through the window, its radiant bridge serving as their only connection across the floor. Sakaeri couldn't build a clear picture of Seraeyu, not when he finally turned and looked at her with an expression that brought her back to a dirty alley in the backstreets of Haebal, a deal gone wrong and a regent brawling below his station.

Seraeyu opened his mouth, inhaling in preparation to expel some thought – compose a precipice of conversation – but then he clammed up instead, mouth thinning in a self-depreciating line.

"I'll leave you to your dinner," he said.

It stirred something discomforting and off kilter.

His eyes averted hers as he strode to the door, waving the Draconguard aside. Dutifully, the sentient bulwark sidestepped the Praetor, then he slipped out the door behind him. Before the Draconguard vacated entirely, however, Sakaeri felt one last lingering stare drift over her. She didn't give him the satisfaction of acknowledgement. Damned Orinian lapdog.

"Praetor, are your chambers not the other direction?" sounded through the thick door.

"Indeed," Seraeyu responded after a long moment. "But I'm not headed there. Leave me be. You've *kept me safe*, as you wished. Now go and drink your sorrows like the rest of the soldiers do when they think no one is looking."

"Praetor—"

"This is the last time I will ask nicely."

" … Understood. Glory be – Goodnight, Praetor."

As the footsteps faded, Sakaeri considered the memory that in the opposite direction of Seraeyu's room was Raeyu's room. She turned to face that general route, staring aimlessly at the wall. Something innocuous yet solemn hung in the air after their departure, and she couldn't parse just what it meant.

Only after long minutes of contemplation, Sakaeri meandered over to the stew, lifting the cloche to scowl at it. She gave a frustrated sigh at the constricted movement the Paladian cuffs instilled, but she dipped a spoon in the liquid, swirling it once in distaste.

"Reunited in a life well-realised," she said.

It was one of the platitudes behind the meal. Sakaeri scoffed and slurped a serving of the frothy broth.

Welcome home, Sakaeri.

CHAPTER FOUR

Patterns start to form when one has enough time to give them thought, and Sakaeri was great at deduction. She was *deadly* at deduction. So, after a fitful sleep in a cold room with a colder ambiance, Sakaeri awoke feeling revived. Her head began to lose the fog imposed by Kaisa's scaly rune, the threads of her scattered mind repairing, and she stared at the horizon beyond the late Oagyu's window, stained orange in the morning's arrival.

Sakaeri could do this. She could steel herself, and she could figure out what had gone awry. Because Seraeyu Thasian was showing too many faces, and there was something that lingered in his presence that did not feel whole. A fragmentation, pulling in different directions. When she looked at him, she saw Jourae's killer – a bloodied fist erupting through a chest – but he rarely gazed back at her, as if her stare alone would burn him from the inside out. And what was that, guilt? No, it was something else.

So when he knocked on the door – a courtesy that he was not obliged to apply – she turned her gaze over her shoulder, waiting. What face would he adopt this morning?

Seraeyu entered quietly, just the subtle twist of a doorknob and the rustle of cloth. This time, a Sentinel flanked him. Sakaeri recognised her as the one who'd threatened her with Haebal's hope, as if that would be a worthwhile thing to scare Sakaeri with. Seraeyu's attention first flickered over to the tray full of dirty dishware, then to Sakaeri's form, framed by blistering pockets of the sunrise.

"You ate your meal," he stated, a soft sentiment in the early hours.

"I did," she responded, equally still.

"I'm glad," said Seraeyu. Sakaeri did not respond.

Seraeyu eased further into the room, and the Sentinel hovered behind him, her visible expression something cross. *People really don't want him alone with me*, Sakaeri considered. *I suppose that's sensible.*

Today, Seraeyu was dressed simply. Just a pressed pair of trousers and a silken shirt, no gems or jewels to speak of. His eyes were rimmed red, either from sleep or something else, and he looked beside himself. A bit ghostly, if Sakaeri had to attribute a word to it. He hesitated where he stood, seemingly torn between walking towards her or the tray, then he decided to clear the previous night's nourishment, his back to her. Sakaeri observed him in silence, wary of her own watcher.

Seraeyu paused when he'd picked up the tray, but still said nothing.

"Did you expect to die, then?" Sakaeri asked, pointed and even.

Seraeyu turned to her, finally, and his eyes shone misery, just as they had the previous day. "When?"

"By the hands of The Bone Soldier."

Seraeyu's brow knit, bewildered. "Who?"

Sakaeri, not letting her indifference fail, continued on, "The man in the mask."

After a long moment, he questioned, "Hana?" And that didn't sit well at all.

Sakaeri felt the gaze of the Sentinel, heavy and hardened upon her profile. Still, she watched Seraeyu as his furrowed brow betrayed his interest, attention rapt, almost single-minded in its dedication. It whispered a buried desperation, and Sakaeri did not relinquish her focus, instead calling to see deeper, further. They may have been able to silence her duet with alicant, but her attunement to her own eyes was infallible; a part of her very being.

His balance was wrong. Seraeyu was all volatile questioning and insecurity, wrapped in a blanket of wispy indecision and a barrier of determination that coloured his entire form with a pearly, impenetrable haze. His consciousness was sewn tight, not pliable as it had been in days long passed. Sakaeri could not divine beyond that initial facia of steadfastness.

Seraeyu was shielding something, whether knowingly or not, and Sakaeri grimaced at the familiarity of it all.

"What do you know of *Hana*?"

Seraeyu was not trained in espionage. He was educated in diplomatic relations, fine arts, and delegated the responsibility of learning the realms' histories if for nothing more than posterity. When his eyes flitted over to the Sentinel by the door, the one who continuously aimed to menace Sakaeri into docile subjugation with her stern gaze, Sakaeri read his confliction, and it was enough to make her curious.

"You heretics defiled that sacred name, one of yours claiming it and pretending to watch over Raeyu Thasian. It was with blind trust that we allowed it, and it was by blind trust that we were spurned," the Sentinel spat, but Sakaeri couldn't bring herself to care enough to turn towards her and her righteous claims.

If Haebal believed that the Sirin inflicted this, it made sense that they would attribute it to *Hana*, the most visible presentation of who they believed to be a hired mercenary. Sakaeri again found herself cursing Aeyun's foolishness, but her focus never strayed from Seraeyu, who watched her with matched devotion.

"Hana is not the threat with which I am concerned," Seraeyu seemed to settle on.

"Praetor Thasian—"

"Hana is—" Seraeyu interrupted the Sentinel. His face screwed up in irritation, and elusive, choice words were instead discarded for: "Frustrating. More of a full hearty idiot than he is any sort of mastermind."

Sakaeri couldn't help the terribly amused cackle that erupted from her then, but she schooled herself just as quickly. "On that, at least, we agree."

It fell quiet. A quick glance to the side illuminated the Sentinel's thinly held containment. Her nostrils flared, a thwarted tongue in her mouth, some retort or sermon swallowed with visible regret.

"You're in better health than before," Seraeyu announced, perhaps not for Sakaeri herself. "I will call on you for a proper interrogation soon."

"I'm giddy with anticipation," Sakaeri said flatly.

They held each other's gazes for another moment, then Seraeyu departed with little pomp, waving the brooding Sentinel out the door with a now uncanny lackadaisical quality, a leftover from his youth.

After that, Sakaeri coaxed herself into a false sense of confidence. Maybe there was more to it. Maybe, somehow, the child in her memories was not lost – or perhaps he was, but he was recoverable. Maybe, just as Aeyun had secrets that laid buried, Seraeyu had answers just waiting to be unearthed.

When Seraeyu returned a couple days later, however, his demeanour was not recognisable as the man who had slowed his gait to accommodate Sakaeri's injuries, nor was it reminiscent of the man who had held his head in his hands or offered her stew.

The man who entered that day did so with a confident, angry stride, the door slamming shut behind him and him alone. There was no greeting nor warning, only his stormy amber eyes sliding towards her and widening, almost as if he didn't expect to see her by the window.

This was not the man she knew. This was the man from the holocaster.

"Seraeyu," she dared, defying her own wit.

A manic, broken imitation of a grin cracked across his face, and a cackle that rang just as unhinged tore out behind it. "Oh, child. How could you be so clumsy?"

"What?" Sakaeri asked, despite herself once more, because this was not Seraeyu. This was *not* Seraeyu.

Seraeyu hummed and ran his fingers through his hair once, staring up at the ceiling, like he was relishing the whole encounter. Only for a moment. Then his gaze settled back, and Sakaeri felt her blood run cold. Her heart thrummed in her chest, rattling for escape the longer their eyes connected. Sakaeri embraced fear without meaning to, its clammy hands squeezing her insides. This was not Seraeyu Thasian.

"And you are Yu-ta, too." Seraeyu scowled as something clicked. "You're the Sirin." He stepped forward, and it looked pained, like every step was wading through thick water. Dark, miasmic energy collected at his fingertips, and his eyes ebbed obsidian at their edges.

Sakaeri stumbled back once, her shoulder connecting with the wall.

This is not Seraeyu. This is not Seraeyu. This is not Seraeyu. This is not—

"None will deny me my right when I have come this far," Seraeyu growled, and Sakaeri felt like her realm became nothing but her own impression and the daemonic presence in front of her. Nothing but hate and grief and disgust, all aimed at her. All pushing down on her, peeling her eyes open to see – *see* how foul her existence was. "Perhaps you mean something." It was whispered, Seraeyu's glaring expression close, his fingers wrapped around her neck. "Will you watch as the light fades from this one's eyes? As I was forced to witness? This is your lesson, child. You do not deny me. I will reach Ka'la'drius – he will know, and we will right these wretched realms—"

Blackened, spindly threads crawled like lightning up Seraeyu's neck, splaying on his cheeks as mirrors of them wrapped up the length of his arm. Viscous, crimson tears pooled in his eyes, a trail slipping down, colouring that side of his face a ghoulish red.

Sakaeri stared on as the veins in Seraeyu's neck tightened, almost a mockery of her own asphyxiation.

"Stop," Seraeyu choked out.

The hand around Sakaeri's throat tightened, sharp nails piercing skin, and Seraeyu's expression faltered. Whatever consumed him shuddered and receded, his grip instead relinquishing as he threw himself back, tumbling bodily onto the floor with a thud. Remnants of Essence buzzed in the surrounding air, his breathing laboured as the sickened inky spindles shrunk way, escaping under his collar.

Sakaeri gasped in breath that she was unaware had escaped. Her back slid down the wall, legs failing to hold her weight.

"Some fucking interrogation," she said, but her voice barely sounded her own.

"I shouldn't have kept you here," said Seraeyu. His words were rough, chaffed by misuse of Essence. Sakaeri was familiar with the symptom now, and it flashed a familiar face across her memory. "I should have known better. Fuck, you almost died."

Her enhanced eyes observed the oppressive energy having abated, washed away by the tepid worry surrounding Seraeyu and his now curled form. His wrists came up to rub away the red marring his face.

Sakaeri breathed in slow. Wait. Watch. Listen.

"Did he know? Did he tell you why he spared me? If his solution was to take my tuning again, well it didn't work!"

"What?"

"Aeyun!" Seraeyu hissed with one last swipe across his cheek. He huffed an indignant sigh. "The damned bastard who seemingly works on nothing more than hare-brained schemes!"

Sakaeri wanted to work through one thing at a time, starting with, "Again? What do you mean, take your tuning *again*?"

Seraeyu hesitated, his fussing coming to a slow, agitated halt. "Like he did the first time. To prevent *this*, I presume."

"The first time?"

"When I was a child – do none of you absolute dolts actually speak to one another? Is it all smoke and mirrors to you lot?"

"What are you talking about?"

"Oh stars, it is. It *is*. And to think, I allowed myself to be jealous, once."

"*What* are you talking about?"

Seraeyu levelled her with a steady stare. "Aeyun did something and

33

took my ability to tune shortly after he arrived in Haebal. In the same way he took it again at the Kaisan Pit. I don't know *how* he did it, but he managed because I cannot tune with alicant anymore, which I guess generally includes the one embedded in me. Usually. Not since leaving the arena."

Mechanically, Sakaeri asked, "Aeyun took your ability to tune, and you can't tune with alicant *anymore*, since he took it *again*?"

"Yes," Seraeyu grumped.

"Aeyun took your ability to tune shortly after he arrived in Haebal?"

"Yes."

"Is Aeyun part Yun? Or … or all Yun?"

"I severely doubt that." Seraeyu's tone matched his unimpressed expression.

"Why?"

"Because—" Seraeyu paused, considering. He tilted his head a bit, like he was evaluating something on Sakaeri's face. "He didn't tell you anything, did he?" It had been a breathy rhetoric, almost sounding in awe. "Just what is he hoping to accomplish by that, I wonder."

Once disparate fibres started to weave together, forming a much clearer picture than iterations she'd scrambled together in the past. For as many knots pulled tight, however, other holes unravelled, leaving gaps in her knowledge. And, if nothing else, Sakaeri loved a good puzzle to ponder.

"What *is* he trying to accomplish?" Sakaeri wondered aloud in reflection. "Why do you know about Aeyun, and what did you mean when you said the alicant embedded in you?"

At that question, Seraeyu looked a bit stricken. He floundered a moment, and Sakaeri found she hated the pierce of pity that met her. "You didn't know?"

Rather than give him the satisfaction of her questioning again, she let fleeting seconds speak her affirmation. He seemed to get the message.

"Sakaeri." Seraeyu sighed, shifting his gaze beyond her shoulder, instead casting it across Haebal's skyline. "We don't have some gift. There is no bloodline carrying power. There is no Bloodsong to be passed down. There is only a lie, and those gullible enough to believe it." He laughed, an ugly thing to be paired with his aristocratic air, held firm whether purposeful or not. "Thasian is nothing more than a name, and the Legacy is nothing more than lore. The scars we carry are from a rite, conducted by the Thasian-nee simply because they are learnt in the art of it, no other reason. Our so-called Bloodsong is nothing but a crystal fused to our bones. There is nothing *special* about the Thasian, other than our flagrant disregard for everything but our placement in the power hierarchy that rules these realms.

"As for Aeyun … Well, he made me a promise. I intend to hold him to it."

CHAPTER FIVE

Aeyun turned over a trinket in his hand, head angled down so that his face remained shrouded under his hood. The make of the item was an odd thing, carved of wood, made to resemble a si'nac – a sly little forest critter with too-innocent eyes – like one might find in the Ou'grobh.

He wondered if the shopkeeper knew it was Da'garu who carved it. Probably not.

"Two or three loaves of this?" Davah asked.

Aeyun was still amazed at how easily he adopted the distinctive Ca'loran brogue.

Debating his selection, Davah stood beside Aeyun, hoodless as his face held no history, no tainted web of fear, attached to it. In his grasp was a fresh-made pan of sourdough, packaged in waxen cloth. As he debated his find, the bell that hung above the small grocer's door chimed, a group of chattering girls walking in. Their footsteps caused the old floorboards to groan, the tremors reverberating heavily in Aeyun's chest.

After a brief internal quandary, Aeyun answered, "Three."

"Right," said Davah.

That decided, two additional loaves were tossed into the basket and, before they reached the till, Aeyun threw in some more cured meat. Just in case. The gaggle behind them ended up huddled around a shelf of figurines, the one that Aeyun had only recently abandoned, giggling about how cute the creatures were. Despite himself, a twitch pulled his lips up at one corner.

"Well, lad, you have some kind of stomach on you, don't you?" The grocer chuckled half-heartedly as he rang up the goods. Aeyun quietly shoved their purchases into the bags that he and Davah had brought with them.

Davah hummed and said, "It's not just for me, of course. I've got a few mouths to feed." The grocer nodded appreciatively, pushing the last of the tubers towards Aeyun.

"Sure, sure. Well, I hope the better half has a plan for all this. I trust there are intentions for it. Composting is all well and good, but you don't want to be wasting the lot of it. Not like we have the spare once the harvest dries up."

"Oh, not at all," Davah said, a smile plastered on his face. "Rest assured, this food is in good hands."

"Aye, aye, sure," was all the grocer responded with, then he tapped the top of the till, where flip cards displayed the total. Davah nodded and dug into his satchel, fishing out a coin purse. He hesitated for a moment, then Aeyun found the bag deposited in his own hand.

Davah still hadn't memorised the amounts attributed to the local tender, despite this not being his first encounter. Aeyun sighed, hoping to avoid the probing look the grocer gave the pair of them — nosey miser — and he plucked out the appropriate coin.

"Here," Aeyun said, dropping the payment on the counter. "Now you can tell her I spent it," he added, an effort to dissuade the grocer's curiosities. It seemed to work, since the man scooped up the pile of payment and wished them a good day.

Outside, Davah nudged an elbow into Aeyun's arm, muttering, "Sorry."

"It's fine," said Aeyun. It was. In the scheme of things, they had much larger worries.

Together, they walked down the cobbled streets of The Hold, bags full of nutrient-rich foods slung over both of their shoulders. The city looked like how Aeyun remembered: rundown and collapsed from a lack of upkeep. Shoddy patches of reworked construction were layered one atop the other, creating an odd mismatch of architecture that appeared as confused as it did unstable. A web of narrow corridors, the city was dissected by two sloshing, murky rivers and one thinly babbling canal. The thick smell of mildew clung to the air, permeating the entire span of the haphazard townland. The majority of the buildings that curved around the hodgepodge streets were grooved together with wood, it being the most abundant resource nearby, but ancient and repurposed stone was dotted around the place. Being the second most abundant resource, dried — or living, in some cases — vines wove themselves into gaps, and they often made up the bulk of support for footbridges crossing waters.

That's not to say that The Hold wasn't a marvel to look it, it was. It was bursting with life, and it was sometimes difficult to tell if it was the people or the plants running the city. Breaking through the potent smell of moss and mush, powdered purity wafted from petals that stretched wide, or tart sweetness from pockets that clustered like pinprick fireworks, fluttering critters chittering between them. It was like the wilds had encroached inwards, and the Holden Folk just let it happen. Lush and vibrant with blooms and blossoms crawling on each corner, the city was like that from children's lore, Davah had said.

Aeyun wondered if there was a reason for that.

"This is still so weird," Davah said, adjusting the strap on his shoulder, his eyes warily following a couple that walked around them in the opposite direction.

The streets of The Hold weren't busy at this hour, early in the morning as it was. But they also weren't abandoned. Sparse, perhaps. The Hold maintained its status as the epicentre of activity on Ca'lorus, most inhabitants lived within its half-crumbled walls. In that constrained radius, Aeyun reckoned it was near the population of Kilrona on Mhedoon. He had no idea how many lived in the Ou'grobh, as if one wanted to stay hidden from the laypeople amongst its shifting tree trunks, they could easily do so with some skill.

However, even those who didn't want to be found could be if someone else's skill happened to up to the task. Aeyun was well aware of that harsh reality.

"Well, it's weird, and it's real," Aeyun mumbled.

His eyes cast over the street, catching on a few more early risers as they came out for a stroll. Just down the next alley was a drunkard, having filled himself up with whatever fermented juice the nearby pub stocked.

Aeyun made a mental note that they were running low on booze.

"It's been long enough and that's sunk in, friend," Davah said, his cadence naturally falling back into a Mhedoonian lilt. "I just meant that we're here. That this is the point we're at."

Aeyun nodded. He could sympathise with the feeling.

They'd been on Ca'lorus for two weeks. Two weeks of angry glares, lectures, avoidance, and forced distance. He hated it. So far, Davah had been the only one not breathing down his neck about his bad choices or trying to keep his distance whenever Aeyun came around. It was welcomed in his current environment. But also disheartening.

Aeyun was back on Ca'lorus, and things had not gone at all like how he imagined. And, if he were honest with himself, he wasn't even sure he knew what he thought would happen. Even so, it wasn't this.

Sighing deeply, he begrudgingly resigned himself to his new routine.

To make things worse, guilt loomed over him like a stagnant cloud these days. Not that the feeling was new, but it was just so much more. Pervasive as it was intoxicating. He expected a torrent of persecuting rain, or at least, to that end, a damning lightning strike.

Like Uruji's newly minted ability to produce little sparks from his fingertips.

Something that Uruji had neglected to tell him, it turned out, was that Jourae had passed down an heirloom dagger to his true-blood son. It had been in the family for centuries, Uruji had told him, and it was only after he'd awoken on Ca'lorus and investigated it that he found the pommel had caved in upon itself, leaving an indent of a stone that was clearly no longer present within its melted hilt, its lost impression visible for anyone to see.

Uruji had not ripped a portal into thin air through sheer will, as Aeyun had proposed, but he'd got lucky, unknowingly calling upon a gate alicant in his possession. And it was all such a fucking joke that Aeyun wanted to laugh until he cried.

Aeyun had asked if his brother's intention had been to find him, and to this Uruji said yes. It didn't make him feel better. Uruji said he'd thought of the resonance that Aeyun emitted, and he wanted them to go somewhere far from the wreckage. He said they'd fallen into the long-forgotten garden of a dilapidated cabin in the woods.

It didn't take a large leap in logic for Aeyun to figure that it was likely his old family home, but he couldn't bring himself to say as much. In fact, he and Uruji had hardly acknowledged any of it yet, Aeyun's obvious unbelonging in the realms. He suspected that a lot of it had been covered by whatever Raeyu must've told him, and the rest by the bits and pieces

Da'garu conveyed. And it wasn't that Aeyun didn't want to talk about it with his brother, he just didn't know how. It wasn't easy when Uruji spent every second moment sighing disappointedly at Aeyun's return to Ca'lorus, offering his repeated discontent that his older brother had failed to listen to him. Again. Just like he always did.

While Aeyun's relationships with his siblings tattered, the two of them got on swimmingly, it seemed. When one found Uruji, Da'garu wasn't far behind. When one spotted Da'garu, Uruji was often only just around the corner, and Aeyun didn't know how to feel about that. It didn't help that Uruji basically acted as her interpreter, either, linking them at the hip more often than not.

Da'garu's muteness was an uncomfortable revelation for Aeyun. Why and when that happened, he'd still been unable to glean, and it made him uneasy every time it burrowed into his mind and lingered, haunting and provoking.

While Uruji was one that berated, Da'garu was one that avoided. She was wary of her long-lost brother; it was all too blatant. And Raeyu was wary of her and Aeyun's tether. Despite Uruji's loose assurances that it was likely how it once was, Raeyu seemed hesitant to be within a stone's throw of him, and Aeyun couldn't deny that he was a bit pussyfooted when it came to it as well. He'd nearly died, after all, so he figured it was fair.

Aeyun rubbed at his chest, the spot where new symbols had been carved by his brother's hands. Runic markings that warded away Essence, he'd said. They'd fade with time and would need to be replaced. A safeguard, in case Uruji's impromptu Silencing failed. If his commune with Essence returned, the transfer would begin again, and Aeyun's life-force would seek to satisfy the agreement made many years prior.

Unbalanced, lacking any reasonable tune with Essence, Aeyun was back to as he had been, his soulsong calling to Vitality with ease, but anything else a struggle. If he'd realised he could have done more with ore in those fleeting months, he'd have tried.

Before his mind drifted into more dangerous territory, Aeyun asked Davah, "Can we stop by the vintner's?" Davah's lifted brow gave away his piqued curiosity. "For you, of course," he said. Maybe it was for himself, too, but he didn't need to voice that.

"I'm always happy to have a bit of drink—" Davah looked up at the pastel-streaked sky, squinting, "—at whatever time of day this is."

There were day and night cycles on Ca'lorus, but the translucent barrier of The Veil sometimes refracted in such a way that it was difficult to tell how much time passed. Most people had tickers in their homes or somewhere on their person. Versions of clocks that counted with flipping mechanisms, not unlike those of a till.

Inside the vintner's shop, Aeyun browsed the shelves, unfamiliar with the available bottles. He was young when he'd last been in The Hold, so any drinking experience he had came from the realms. Davah sidled up to his right, scanning along with him.

"What's that red one?" he asked.

With a shrug, Aeyun whispered back, "I don't know."

It earned him a bemused look from the other, but Aeyun scoffed and pushed it into Davah's arms. They grabbed a few more bottles from sections near reasonable price labels, then they scuttled to the till. Behind it, a woman with scraggly hair stood, her eyes boring into them, following their movements.

"Don't get out of the Ou'grobh much, do you, folks?" She murmured, calculating their fee. Aeyun tried not to let his posture stiffen. From what he recalled, some Holdens didn't take well to those who lived in the forest. "I'd be filling myself up with this too, stuck out there. Don't know how you do it."

"What makes you think we're from the Ou'grobh?" Davah dared to ask. Aeyun had a sudden desire to smack him for it. The woman at the till leered up at Davah, and Aeyun tried to angle his face away as best he could. "Anyone as cagey as your friend here isn't from these streets. He's walking around like he has something to hide."

"His ugly face is all," said Davah. It earned a chortle from the vintner, who slid the bottles towards them.

Aeyun, still in possession of the coin purse, took out the required amount and exchanged his sister's tender for their vices. He'd have to figure out a way to make them more coin, especially if they were going to be around longer.

And he suspected this to be the case.

Out in the open air once more, Aeyun chided, "You called me handsome once."

Davah chuckled as he resettled the now heavier bag on his shoulder.

"No, no my silly enigma. I said that Saoiri called you handsome, and that I agreed," Davah informed him, like it was any sort of correction. "I remember, because afterwards your drunk arse nearly fell off your chair trying to say that you weren't, and that there were far more handsome people on Raenaru." He gave Aeyun a look. "Now I see that you were thinking of someone in particular, weren't you?"

Aeyun pointedly ignored both his question and the heat that flushed his face.

"Have a thing for the Thasian gal, hm?" Davah asked, a wide grin wrinkling his freckled cheeks. "Makes sense."

Aeyun grumbled his annoyance, but otherwise didn't comment.

The Ou'grobh greeted him with its familiar tune, beckoning them into its rustling forested lands as they exited the city gate. Davah grabbed onto his arm, fingers digging in. *Someone* clearly did not want to get lost in the shifting trees. Aeyun felt the exhilaration of his Vitality buzz to life as they took a step forward, a breath of satisfaction settling into his lungs.

Anticipation thrummed through his body, tingling in a circuit with each step. The woods were foggy, the morning's lingering dew having moistened the atmosphere, seeping into the terrain. The ground was muddier than normal, likely due to the previous day's rain, and Aeyun, now privy to stretching horizons, had yet to demystify the mechanics of weather systems amongst The Veil.

He'd thought nothing of it before he'd experienced the great expanses of the realms. Now he wondered how such an isolated realm even had pressure drops and temperature changes. None of it really mattered though. Not to him, not to *now*. His boots dug into the softened ground all the same, presenting a heavy squelching sound each time his foot lifted.

Davah could have easily avoided the same fate, being from the most waterlogged realm Aeyun had ever encountered – perhaps aside from Tenebrana, which was a whole different kind of sludgy – and he was sure that the man could nimbly take steps in the practised manner of one who'd become accustomed to that kind of environment. Despite this, Davah's boots splashed into the mud right alongside him. Aeyun wondered if it was from an attitude, or if it was him matching Aeyun's stride.

"It shouldn't be too much longer now," said Aeyun.

He hoped the assurance would quell some of Davah's doubts. The biting nails in his forearm told him otherwise.

Finally, after many long trudges, an *ah!* sounded from the leech at Aeyun's side.

"We're here!" Davah exclaimed.

Aeyun could hear the relief that dripped off the statement.

The grotto itself was as damp as the forest, stagnant water rippling as little critters jumped from one waterlily pad to the next. Pushing aside some low-hanging roots that dripped over the edges of an outcropping, Aeyun gestured for Davah to walk into the cavernous space there. Upon entry, Aeyun's eyes were drawn, as always, to the ethereal blue-hued ore that peeked through crevices in the stony walls of the cave.

In his previous life, he wouldn't have given them a second thought. With the experience he now had, he wondered what type of attunement lay hidden in their core. Regardless of his own curiosity, he'd still not allowed Davah to pluck one from its resting place. He was sure that he would try, if he hadn't already, but he'd not done so on Aeyun's watch.

The ore kept the small, humid passage alight with a cool glow, and Aeyun permitted himself a moment to stare at a cluster on the ceiling. Complemented in the lowlight, iridescent mossy patches and white, tongue-petaled flowers were painted across the cave walls, nestled comfortably in corners. The cave itself wasn't very deep, nor extensive. It only took a short meander, then they were emerging on the other side. Back under the hazy light of the morning, a large building took shape before them. It was cradled in a lush glen, flanked by a waterfall that fed into a gurgling pond.

The building gave the impression that it was once remarkable, its twisting architecture a shameful impersonation of the marvel it must have been. Now, portions of it lay tumbled, and wooden slabs offered a patchwork mend on holes that punctured the half-crumbled stone. Elegant carvings had lost their faces, and runic archways had been haphazardly repaired with replacement symbols that stood in contrast to their more ancient neighbours. The grounds, presumably once maintained, had a wild feel to them now, and a lingering, pungent air gripped the whole area, as if the water pouring in the distance hung invisibly, interwoven in intangible striations.

There was a tragedy to The Hold that Aeyun could easily pick up on after his return. But this building, the ancient a'teneum hidden in the Ou'grobh, seemed like it was lost to time. Abandoned and forgotten.

No one was pottering around the grounds, so Aeyun figured they were among the building's manuscript-lined walls instead. He tried to ignore the sneaking premonition bubbling behind his chest, something mild and meek. As they reached the broken doorway, it felt like lead dropped in his stomach. A distant dread manifested, and he still wasn't sure why that happened every time he returned.

"We're ba—ck!" Davah called in a sing-song voice, cupping his hands around his mouth.

Aeyun grimaced. After a beat of silence, Davah shrugged and walked further in, this time leading them all the way into the inner belly of the decrepit archive. A true tomb for tomes, Aeyun considered.

All around him, Aeyun could feel the devastation that once wracked the building. He could imagine that once there were no neatly laid books. No rows of pristinely kept shelves. That there was mostly rubble, poking roots and vines, and the occasional scurrying of scavenging creatures, hidden in shadows and crevices. A chilly feeling sank into his bones at the image. But it wasn't real. It wasn't what he saw now.

The a'teneum of the present had portions of eaten-away stone, and wood, roots, and creepers still clung to walls and crevices, the greenery appearing pleasant among the volumes of manuscripts and grimoires and texts that climbed in layers of shelves beside them. Always alight, the fire in the hearth reflected warmly across the interior, washing the room in a soft glow. Reaching up to the atrium ceiling – a mess of broken glass and knotted vines – pillars rose elegantly, runic symbols tracing up the wood.

Aeyun tried not to think of Uruji panickily scraping one back into place.

"Aeyun."

The call grabbed his attention. Aeyun found himself turning towards its origin, where Raeyu stood peeking out from the entryway of a stairwell. Her sun-drenched, golden gaze locked onto his, and she gave him a smile that didn't reach her eyes.

"You're back," she said, and it sounded happy.

"I'm back," he said, and he hoped it sounded glad.

There were too many bodies for the dusty furnishings to accommodate, so Aeyun had settled himself on the edge of the hearth, sat on the corner of the stone there. Davah was next to him on the wooden planks of the floor, a blanket folded beneath him for comfort. The rest of the ensemble was dispersed amongst the furniture.

Gama-of-Yun, of course, laid still but breathing steadily upstairs. As he had for a long, long while, Aeyun came to learn. Apart from Aeyun's interference.

Aeyun swirled his fermented drink, watching it paint the inner rim of his cup mauve. The fire crackled behind him and, across from he and Davah, Uruji's chatter with Raeyu – and presumably Da'garu – filled the background, adding to the static buzz in his head.

Davah was humming something under his breath, his attention on the network of vines weaving across the rafters of the atrium. Aeyun took a sip of his drink and observed the other three. Da'garu was moving her arms animatedly and Uruji was, somehow, able to recount the story she was telling to Raeyu.

Likely because he was with her, for whatever the journey was.

Feeling like he was intruding, Aeyun sighed lightly and took another sip.

"Aeyun," Uruji called suddenly, and Aeyun snapped his head up. When his eyes caught his brother's, Uruji gave him an expectant look. About what, he wasn't sure. Beside Uruji, Da'garu was eying the drink in Aeyun's hand, frowning at it.

"What?" Aeyun asked, since nothing else seemed to be progressing the conversation.

"She said that's really strong," Uruji tipped his chin towards the bottle on the table, the same as what Aeyun held, and Aeyun's eyebrows lifted, incredulous. Down by his knee, Davah muttered something like: don't I know it.

"And?"

Uruji's answering expression was just as disbelieving. His gaze shifted over to Davah.

"What'd you do to him this past year?" he asked, likely because Aeyun was more grumbly and defiant than he recalled.

Aeyun understood – truly he did – because Uruji probably remembered Aeyun as he was when he was righteous and audacious, tackling challenges head-on and trying his best to be a reliable figure in his life. Until he wasn't.

Davah didn't do himself any favours by lifting a hand to salute them with a wink, teetering slightly, then catching himself, unbalanced. Out of the corner of his eye, he saw Raeyu's gaze latch on to Davah with a glint of something Aeyun couldn't quite place, but it felt a lot like disapproval.

Aeyun sighed and looked upwards. He couldn't look at any of them. Not in the eye.

What he didn't expect was – a few minutes later, when he'd gone back to idly sipping his drink – for Uruji to stand and stride over. Aeyun also didn't know how to feel about Da'garu's eyes watching his brother's back as he went.

"Hey," Uruji said, sparing a glance towards Davah, who was now leaning back with his eyes closed, still humming a tune only he seemed to know. "Can we talk?"

Aeyun flit his gaze between his brother and the room's other occupants, all of whom appeared to be trying their best to act like they weren't paying attention. He didn't know how to interact with Raeyu anymore, and he certainly didn't know where to start with his sister. The drink in his hand was suddenly feeling too light.

Aeyun stood, ignoring the subdued spin of protest from the room, and he vaguely waved a hand in Davah's direction. "Watch him?" he asked the floor, perhaps Raeyu. "Yeah," he said to Uruji, then walked towards the table, intending to get another refill.

"Ae—"

"I said yes, Uruji. Just—" Aeyun didn't finish, instead grasping at the neck of the bottle and tipping the liquid into his cup. He numbly watched as it splashed against the inner rim. "Okay, let's talk."

Aeyun ignored the gazes that trailed after him as he walked towards the a'teneum door. He wouldn't mind fresh air. Inside was suffocating.

Ca'lorus was suffocating.

"Hey," Uruji said again once they were among the dimly lit flowers.

The light from the thinning portion of The Veil filtered down, bouncing off the waterfall in the distance, reflecting across the meadow and around the glen. Aeyun looked up, but he saw no moon. It usually wasn't visible, only winking into the highest portion of the sky if one were lucky enough to catch it at the right time.

"Hey," Aeyun said back. He walked out a bit further and sat down, patting the grass beside him.

Uruji stared for a moment, then knelt down beside the wilderlilies. "We haven't really …"

"Yeah, I know." Aeyun twisted his drink, watching it swirl. "I know."

"How have you been?" Uruji asked, and Aeyun briefly considered that he should be the one asking that.

In fact, he *really* should be. So, he did. "How have *you* been? After father …"

"Oh," Uruji said, then it was silent.

Aeyun looked over and saw that Uruji was watching the water crash down in the distance, filling the seemingly endless pond below. Pyreflies, or something similar to them, danced in the air, and Aeyun spied one that floated a bit further from the pack.

"I'm not sure. It still doesn't seem real."

Aeyun didn't find that hard to believe. Uruji had been stuck in the a'teneum, among these grounds, for the better part of a year. It'd be easy enough to pretend that nothing outside of it was real, or that it existed at all.

Uruji hadn't even seen The Hold. Neither he nor Raeyu had, since they looked too out of place, both sporting horns that were too obvious. Too

43

foreign. Aeyun knew first-hand how fearful the people of Ca'lorus could be when faced with the unknown. It was better that they don't provoke suspicion. Unfortunately, that left them with very few places to go.

"I'm sorry I wasn't there," Aeyun finally said.

After a long moment, Uruji asked, "Why weren't you?"

Uruji picked at a blade of grass, and Aeyun felt something inside him tear with the fibres of it.

"You weren't told?" he wondered aloud.

Uruji looked up at him, curious. "Your friend, Davah, said he wasn't getting into all of it. That it should come from you."

Aeyun scoffed. He took another swig from his cup and grimaced as it slid down his throat. How was he meant to tell his brother that he'd ended up exactly where he'd intended, but with nothing as it should be?

"I, uh," Aeyun trailed. He paused and offered his cup to Uruji. "Sorry, do you want some?"

Uruji cautiously sniffed at it, looking very much the son of a bureaucrat. He glanced over, resolved something, then took a gulp of it. His face twisted between interest and revulsion before finally settling on indifference.

"Not as bad as I would have thought."

"Ah, well. We've no rolling vineyards of Lu-Ghan here." Aeyun took the offered drink back, resting it down for the moment. "I thought it was time to find *here*. To find Da'garu," he said, and even as it rolled off his tongue, it felt like a half-truth. "To be honest, I wasn't even sure she was alive until I saw her through the rift. I also left because Oagyu was growing tired of me, his goons out to track me. I could sense it. I knew that if I stuck around that it wasn't only me in danger, but Raeyu.

"And I guess I wanted to know if I was mad. If I'd created Ca'lorus in my head, and everything that happened here. If there really was a whole realm out here, or if I'd conjured it up in my mind after witnessing something awful in my youth."

"Da'garu said her parents died," Uruji said, voice quiet. Aeyun nodded, morose, and his gaze was drawn back to the drink in his hand. "So, I guess that means that your—"

"I *am* your brother," Aeyun told him, resolute. "In every way that matters, and father was my father, in all the same ways." He felt like it needed to be said, and when he turned to Uruji, he was met with a contort of sadness.

"You will always be my brother, Aeyun." Uruji took a deep breath in. "But I want to know A'vor, too. And who you are, as one." He placed a hand on Aeyun's shoulder. It felt heavy. Grounding. "I want to know who you were, and who you've become. *Because* you're my brother."

"Okay," said Aeyun. "We can do that."

Uruji nodded, then he extended his arm. "Give me more of that dreadful drink."

Aeyun laughed and passed it over, giving Uruji a playful nudge. He sat quiet for a moment, enjoying the sounds of the water and the forest beyond, then he hummed aloud.

"You've been looking out for Raeyu? And Da'garu?"

"Honestly, Aeyun, it's more like Da'garu has been watching over us." Uruji shook his head, an amazement crossing his features, and he passed the drink back over. "She's really something else. It's mad how resourceful she is, and I'm pretty sure she can talk to animals through her mind or something. You call it Vitality? Through that, I guess."

Aeyun listened intently as Uruji gushed about Da'garu and her abilities, as well as her keen senses and self-sufficiency. It was heartening, in some odd and disconnected sense. There was a pride there that filtered in, but it was tinged with a rotting regret.

"You know," said Uruji. "I have some theories about all this Vitality and Essence nonsense."

He stood and snatched a stray stick, traipsing back towards a bald spot of dirt near where they sat.

"Okay, so, I think it might be like this: we have alica, threads of power that manifest elemental energies, held within our alicant, right? But if we distil alica as a force in and of itself—" he dragged one end of the stick in the dirt, carving a solitary straight line. "It is a spectrum of elemental power, ranging from fire to wind to water to the very soil we stand, and various combinations as such to produce nuanced mutations." He tapped just beside the line, glancing at Aeyun. "This is that: alica, one axis." He then pivoted and drew a line perpendicular of the first, through its middle to create a cross. "This is our second axis: boggling manifestations that do not fit the schema of alica manipulations. So, here," an indication was made towards the bottommost end of the second line, "is Essence. Destructive, unfolding, and wild. Perhaps the very essence – hence the name – of the stuff that is life." He drifted his bark-peeled implement towards the top of the second line, taping there. "And maybe *this* is Vitality, as you name it. The antithesis of Essence. Generating, yielding, and compelling. The second hand of creation." He looked back at Aeyun, gauging him for a moment. When no response was forthcoming, Uruji continued. "If this is true – if this is a visualisation of these axes of power, alica being elemental, then *what* is this axis defined as?" He contemplated the Essence-to-Vitality line. "This strange, cosmic push and pull?"

Uruji stepped back once, then toed forward and created a large demonstration of a circle surrounding both lines.

"And what does it exist in, these manifestations? What is their cradle?"

"Does that brain of yours ever rest?" Aeyun asked amicably.

Uruji smiled. "Da'garu made it seem that I remind her a bit of Gama-of-Yun, when he was awake."

"Was it Gama who looked after her?" Aeyun had suspected as much, but he still wanted to know for sure.

"She made it seem like they looked after each other. That Gama-of-Yun is a bit forgetful?" Uruji asked as he discarded the stick and shuffled back to Aeyun's side.

"Yeah." Aeyun could remember the man losing track of his thoughts time and time again in his youth. "So," he began, knowing that it was a topic he wanted to breech, "other than you getting uncomfortably chummy with Da'garu—" Uruji looked mortified and affronted all at once, "—anything to add about Gama-of-Yun?"

"Right." Uruji sighed. "Do you know what he is?"

It wasn't the response that Aeyun expected, so he asked, "What do you mean?"

"He doesn't age, right? So, what is he?"

Aeyun hadn't really thought about it. And he also hadn't taken a good long look at Gama-of-Yun since being back on Ca'lorus, mainly due to his guilt for having hijacked his body before. Thinking about it now, though, he hadn't aged, had he? And that was … odd.

"Honestly, I thought he was just a man," said Aeyun. He took another sip and realised the cup was nearly empty. "But now I don't know, especially not after—"

His sentence ended abruptly as his thoughts drifted to Seraeyu.

Seraeyu, who was manipulated by a Yun, he'd said. Sirin. Seraeyu, who was left alone for almost a year now to do her bidding. Seraeyu, who Aeyun had promised he'd be there for. Seraeyu, who everyone thought was a gone-mad warmonger, except Aeyun, who knew.

That responsibility sat weightily. And he hadn't told any of them yet. He didn't know how, and he didn't know where to start.

"Aeyun?"

"I don't really know," said Aeyun. "But he's not a god."

"No, I suppose not," Uruji conceded, then all fell quiet. "This year has been tough on you, hasn't it?"

Aeyun shook his head, offering a mirthless chuckle. "Yeah, I think it has. But … not just me. It's been rough for everyone."

Uruji's hand found its way back to his shoulder and squeezed, offering a small comfort in the night's stillness.

Long after Uruji had returned inside, leaving Aeyun to his peace and quiet when he'd said he'd like the time alone, Aeyun was laid back in the flowers, looking up at the refracted starlight spread across the expanse of the curved sky. Still feeling alcohol coursing through his veins, he lifted a hand up, stretching it towards the darkest spot above him, reaching for a boundless plane he wasn't sure could be found beyond.

"Are you there?" he whispered, closing an eye to focus better. "Can you hear me?" Silence answered him, and he spread his fingers further. "If you can, I'm sorry. I'll still figure it out, like I said I would. I've not forgotten." Aeyun frowned and let his hand fall over his face. "I won't forget."

"Who are you talking to?"

It was Raeyu's voice that had called, and it startled him enough to surge upright and twist towards her. Her silhouette was carved among the light breeching the a'teneum's doorway, and her presence carried the same pensive calm it always did. Like she was far ahead of what Aeyun perceived, always looking backwards, knowing.

She gave him a cautious smile, too far to touch.

"I—" Aeyun gathered his thoughts. "No one. Just myself."

"Oh," she said, folding her arm behind her back. Aeyun eyed the empty space where her other arm should be, and he felt a lurch in his stomach, churning with shame. "Well, that's okay. You can keep doing that if you want."

"I don't need to keep talking to myself, Rae." Despite himself, he snickered a bit at the notion. "I'm fine, thanks."

They stayed that way for too long, Aeyun half-turned to her, and Raeyu looking down towards him from an uncomfortable distance. Aeyun finally took it upon himself to stand, but Raeyu lifted her hand in apology.

"No, no, I'm sorry! Stay," she said. "I didn't mean to make you get up. Stay, I can leave."

As she turned on a heel, Aeyun reached out and said, "Raeyu." She stopped and looked back. "Don't go." She looked like she'd protest again, so he followed it up with, "I'd like you to stay." Then, "I miss you."

"I miss you, too," she said, voice trembling. Raeyu looked down, and when she looked up again, her eyes were glassy. "I've missed you."

"I'm sorry," he said, but he knew it wasn't enough. The emptiness in his chest ached, and his hand still hovered in the air.

"I know," she told him, then she wiped at her nose. "Can I watch the stars with you?"

"There are no stars."

"It doesn't matter," Raeyu said, dropping herself down to the ground, laying back.

Aeyun looked at her, a smile pulling across his face, then he laid back as well. He shifted his body to be parallel to hers, even if they were too far to be next to each other. She reached out her arm, dropping it across the grass, and her head lulled in his direction. Aeyun copied her with his right, connecting with her gaze.

"The stars are pretty tonight," he said.

A smirk twitched on his face as her cheeks coloured.

"I thought you said there aren't any?"

"I see one," he told her, and she smiled back at him with a laugh.

It was a fleeting moment, and soon enough Raeyu was standing, telling him that she was going to get some sleep. That he should as well. Aeyun agreed, but didn't get up. Instead, he wished her goodnight, and she did the same, traipsing back towards the entrance of the a'teneum. He watched as she disappeared inside, and the warmth of the evening felt like it followed her into the threshold.

He looked up at the sky again and gave a wry chuckle when a sliver of the moon peeked through the darkness.

"Do you watch the others, too?" Aeyun asked it, subdued. His thoughts wandered, guilt filtering across the lunar luminescence. "Am I supposed to tell her?" he pondered, even quieter. "Do you want me to?"

He hadn't realised when the world became darker, shrouded in inky fog. He hadn't realised when his vision became a bit more radiant, or when the realm fell out from under him. He did realise, however, when Seraeyu's voice rung out.

"Starry sky, do you always speak in riddles? It's infuriating."

Aeyun startled, eyes wide. "Seraeyu?"

CHAPTER SIX

Sakaeri stared at the Yisuna mask, and it gazed back at her, unfeeling. She trailed a finger down its glazed finish, elegant patterns etched onto its exterior. Lips, a mulberry purple, whispered no insights, and eyes, ore-refined and lined with charcoal, communicated no indication of how this would go. How she should adapt.

With a heavy sigh, she lifted the guise to her face and stared in the mirror. What met her was an expressionless expanse of pearly ceramic, adorned with a regretful impression of horns that shrouded her own blunted nubs of cartilage. Translucent panels shielded her eyes from view, and she studied the face of a killer. As she returned the mask to the counter, her hand shook. She willed it to stop its trembling.

A knock at the door had her jumping, a reaction that should have been long abandoned. She turned to watch as Seraeyu entered, his aethereal signature as volatile as it was docile, a contradiction standing in once piece. At first, he said nothing, simply sharing a resigned grimace with her, then he gestured towards her outfit of battle garb, all reinforced weaves and dark shades of black and grey. It was the boots, heavy-treaded and steel-toed, that she held a personal preference for.

"You look the part."

"I am the part," Sakaeri retorted. After all, the appearance she was emulating was based on her very band of merry, dead mercenaries. "Are you sure about this, Seraeyu?"

"No," he said, and Sakaeri couldn't help but think it too honest. "I'm not sure about anything, but we cannot have the realm eager to see you executed." Seraeyu sighed, running a hand through his hair. "And I cannot do this alone."

"I suppose you can't."

Another knock resounded, further this time, and both of them turned in the direction of Raeyu's bedchamber doors.

Sakaeri wasn't quite sure about how she felt regarding her new designation to the elder Thasian's room. After the incident in Oagyu's old chambers, Seraeyu had instigated her move, freeing her from her restraints, and Sakaeri still hadn't been able to bear interacting with Raeyu's old things, frozen in time since her disappearance.

Raeyu's room was peaceful and light, faced towards the sun. Books, gathering dust, were cradled among shelves that sat beside a chair, one knitted blanket tossed across it, a remnant of an unworried action. Scattered among the walls were pictures that Sakaeri hadn't dared to inspect, but smiling faces blurred in her periphery all the same. There was also hung weaponry, relics passed to a generation younger, and troves of jewellery and metal wares that ranged from ostentatious to understated. Sakaeri was sure there were more than a few pieces from Aeyun among them. There were also large blank spaces filling the room, and it was within them that Sakaeri felt both the most solace and the most pain.

Stood in Raeyu's ensuite, Sakaeri retrieved the mask once more and fastened it around her head, clipping it behind her neck. She didn't say a word as she walked by Seraeyu in the doorframe, though he respectfully made room for her passing, and she studied the weaponry pinned to the walls. A dual-sword, latched as one but dividable into two thin blades, stood out to her, its hilt wrapped in sturdy leather. Using the blunt end, and ignoring the loudly hitched breath behind her, she smashed the display case holding the Thasian-nee-made replica of the traditional war fan, composed of several detachable blades and a hidden knife. A homage to an ancient art.

"Was that necessary?"

"Am I really a Sirin without my projectiles?" she bit back just as easily.

The knock on the door rapped again, this time followed by a Draconguard's call of, "At your word, Praetor."

It was the same who'd been so openly determined to follow Seraeyu the other day, unrelenting when he barrelled into Oagyu's room behind the current most powerful man in not only Haebal, but the whole of Raenaru. *Bold, this one.*

Seraeyu cleared his throat, and when Sakaeri secured the last of her weaponry to her body, he called out, "Please proceed."

The door opened, revealing the stiff-postured Draconguard, glaive held staunchly in attention, flanked by several other Orinian grunts. Even more Raenaruan Sentinels, the ones of highest distinction, stood waiting, their gleaming, pearly armoured shells announcing their elevated ranking. Seraeyu stepped around Sakaeri, his silken robes dragging, the embroidered stitching glistening ethereally. It twisted in mournfully beautiful patterns across the length of fabric.

He looked every bit the solemn monarch, his steps echoing as silent militias dutifully parted for him. Seraeyu did not look back this time, trusting Sakaeri to follow, and she watched as he gained a bit of distance. She watched as his shoulders straightened and his head held high. As his arms settled inwards, betraying the clasping of his hands.

Sakaeri steeled herself. Their eyes, judging and calculating and expecting, meant nothing. What mattered then was only the small gap of distance between her and the Praetor – between her and Seraeyu Thasian, son of Paeyuni and brother to Raeyu, ward of Uruji Thasian-nee, the elusive answer that still bound Aeyun to the realms – so she elongated her stride to shadow him, narrowing her focus to his aid.

"What are you saying, Seraeyu?"

"Do I have to spell it out for you? You aren't daft, Sakaeri," he said, allowing himself to sit cross-legged on Oagyu's floor rather than bothering to stand.

Sakaeri searched his eyes. For what, she wasn't even entirely sure, and then she let the words sink in. There is no Bloodsong. There is *no* Bloodsong. Only scars from a rite, performed by the Thasian-nee, to embed a crystal and fuse it to their bones. Hadn't Aeyun even admitted that much, months and months ago? He had, but he *hadn't*. He'd said no such confession about the lack of innate power among the Thasian. Scars, demarcating the ritual that bound some nebulous, great power to their very being.

"Is that why you ripped her arm off?" It had escaped Sakaeri without a filter, and the belated terror of realisation reflected on Seraeyu's face.

"I *what?*"

Something Sakaeri wasn't privy to, some recount of horrors Seraeyu faced alone, played across his wide eyes. Sakaeri swallowed an uncomfortable feeling. This Seraeyu, who stood in direct contrast to the man who had barged into the room, was broken in a way that felt too familiar, too similar to Sakaeri's own cracks and fissures.

"Seraeyu, when you asked me … if I was there. About what you did. Do you …" Stranger things had been true. More convoluted realities given a reprisal. "Do you know how this all started?"

"I know how it started," Seraeyu admitted bitterly, and Sakaeri wasn't entirely sure what to do with that answer. "I, like a fool, played into the hand of a daemon."

With little in the way of warning, he tugged at the fabric of his shirt. She was presented with an embittered, vile web of inky tendrils that culminated over his heart, the bundle of it looking angry and aggravated against his skin. She knew what that meant; that something was eating at him, feeding off his very life-force, just like the marks that Aeyun and Raeyu shared. Except his looked like Raeyu's arm, albeit more enraged and alive.

"Who is that connected to?"

It seemed the question gave Seraeyu pause, since he tilted his head, looking at Sakaeri with thin curiosity. "So, you know it's connected to someone, but not about the Bloodsong?" Sakaeri didn't deign to answer him. "It's connected to a fragment of an ancient soulsong, just as Raeyu's is – was connected as well."

"The crystal?"

"The crystal," Seraeyu confirmed, gloomy.

"The crystal – the soulsong fragment – is the Bloodsong?"

Seraeyu looked like he was trying to parse out something in his head again, but he simply nodded his affirmation at the deduction. "You … you said I took, um, I took Raeyu's arm?"

"You did," said Sakaeri. There was no room nor time for hesitation. That was a fact of the circumstances that led here, and she had no leeway for fragility.

51

However …

"She's alive."

The sigh that left Seraeyu nearly overtook his whole body. He nodded, closing eyes that glistened, watery at their rims. "Thank you," he breathed, and Sakaeri hummed. "I don't have her crystal, though. If I wanted her arm, don't you think I would have wanted the source of power within it?"

"You? No. The daemon that walked through that door? Yes."

"You believe me?" Seraeyu asked, and there was something far too raw behind it. Sakaeri, however, did not look away. She would not turn away from this.

"You are many things, Seraeyu Thasian, but that vengeful being is not one of them."

Seraeyu looked ready to burst into tears, but instead he nodded once with a deep breath. Sakaeri hated the sight of it. Once, back before these troubles, Seraeyu was a man who would express himself as freely as he was able. He did not hesitate to be emotive, only dulling himself when in the presence of his father or other foreign dignitaries. This person before her, though, was tamed in a way that made Sakaeri wrong-footed. A soldier who had trained himself to compartmentalise until he could break down in peace. Watching it hurt in the worst way.

"There were two, and Raeyu had the other one. If this daemon residing in me aimed, and succeeded, to seek out the other, why would she not have kept it? Used it?"

"What if it was useless?"

Seraeyu's focus shifted past Sakaeri, scanning the horizon. She doubted he would find answers there. "If … there was nothing to be found? I imagine that would be … very bad."

"Why's that?"

Seraeyu visibly swallowed. "Her attachment to whoever was supposed to be there was consuming. If it was lost, somehow, it likely only fuelled her hate. Her revulsion for all who may have influenced the disappearance of that fragment."

That look was back again, the cycle of nightmares that flowed behind his tired eyes. Something that sunk its claws into him, reminding him of moments he couldn't seem to escape. Sakaeri reached forward and placed a hand on his knee.

"Seraeyu." The call was grounding enough that it brought him back. She released her hold and leant away. There was something she wanted to know about this broken vessel in front of her. "Do you know what happened to my father?"

"Your father?"

Ah, she thought, *so that was one thing he had not figured out.*

"Jourae Thasian-nee."

There was a beat of silence, then she couldn't watch as his face crumbled. She instead angled her vision towards the lofty ceiling, bright in the morning's light.

"Your father was Jourae-nee?" he asked, and it was fractured in the air between them. "I … I don't know. But I don't think … Sakaeri, I'm so sorry, I don't think he's with us anymore."

And there it was, laid out plainly before her. Wetness prickled at her eyes until trails curved down her cheeks and dripped from her chin. *Starry sea. He doesn't even know what he's done, this poor wretch.*

"Sakaeri …" It travelled across the room, and she pinched her eyes closed. "Sakaeri, I'm so sorry you had to find out this way."

"Yeah," she said, and the word caught in her throat. "Me too."

Seraeyu not only didn't know that he had ripped his hand right through Jourae's chest, but he wasn't aware that Sakaeri had been there to witness it, nor that he was apologising for the death of a man he so brutally murdered. Or, perhaps he did know, that he had been the cause of Jourae's demise. That the thing that lorded over him had instigated it, but he didn't know his very active role which Jourae's children witnessed.

Jourae's death was nothing more than an achievement for this daemon within Seraeyu, tethered to his soulsong, and it left Seraeyu with the unwitting fallout of its actions. Not just that, but Seraeyu, plucky and undeterred and full of sass, had been robbed of his tuning from a young age. By Aeyun who, remarkably, was unable to tune with ore. Who could still tune with his other *not-Essence*. Who could only tune with Essence once Seraeyu had broken whatever hold had been placed upon him. Who, somehow, had survived a ritual that was meant to exchange his life-force to sustain another's. Who had returned to his birthrealm, where Raeyu and Uruji reside – Uruji, a Thasian-nee trained in arts of rites and skilled enough to perform feats thought impossible – and suddenly Seraeyu is unable to tune again, his call to alicant diminished, as it had been in his youth.

But not his Essence. That remained. And it remained *strong*.

Sakaeri wished the pieces didn't fit. That she couldn't determine the breadth of the imbalance that tied them.

"How do you know about Aeyun? What did he promise?"

"I can find him sometimes, among the endless void. I didn't know why, but since … There's just this awareness there, and it's constantly seeking."

"Like a part of you, missing?"

"Yeah," Seraeyu said in a tone that spoke to his hesitance to admit that much. "He promised to fix it; not leave me to contend on my own. To end it, if it came down to it. Maybe that job can fall to you, though, if you'll have it." A discordant laugh rang out, a tired acceptance to what he deemed an inescapable fate.

"That cheeky bastard," Sakaeri groused, disbelieving. She wondered the timeline of this, and just what was going through Aeyun's head when he'd relegated himself that duty. How long had he been aware that Seraeyu was a victim in a grander game? "When had that promise been made? Had you always been able to cross the in-between to communicate like that?"

"No," Seraeyu said resolutely, and it was the first time Sakaeri let her gaze flit back down to him. "No, not before all this. And I don't really know. It was within the last year that we spoke, but my cognition was never clear. I didn't know when things occurred, just that they did. I feel like I've been mostly comatose for what has been, apparently, nearly a full cycle around the calendar."

"Ah."

"Sakaeri?"

"I was with him, for a time." A scowl befell her. "He didn't say a damned word."

"Of course, he didn't."

"Of course, he didn't," Sakaeri echoed. "Well. My sincerest apologies, I can't take the mantel of that duty to end you. And neither can I let you handle it yourself." She gathered her limbs and stood up, debating for a short stint before stretching her hands out to assist Seraeyu off the floor. "Aeyun was at the Kaisan Pit, yes. But I've lost contact with him."

As Seraeyu gently took her palm in his own and allowed her to lift him, he shifted his focus to the floor, far too obvious a tell. He must have known it, too, because when he looked back at her, he said, "I think I heard him last night."

"Oh?"

"I think he was drunk."

It had come out so flat and unimpressed that Sakaeri barked out a surprised laugh.

Yun of the stars. Help me through this.

Seraeyu was connected to Aeyun was connected to Raeyu. If one cog broke, the others would soon crumble, unless Raeyu lived singularly, due to Seraeyu's demise and Aeyun's sacrifice. There may have once been a time where Sakaeri had stoned her conscience and silenced her thoughts, plunging a blade into Seraeyu's cursed heart. Thus would repair Aeyun's missing attunement, returning it from whence it had been banished, some confounding action he'd taken in his earliest days on Raenaru. Thus would rekindle the ritual to exchange his life, the *entirety* of his life-force in full, to sustain Raeyu's own where it had faded years back. It would allow for the extraction of half of his stretched soulsong, the indescribable unknown, from where it was cradled and locked, interwoven within Seraeyu. And Seraeyu, inexplicably connected and buried within Aeyun's soulsong, as well.

There may have once been a time, and Sakaeri mourned for the lost girl who would have thought herself capable of that without repercussion. Who would have thought she'd have achieved that goal without tearing herself into pieces, drowning in the morbid reality of what she'd done. Now, armed with an acceptance for compassion, and propped up by a promise she made to a man who lay dying in her arms, she would stand by all of these incorrigible idiots and love them the only way she knew how. No harm would come to them if she could help it, even if that meant barring them from their own stupidity.

Sakaeri would not stand idle and lose any further members of her misfit, miserably fortuned family. Not again.

"So, how does a Praetor justify an alliance with a Sirin who's accused or treason?"

Seraeyu smirked, and Sakaeri returned her own wicked smile, finally reminded of the mischievous persona that slotted right into place in her memory. For all the trauma, he still lived in there somewhere, ready to make a play. And for how desolate the walls of the Tower had become, they grew just that much more familiar in his dastardly reflection.

"A Praetor of any worth knows to keep his friends close." He sent her a purposeful, almost gleeful look, just like those rare occasions when they'd combine their efforts to outsmart his sister and the Thasian-nee boys in days long passed. "And his enemies closer."

Seraeyu's steps echoed, and Sakaeri considered it a sorrowful sound. This procession was not one that he should be walking alone. As his footfalls resonated off high ceilings and marbled floors, he was saluted by every Sentinel he passed, their hands perpendicular over their hearts in a sign of thanks and respect. She wondered how many of them actually meant it. Especially when he had a tail of Orinian Draconguard and a select few hand-picked Sentinels. The group of them had fallen in line behind her as they walked towards their destination, and she felt the weight of their gazes on her back.

Sakaeri didn't know how far the rumour of treasonous Sirin had gone. She'd assumed it had been Seraeyu, presumably in a sort of fugue state himself, who'd done the accusing. But to how many? And how long had that accusation been left to grow? Was it only certain militant ranks privy to this allegation? Or had it become more common gossip among the masses?

It was unfortunate that Seraeyu was just as ill enlightened.

Seraeyu, however, continued on. And she would be doing both him and herself a disservice if she pretended like she didn't admire him for that. He'd become *something*, through all this. And while the extent of just what that something is was yet to be seen, she found herself curious to witness what would eventually be rendered. Seraeyu, it seemed, had the weight of the realms draped across his shoulders, and yet he still stood, resolute.

The young Praetor slowed to a stop before arching doors, a golden plaque demarcating the room ahead as the *Yunae Suite*, the largest and most grand of the meeting rooms among the Tower. As he stood there for a moment, Sakaeri found herself wondering, and not for the first time, just what was going through his head.

For him, it had been maybe a month and some change since he'd only been the second son, obscured in the shadow of his sister. But now, his tyrannical father was no more, and his revered sister was nowhere to be found. His hired hand was severed, lost to a battle he doesn'tt remember, and half his soulsong was locked away in someone who had disappeared from the known realms.

Now, it was only Sakaeri who'd reclaimed a place by his side.

She did not know what terrors he'd endured, what experiences were forever branded in the darkest corners of his mind, but the Seraeyu before her was something more than the one she'd once offered her aid to, years back, which may as well have been a lifetime ago. That Seraeyu had adamantly denied her offer of assistance. This Seraeyu requested it. This Seraeyu was learnt in the follies of stubborn pride. This Seraeyu was wiser.

He set his shoulders and pushed the doors open, entering into a space full of expectations and arduous political navigations that he'd not before had to contend with. Not alone. On the opposite end of the long negotiation table, revealed with the widening of the egress ahead, the Draconian king sat with a carefully blank look upon her painted face, every flaw hidden to reflect nothing that could be misconstrued as an insecurity, her most loyal Draconguard flanking her position.

"I have been waiting, Praetor Thasian," the Dracon said.

"A pleasure as always, Dracon Rhodan," said Seraeyu. It held more weight than it should have when he followed it up with, "As you can see, I have arrived."

CHAPTER SEVEN

"You have brought a guest," the Dracon said, indicating towards Sakaeri once the doors were latched shut.

The space was full of high-ranking officers from both realms, suited up and helmets in place. Once the room was appropriately cordoned off and sealed, the Draconguard who'd escorted Seraeyu filed around the table to align themselves beside their Dracon. Similarly, the Sentinels who'd followed their Praetor did the same. Sakaeri had strategically placed herself behind Seraeyu, ensuring her mask would stare stoically at Orin's leader throughout the entirety of the occasion.

Seraeyu allowed himself a moment's reprieve as he settled into his opulent chair, crested with a depiction of a metal-twisted weeping tree. Sakaeri shifted minutely to the side, opting for a better observation angle. She spied his profile, noting the tightening of his jaw, and how the aura around him grew dense; nervous and agitated.

"How much do you know of our traditions, Rosalyn?" he asked, and Sakaeri found it very bold indeed that he decided to address her by her forename and forego the formalities that the Dracon seemed so adamant to adhere to.

Unfazed, the Dracon offered a tight smile and threaded her fingers together upon the table. "I suppose that would depend on the given tradition, *Praetor*."

"I suppose it would, yes." Seraeyu nodded, slipping into a bored persona that Sakaeri had seen him adopt when the media hawks came to scavenge for stories. "Among many a record, there have been recounts of a band of highly skilled and secretive mercenaries who have come to the aid of the Legacy. While not restricted to the Thasian in servitude, this group of formidable allies has proven time and time again that their allegiance is to a higher calling: preserving the sanctified agreement between the Herald Hana and the Auspicious Yisuna."

Well, that ... that just wasn't correct. At all. Assuming he spoke of the Sirin.

"It's said that Hana, guided by the words of Oracle Yisuna, brought about prosperity across Raenaru, forming what is now the Raenaruan Council from respected representatives across our realm's regions and then taking on the role of Praetor himself. As the stories go, he sired a child with Yisuna, favoured by the Yun, who was gifted with great power, held within the very confines of their blood. Can you guess which lineage this child begot?"

"The Thasian, Praetor," the Dracon responded, patience held as thinly as her lips.

"Hm, yes," Seraeyu said, and Sakaeri thought he sounded particularly bratty. "And thus, it is said, the Legacy was borne of the sacred union between our blessedly revered Hana and Yisuna. The Sirin, my dear Dracon, are the flock who protect the sanctity of this union, and therefore …" He offered a hand to the air in front of him, urging the Dracon to fill in the gap. When she didn't, he sighed and continued on. "Yes, Rosalyn, you are correct. At its core, the Sirin are obligated by oath to the Legacy and therefore the praetorship."

"So what was it then, Praetor, that influenced you to seek your Sirin? If I do recall, you requested that I report any sightings of these mercenaries to you."

"Ah," said Seraeyu. Ever the performer, he grinned, smug and proud, and leant forward to rest his chin upon his palm. "Astute, as always, Dracon." He hummed and there was a twinkle in his eye that Sakaeri wasn't sure she liked. "As you well know…" The pause was too long as he looked directly at the Dracon, unwavering. "It only takes one rotten fruit to infect the rest. I would like to cleanse my Sirin of any rot. Surely you can understand that."

The Dracon said nothing, but Sakaeri could see her shoulders tense and … what was that about? Did Seraeyu know something about Rosalyn Rhodan? Or the Orinian realm?

"My Sirin simply need a reminder of their oath and their mission. I am not an unreasonable man, Rosalyn. Those who have remained loyal, and those who seek to come back into the Legacy's embrace, will be given the chance to do so. And, as I understand it, it's within the Sirin tenants that they, shall we say, take care of rogue actors."

And wasn't it interesting that Seraeyu would know *that* bit of information? Sakaeri would very much like to know why he did. In fact, Sakaeri would be very eager to find out how much of what slid from his mouth was purely based on conjecture and lies, and how much of it was just twisted versions of the truth he knew. Or perhaps thought he knew.

"Am I correct in my assumption that this is a Sirin who is glaring at me right now?"

Sakaeri thought that glaring was a bit of a dramatic overstatement, but sure. Her mask probably did have that effect, she supposed.

"This is Yisuna," Seraeyu stated simply.

The Dracon glanced up at Sakaeri's face and squinted, as if that would help, then she looked back towards Seraeyu. "And have I, perhaps, met this Sirin before?"

"This is, and will henceforth be known as, Yisuna," Seraeyu said once more, a little firmer than he had previously. The Dracon frowned and dipped her head once in a show of acceptance.

"Very well, Praetor Thasian." The Dracon pursed her lips, only a brief and fleeting thing, then she sighed in a put-upon manner and drummed her fingers on the rich ashenwood before her. "I will make the further assumption that nothing of use to our efforts was gleaned then. How very droll that your internal affairs have been at the heart of such a ruckus. I do find it odd, however, that nothing would have come to light. Given what we'd witnessed, and with whom she kept her company."

"Yes, that," said Seraeyu.

Sakaeri felt the muscles in her neck coil with tension, and her fingers were itching to grab a hold of the hilt of the sword strapped to her side. The delighted look of capture upon the Dracon's face was not one Sakaeri wanted directed anywhere near Seraeyu, so he better find a way to use that wit he always seemed to keep handy.

"It seems there are those who would paint me poorly," Seraeyu said carefully.

He leant back and placed his hands in his lap, clasping them together. Sakaeri wallowed in a fleeting, melancholic thought of *Seraeyu* ...

"Some who would make false claims in the hopes of turning tides to their favour. This encounter was ... unplanned. And it was opportunistic. And it was rectified." Seraeyu tilted his chin, eyes connecting with Sakaeri's, despite the refined ore that divided their gazes. "And I am honoured that Yisuna stands here as my guardian."

It occurred to Sakaeri that she should probably prove this. Seraeyu gave her a small, tired smile, something just between them in the heavy atmosphere, then he closed his eyes for a short-lived respite, preparing to face the Dracon once more. But Sakaeri hadn't responded yet. But Sakaeri hadn't ...

She realised that Seraeyu didn't expect it. He expected *nothing*.

He did not ask that she prove her loyalty, nor her respect. He hoped for it, but he did not demand it. Seraeyu only held onto a vague wish that she would walk by his side until whatever this nightmare was reached its end. Or at least that she would not leave him to the whims of the daemon who fought to control him. Seraeyu still felt alone.

Flashing recollections called to the front of her mind. The visage of a young boy, sulking as he watched the rest of the Thasian progeny step into the confines of an armoured land-skimmer, ready to set off. Without him. The way he'd stare at the horizon, like it did not promise opportunity, but something suffocating instead. The hours he would spend on the rooftop, running drill after drill until Uruji was sent to fetch him. To say it was time to rest for the evening, and that Uruji was needed back at the smithy. Or back home.

Home. A word that Seraeyu had perhaps not thought kindly of for quite some time.

Why hadn't he accepted her offer of protection in their youth? At least then they would have been alone, together. Sakaeri had her not-home home. But really, she dared to let herself wonder, what built the foundations of *home* for Seraeyu? Or even for Sakaeri?

Seraeyu adopted a wry twist to his lips, something aimed at himself, then was ready to address the Dracon again. Tossing caution to the wayside, Sakaeri curled her fingers around his arm. He flinched and turned back to her, a silent question on his tongue, a slight raise to his brow.

Sakaeri withdrew her hand and instead saluted it perpendicular over her heart.

Soft but resolute, she said, "You have my trust."

Seraeyu looked a bit overcome then, if only within the uncertainty in his eyes. He nodded to her and responded just as gently, "Then I will make sure I continue to earn it." After a fortifying breath, he turned back to the Dracon, and Sakaeri liked to think he looked just the smallest bit sturdier. "Unfortunately, these events have not revealed anything new, except for what we all witnessed, together."

"That is not at all what I wished to hear," the Dracon said. "However, we do not always get what we wish, do we?" She cleared her throat and rolled her wrist, as if the whole affair would be waved away with it. "I will leave you to your own summations regarding your Sirin. Our compatriot seemed particularly unwilling to relinquish his grasp, but that is between you and him. To me, it truly makes no difference, and I wish you the utmost luck cleaning up what looks to be a messy kerfuffle, indeed. What matters to me, Praetor Thasian, is that you still intend to uphold our agreement."

Seraeyu barely let a moment pass before he said, "Of course, Dracon Rhodan."

"Very well." The Dracon did not spend long ruminating on this, and Sakaeri wondered just why that was. In her experience, it meant that contingencies were in place should things go awry, or that the Dracon was not in a position to presume that Seraeyu meant anything other than what he said.

"On to business, then. We've made progress on Mhedoon. I've received reports that the rebellions have quieted, and the citizens generally let the soldiers go about their work. Investigations into the explosion at Caiggagh revealed that there was a vessel bought there the same day, just before the event occurred. The vendor decided to be a bit more transparent this time around, after some encouragement. There was no name for the record of sale, but he said he thought he recognised the man who bought it. Apparently, he's involved in the ore trade."

Oh, fuck. Bloody stars-damned idiot.

"Does that sound at all familiar?" she asked Seraeyu, who shook his head in the negative.

It occurred to Sakaeri that no, it genuinely wouldn't, would it?

"It could be entirely unrelated, but we will continue to look in. Something else …" The Dracon paused for a second, considering, then she sighed in that put-upon way again. "He said he's the spitting image of someone who should be, by all rights, buried under the sea. This vendor had a past on the waters, a retired profiteer, you might say. He said this man looked remarkably like a child under the tutelage of the Dread Pre'ach'an."

Why did that name sound like something Sakaeri should know? It was just there, just within reach, but—

"That's impossible," said Seraeyu.

"One must wonder, though."

"I saw that vessel sink with my own eyes." Seraeyu grimaced. "There were no survivors."

The Dracon watched him, then hummed lightly. "Perhaps you are correct."

"And the rest of what you're searching for?"

"Unfortunately, no progress has yet been made. It seems the seas of Mhedoon are a mystery, and many secrets are hidden beneath its waters. Our expeditions have been rather fruitless. When do you plan to allow refugees in? Our cities are overburdened."

The last portion of her statement caught Sakaeri off-guard, its transition swift and tactless. A glance towards Seraeyu shown him mirroring surprise.

"We have ... spoken of this," Seraeyu's response was slow, considering, and the Dracon took it as hesitancy.

"I understand your predicament, but it has been months since the last incident, and our cities do not have enough subsistence to sustain the strain the citizens of Paladi have placed upon them. You know very well that I would not ask unless absolutely necessary. I have proven my worth, I believe, and my Draconguard have proved a valuable asset. My kind gestures can only be stretched so thin, Praetor." The Dracon held an absurdly constipated look for a breath, then she said, "Seraeyu, I ask you as the Dracon and as an old acquaintance. My people needn't suffer this long. I have catered to your fancies. We have solidified our treaties. Together we shall reform and shape the realms to a better tomorrow, but for that day to come, I need my people to survive to see it. Your borders may still be closed, but they need to be open to Paladians. Your forges will know no better smiths, and with the Thasian-nee gone—" She paused, peered at Seraeyu's frozen expression, and read something there that had her saying, "Forgive me, I did not mean to remind you."

"I must ... speak to the Council. About the citizens of Paladi who need refuge," Seraeyu said, and the Dracon looked encouraged, almost younger in a way. Sakaeri tried to parse her age under all that painted skin. "I will send word, when a plan is in place."

"By your grace, Praetor Thasian," the Dracon said, bowing her head. She delicately lifted a hand to the side, awaiting her most intricately armoured Draconguard to offer their own to assist her as she rose. Seraeyu moved to stand on his end of the table as well, silently observing the Dracon as she said, prim but oddly hopeful, "I will await your word."

CHAPTER EIGHT

The rush down the hall may have looked a bit odd after the meeting, stilted strides and tripping feet, but Seraeyu had waved off their entourage. Even that hovering Draconguard and sneering Sentinel. He'd not said a word, only pulled at Sakaeri's wrist once before letting go and sweeping down the hall. She wasted little time chasing after him, because that meeting was a whole lot of nonsense that really needed to make a whole lot of more sense.

The closer they got to their destination, which seemed to be Seraeyu's childhood bedchambers this time, the quicker his feet fled, his silken robe ruffling low to the floor. He kept his head down, barely acknowledging the Sentinels they passed, and Sakaeri fought to keep pace.

Seraeyu was *quick*. Had he always been this fast?

Antiquities and faded tapestries melded in Sakaeri's periphery, the hallway feeling like one limitless path until finally Seraeyu flung his door open and strode into what remained of the shrine to his youthful days passed. He slipped by the framed, pressed flowers hung on the wall – a loving gesture from Paeyuni that once lined his nursery – and he swivelled around the haphazard pile of battle implements carelessly heaped near the foot of his bed. His entire room was a reflection of gentle corners and sharpened edges, like it was in a competition to see which could outshine the other, and clothes were just *everywhere*. The absolute state of the place wasn't much better than how Oagyu's room had first appeared, before Sakaeri so helpfully ensured that everything had, and was in, a place.

Seraeyu did not turn as she shut the door behind her, instead he curled against the glass of his window, giving her a sharp *turn it off* when she'd flipped the light switch. He let out a strangled sort of noise and caved in on himself, clutching at his chest. Sakaeri stalled her progress towards him, subtly testing her attunement to each of the jewelled adornments that Seraeyu had so graciously gifted her.

Seraeyu voiced a long, tired lament, then he gritted his teeth and held a hand out to keep her from approaching. "So," he managed between wheezes, eyes still screwed shut. "I guess Paladi erupted while I was dead to the realms."

When he laughed, it was manic. More than a bit concerning, actually.

"Seraeyu, are you alright?"

"J-just give me a moment."

A strange sort of gag crawled from Seraeyu's throat. He pressed harshly upon his chest and gasped in air, his eyes opening and reflecting deep, endless obsidian, little white streaks cracking through them like bloodshot veins.

Sakaeri was not interested in taking chances, so she tuned with the pristinely faceted ring upon her finger, thrusting her palm forward to force a pinning gale against Seraeyu's form. It was the silence that was the most off-putting, Seraeyu's grunts of discomfort cut off abruptly. His fractured gaze instead bore into her, and his stony expression slowly dissolved into something creeping and frigid.

They stared at each other, and Sakaeri almost felt like it was a sick game being played. Just as stark as the silence had been, Seraeyu's hoarse cackle startled.

"Fancy meeting you again, *Sirin*," Seraeyu's voice spat, and his broken laugh devolved into a choked sort of cough. Seraeyu eyed Sakaeri's stoic resolve and said, "Useless. Foolish." Then interest in Sakaeri was lost, and instead Seraeyu's head turned to gaze out the window he was pressed against. "*Cah. Ca'ou. Uo'ca, Ka'la'drius … Ca … e'ju, a'gara? A'gara'ne.*" Seraeyu's hand flattened against the windowpane. "*'Om, bah da'ju'ne a'gara.*" A grimace befell Seraeyu's features, and then a final miserable, "*Cah …*" drifted from his tongue before he slumped.

And Sakaeri did not know what to do with *that*, because those words, lyrical and flowing, sounded like *Aeyun*. It was a shame, really, that she couldn't even begin to decipher what that could possibly mean, since Seraeyu was gasping again and groaning as the inky miasma receded from his eyes, his gaze gradually coming to lull into connection with hers, the tune sloughing off as Seraeyu crumpled further.

"So," he pushed against the floor with his heel to right himself, but only managed to slip a bit further, exertion blossoming on his cheeks. "As I was saying, Paladi seemingly erupted?"

"What the *fuck*, Seraeyu."

"That was nothing, barely a break of control," Seraeyu said, brushing some hair aside from where it had fallen astray across his forehead. "Handled. Done. Let's move forward."

"But what was that?"

"You've seen it before."

"No, Sera, no I haven't. That daemon spoke like Aeyun does; a descantation, but nothing *happened*." And wasn't that just the truly boggling thing? The parasite within Seraeyu took over, but only barked a bit and then seemingly … whinged?

Seraeyu regarded Sakaeri for a gruelling bout, still huffing.

"That's Aeyun descanting?"

Something felt stale in the air. Sakaeri chanced moving just the smallest bit closer to squat down beside the felled Praetor. Was her statement really all that surprising?

"Huh," he said, as if he'd just divined something odd.

She let him have it for a minute. Only a minute, though. "And?"

"His mother mustn't Ube." It wasn't a question, not really, but it was phrased like it should have been, despite being weighted with too much conviction. Seraeyu, ever the sleuth, just raised a brow at her. "Ah, I see." And then it was like more tumbled into place, and he followed with an even softer, "Ah, I see. Of course she wasn't." Gently, tentatively, his fingers stretched towards hers and took hold. He pulled their threaded embrace to his face and rested his cheek upon it, eyes closing. It reminded her of youthful gestures, lost in memories of times long passed. "Sakaeri, I'm quite tired."

"Sleep then," she found herself instructing, receiving a quiet hum in response. "We'll talk about Paladi when you wake. I will ... help you through this, Seraeyu."

"I'm grateful for you, Sakaeri," he said, forcing himself off the floor and unthreading their hands so he could collapse into his mattress. "Truly."

It wasn't instant, but Sakaeri watched him settle into a quick slumber, covers half strewn.

Seraeyu Thasian, she thought. *You are not given nearly enough credit.* She stood and adjusted the blankets into something more comforting before she stepped a few paces back and sat against the windowpane he'd only just abandoned. *And you have grown to be someone admirable, I think. At least one of us has. And isn't it funny that it's you?*

Seraeyu shivered a little and dream-lethargic fingers grabbed at the chain around his neck, the one with the too-small ring. The one he never took off; Paeyuni's sentimentality towards her once-young son. Always shielded, a permanent staple under all his aristocratic adornments.

Paeyuni loved both of you, but stars did she adore you, Seraeyu.

Seraeyu's short-lived panic abated once his hand encased that decade's old gift.

Raeyu tried, Seraeyu. I know you know that. But she could never be Paeyuni.

The light from the window shone on Seraeyu, its gaze peeking out from behind cloud cover, filtering across the quiet space. It almost read like a soliloquy, a testament to how still a moment could become, a glow illuminating the pieces left behind.

You've been trapped all this time, haven't you? Stars, Seraeyu. I swear on my life, you'll never be trapped again.

We'll never be trapped again.

"No."

"Sakaeri," he said, and she hated the way it sounded like he was reprimanding a child.

They stood on the now reinforced rooftop of the Thasian Tower, its reconstruction sitting in sharp contrast to the aged slabs of stone that once formed the majority of the space. Sakaeri had decided to very much ignore the memories that slammed into being when she'd stepped into the open air, instead opting to focus on Seraeyu and this *stupid* request.

"I can't exactly go traipsing around out there, but I desperately need to know what's happening on the ground. What Haebal City *is* now. Please." Seraeyu snatched up her limp-hanging hand and caught it between his own. "It's all I ask. Just for a little while."

"I will not leave you with—"

"Praetor, you summoned me?" The surly Sentinel emerged from the stairwell, visor flipped up, attention zapping towards Sakaeri. "Is there trouble?" She eyed their attached grasp with a poorly corralled frown.

Stars, this woman did not navigate Sakaeri's nerves with *any* finesse.

Seraeyu gave a tired sigh and patted at Sakaeri's hand once before letting it go. It flopped back to her side with little ceremony, and Sakaeri instead chose to focus her shrouded gaze upon their interloper.

"No, no, nothing like that," Seraeyu assured, which seemed to do little in the way of assuaging the soldier's concern. "I was simply looking for some company while I send Yisuna here on a small errand."

That seemed to snap something to attention, and the Sentinel sputtered out, "On her own?"

"No, Koali, not alone—"

As if on cue, that contentious Draconguard slipped into the space behind the Sentinel – or Koali, apparently – and sidestepped to the right, offering a respectful dip of his head when he'd spotted Seraeyu in the distance. Seraeyu's grin was almost dazzling then, and it made Sakaeri think that she was missing something.

"Ah, just who I was waiting on. Draconguard Jaspen."

"No," both Sakaeri and Koali said at the same moment, and *ugh*.

Jaspen looked confused then, his helmet held under his arm, darting gaze swapping between the odd mix of individuals before him. "Praetor Thasian?" He asked, respect somewhat undercut with uncertainty.

"I have a very important task for you, Jas," Seraeyu said, absolutely smug, and Sakaeri tried not to cackle at the balk that befell Koali's face. "Will you please accompany my dear Yisuna on her errand into Haebal?"

"Accompany the Sirin into Haebal?" he repeated, as if that couldn't possibly be what had escaped the most esteemed Praetor's mouth.

Seraeyu hummed and said, "Indeed, if you could please do just that. You're so very good at poking your nose where it doesn't belong. I figured I'd invite you along to this one, you know, to give you a bit of an edge."

"Praetor Thasian, are you sure—"

Whatever Koali's sentiment was became lost when Jaspen fell to a knee and devotedly responded, "Of course, Praetor Thasian. I would be honoured to have this task."

"*Stars*," Seraeyu muttered lowly enough that it was surely only Sakaeri that heard. "Ah, lovely. Now with that settled, Koali, I would love to run some drills with you. Surely you'd be glad to help me hone my practice, should the need arise that I make use of it."

"I – Yes, Praetor, I would be grateful to assist."

Sakaeri slouched a bit to the side to better match Seraeyu's height and whispered, "I do not like the idea of leaving you here."

Seraeyu smiled sunnily at her and, too loud to be secretive, said, "Well you'll just have to get over that, won't you?"

If the walk down the stairwell had been awkward, the descent down the elevator was gruelling. Sakaeri stood across from the-Draconguard-now-known-as-Jaspen, her stance wide and sturdy, head held high. He, in turn, stood in the opposite corner, tall with his chest puffed out like some posturing fiend. Each click of a floor being passed felt like a test drawing to a close. Who would crack first? Because it sure as the stars wasn't going to be Sakaeri.

It was nearing the middlemost point of the journey when Jaspen cleared his throat.

I win, resonated smugly across the most petty corners of her mind.

"Sirin Yisuna—" and wasn't that awfully formal "—I will not pretend to know the circumstances under which Praetor Thasian has absolved you. Despite this, I would like you to know that ..." he trailed, and this little intimidation attempt was almost endearing in an annoying kind of way. He was a tenderfoot, wasn't he? He looked young when his helmet wasn't screwed on like he'd lose it otherwise. Jaspen, she suspected, was not really learnt in the grim games played in shady offices. He gathered his resolve and said, "That I am watching you."

"You're oddly devoted to Seraeyu for a Draconguard."

Jaspen's shoulders stiffened, and she'd be willing to bet he grimaced under that gaudy helmet of his, but he proudly professed, "Praetor Thasian is a valued ally to all of Orin. I would be remiss to not show respect."

They just passed floor five and Sakaeri saw a dwindling opportunity. "Ah, yes. With the events at Paladi, strong allies with welcoming cities are indeed valuable, aren't they."

"I would appreciate if you weren't so dismissive, Sirin Yisuna," Jaspen said, and it was too flat. Too measured. "Some of us have families – parents, sisters, brothers – who have become wards of the realm. They need somewhere to feel safe. To keep their bellies full and not worry what personal effect they might find mysteriously missing from one day to the next." The elevator ticked past the second floor. "Some folks don't like to share as much as they ought to."

When the doors finally slid open with a loud ding, Sakaeri watched Jaspen stride ahead a few paces. She decided she didn't despise him as much as she had at higher elevations.

When she finally entered the grand lobby of the Thasian Tower, the realisation hit her in full force that she had not seen these sights in so very long, much less walked these paths. Haebal City had been one big enigmatic question mark, and looking at the black marbled pillars and gold-plated corners of this building she once called home struck something piled beneath the dust of nostalgia. She honestly hadn't realised she'd paused until Jaspen had doubled-back and stood at a safe distance, asking, "Is everything alright, Sirin Yisuna?"

"Yes," she said, and couldn't decide if it was the truth. "Drop the *Sirin* bit."

"As you wish, Yisuna," Jaspen replied, and she swore she heard a grimace.

The lobby was lined with Sentinels, more than there had been in her recollections, and they all watched the pair of them in varying levels of brazen interest. Just what was the dynamic here, Sakaeri wondered. There was only one pair of Draconguard on this level, crammed in a backmost corner and chatting like they had something to hide. Maybe they did.

Perhaps, then, the majority of Draconguard who seemed to have an enduring presence within the Tower held a level of their own? Maybe they were not meant to be as visible as they were apparent within the Tower walls? Sakaeri glanced at Jaspen.

Maybe Seraeyu shouldn't have sent a Draconguard to go traipsing with her through Haebal.

"You Draconguard have become a permanent placement here, I see," she said, digging.

Jaspen actively ignored the attention they drew, strictly marching towards the lobby doors. "Not permanent. Praetor Thasian had asked for a despatch ahead of the – that *event*." It was spat with such vitriol that Sakaeri's head twisted towards him on instinct. "Usually it's only a small group of us. A diplomatic envoy, really."

"Ah, so you're not a foot soldier," said Sakaeri.

"I am as much as any other Orinian. We all adhere to the mandate, undertaking training to uphold Orin and our realmsmen."

"What's your rank?"

"Draconguard, former second lieutenant of the artificers' division." It was all he was able to say before they neared the exit and the Sentinels who guarded it, their stares piercing, even through their visors.

"Good morning," one of them said, and the tone conveyed anything but.

"A pleasant day to you as well," Jaspen said cordially, and Sakaeri held back a cringe at the formality of it.

The two Sentinels seemed unmoved, one of them sniffing. It somehow sounded ornery to Sakaeri's ears. While Jaspen waited in what appeared patience for the Sentinels to release the lock on the door, she smoothly offered a Raenaruan sign of thanks to each. Even still, when she'd straightened back up, neither Sentinel moved.

"We'd wondered where you'd all gone, you know," the one on the right said, not quite miffed, but not far from it. The one of the left nodded in agreement. "Couldn't really have picked a worse time to disappear." There was a subtle shift of a shoulder towards Jaspen, who didn't react if he'd noticed it. "Lots of new faces, not nearly as many old."

To be fair, the Sirin did not have a face. They were phantoms that stalked shadows, wraiths that disappeared with the wind. The only face these Sentinels would know was Hana's, who was not a Sirin at all. But now, Sakaeri was emulating Hana was emulating the Sirin, and at which point did one stop pretending and become? Sakaeri, after all, was a remnant of those slaughtered spirits.

Hana, however, never spoke. So she had to wonder why these two expected *her* to.

"Yisuna mask, huh?" the one on the left finally spoke up. "Hope that doesn't mean Hana's gone for good. Maybe he was up there after all." And it wasn't said cruelly or in a mocking tone. It sounded like a lament of a fate long transpired. So rumours of treasonous Sirin had not even made it to the ground floor of the Thasian Tower, it seemed.

Good. That was good.

"Nice to have one of you back," the rightmost one chimed in. "Things have been … just real odd. Real weird. It'll be good for the city to see a bit of old Raenaru again."

"Bit of a strange pair-up, you two, though," the left one stated, and Sakaeri did not disagree.

She stepped minutely to the side and gave each of them the sign of Raenaruan thanks again, this time adding the crossing of her left hand to mirror the gesture on the opposite side of her chest, something usually only done in ritual. An outdated version of greater gratitude and respect, though these two would certainly know it from the plays that ran during annual festivals, or if they were men of faith and went to the seldom-opened shrine in the city, or any of the old temples dotted across Raenaru.

As expected, they recognised it immediately, and one of them even chuckled a little.

"Alright, alright. Brooding and silent, must be a Sirin thing."

They both offered her, and only her, a return gesture, then the doors were released and Sakaeri was free to roam. It felt childish, the excitement that swirled in her stomach, though some of it was mixed with dread. As she stepped out into the courtyard, Haebal City greeted her with towering buildings and the din of the daily charade. Beyond the brambles and the wispertrees, beyond the blooming popperlilies and fernberries, beyond the reinforced walls and heavy iron gates, Haebal City *lived*.

CHAPTER NINE

"Why here?" Jaspen asked as they slipped into an alley beside the boarded-up Thasian-nee smithy.

The journey through Haebal's glimmering Cheyun District had been uncomfortable, full of phantasms of moments long passed and quickly averted glances from bumbling city-dwellers. As soon as Sakaeri had left the confines of those sprawling gardens encasing the Tower, she was struck with a biting and uncanny image of a city troubled with unspoken concerns, all spread thickly throughout its winding paths and perfectly composed storefronts, modelled after prosperity itself. Haebalians seemed to have adopted the tendency to either trudge their feet in some sort of defeated gait or hasten their footfalls to escape the future that chased them. It was odd and so very different from the city she'd known in her youth, full of vibrancy and confidence. Now, only a drab interpretation of it presented, somehow pairing well with the grieving cries of the mid-morning chimes, sounding from the shrine sat on the border of Penthyun and Danu, locked up tight so that the clergy could practice in peace.

There were a few folks who stared more directly than others, a stilted sort of curiosity painting across their faces as they eyed the emblazoned plates of the Draconguard's night-shaded armour beside her twilight cloak and ceremonial Yisuna mask beside him. Cheyun was largely a place of business and governance, so there was not an abundance of children around on any given day, and in this quick jaunt Sakaeri had only seen a few, one of whom was forcibly tugged from her and her unlikely companion by a father who cast suspicious appraisal across their way. There was something left to rot on Haebal's streets, and a part of Sakaeri wondered if the city would ever truly be cleansed of it.

"Well," Sakaeri began, easily falling back into her slinking Sirin choreograph, melding with the shade tucked between crates and alleyway debris, shoved where it wasn't visible to the naked eye. Something about that felt kindred, whether she wanted it to or not. "Seraeyu wanted me to make sure of a few things," she said as she eyed the window on the third storey, the one she knew led into the Thasian-nee's kitchen.

"And this involved breaking and entering into the second house of Thasian's old place of business?" Jaspen whispered, perhaps a little harshly. The both of them jumped when a fencat sprinted from a pile of rubbish set deeper into the narrows, its bony body leaping frenetically to escape their intrusion.

"Just shut up and keep watch."

"Excuse me?" Jaspen didn't relent. "I was sent *with* you, Sirin Yisuna. As such, I will go where you go."

And yeah, she hated that. And Seraeyu had not sent her to her late father's home specifically, but rather on a reconnaissance run of Haebal City in general. However, the Thasian-nee residence was indeed housed within those sprawling corridors, so …

She also knew that the Draconguard was there for one of two reasons: to not arouse further suspicion on her person as she ran amuck on her own, or so that she could pry answers from him by asking questions that Seraeyu *should* know the answers to but doesn't. The meeting with the Raenaruan Council was set for a few days' time, representatives from all the main regions called to convene at the Thasian Tower for what seemed to be the first time since the fall of Oagyu himself. The daemon must have told them to fuck right off and leave the politics to her, which presumably did not cast Seraeyu in a favourable light to the Council.

Not that they could have done much about that in the first place, the way they already grovelled at Oagyu's feet, heeding his decrees.

"Well, pardon me if I don't feel comfortable inviting a *Draconguard* into the late head of the Thasian-nee family's home."

"You'll forgive me if I don't agree that this can reasonably be interpreted as *an invitation*."

Sakaeri levelled his ostentatious, gleaming helmet with an unimpressed look that Jaspen could neither see nor react to. "How would your metal arse get up there anyway?" When he didn't comment, she continued with, "Look, I'm going up there and you're staying down here. And then we can have a nice stroll around some of the neighbouring districts and you can catch me up on all the goings-on over the past while."

"Sirin Yisuna—!"

It was too late. Sakaeri had pulled upon her tune with the misty verdant jewel lodged in one of her rings – and wow, crystals and gems really were a game changer, the tune duetting with her own innate melody, procuring a pleasant thrum instead of that grating brush that came with raw, unrefined ore. A zephyr manifested with a swirl under her feet, and she crouched low before propelling herself forcefully with the assistance of cradling wind. The jump had flung her slightly too high, past the next floor's landing, but she lurched out gloved hands and latched onto the bars of the targeted kitchen window on her descent, digging in and holding tight as her body's weight swung towards the tiled siding. The funny thing was, if there *wasn't* a grate on the window, she wouldn't have been able to find purchase at all. So much for deterring thieves.

Far below, Jaspen muttered something that Sakaeri couldn't care to parse, and she instead focused on changing her tune. There was a unique quality to the pendant hung from her necklace, another adornment lifted from Raeyu's stash, which held a crystal Seraeyu said was mined from the tunnels of Paladi, scarce and ancient, compressed and formed over years unfathomable.

Adamantine was a rare gift indeed.

Focusing on it, looping her consciousness around threads of a tune that lay dormant, she held it close, asking the whispering ballad to lend her strength, just for a little while. With concentration, the bars on the window began to crunch inwards on themselves, her grip quickly swapping to the handles of the window itself, and soon the wrinkled metal was crumpled and clattering on the stone below, just beside Jaspen's feet. Commanding the window's latch to spring open was a simple flick of her finger, then the duet calmed, fading into aether.

Potent, Sakaeri considered, *and very useful, but also draining, that one.*

She nudged the window open and hoisted herself up, sat halfway into the darkened kitchen when she glanced back down at the abandoned Draconguard below. He was still looking at the crushed metal littering the space by his toes. "Stay put," she ordered, and his head snapped up to meet her gaze, but he remained eerily silent. "Right, then," she muttered to herself, climbing the rest of the way into the stale abode.

Tucking her limbs through the curtains, she was greeted with a dark room, quiet with disuse. Her vision adjusted accordingly, and it caught on things like one chair pushed a little further than the rest, someone having left the table a bit too carelessly to bother. A vase with wilted stems of something that had long since lost its petals. Dishes having been left to dry, instead gathering dust in this husk of a room that once sung with warmth.

Warmth, that's what it needed. That would help.

Sakaeri gently stretched her attunement to the dormant ore gathered in lighting fixtures, urging them to glow ever so softly. Anything harsh, she thought, did not have a place in this moment. With the brightening of the space came the illumination of further little details she'd missed. The cabinet door left ajar, the withered herbs by the sink, the note sat next to the breadbox. Transfixed, she felt herself lured to the message there, the very air surrounding her feeling weighted. Some final words, left behind when nothing else was.

When she'd loomed over the scrawl, it was the bloodied, now rust-brown prints upon its edges that yanked her heart into her throat. Because, bloodied? Why would they be bloodied? Then there were little distortions across the wafer material, like small drops had been scattered as someone read the message. The message that only said: *Don't forget to eat breakfast before joining us! Love, Uruji.*

Sakaeri read it once, twice. Three times until she felt like she could breathe again.

Bloodied hands? It certainly hadn't been Uruji himself, since he'd warped himself to another realm entirely. And it couldn't have been Aeyun or Raeyu, and especially not Jourae since … since …

That left … Seraeyu?

Seraeyu had been here? Wouldn't he have said so?

Or did he not know? Had he not been *him*? But then, why weep for the man murdered? Why cry at all?

Sakaeri backed away from the note, wary as if it were poison. Another piece to the grander game, whatever it was that they were playing. She wasn't sure there would be any victors in the end, just the destruction of greed and vanity left behind. Sakaeri allowed herself one fortifying inhale. It was time to move on.

She twisted on her heel and strode to the kitchen's door, nudging it open. As it creaked, maw widening, Sakaeri peeked into the space beyond. A room for gathering, enjoying idle conversation and laughter, neither of which bounced from its walls for far too long. Easing the same calm glow here as the room prior, she stepped light-footed, sounds other than settling wooden planks too much like a screech in a silent mausoleum. The piano by the window looked lonely, un-played and covered in a film of settled grey. A book that had once been the current fancy of either Jourae or Uruji rested crookedly atop a side table, its last moment of glory demarcated with an eared page.

Standing there in that liminality, stuck between the kitchen, the living room, and the entryway with its stretching stairwell, Sakaeri recalled standing in Raeyu's old room. In Oagyu's room. In Seraeyu's room. In a temple full of dead Sirin.

How many places would Sakaeri stand where its testament was to persons lost? Was it the realms' retribution for the life she chose? For the lights she'd snuffed out? Or was that just the cold reality they all existed in? Forever cycling, forsaking all who lost momentum.

Sakaeri shook it off. It had no place here, those thoughts.

She meandered to the stairs, restraining herself from trailing fingers across various oddities that meant something to someone in this preserved visage of a household once thriving. It wasn't clear who preferred the prime placement of the kitschy sabermaw figurine, but one of them liked it enough to place it beside a picture of Uruji and Aeyun, both laughing raucously at something beyond the frame. Next to that was an image of Jourae looking like a mountain beside an adolescent Uruji, who was beaming as he held up a beautifully faceted gem. No doubt one of his first major achievements.

Sakaeri allowed herself a moment to stare. Then she moved on.

Always moved on.

Each step up felt like a retracing of Jourae, of Uruji, of Aeyun. Each step up felt like a new stone had been shackled to her ankle, every footfall more taxing than the last. When she made it to the landing, she stood there, hand gripped upon the rail lest she fall back or retreat.

Slowly, and ever so cautiously, she spied into rooms that she'd never once entered. Uruji's was tidy, and that seemed fitting, tomes filed meticulously, desk clear of clutter. Aeyun's was ready for his return, as it had been for nearing two years to that day, bed made and the chair in the corner looking lived in, almost as if someone used to sit in it regularly, waiting. The last, Jourae's, was cold.

It wasn't tidy, not really, miscellaneous assortments of little knickknacks about the place, maybe presents. It wasn't ready for his return, not traditionally, since the bed dressings hadn't been tucked back into place. It was cold. Unused, forgotten.

And *Yun of the stars*, how was she supposed to look Seraeyu in the face on her return? How was she meant to, when her mind kept repeating those last moments to her again and again and—

She shut the door. She walked down the stairs and continued towards the smithy, unsurprised to find it picked clean of anything that had once graced its smelter. She doubled-back towards the kitchen, not allowing herself another inspect of the note.

It was not her place. It never was.

Sakaeri swung her legs over the windowsill and intended to use that adamantine to weld the window shut for good. Making good on that plan, she propelled herself away from the sealed egress and tuned a gale to soften her landing.

And then she moved on.

CHAPTER TEN

Aeyun sat in the tower where Gama-of-Yun laid peacefully, his chest rising and falling with evened breaths. He stared at the face he recognised from his younger years – a straight-sloped nose, shallow cheeks, the sharp curve of his brow – Gama-of-Yun had seemingly not aged even a single year. It was strange, considering Gama-of-Yun didn't look like a god. And he certainly didn't act like one, from what Aeyun recalled.

He still didn't believe that Gama-of-Yun was a god at all.

"You called to me," Aeyun murmured. He plucked at lint on his trousers and frowned, glancing back at the comatose man. "I know you did. I heard you, in the in-between."

There was no response, only the muffled noise from the floors below and the rustle of the woods beyond the window.

"I don't know what you wanted – what you want." Aeyun frowned. "Do you know her? Sirin?" He breathed in, frustrated. "Do you know how to get rid of her?" A pause. "Are you helping her?"

His next inhale shuddered.

"Who is Ka'la'drius?"

Something pulsated around Aeyun, then it rippled across the realm. Runes on the walls shrivelled up, and Aeyun *knew* this. He recognised this, remembered it. He stood, alarm clawing up his insides, swift and biting. There was a shuffling to his left, and when he looked, he was terrified to see that Gama-of-Yun had moved, his eyes now open.

"Ka'la'drius," Gama-of-Yun repeated, slow and lethargic. Aeyun watched in morbid fascination as opaline eyes flickered towards him. "Ka'la'drius?"

"Ka'la'drius?" Aeyun repeated back, quiet in questioning, lost.

What had he done? What was he supposed to do? This man who hadn't moved a muscle – with one exception – in years was groggily regarding him, saying a name that Aeyun had only learnt recently.

"Ka'la'drius?" Gama-of-Yun said again, and a dreadful feeling sank in. "You are Ka'la'drius?"

Gama-of-Yun began to sit up until he winced, a small trail of crimson seeping from his tear duct. Heaving in hastened breaths, Aeyun backed away.

"Da'garu." He hoped she was back from her trip to the trader. He hoped she was back and that she would come to his call. "Da'garu!" Gama-of-Yun swiped at his face, baffled by the smudge of red that rubbed off on his wrist, then he made to stand but quickly crumpled back down. "DA'GARU!"

Gama-of-Yun's eyes flashed, black starting to seep into their corners. It wasn't long before heavy thumps indicated someone running up the stairs, then Da'garu was rushing through the door, huffing. She paused in the frame, mouth dropping at the sight of Gama-of-Yun, then she dove forwards, grabbing his head in her hands.

The ink in Gama-of-Yun's eyes teased recede, and they became opaline once more before fading to white. Then they appeared as the murky brown that Aeyun remembered them to be. Gama-of-Yun's wavering gaze landed on Da'garu, his brow furrowed in bafflement.

"Da'garu?" he asked hoarsely. Not a moment later, Aeyun nearly felt his heart stop when Gama-of-Yun looked over and called out a gravelly, "A'vor?"

Gama-of-Yun was worse than Aeyun remembered. He may as well have been brain-fried by one of the Thasian lightning strikes for how well — or not well, rather — his mind seemed to work. He was more than just forgetful; he was bewildered by the simplest things, often lost in his own musings, and he seemed to lack any sense of time.

After calling out *A'vor*, he asked how Ca'rud and A'ru were. Of course, the question met silence, then Da'garu's eyes flickered, perhaps conveying something to Gama-of-Yun. Something silent but heard by the recipient. Unable to contend with the development of it all, Aeyun gave them space and absentmindedly wandered down the stairs.

"Aeyun?" Raeyu's voice drifted to his ears from across the room. He looked her way, but his focus didn't steady. "Are you okay?"

"Uh, I—" he gestured vaguely to where he'd emerged from. "Gama is awake."

"The god's awoken?" Davah asked. Aeyun couldn't tell if he was joking.

Aeyun kept stumbling on — he wasn't even sure where he was going — and he saw Raeyu move towards him in his periphery, but she held herself back. Uruji, however, had no such reservation. He followed Aeyun out into the glen. He didn't ask or make any commentary. Instead, he simply stepped in time beside him. He didn't even question Aeyun when they neared the mouth of the cavern.

Shaken, Aeyun decided it was the right moment to speak.

"Uruji," he said, and his brother looked up at him. "Stay with them. Stay with Da'garu. If Gama does anything strange—" his mind was plagued with thoughts of Sirin, "—do whatever you need to do."

"What do you mean?" Uruji asked, a concerned note overtaking the question.

Aeyun's mind felt like it was spinning, ripping apart. He had to leave. To get out. He couldn't be next to all this, struggling to tread water in an endless sea of a push and pull that never seemed to stop. He needed quiet. And he needed to be away from the stares.

"I'm sorry, I—" Aeyun shook his head. "I'm counting on you," he said, and he felt guilty as soon as he did.

Uruji fidgeted, seemingly unsure of what to say next.

"Where are you going?"

"I don't know," Aeyun said, and he left those as his parting words while he dipped into the cavern, the a'teneum and all its questions left behind him.

The Ou'grobh in the evening was mysterious as it was menacing. The streaky glow of the night slipped across the surface of The Veil, casting an ethereal glimmer across the forest canopy. Aeyun let his first step take him deep into the wood, far from it all. A tightness grew his chest, ready to burst, and he stepped again, the trees thrusting him through dense foliage. One more step and he was running.

Running, running, always running.

When had it all gone so wrong? It had actually gone right, hadn't it? Here, together. So why did it feel so wicked, the way things were? Why did he feel stained? And why did it all terrify him to his core?

In the depths of his soulsong, the truth murmured dissonantly.

This wasn't it. There was more to be done. And Aeyun wasn't enough to get it done. He failed again and again and again. And those who he was meant to protect, to safeguard from all the atrocities the realms wished to subject them to, had suffered the worst. And Aeyun wasn't enough. He couldn't be enough. He didn't know how, and he wasn't doing anything right. Every step he'd made was a cut and every leap he'd jumped was a gouge. He couldn't do it. He couldn't do it, and he wasn't enough, and he couldn't understand—

Aeyun tumbled gracelessly when the Ou'grobh spit him out into a clearing, overgrown with weeds and wilds. As he rolled to a stop, his bare arms caught on loose twigs and thorns, scraping against them, little nicks left where they'd bit indiscriminately into inky and unmarked flesh alike. He groaned and pushed himself up, peering at an old cabin and a forgotten garden.

He was home.

Aeyun shakily stood and looked at the bones of his childhood. The wood had stains of ashen edges, a distinct indication that a fire once raged there, and the hand-laid fence that his father had put up was broken in several places. Kicked in, if he were to guess. On the far side of the garden were two stones, symbols carved atop them.

Trembling, Aeyun walked over to them.

Mother, one indicated. And the other, Father.

Aeyun fell to his knees before the stones, a strangled sound erupting from his chest. He placed a hand on either rock, knelt his head down, touching his forehead to the dirt.

Mother, the stone said, because Da'garu probably didn't recall their names at the time. A loud sob slipped from his throat, lodged their chokingly, and his chest constricted with a painful lurch. He'd left her here alone, among the mayhem and the wreckage. To discover it all herself. To deal with it all herself.

When had she found Gama-of-Yun? Or when had he found her? Had Da'garu lived in this burnt husk of their old home for days? Weeks? Years? When had she lost her voice?

"Fuck," he breathed out, sniffing loudly. "Fucking, dammit!"

He didn't deserve to call himself her brother, or family at all.

And he'd done it again, just now. Leave those he cared for because he couldn't handle it. He was pathetic. He was disgusted. He was—

Aeyun opened his eyes to a smoky sea of black. Essence flowed around him, little pockets of collapsing energy visible through fractured, bodiless walls and nonsensical layers. It was the same maze from then, when Essence abandoned him. Aeyun felt his gaze light up with a familiar, comforting radiance.

Somewhere, an echo dripped, its origin too ambiguous to determine a direction.

He knew what he was looking for. Listening, grasping onto small reverberations that wove through the nothingness, Aeyun stood, rubbing at his eyes. He let intuition guide him, beckon him, and he circled around the maze, steadier than he had been the last time. A song carried across the haze. Aeyun wanted to find it.

For seconds or hours, he couldn't tell, he wandered between the unforgiving miasma until, finally, he found its centre. It pulsed and there Seraeyu sat, clothed in casual attire, looking a far cry from the holocaster image that plagued the capital cities across the realms for the past year. His eyes were closed, his head angled down. He almost appeared as if sleeping sitting up.

Slower now, Aeyun approached. He dropped to his knees before him. Not daring to speak louder than a whisper, Aeyun said, "Seraeyu."

Seraeyu's chin lifted, his eyes opening. They were a deep, inky obsidian, devoid of any splash of ivory or sprinkling of light.

"I hear you," Seraeyu said, looking but not seeing.

"Is she awake?" Aeyun asked, watching for signs of clawed fingers wrapping around Seraeyu's skull. They didn't, and Seraeyu gave a lazy indication of denial.

"No, she's been quiet."

Those words were all it took for Aeyun to reach out and grab Seraeyu's wrist. When he did, he felt the vibrancy of his own vision dampen, and he watched as little pinpricks of white appeared in Seraeyu's eyes, populating them like stars.

"Hi," he said, but he wasn't smiling.

"Hi," Aeyun responded.

"You look like a wreck," Seraeyu admonished, and Aeyun felt like he was scrutinising his form, even if he couldn't track his pupils.

"I feel like a wreck," said Aeyun.

"So, we're just going to pretend like this is normal?" Seraeyu said after a long bout of silence. "You know, I heard you the other night, too. How are you doing that?"

"I don't know," Aeyun admitted. He barely remembered speaking to him the previous night, anyway.

"You sounded drunk," Seraeyu commented.

Aeyun fought the urge to flinch away, sure it would break the connection.

"I was ... a bit."

"Right. I hope you're enjoying your holiday, then," Seraeyu said, but he didn't pull away. He sat still, patient and waiting.

"It's not a holiday," Aeyun told him, a simmer of frustration boiling.

"I'm sure it's not."

While his tone was biting, Seraeyu's message wasn't sarcastic. He seemed well aware that, whatever he thought Aeyun might be doing, it wasn't a restful occasion. The issue, though, was that Aeyun *did* feel too idle.

"Talk to me," Aeyun said, and he couldn't quite mask the desperation.

"Why?"

"Are you okay?"

"It was you, right?" Seraeyu asked, his hands turning to curl around Aeyun's wrists in turn, their vice almost threatening. Aeyun knew – burdened with a horrible premonition – what was coming before it left Seraeyu's lips. "You're the reason I can't tune?"

"Seraeyu—"

"Why'd you do it?" he asked, and Aeyun stared at the face of the man he'd doomed to be deemed Untuned many years passed. "I can feel your presence in whatever it is that clings to me. Like it was leeched from your very soulsong. I didn't know why you fascinated me before, but I can feel it now. I hear it, incessantly."

"I fascinated you?" Aeyun caught on to what was likely the most innocuous notion of that statement. Seraeyu groaned and shook Aeyun's arm a bit, annoyed.

"*Really?*" He stopped his tugging. "Why'd you do it?"

"Can you tune with ore anymore?" If he couldn't, then—

"Not really, no," Seraeyu said, a frown etching grimly.

"Oh," Aeyun responded, and Seraeyu groaned again.

"*Starry sea* – Aeyun!"

"I can't, either," Aeyun told him, despite being unsure if he should reveal such a fact. "Tune with ore, I mean."

"Why'd you do it?" Seraeyu asked again, and Aeyun swallowed a dry tongue.

"It wasn't fair to you," he said, and he was frightened to find out what Seraeyu's reaction to his admission might be. Seraeyu watched on, silent. "We wanted to do what was best—"

"We?" Seraeyu interrupted, his grasp loosening slightly. "You and ... Raeyu? Of course, she put you up to it. Of course."

"Don't misunderstand; she wanted to protect you," Aeyun was quick to say, but Seraeyu was slipping away.

"Protect me," Seraeyu said, incredulous. "Well, look where that landed us!"

Just as the connection was nearly severed, Aeyun adjusted his grip and pulled him back. Seraeyu blinked at him, a bit closer than before.

"Don't pull away," said Aeyun. Quieter, he added, "Please."

"Don't do that," Seraeyu told him, volume matched to Aeyun's. "That's not fair. I'm mad – I'm rightfully *livid* with you, and my sister – don't make me feel bad for you. You can't make me feel bad for you right now."

"I'm not trying to—"

"But you are!" Seraeyu interrupted him, exasperated. "I – Aeyun, you seem – how am I meant to be mad at a man who looks as broken as you do?"

Aeyun didn't know how to respond. Anywhere other than Seraeyu was a mist of blackened walls, full of swirling haze, so he instead focused on his own hands and where they met Seraeyu's wrists.

"I am angry at you," Seraeyu declared, and Aeyun watched as sharp nails dug into his skin. "And I have every right to be. How could you take away something so precious, so integral to my very being? You took away my defences, Aeyun! I was never given the right – the opportunity – to prove the realms wrong. Instead, I was relegated to the sidelines. I became the reason, in truth or not, for all my father's troubles." The fierce clawlike points of his nails poked in, leaving little rings around their impression, but then the pressure abated and Seraeyu's fingers loosened, shifting. "You don't know what the fuck you're doing, do you?"

"No," Aeyun said, finally looking up. Seraeyu's gaze searched his.

"Where are you?"

"At my parents' graves."

The reaction was a mix of conflicting emotions. Pity first, then confusion – likely because Seraeyu still regarded Jourae as Aeyun's only father – then a morose sort of curiosity wove across Seraeyu's features. But he didn't ask.

"Are you okay?"

Aeyun considered the question. Was he? Probably not. In fact, he was sure he was very, very far from being okay. His morbid chortle undoubtedly communicated that well enough.

"Are you alone?"

It was a simple quandary. Aeyun both was and wasn't. As his gaze traced Seraeyu's face, concerned and beckoning, he was reminded that Seraeyu was alone. Truly alone.

"What about you?" he asked, and Seraeyu gave him a tight smile.

"Tricky, trying to turn it around like that," he said. "But okay, I'll bite. If you don't want to talk about it. Because I can't attune with ore as freely as before, I've been in control, for the most part. I think the daemon is finding it difficult. Not that I have any clue what to do, though. There are a lot of corrupt actors that I'm now in a game with. If the daemon doesn't kill me first, I'm sure they will if I screw up. I've never been so in over my head in my life." He gave a mirthless laugh. "I never wanted this."

"Wait," said Aeyun. "You're in control more? Is – is Sakaeri with you? And what do you mean the daemon might kill you, or that they will?"

"Sakaeri is here, yes, if not a bit under-informed from your own adventuring. I am very fortunate that she's here, though." Seraeyu retreated, his form sagging, glum. "It's been complicated. But she's here, and hopefully safe." He pursed his lips, thinking for a moment. "As for the control, well … back before, sometimes it was like I was a passenger, watching. Other times, it was like I blacked out, or it was all hazy, only to come to and something else unspeakable had happened. Now, I seem to command primary agency. Like control has swapped – only sometimes her. But she's done so much damage.

"She disappeared a lot of people, and she created these networks across the realms. I want to call off Orin – did you know they've occupied Mhedoon? – but I don't know how. The Dracon is breathing down my neck and she has Draconguard in the Tower, watching me. I think … I think Paladi erupted? And none of them know I can't tune anymore. I have a meeting with the Council in a few days, and there's the Lu-Ghanian Ministers. They've sent their Sentinels en route as well. And then there's that awful man, Kaisa—"

"Kaisa's been visiting you?" Aeyun said, and he wasn't entirely sure why that name alarmed him the most out of all those figures, but it did.

"Not yet, but he surely will."

"Are you safe?" Aeyun asked, and Seraeyu gave him another tight smile, just as he had before.

"I mean, not really, Aeyun. I'm fucking terrified. I genuinely don't know what to do."

"And you think daemon'll kill you – why?"

Seraeyu shrugged. "I'm not her ideal host anymore. I don't know how she broke through your cursed tune—" Aeyun didn't miss the glare aimed his way, "—the first time, but she can't seem to do the same this time."

Aeyun rolled the thought over in his head a few times. "You can tune with Essence, you know." Seraeyu's eyebrows rose, but he didn't respond otherwise. "That's why you can't tune with ore. I used to think it was because – anyway, it doesn't matter. You're unbalanced, because your call to Essence … it's compounded with mine. I can barely hear it now, its song." He took a deep breath, then sighed. A weight felt lifted, and he said, "You have my Essence, and I have your Vitality."

"Your Essence was exchanged for my … Vitality?" Seraeyu questioned, then a disconnected, sardonic smirk spread across his face. "So, you're saying that we are perfectly unbalanced, in equilibrium, together?"

Aeyun blinked and huffed out a wry laugh.

"Yeah, I guess."

"How very strange," said Seraeyu. "What an odd thing for you to have done."

"At the time, I didn't know it was what I'd done."

Seraeyu's features contorted at that, reflecting unspoken bemusement. It preceded a companionate impasse, one where Aeyun began to feel quietly dissected.

He broke it by asking, "Should I tell her?"

"No," Seraeyu said, catching on right away. "You still might have to kill me."

"Ser—"

"You might. And she wouldn't be able to. Not if she knew it was still me."

Aeyun couldn't fight him on that. He was right. Raeyu loved her brother dearly, and she'd never be able to put him to eternal rest, especially if she knew that he was still there, a prisoner of his own design. Or, in part, *their* design.

Seraeyu's eyes caught on something behind Aeyun and, not a second later, Aeyun felt a presence invade his senses.

"A'vor," a voice rung out, and Aeyun instinctually knew it as Da'garu's. What almost surprised him more, though, was Seraeyu's jump at the name, meaning he'd most certainly heard it as well. *"What are you doing?"*

"Who—?"

Aeyun cut off Seraeyu's question with a terse shake of his head. He gave him an apologetic look, then he began to lean away. Seraeyu clung tighter for a moment, perhaps out of spiking insecurity, and Aeyun gently picked up Seraeyu's lingering hand that was latched to his wrist. He held it for a moment, hoping to suggest that he wasn't abandoning him; that he would be back; that Seraeyu wasn't alone. Then he allowed their grip to slip apart, the hazy maze dissolving around him.

Back on solid ground, back upon the graves, Aeyun blinked the realm into focus. He turned around to look at his sister, whose eyes were glowing a ghostly white.

Before he could even consider the significance of her knowing where he would be, he said, "You spoke to me."

To that, Da'garu looked desperately confused, only shaking her head once in the negative. But she had. He'd *heard* her, crisp and clear, as did Seraeyu. Her gaze trailed down to the stones before him, and she frowned. Hesitant, she reached out a hand, a gentle coaxing to get back on his feet. She jerked her head to the side, indicating her preference that they leave this place, and that they do so together.

Not one to waste an olive branch where it was given, he accepted.

By the time they'd reached the a'teneum, Aeyun was dreading facing his companions. He'd fled in what was likely a very pivotal moment, and he was ashamed. More so, he was overwhelmed. He felt like he was being pulled in several directions, and he didn't know which way was up.

What was he even trying to accomplish anymore?

When they entered the ages old building, he felt the pressure of everyone's stares.

He didn't know why it made his skin crawl when he saw Gama-of-Yun sitting in an armchair by the fire, a book laid out in his lap. But it did. The oddly unaged man looked up then, mystified and unabashed as he watched them.

"Do I ... ?" Gama-of-Yun asked, his brow twisting in thought.

"Gama-of-Yun?" Uruji questioned, cautiously. Gama-of-Yun looked over at him then, and the confusion on his face only grew. Suffering a wince, Gama-of-Yun put a palm to his temple and stood up, gently depositing the tome he'd held on the cushion of the chair.

"I think I might lay down. Da'garu, I'm going to lay down. You'll be okay on your own today? I think our trip to town may have to wait till morning," he said, nodding to himself. Aeyun glanced towards Da'garu to gauge her reaction to that, but her own expression was bereft of understanding. "Oh," Gama-of-Yun said as Davah deftly moved out of his way. He blinked at the man. "Oh, Davah, do not feel bad. A journey awaits us all." It was said kindly, generously, and it left Davah staring wide-eyed after him as Gama-of-Yun ascended the stairs, muttering to himself on his way.

"I didn't—" Davah spun towards Aeyun, alarmed. "I didn't tell him my name," he said, then he twisted his neck to crane a look after the fading steps. "I ..."

Despite himself, Aeyun turned to Da'garu again, an unspoken question hanging in the air. She just gave him a brief shake of her head before busying herself with grabbing some food left out on the table. If Aeyun interpreted it right, that meant that Da'garu wasn't sure why he was so curiously befuddled either. What it didn't communicate, however, was how long he'd been like that. Judging by Da'garu's lack of reaction about the commentary around a trip to town, Aeyun figured it may have been too long. Because surely there was no actual plan to enact that little jaunt.

"Aeyun?" Raeyu called, and his stomach dropped. He looked at her, heart pounding, rattling around his ribcage in a sickening ricochet. "Are you okay?"

It was a question he was tired of hearing.

Aeyun was tired of being asked if he was feeling alright. Or if he needed anything. Or if he wanted to talk.

It wasn't supposed to be like that. He was meant to be the pillar. He was meant to be the one who took the brunt of the worry, who shouldered it, so that others didn't have to. And if he felt like a failure before, he felt even more like one now.

So, instead of saying that he felt like he was drowning – instead of saying that he wanted to scream and cry and rest his head on someone's shoulder – he said, "Yeah, sorry to worry you." He plastered on a smile. "I'm fine. I just needed a moment." Da'garu tilted her head then, brow arched in curiosity. Aeyun very much suspected that she saw right through that placation. "Just some air to clear my head. I'm good."

"Okay," said Raeyu. Her eyes were gentle and her smile welcoming, but Aeyun felt like he was falling backwards. "If you say so. I trust you." His heart sank further until he could swear it felt like it was bleeding out from the soles of his feet.

"Yeah, I promise. You don't need to worry about me. I'm feeling a lot better."

"I'm glad," she said, and it seemed so genuine that Aeyun had to fold his fingers into his palms, nails digging into the flesh there.

"I'm always okay in the end, you know that." Aeyun grinned and forced out a laugh.

"We're here, though, if you need us," Raeyu said, but he could already feel the weight of her worry fading.

Aeyun went through the motions of rubbing the back of his head sheepishly. "Yeah, I know!"

"Wait, Da'garu—!" Uruji called, and he spared Aeyun a quick, apologetic glance before he followed Da'garu out into the glen, where she'd silently disappeared. Aeyun took a long-suffering breath through his nose. He turned, wanting to be alone.

Instead, he caught Davah's gaze. His companion watched him intently, something connecting there. An understanding that Aeyun couldn't shake.

Aeyun just wanted to sleep.

He started towards the stairwell. As he passed Davah, the man's face taking on that grave look it did when he just *got it*, Davah said, "I won't pry, but ..."

"I know, Davah," Aeyun said, letting a hand fall heavy on Davah's shoulder. "Thanks." He meant it.

Without another word from either of them, Aeyun traipsed up the stairs, aiming to find one of the rooms the group of them had been rotating in and out of during their stay – there wasn't enough space in the a'teneum for them all, not really, so accommodation was often first-come-first-serve. With the exception of Gama-of-Yun, of course.

Aeyun cast a wary eye towards the uppermost turret, where Gama-of-Yun was resting. Telling himself that he didn't have the mental fortitude for it, he instead veered towards one of the rooms to the left, where a bedroll was laid out. He'd leave one of the nicer rooms for the others.

He stepped in and slid the door closed, toeing off his shoes. Padding across the room, he shed bits of clothes as he went, letting himself breathe. Aeyun was exhausted. Beyond the window, he could see the thinned, filmy sky of The Veil. He frowned at it.

He wanted to see the vastness of the starry sea. He wanted to see the moons that smiled down upon Tenebrana, and he wanted to watch the sun rise over the waters of Mhedoon. He wanted to witness the majesty of the in-between, and he wanted to immerse himself in the buzz of Haebal. He wanted more, and he wanted all of it.

Feeling constricted, he pulled off his undershirt in a frustrated motion. His head hung with a groan of irritation, then he spotted something that shouldn't be there. Or rather, something that should be there, but was absent.

Unmarred skin, rune-free and clear around that ever-present Essence scar that demarcated the location of his heart. "Oh," he said. "*Stars*, dammit."

Uruji had said that if he came into contact with Essence that the runic wards would fade. That his elementary studies of the runic arts, learnt from the books that lined the library's walls, wouldn't be enough to hold up to it.

But it was meant to happen slowly. Chipped away over many moments, not seconds.

Aeyun guessed that Uruji hadn't counted on his old ward wiping the runes away in one go, with one touch. He guessed that Uruji wouldn't have even considered that Aeyun would be speaking casually with the man who tore a hole through their father's chest, and he guessed that Uruji didn't even know that he'd banished Aeyun's attunement with Essence back whence it came, curled up inside Seraeyu's soulsong.

Aeyun restlessly scrubbed his hands down his face. Nothing was easy.

CHAPTER ELEVEN

Jaspen hadn't said a word since they'd left the Thasian-nee smithy. Not even when they breached the threshold of Cheyun and Penthyun, its main corridors depressingly barren where they had once been thriving. Sakaeri supposed that barricading a people from the realms would concede that, supply chains being disrupted or broken entirely. In fact, there were definitely a few new *unit for sale* signs than she recalled.

No, throughout the entire trip from one district to the next, the Draconguard remained silent. Stoic. There was no idle chatter, not as they passed faces that Sakaeri recognised but couldn't quite place, nor when then traipsed over The River Souyi, its waters babbling against rocky ledges, its narrow passage drowned between towering blocks of opulent structures. It wasn't until they neared Danu that Jaspen spoke.

"That alicant," he said, and wasn't that just an obtuse way to start a sentence. "It's illegal."

"Not sure what you're referring to, kid."

"Adamantine," he whispered, and Sakaeri wondered *why*, honestly. The streets were gloomy and sparse, not many making the trek from the tree-lined boulevards of Danu into the once-spectacular Penthyun. "And I would appreciate if you refrained from calling me *kid*."

"I will call you kid if you spout nonsense. The Treatise of Fair Tune, as written by the Autonomous Region of Tarnin, did indeed succeed in making the possession or use of adamantine without an express and *ridiculously specific* licence illegal, and it also made it impossible to trade or refine. However, these are laws which apply only to Orin, since that treatise's governance cannot extend to dominions where the given authority did not sign said treaty." Sakaeri flapped a hand as she prattled, preening a little in what felt like undivided attention oozing from the novice Draconguard. "In theory, adamantine should not exist beyond Orin, and yet ... If this alleged alicant was, let us imagine, gifted to an individual who had no tracings of its origins, ownership having previously been held under someone of Raenaruan descent, presumably in their lineage's possession from perhaps a time since before the treatise was even in effect, well. That's perfectly fair and legal until any one owner steps foot on Orin with the alleged alicant in their possession, wouldn't you agree?"

"That's *smokeserpent spit*."

The laugh that burst out erupted from her diaphragm, so quick and unrelenting that she took a moment to steady herself on the peeling bark of weeping whispertree, its amethystine tendrils dusting the pathway ahead. "Smokeserpent spit or not, I'd bet coin that would hold in a Court of Council." Though, she sincerely hoped there would never come a time her testimony would be needed at such a proceeding.

"The Praetor must place much trust in you," Jaspen said, and it came across as an odd mix of curt and contemplative.

Sakaeri let herself settle into the moment, scanning the lanes ahead. If they didn't turn towards the several sprawling estates, they would instead end up in neighbouring Gyuyu or Narui, or the leafy forest Aeyun and Raeyu had seemingly claimed as their own a lifetime ago. There were still little signs of life here and there, like a young mother with a pram or someone exercising their tamelynx. It was when a child whirred by on his bell-chiming cycle, screaming to his lagging friend to *watch for the clinker!* – who she presumed to be Jaspen – that Sakaeri sighed. Well, she'd have to pick one of those destinations, wouldn't she? And she really needed to start getting answers.

As it turned out, she didn't have to make a decision at all, since Jaspen apparently elected to take the initiative to direct them towards the gardens bordering the forest.

"If we're to talk about unpleasant things, it may as well be surrounded by something decidedly more pleasant," Jaspen explained.

Sakaeri chose not to enlighten him about her admittedly not pleasant memories in those very gardens.

As they neared the botanical enclave, residential units became fewer and far between, transitioning smoothly into what became a thriving epicentre of biodiversity. Paths wove throughout carefully pruned bushes and ponds rippled in response to hanging threads of whispertrees and sweetblossoms alike. There was a serenity carried upon the flittering breezes, enough to beckon a few others who wished to bask in the peace of nature, finding themselves a spot where they might read or picnic or simply lay daydreaming.

Sakaeri, however, found her eyes drawn to the far pond where relentless mushrooms grew on its edge, there since two of the people who knew her most nearly bled out from the gouge of her blade. She stared at it. She would not hide. Not from her past, not from her future.

"What do you want to know?" Jaspen asked, and she thought it remarkably amicable.

"Everything," she answered honestly.

Jaspen had only just finished telling her that Paladi had, as suspected, erupted after a quarter year of devastating quakes. It had only been a couple months since, but the once-grand caldera-tunnelled city was now nothing more than a molten cast of itself, entirely uninhabitable. And this bit of information had come after his relay that the Lu-Ghanian Sovereign Coalition was ready to wage war on the Unified Ministry of Lu-Ghan, so no wonder the ministers aimed to visit. *And yes*, it was true that the Orinian Draconguard was sent to assist – Jaspen did not comment on her interjection of *invade* – Mhedoon in light of the copycat attack at Caiggagh.

Apparently, both Tenebranan and Quingan authorities had consistently dodged the Dracon and Seraeyu's attempts to ally, as far as Jaspen knew. Which could have admittedly been a somewhat shallow knowledge pool, given his removed position within a simple peacekeeping envoy. Before she could pry into how Kaisa fit into this reeking mess of politics, a frosty premonition had the nape of her neck prickling.

She tensed where she sat on a bench beside Jaspen, refusing to turn and give whoever it was that marked her the satisfaction. She just *knew* it had to be the same cloak that clocked her from the docks in Keou. That, or it was some compatriot of theirs.

"I'm here for them," Jaspen said, and it got jumbled in Sakaeri's broken concentration.

"Who?"

They're behind watching. Waiting. Listening.

"My family. They've been delegated to Mercur because of my service, but even the capital can't house them forever."

"You're trying to get them moved. Here," she realised.

They're moving, finding a better vantage, slipping through the brush like a spectre.

"It would be better for them, I think."

"I'm not convinced anywhere is safe, not really."

They're preparing, setting up their trajectory.

"I believe in a more secure future. I believe in who I think Praetor Seraeyu Thasian to truly be."

There was barely a break in the floating mist above the flanking pond, its humidity cut by the blades of two sharp dirks, aimed at the tender junction of neck and shoulder. Perfectly pitched to pierce right where armour was weakest for mobility. Sakaeri was flipped and twisted before the honed instruments even passed the middle point of the pond, her war fan spread to block the prick of impending death before it met Jaspen, her own body well out of the way when her intended dirk whistled past and lodged itself in the grassy terrain just beyond the bench.

Jaspen startled and barked an exclamation, hand flying towards his leaning glaive as he jerked to mirror her twist, twitching back once more when he was met with an eyeful of her flared fan. Sakaeri instead watched the woods and the shadows that crept within them. Her sharp gaze tracked a presence just beyond what the naked eye could see, but her focus tuned towards the warped chill that lingered there, locked up tight and barricaded with a sheen of not regret but duty. Some putrid combination of undertaking wrapped around sorrow and shame aimed at her. For her, or perhaps *because* of her.

You must scrub the slate clean.

When their presence faded to the wind, like a forgotten and stray thought, Sakaeri loosened her stance and latched her war fan back to her belt, turning to fetch the discarded dirks.

"Seraeyu Thasian," she said, feeling Jaspen's wary, cautious eyes follow her movements, "is Haebal's only hope."

As she dislodged the blade snug deep in the dirt, the one meant for her, she brushed her thumb across the etched Sirin wing upon its hilt. Standing, she stood and held the blade close, pommel up and tip down, cradling it to her chest. Another lifetime lost. Her grip tightened.

So be it.

"It was ... one of the bad ones?" Jaspen had finally gathered the courage to ask when they'd quickly made their way back into the bowels of Danu.

Together, strides matched and in closer proximity than she would have preferred, they side skirted the main corridors, melding into the narrows that slithered a path towards the sages' hallowed compound. *One of the bad ones*, she entertained the notion.

"Well, it was certainly someone who would have rather seen our blood run, if that's what you're asking."

And that wasn't good at all. So, in that sense, their assailant was *one of the bad ones*. Was she considered having gone astray? Had she missed something, some convergence of those who remained, or was she seen as compromised due to her time at The Pit? Sirin weren't meant to suffer capture and escape, but annihilate. She knew that. But the Sirin were *dead*. The Nest was ravaged. Anyone, any stars-blessed soul who evaded that premature slaughter, had vanished.

So why target *her*?

"That blade you picked up." He offered a clipped gesture towards the dirks tucked into her belt. "It bore the same symbol as one that struck a Sentinel maybe a month ago. You're familiar with it?"

Wasn't that just too strange? A Sirin, targeting a Sentinel?

"Have these attacks been commonplace?" She darted around the next corner, concentrating. The tree-shaded crevice offered little respite, just a place to cast an investigative eye across Danu's solitude. Sakaeri had already used a lot of her energy. Her soulsong sung only softly now, so she rather hoped there wasn't a confrontation on the horizon. "And the targets?"

"Isn't that obvious?"

What kind of blasphemy was that?

"Seraeyu?"

"My understanding is that a squad of Sentinels had tracked a suspect to Narui. It turned out to be a false lead, but they've been searching since the first altercation. That happened a good while back, before my envoy arrived."

Sakaeri watched a couple totter down a stony path, too enamoured with one another to be any sort of active threat. "There have been repeated assaults against Seraeyu?"

"Yes."

"And what happens then, when this occurs?"

"The Praetor is protected by his escort, or he takes matters into his own hands."

"Meaning?"

"Before our envoy arrived, I am informed that interrogations took place, managed by the Praetor himself. Anything I've been witness to, the Praetor deflected with ease and returned to safety within the Thasian Tower. His barricade of Essence was a near constant defence around its walls, but now ..."

They were nearing the ecclesiastic grounds now, twitters echoing from birds behind its impervious walls, stood stalwart against the residential meanderings before it. A misplaced trepidation hung in the air alongside the season's perfuming blossoms, and Sakaeri suddenly felt out of place. Discomfort draped across her shoulders, urging them inwards, and she found her gaze trailing up the dividing bulwark.

The noontime bell tolled as she studied the glyphs and crude impressions of elemental design atop the high ridge. It wasn't the subtlety in the swirl of water or the simplicity of the striations representing wind that choked the breath from her throat. Beyond those, professing a connection only to those who knew what to recognise, she stared at a sun and its feathered rays, carved just above the bolted-shut doors. The very same divine symbol that bore on the shrine crumbled to pieces below Mhedoon's ocean. The very same that adorned the sanctuary she'd considered her not-home home; the forgotten Temple of Sirin, Yisuna's sacred birth and resting place.

But the sages had turned their backs to the Sirin. Locking them out alongside the rest of the realms. That symbol resting there had never meant anything because any significance it held was long dismissed, severed with any goodwill harboured between blades and prayer. It never meant anything.

It *never* meant *anything*.

Unless it did, once the Sirin lost. When those who remained answered a neglected dirge, seeking asylum in a remaining stronghold. And, very suddenly, it meant something.

It would now more than ever beckon those lost, and perhaps it always did.

"Have any sages visited the Tower?"

"The Auspicious Cleric Jugaeya sent word of a visit this evening; a meeting to discuss the preparations for your Festival of Hana in the coming fortnight? The message was delivered early this morning. I'd volunteered to be the delegated Draconguard present."

Sakaeri tore her gaze from the damnable depictions far above and scowled at him behind her mask. "You're far too involved and in the know for any old Draconguard envoy."

"I simply wish for the Praetor's safety and continued prosperity."

"So you keep saying," she muttered. "We'd best get back and have a chat with the *Praetor*. And Draconguard – what's your surname?"

"Verdanta."

"Draconguard Verdanta," Sakaeri continued, squeezing herself out of the gap she'd melded into beside a retaining wall and a mature, knotted weeping tree. "Do not trust the clergy."

She felt his eyes track her as she slunk back towards the shaded passageways that winded through terraced estates. "Understood, Sirin Yisuna."

For none shall recall, the haunting tenant wriggled into her thoughts.

But Sakaeri rose from the ashes, and she would sooner suffer the fabled pyrewing's fury for all eternity than forget and be forgotten. Sakaeri was not collateral to be cleaned. She was not a corrosion so easily snipped and discarded.

Sakaeri was the daughter of Ube of Krunan and Jourae Thasian-nee. Sakaeri was the girl who escaped the streets and the woman who found her own footing, forever rising. Sakaeri was the persistence it took to stay alive, and she was the courage it took to forsake fruitless grudges. She was perseverance, and she was fortitude, the living embodiment of vigour.

Sakaeri was steadfast, mind and body, and she was ready.

CHAPTER TWELVE

"Where is he?" Sakaeri asked as Jaspen stepped up behind her.

Koali looked over from where she was considering a newly placed rack of weaponry, the scene around her seemingly set to accommodate a training regime, arranged with dummies and all. Her visor was flipped up, so Sakaeri got a great view of her soured expression as she abandoned her ministrations in order to address them.

"Praetor Thasian will return shortly. He'd left for a bath a bit ago, wanting to refresh before going through another bout of exercises."

"A bath?" Sakaeri asked. "In between practice stints?"

"Did he look well?" Jaspen questioned beside her.

Strange. Why would he ask that?

Sakaeri glanced at him, but his helmet covered any hints that may have otherwise offered insight. He only stood there, rigid and disciplined, line of sight directed unwaveringly upon Koali. The Sentinel's eyebrows furrowed, creasing the space between them, then she settled on something near a half-glare.

"Are you suggesting I worked him too hard?"

"No."

"What *are* you suggesting, then?" Sakaeri asked, hesitantly curious. Jaspen did not turn to her. Their debates became irrelevant anyway as, just then, Seraeyu exited the stairwell, closing the door softly rather than letting it slam shut.

"Praetor Thasian," Jaspen said, and the way it was spoken held something within it. What that something was, Sakaeri couldn't quite determine.

A delicate and cautious thing, perhaps.

Seraeyu didn't look up at them right away. He instead continued to stare at his hand, rested upon the door handle. An uncanny urgency welled within Sakaeri, urging her to manoeuvre around Jaspen to reach Seraeyu. As she approached he appeared entirely as he had when she'd left hours ago, the same attire and all.

She bent her knees to fall into the line of his gaze. As she did, she spotted a stray rivulet of crimson that hadn't yet been rubbed away. Silently, she swiped at the evidence on his face, the edge of her thumb disappearing the weep of aether. His golden irises, deeper than Raeyu's but reflecting the same buried anguish more every day, met hers.

"There's somewhere *else*, isn't there?" It was spoken so softly it could have been carried away on the breeze. Sakaeri's hand froze upon his face.

"Why would you ask that?"

"They can never come back," he said, and it hurt a little. "*A'vor* and the rest."

"*A'vor?*"

"It's not descanting, Sakaeri. It's a language. It's *her* language."

Every tangential thought, every reverberating question she harboured, cratered and fell into oblivion. Her mind struggled to revive once more, aiming to make sense of a language she'd heard spoken time and time again throughout her life. A language that persuaded Aeyun's odd form of tuning, not the fabled descantation. Not in the way she understood it. Words, bargaining with the very fabric of whatever the realms resided in. Lyrical hymns that held meaning, that said something more than a command and, for the first time, she found herself wondering what it was he always said. What it was he begged the unknown to do again and again, its will gracious enough to concede every time.

But it wasn't only him. He'd called to that strange, wild woman shown through the rift, using a similar intonation to the ancient Mhedoonian tongue. A similar dialect to the ancient Mhedoonian language. Aeyun's actions, alike to the terrifying visage upon the forgotten soils of Beldur, were as if they followed the same directive. A gate once connected, a woman emerging, devastating a population, wielding power similar to the Thasian.

It was not analogous. Not entirely. But there had been a sunken, crumbled temple. And it was all similar; similar, but not entirely.

How deep did the fissures go?

"How many secrets does my sister keep?"

"I don't know," Sakaeri answered, and *stars* did that twist a knife in her heart.

"Praetor Thasian?" It was Koali who called this time, closer now that she'd moved in towards Jaspen. The Draconguard stood in place. He was still, not a question voiced. But there was a lingering tension to his limbs, too stiff and too measured.

Sakaeri's arm fell back to her side as Seraeyu adopted composure from that mysterious reserve he always seemed to have ready.

"Thank you for waiting Koali, and good to see you back, Jaspen." It sounded too formal, forced. "I'm sorry, I don't think I'm quite up for continuing our practice. I—"

"Actually, Seraeyu," Sakaeri interrupted, clearing her throat. "Our friendly Draconguard Verdanta and I have something we need to discuss with you."

"Oh?"

"There was an incident—"

"I knew you shouldn't have been sent into Haebal! What have you done?" Koali snapped, her fingers inching towards the hilt of her sword.

Sakaeri barrelled on, "—which we need to report."

She tugged one of the blades free from her belt and held it out, its winged emblem on display. Seraeyu looked at it, then glanced back up at Sakaeri, puzzled.

"This and its pair were tossed at us while in Danu. It has the same etched symbol as the knife that struck a Sentinel a while back. The same attack that launched an inquiry, which lead to the incident in Narui."

"Ah," Seraeyu said, then he followed it with a more illuminated, "*ah*. Yes, that makes sense." She caught his grateful nod, communication that he put together the pieces she'd laid out for him. "The same symbol, you say? Aimed at you two? Are you both alright?"

"Sirin Yisuna fended off the attack," said Jaspen.

"This is …" Koali's voice tapered off, her eyes flickering between the weapon still presented in Sakaeri's palms and the Yisuna mask on her face. "But you're …"

"Perhaps the attackers are getting bolder now that your barricade of Essence is lifted. Not only targeting you, as they have been, but those who may be close to you," Sakaeri said, still aiming to fill the gaps in Seraeyu's knowledge. "This is, as both of our acquaintances so curiously and accurately suspect, a Sirin blade. Take from that what you will."

Seraeyu stared at her, his expression carefully blank.

He finally said, "I see."

"This is … troubling," Koali muttered.

"Praetor, you have a visit from a sage this evening, don't you?" Jaspen asked, untangling himself from whatever trepidations had plagued him. "Are there any particular preparations that need to be made in advance? Is there any way I can help?"

"Yes, the upcoming festival," Seraeyu said, nodding absently.

"This is the first you've heard from them during your time as Praetor, isn't it?" Sakaeri asked helpfully, and Seraeyu glanced her direction once more. "I suppose they've decided to rekindle some old traditions in preparation for the grand event." She purposefully twisted the dirk in her hand once before catching his eye, pausing once before sheathing it in a leather loop. "You know what they say. Keep your friends close, and all."

"Right," said Seraeyu. Something darkened in his gaze, but it was quickly quashed and discarded, instead replaced with a reporter-ready smile. "Well, we'd best make sure to give them a warm welcome. After all, they are our neighbours here in Haebal, and the Festival of Hana is important to many of the city's denizens."

"A delegated Draconguard will be there." Sakaeri jerked and thumb towards Jaspen. "This one."

"I'm happy to be of service and perform my duty as an emissary between our realms."

"My impression is that Draconguard Verdanta will be *most* attentive. He and I passed the compound on our way back. I'm sure he'd agree that it was an enlightening experience."

"I have listened closely to Sirin Yisuna's words about your clergy's aspirations."

"I see," said Seraeyu. "Koali." He turned to the Sentinel and gave her a kindly smile, which the woman seemed to melt in. And *frigid void*, if this soldier couldn't become any more of an embarrassment. Where was her decorum? Why in all the realms was she *this* endeared to Seraeyu? "Could you please organise preparations within the arboretum for our visitors this evening? We will receive them there. I believe that environ will serve as a good medium for this chat. Vibrant and full of life, as the Festival of Hana should be."

"A … a beautiful sentiment, Praetor Thasian." Koali returned his smile, but it seemed lacking. Bogged down with doubts, she briefly flitted her focus to Jaspen before landing it on Sakaeri. "You will watch over the Praetor?"

"With my life," Sakaeri responded.

"*Yun guide me*," Kaoli muttered under her breath before she gave Seraeyu the designated sign of thanks. "May your will be mine," she told him, then she flipped down her visor, took a centring breath, and slipped past the group of them to make her descent.

There was a bout of silence after her departure, the three of them watching the closed door like it would fly open again. As if it would present answers to all the questions hanging in the air. It did not, however, and Sakaeri sighed because *ugh*, wasn't this just her luck. Convolutions upon convolutions. It seemed the realms liked to make her suffer for a laugh.

"I can tell you with high confidence that the assassins and the sages are in league."

"Buy *why*?" Seraeyu voiced, and it sounded much more like him and not *the Praetor*.

"Call it a hunch."

"The sages have been allied to the Legacy for millennia. You'd think they'd be more motivated now than ever to protect that."

"Yes, if something should threaten the *Legacy*, you'd think they'd be quite keen to address that," Sakaeri said, circling around him to gaze at Haebal's skyline. The sun reflected gleamingly upon its expansive networks, creating a bright sheen across the rooftops.

"Well, *shit*," Seraeyu said, and Sakaeri found herself joyously revelling in his continued break from praetorship, something about his more natural levity comforting.

"Praetor Thasian." And there the Draconguard was to ruin the moment. "I've been meaning to … ask you something."

Seraeyu gave him a tight-lipped look which was likely meant to be another smile. "Yes, Jas?"

"You don't remember, do you?"

Finally, Jaspen removed his clunky, over-designed helm and fixed them both with a stare that pleaded answers. Sakaeri wasn't sure what to do; pull Seraeyu behind her or watch whatever this was unfold. It was something about the honesty swimming there, swirling around the sapphire of his irises, that had her faltering. Jaspen stepped forward once, then he fell to his knee.

"Seraeyu Thasian," he said, and no matter how desolate the name was when it left his lips, it did not deter from how odd it was to hear it come from him, a Draconguard. "Since I have been in this realm, I have watched you fall apart again and again, fighting a battle with a curse that would puppet your limbs, speak with your tongue, but was not *you*. I've known since the night I found you here, when you – do you not remember?"

Seraeyu did not move. He barely breathed. "What are you talking about?"

"When you nearly dove to your death, Praetor," Jaspen said, and it came out cracked and hoarse, his head angled down to allow Seraeyu the time to process in privacy. As much as he could have here.

Sakaeri didn't interrupt. Whatever this was, it was Seraeyu's revelation to have. But she would be there, waiting, when he was ready to face what it meant, together.

"I – what? When?"

"Commander Ephrite had escorted our envoy. The night we arrived I'd come up here for air and cigarette, to – to look at the stars, I don't know. We can't see them on Orin." Jaspen shook his head with a grimace and somehow sunk further towards the rooftop. "You were there, just on the edge before it was fully reconstructed. You were standing there, looking down, and when you'd turned to face me, you asked me to drive my sword through your heart. When I didn't move … you let yourself fall back. I only just barely caught you.

"I thought maybe now you'd remember, since you seem more the master of your own mind, but … you don't."

"Stop," said Seraeyu. He'd raised his hand to his head, pressing against his temple. "I don't remember this – I don't." He opened his eyes, squinting, hunched as if he might topple over. Sakaeri positioned herself to his flank in case he did. "I don't … there was a night, I think, and you came up here. But you apologised and left when you saw me. You didn't stay; you left."

Jaspen did look up then, a pained grimace pulling lines around his mouth. "I stayed, Seraeyu Thasian. Every time you unravelled."

"I can't remember. It feels hazy. Like … like the memory is diluted. It's – *stars* – how much of my life has been painted over?"

Sakaeri decided it was time to stop playing bystander. She took his hand, stilling his trembling fingers when her own wrapped around them. "While a bizarre ally, we could stand to have more people beside you, Sera. Truly beside you." Sakaeri swapped her focus to Jaspen. "Why didn't you report it?"

"At first, I'm ashamed to admit that my motivation wasn't altruistic. Seraeyu Thasian is one and the same with Praetor Thasian, and I've told you of my family's circumstance. We *need* the praetorship aligned with Orin to open Raenaru's Gate to refugees." Jaspen paused, offering a meek sort of attention towards Seraeyu then. "But every time it happened my eyes saw less the terrible lord of this realm and more a man caught up in a nightmare. I vowed to myself that I would not let you fall apart alone, that you would not be forsaken and devoured entirely by your curse."

"I don't understand," Seraeyu said, stumbling back, inadvertently hitting Sakaeri's shoulder. His grip tightened. "Why would you vow that? Why take the risk at all?"

"Why let an innocent man suffer?"

The question seemed to dissolve Seraeyu's response, whatever it would have been. Instead, he leant heavier, and Sakaeri compensated with her own weight.

"You weren't always … lucid. I'd remind you who you are or tell you stories about Orin." Jaspen frowned again and looked away, unable to face whatever expression Seraeyu had. "When you were there, you'd ask for it to end." Sakaeri felt rather than heard Seraeyu's hitched inhale. She grimly wondered what aspect it was a reaction to: his question, or the fact that the morbid request was repeatedly made known. "And then you started asking for Aeyun, but I know no one of that name."

"*Cheeky bastard*," Sakaeri grumbled.

It urged a desperate sort of laugh from Seraeyu.

"Well, thank you then, I suppose. I really … I don't know what to say."

"Tell me how I can help, that's thanks enough."

"Okay, Jas," said Seraeyu. "Let's start with handling this Cleric visit, and then perhaps tomorrow you can catch me up on the last year of my life. I think that'd be quite a good thing to know, wouldn't it?" His tone was a little sardonic and a smidge depreciating, but it was a Seraeyu that Sakaeri recognised. She now knew better than to take that for granted. It seemed she and this rookie Draconguard were slotted in place as Seraeyu Thasian's dedicated wardens, as unlikely an outcome as that may have once been.

But Sakaeri would take her blessings where they manifested.

Jaspen, as he bowed his head low and stood in night-shaded armour that glistened beneath the sun's rays, was a second beacon of hope in what felt like increasingly dire times. And hope, Sakaeri considered, was something they all desperately needed as they rose to face whatever fallout loomed on the horizon.

CHAPTER THIRTEEN

"Ah, our Praetor has graced us with his presence once more."

Seraeyu, dressed in a sharp charcoal-hued overcoat, horns and shoulders draped with decadent adornments, entered the cavernous centre of the overgrown reception area, renouncing the antiquated scarlet robes his counterpart held an affinity for. The designated meeting space was snug in the middle of the sweeping arboretum. A long table, littered with gleaming shards of ore, made up the distance between the Praetor and his guests.

Striding in behind him, Sakaeri's eyes darted across the lush interior, casting over the knotty, vine-webbed glass ceiling to the blossoming perennials and the glowing curl-tailed stalks that interwove between shrubs and creeping lianas. The entire atmosphere felt enchanted, buzzing and drunk on powdered humidity and the bottled intensity of tightly held power. Stood behind the opposite end of petrified wood, carved across its great expanse as a ringed and varnished plank, the Auspicious Cleric Jugaeya, old and shrunken, was clothed in a heavy mantle of carmine shrouds. He considered Sakaeri's arrival with little in the way of recognition. Several golden-threaded, onyx-robed acolytes stood in the fringes, resembling more pious versions of the Thasian's housemaids – the likes of whom seemed to have disappeared entirely from the Thasian Tower. Koali stood sentry at the sage's side, having welcomed the clergy upon their arrival, and a handful of other Sentinels lined the fertile paths around them, hands lifted in Raenaruan solidarity and respect.

Jaspen settled into a space near where they'd entered as Seraeyu and Sakaeri made their way to the table's head. His place was not an active one here, only that of an observing outsider. He knew that, and he did not push his presence. Instead, he quietly sank into the background. Watching. Waiting. Listening.

Perhaps Sakaeri would've considered taking him under her wing in a different lifetime.

Sakaeri took her position at Seraeyu's shoulder, her mask secure as she stared down their saintly visitors. In her mind, she counted her instruments of war, keeping a careful catalogue of their locations on her body should the need arise. Externally, her shoulders squared and her stance widened, sturdy, with her gloved hands held firmly at the small of her back. Why would the Praetor's shadow salute when it need only loom, patient?

"I am most honoured to receive you. The sages' absence has been long, Auspicious Cleric Jugaeya." As Seraeyu spoke, the surrounding branches shuddered, rustling in resonation across the lofty atrium. Sakaeri wondered whose, if anyone's, influence that was. "The Legacy has indeed been carried on my shoulders alone in the interim."

"Accept our most humble condolences for what you have carried, Praetor Thasian. Be assured that we have nothing but the best interest of the Legacy in mind. As circumstance has dictated, the stars have not aligned for us to meet and speak after the ill-fortuned calamity."

"I am aware of your devout interests, thank you Auspicious Cleric Jugaeya. The sages' priorities have always been ensuring the sanctity of the Bloodsong."

Sakaeri was sure many in the room picked up on the wooden atmosphere as the two exchanged loaded words wrapped in pleasant tones. She, however, did not flinch. Before them, the elderly sage looked down his nose in scrutiny before he seemed to catch himself, schooling his expression into practised indifference once more. His worn knuckles wrapped around his bell-strung staff, jiggling it once, and the rattling leaves quieted, blanketing the arboretum in silence.

Ever so slightly, the old man's eyes narrowed as he asked, "I beckon our Praetor, Seraeyu Thasian, son of Paeyuni and Oagyu Thasian, to heed our advice, if he is willing to humour the counsel of a lifelong Cleric."

Seraeyu was still for a moment, and Sakaeri could read the conflicted duress wrapped tightly around his form. Opposite him, the sage's aethereal signature read as an impenetrable opaque, as many among the clergy often did.

Her wonder at Seraeyu's reaction did not go unsatisfied long, as he opted to say, "The Praetor receives counsel elsewhere, though you may speak freely if you wish."

The reaction was immediate, the sage's expression shuttering, a stony gaze replacing his contempt-tinged suspicion. "Perhaps we will speak with the Praetor at a different time on these matters. Today's occasion, as proposed, is to discuss the nearing Festival of Hana, a most revered occasion in our city and in fact across all Raenaru."

"As is my understanding."

"It would be a shame to see this year pass without its tradition realised."

To that, Seraeyu said nothing.

It was a ploy, Sakaeri had deduced, recognising the way Seraeyu's aura fluctuated contemptuously. Seraeyu had decided that it was in his best interest to play the daemon chained around his heart rather than let the clergy know that he had wrangled back majority control. Maybe Seraeyu had recognised something she had not, but he was certainly hedging his bets when the sage mentioned *tradition*. Maybe Hana held more meaning than the star-crossed tales of old. Or perhaps it was a reference to the Council of Raenaru, whose visit they would be expecting soon. The herald, Hana was referred to, forming the praetorship.

Indeed, the *tradition* to be realised could mean a good many things, but Seraeyu smartly held his tongue to not oust his dubious understanding of just what that was. Sakaeri, she found, was inordinately proud of his tactical manoeuvring, for some inane reason.

"On behalf of myself, the sagely order, and citizens of this bright beacon that we call home, I would beseech the Praetor to host the Festival of Hana so all can spectate and enjoy merriment that has very much dwindled in these passing months. Surely, not all times need be so dark. The Legacy stood for the laypeople in days long past. It is not soldiers and warriors who walk those streets beyond the Tower gates, but ordinary people. Civilians seeking a few brief moments of respite with their loved ones. I'm sure *you* … Praetor, understand."

Something in that entreat had Seraeyu's fingers curling into his palms. The jewels upon his horns jingled as he tipped his head to the side, only slightly. A cruel sort of grin cracked across his face that made Sakaeri question if he was still, in fact, Seraeyu at all. But there was no cracked film eclipsing his eyes, no creeping poisoned veins, and no strange language spewing from his mouth.

This was Seraeyu, and it was his intention to make the clergy squirm.

"Have the festivities. As you do, I will continue to construct brighter future. One that is *just*." And the way the word unfurled from his tongue it was like a decree uttered with absolute authority. It seemed to have the desired effect, the Cleric Jugaeya clutching firmly at his staff, a deep inhale taken through his nose.

"And so shall we continue," the sage said, something regretful in the sentiment. "I believe we have discussed all that needs saying." He shuffled away from the table's edge and gathered his acolytes, preparing to leave. "May the Thasian always overcome, and may those lost always find a guiding light back into the embrace of the glorious Yun."

A crackle brought Sakaeri's attention to Seraeyu's palms, miasmic sparks dancing dangerously there. As the representative clergy swept past them, she felt one of the acolyte's gazes latch onto her though their darkened veil, the length of it shrouding their face. It was like being marked all over again, and she turned her head to the side ever so slightly to return their glare. Slowly, watchfully, her arms crossed back to her front, ready to unsheathe a weapon should the need arise. If this was a Sirin, though, it would not. The moment would pass, but two predators would be left with the burning scent of prey in their nostrils, ready to bear fangs in darker alleys.

The acolyte glided by, appearing unbothered, though Sakaeri could read their aura as locked up tight. Still, it failed to tame the little spikes of adrenaline that crept from a smoothed veneer. A Sirin in holy clothes, the infiltrator led the procession for Cleric Jugaeya's departure.

On close inspection, Sakaeri noticed the sage's staff chiming with small bells, jostled with his every step. When he ghosted by, Seraeyu's crackling essence fizzled and dampened, only to flare once more once he'd passed. An escort of Sentinels departed behind the clergy, intent to see them to the gate. Koali, ever the dedicated Sentinel, dutifully left with the escort, though Sakaeri was sure half her mind stayed behind.

Seraeyu's facade wilted. He winced, shaking out his hands, as if that would calm the erratic energy that pulsed around them.

"Please accept my thanks to those of you who have dedicated your time to this meeting," Seraeyu addressed the remaining Sentinels, his calm held but only just. "I would like a moment to ruminate here, so please do allow yourselves the courtesy of an evening unchained to duty. I will see myself to my quarters later. Dismissed." The remaining half-dozen Sentinels did not lower their rigid sign of respect over their hearts, nor did they make to remove themselves from the vicinity. Seraeyu, whose composure was ever-slipping, let loose something of a snarl and viperously snapped, "That was not a request but a directive. *Dismissed.*"

Hesitantly, the surrounding militia lowered their salutes and offered respectful acknowledgements of *Praetor* as they exited one by one. Soon Seraeyu was left in the company of Sakaeri and Jaspen, the Draconguard having graciously ensured all onlookers had vacated. It was only three in the atrium alone.

Smoky, flickering black wisps of unmitigated force were coursing from Seraeyu's fingers, slithering up around his arms, his breath heaving quickly. "Sakaeri."

Sakaeri was by his side in an instant, hands gripping upon his shoulders before she lurched back at the biting sting of it. "Seraeyu, what do I do? I don't – Aeyun. He's dealt with this. Aeyun would know."

She scraped her mind for something, anything, that would help soothe the miasma erupting from Seraeyu. It looked near identical to the vestiges of the in-between that tried to consume Aeyun on Mhedoon, so it was … was it raw Essence? What combated raw Essence? For Aeyun, he'd instinctively seemed to emit some sort of seeping *not-Essence*, then he slept it off. But Sakaeri didn't *do* what Aeyun did. She was never taught.

"Praetor," Jaspen said as he too huddled close, arms twitching but not reaching. "Can you not sedate it? It never spread like this …" He had his helmet removed, grasped harshly in one hand, a lingering tightness betraying his concern even more than his wavering voice.

Seraeyu grimaced as he crumpled against the table's edge, his eyes ebbing black, his nails digging into the varnished wood.

"Why can't I control it?" Seraeyu asked, gritting his teeth as he groaned in pain. The zapping miasma coursed across his chest then, connecting a circuit between his arms, bolts ripping across from one hand to the other. He groused, "It's *too much!*"

"Aeyun's not-Essence, Essence!"

"What?" Seraeyu growled in response, trying not to sink all the way to the floor.

"His not-Essence, Essence! It counterbalanced it, this, but you – can you not? *That cheeky bastard!* Can you not call upon it?"

"Vitality?" Seraeyu asked, voice pitched from a losing battle, angry dark streaks now chewing at his neck as shadow washed the whites of his eyes.

"Vitality?" both Sakaeri and Jaspen asked at once, expressions mirroring confusion.

"*Fuck*, no, I can't," said Seraeyu. "Because the *arsehole* commandeered it again."

"He has your …" And suddenly Sakaeri's theory was confirmed, but starry sea above, she wished it wasn't. It wasn't that Aeyun had banished Seraeyu's call to the Grand Symphony, but that he had stolen Seraeyu's duet with not-Essence Essence – Vitality, Seraeyu claimed. Caged it. But the Great Starry Sea acted in even scales. No order without disorder, her pilfered manuscripts had said. No take without an equal give. Aeyun's actions had ripped *two* soulsongs in half. Not just one.

And, that fateful night, Aeyun never had a whole soulsong to sacrifice to Raeyu at all, had he? Bloody *stars-damned fool.*

"Well, call to *him*. Would that work?"

"I *can't*," Seraeyu bit out. "I don't know—" a guttural noise that she hoped sounded worse than it felt escaped him, "—how!"

His eyes were nearly starless voids now. The plants and ore around them began to quake, energy roiling from Seraeyu's form in droves. Sakaeri's heart pumped wildly, and her head kept repeating *this isn't how it ends* and *the aether won't take him*. Seraeyu curled in on himself in agony. He looked all at once like the child who stood alone in corridors, no one around to offer comfort when the realms moved at breakneck speed, demanding the attentions of those stronger and more influential. No one left to soothe the forsaken.

Sakaeri threw herself around his shivering form, drawing him close and pressing his head to her, unwittingly collapsing him against the scar Aeyun had seared into her skin when he disappeared Kaisa's putrid, enslaving rune. The crushing force leeched to her, surging across them both and she rumbled something low in her chest to dispel the discomfort.

"Let me share your pain," she said, clutching him tighter. "I'll help you. We'll conquer this together, Sera."

She squeezed her eyes shut to block out the blistering chill that encompassed those sinister bolts. When she'd opened them once more her vision had gone radiant, the realm looking incandescent and flowing and *wild*. Where she held Seraeyu shone a milky sheen, softening the erratic thorns of Essence. Time itself felt incomprehensible, and all Sakaeri knew was the heavy burden of power pushing and pulling between them, stray threads of *Seraeyu* getting caught up in the mix of it.

"*Wait*," Seraeyu said, but she wasn't sure where the vocalisation came from, since it sounded like it rattled in her head. "*Wait, she'll wake!*"

And then he was pushing back from her, and they were stumbling apart, the glow in her sight fading, Seraeyu looking at her with this strange, alarmed amazement. His eyes were once again reclaimed his own from the depths of the aether.

"Divine alica around us," Jaspen whispered, drawing their attention. He shifted back a step or two, gaze flickering between them. "What have I just witnessed?"

CHAPTER FOURTEEN

No one had spoken for far too long.

The atmosphere weighed heavy, and Sakaeri was busy trying to tape together smashed pieces of a puzzle that came from different pictures. Aeyun was not Jourae's blood, but he tuned with *Vitality*, as it was apparently referred. The Thasian did not have a Bloodsong, but an ore which encased some kind of sealed daemon, from whom they drew their power. Essence and Vitality were not meant to be within reach, but she had witnessed time and again that they very much were. And her eyes did not deceive her.

Sakaeri had been attuned to that nebulous not-Essence Essence. Just now. Just here.

What's more, it had felt as if she had not only eased the erratic resonance that poured from Seraeyu, but that she had absorbed it. That she had taken in its excess, and it was like something keened at the additional buzz of energy filtered through her. Like that wielding of aether was instinctual as much as it was borderline euphoric, odd in its sense of utter connectedness. Like something intangible was understood, comprehended until it washed away once more when attunement dissipated.

It had been intoxicating. And her eyes were not bleeding. In fact, she felt grounded. Powerful. There was something in her that wanted that feeling back. That enticing collision of creation and destruction. That unfathomable sense of vast aetheral liminality.

"Seraeyu Thasian," said Jaspen.

Sakaeri looked away from the effervescent curl of vines she'd stumbled back towards ages ago, instead heeding the other two in the arboretum. Seraeyu had settled himself upon the table, his head having now lifted from his hands. Jaspen stood exactly where he had been, seemingly frozen in stiff misbelief.

"What I have observed in my short time at your side is beyond what many in the realms believe possible."

"And you?" Seraeyu asked, voice once again rasped. "What do you believe?"

"I believe there is much I don't understand."

The steady drone of humidifiers filled a reverent gap, and Sakaeri wondered distantly what was to come. Because as much as everything else had felt like a pinnacle of *something*, these moments felt like her own personal revelation. A point of no return, a shift in what it meant to be Sakaeri of Krunan, of Thasian-nee. What it meant to fill the space between her head and her heart and her will.

A deep, ghoulish thing whispered that Sakaeri wasn't meant to *be*. But she had been, and she is. And how was she meant to feel when, in that moment, she fancied herself a *god?* Limitless, infinite. Comprehension beyond, unbounded. A moment of … something indescribable. *Ah-ka.*

She watched as Seraeyu lifted his chin in defiance; towards what, she wasn't sure.

"I have done abhorrent things, Jaspen." It didn't garner much reaction. "Despite what or who you believe me to be, I am not so entirely different from this daemon you've witnessed. I have held ill intentions. I have had cruel whims. I am not infallible." Seraeyu crossed one leg over the other and gave the soldier a wry grin. "I am no glowing saviour, so please don't paint me as one in your mind. I am a man whose ambitions and woeful ignorance have eaten him alive, and I am nothing more than what remains."

"You are better a man than you think."

"I'm not so sure of that," Seraeyu muttered. "What would you sacrifice for my favour?"

This face, the one that had settled somewhere cold and unforgiving, was one of the newer iterations Sakaeri didn't quite know how to place. It was something that had been there, but now it had spread, creeping into facets that carved a chipped and fractured whole.

"Who are you without your Dracon?"

How very curious. This was both Seraeyu and the Praetor. *This* was Praetor Thasian. And this was dangerous. But Sakaeri would remain in the shadows. As Jaspen pondered his response to what was indeed a loaded question, Sakaeri pondered the quickest way to dispose of a Draconguard. Because he would never be Seraeyu's downfall.

"My loyalty cannot be bought, Praetor," Jaspen seemed to settle on. Sakaeri considered the sword in the scabbard at her side. "It can, however, be earned."

"That also means it can be lost."

"Yes, it does."

"And what would you do, when you find things you wish you didn't know?"

"I will learn how to deal with revelations as they come."

"Should you dislike those revelations?"

"The realms are not black and white, Seraeyu Thasian," Jaspen said, holding a remarkable calm for how agitated the words tumbled out. "And adamantine is legal until it isn't."

Amusement curled Sakaeri's lips. *How adorable.*

"What's that supposed to mean?" Seraeyu asked.

"That Draconguard Verdanta is yours outside of Orin," Sakaeri answered for Jaspen, who simply stared back, mulish. "Our very own little smokeserpent."

Jaspen held his breath, then exhaled in one tired push of air. "I could really use a smoke," he grumbled, his shoulders drooping in a way that looked at odds with his armour.

"I don't think I have the luxury of expecting more than that," Seraeyu said as he leant back, peering through the vine-twisted glass above. "I can only hope that resolution comes before extents are tested. Though, I must warn you." Seraeyu lulled his gaze back. "Even I'm not sure of this story's gnarled end. And you—" Sakaeri hadn't expected him to turn to her, a deliberative quality to it. "You ..."

"Will not leave you," she finished for him. He gave her an inscrutable look. "They have each other. You'll have me, for however long I'm needed." Raeyu would want her brother to have something secure at his side. And Seraeyu did not deserve to contend with this on his own. "Sorry you're stuck with the rubbish."

"You were never rubbish," he said so immediately that Sakaeri truly couldn't convince herself he thought anything otherwise. "You've never been rubbish."

"I've also never been a saint."

"I never needed saints in my life," Seraeyu said with a mocking smirk. "They're all liars and cheats."

"I should be happy I'm no Yun worshipper," Jaspen murmured between their banter. And that *was* something, wasn't it? For some reason, it had Seraeyu barking out a laugh.

"I should certainly hope not!" He sobered and continued on, "There are things I must look into. Though, I'm not sure if I have the stomach for it tonight. Jas, I would like to ask you something." The Draconguard stood at attention and Seraeyu opened his mouth, hesitated, then said, "Over these past months, what has been—" He paused again, glancing away. "What have my interactions looked like, with others? And with Yu-ta specifically?"

"You seem very driven. In all appearances, you have presented yourself as a cautious, determined lord with very few whom you hold in close acquaintance. You've been distant from your populace, often relegating Sentinels to act on your behalf. Much of your time is spent in the Tower." Jaspen seemed to sieve through recollections before saying, "I don't believe I've seen you interact with a Yu-ta besides Yisuna—"

"Sakaeri," she corrected on impulse, and he gave her an odd look.

"—but I am aware that you held interrogations prior to my arrival, and I believe I've heard some of those folks were Yu-ta. You reduced your staffing severely after the incident at the Tower, and I have really only seen you speak with those who forwarded an aim."

"Interrogations?" Seraeyu's complexion looked dulled, pallid and emptied.

"There are not many Yu-ta folk around the city, really. Many of them may have fled, after what happened. Likely fearing a similar fate by association, no matter how miniscule a chance."

Seraeyu said nothing, but it was everything else that screamed at Sakaeri. She knew that look on his face. She'd seen it among the Sirin. After their first fatal job. Or after a mission gone wrong. That blank horror that masked wicked visions of vile circumstances. Oh, Seraeyu. *Oh*, Seraeyu, what had he witnessed? What had he endured?

He knew why the Yu-ta were scarce. She was sure of it. She could only hope that he didn't know intimately and in detail, because it was likely a gruesome tale. But, somehow, she did not think the realms pitied Seraeyu enough to save him from those revelations. His sickly appearance reflected as much.

"Draconguard Verdanta." Seraeyu's swap to formal address did not go unnoticed. "What do you think has occurred here?"

Jaspen, who'd already been tense, stilled entirely and with a sharp, steadying inhale. "There are many unsavoury characters in a game surrounding this Tower. Outside of the incident at Caiggagh, nothing seems to point to an external source. I have not ... invested time into realising any suspicions."

So, Jaspen was no saint either, it seemed. He had his priorities, and that's where his sight ended, a veil being cast over everything else. What an odd soldier, this one. And *Caiggagh*. She figured it was connected. Was probably Kaisa causing a ruckus. At least those stupid smugglers seemed to make it out alright.

"Caiggagh? What *did* happen at Caiggagh?" Seraeyu grasped onto it. Sakaeri couldn't blame him, latching onto anything that would tear him from his own mind.

"An explosion, not unlike what happened here. It damaged the docks and killed a handful of bystanders. Commander Ephrite was with you when news arrived. Witnesses say it was unlike any they've seen. Like—" Jaspen's gaze trailed to Seraeyu's hands "—Essence itself."

Seraeyu's eyes widened, his entire posture pulled rigid.

"And there is ... no named culprit?"

"No. You and the Dracon have been investigating that."

Seraeyu said nothing, so Sakaeri decided to interject. "Kaisa had been there. I'm not sure why you're looking into it, really, since you've been so chummy."

The Praetor – Oagyu's son – melted away and instead it was Raeyu's brother who looked at her. He slowly shook his head, then lifted his gaze to the stars far above the atrium.

It was a strange reckoning when she realised that was all it took for her to understand. It hadn't *been* Kaisa. Of course, it hadn't. Somewhere across the Great Starry Sea, she wondered if *he* knew his shame was coming to light.

Aeyun never was any good at making decisions on his own.

CHAPTER FIFTEEN

It was surprisingly difficult to find privacy amongst the a'teneum.

Aeyun had swiped a dislodged copy from the books Uruji had piled on the corner of a desk, hoping to find one that outlined the runes that were now missing from his chest. He'd barely even had a second to crack it open without someone passing by or asking what he was doing. Studying to replace the runes he lost talking to Seraeyu wasn't something he wanted to disclose.

Finding solace in the cave that connected the glen to the grotto, Aeyun had snuggled himself into one of its corners, near a bushel of glowing, tongue-petalled plants to keep the pages illuminated. As he leafed through, he soon discovered that the book he'd taken was not what he needed – there were no warding runes outlined in its chapters – but it did have some interesting detail about some of the local flora and fauna. Who knew that the vines twisting throughout the hold were actually networked beneath the entirety of the Ou'grobh? Well, Aeyun did now.

A clatter of shifting pebbles made him glance up. Just around the next bend, Aeyun could barely see Davah as he began hesitantly reaching towards what could only be assumed to be a loose ore.

"Ah, ah!" Aeyun called out, like he was scolding a child.

Davah spun so fast he nearly toppled over. "Stars above, friend. You'll put me in an early grave," he said as he recovered his breath. Curiously, he wove further into the stony hollow, coming to stand before Aeyun. "What are you doing in here?"

Aeyun shrugged, haphazardly lifting the book in the air for Davah to see.

"*A'on'nac da'a'Ca'lorus?*" Davah questioned, and Aeyun twisted the bound tome in his hands, spotting the title he'd clearly missed before. If he'd realised that it mentioned creatures, he would have grabbed a different one. "Is that something about fiends?"

"Fiends?" Aeyun couldn't help his bubble of laughter. "No, just animals and things. Those that inhabit Ca'lorus." Davah nodded slowly, obviously trying to connect that nugget of information back to his knowledge of the ancient Mhedoonian tongue.

As he settled on the dirt beside him, Davah asked, "What's got you curious in that?"

Aeyun considered the book in his hands, then he looked up at Davah.

Davah wasn't looking back, his eyes instead roving over the oddities of the cave. Aeyun wondered if Davah often disappeared here, when he couldn't be found.

Of the people Aeyun was surrounded by, he wondered if he could tell Davah more. Unlinked to the Thasian, perhaps he could be a safe confidant. After all, if they still needed to kill Seraeyu …

You Yu-ta hunters?

The question asked under a sweltering sun rang in his head, and Aeyun frowned.

"Any luck with Saoiri yet?" he asked. Davah was still in possession of the communication stone linked to her, somewhere on Mhedoon. Davah shook his head, morose.

"No, not yet." Davah picked up and tossed loose gravel, watching it clatter in the distance. "I haven't asked yet, and I don't really know the state of you, but do you think …"

"I'm trying to figure out how we might get back," Aeyun assured him. Every moment, it was on his mind. "I'm sorry you've been dragged so far."

"Hey," Davah said, finally looking at him. "I made the choice to stick around, didn't I? Don't you go blaming yourself." He tsked, shaking his head. "Honestly, friend, sometimes you take on too much – you're one man."

"Yeah," said Aeyun. He didn't know what else to add.

"Are you—?" Davah's question halted, his face twisting up, like he was figuring out an adequate pivot. "Want to get out of here for a bit?"

Aeyun didn't even have to think before he said, "Yes."

"Woah," Davah said as his fingertips neared The Veil. Aeyun watched as the strange wall rippled and bounced where Davah had touched it. Its reflective surface undulated and distorted their figures, making them appear warped.

It had been a long time since Aeyun had peered at his own image. He'd taken his hood down when they'd neared the barrier, secure in knowing that it was just the two of them present, so it allowed him to take in his own tired eyes and frown-marred features. He looked sleep-deprived and weary, and he was starting to understand why everyone was always asking him if he was alright. Something else he noticed was how his once gangly but lithe physique had become more muscled but also conversely deflated, like if the bulk wasn't there he'd be verging on emaciated. Maybe he should eat more.

"It's weird, isn't it?" Aeyun asked Davah to distract himself. "Here's where Ca'lorus stops. It just ends." Aeyun paused, his hand lifting towards the thickest part of the wall, far from its tapered curve. "But I've seen the realms, and it seems—"

"You think there's more," Davah asserted. Aeyun nodded.

"There has to be, right?" Aeyun's finger trailed down its surface, and it dipped like silk, but tingled like cool water. "But it's difficult to reconcile. If there is – more, I mean – then why?" He took his hand away and looked up instead, watching as pastel colours flit through the odd film that rose high over their heads.

"That I certainly cannot answer, my favourite enigma," Davah said, copying Aeyun and tilting his chin up.

"I feel stuck," Aeyun blurt out suddenly.

"Oh?"

"Here I am, back in my birthrealm, and nothing. We're here, I'm still alive thanks to my brother's genius, my sister barely looks at me, I can't spend more than five minutes with Raeyu without one of us running away in fear that—" Aeyun stopped. He'd still not explained that to Davah yet. "We're connected, me and her."

"Yeah," Davah deadpanned. "Kinda figured that when we arrived and your *everything* looked like it was trying to zap over to her."

"Oh."

"But it's not like I *actually* get it," Davah clarified, an invitation.

Aeyun glanced over, shuffling anxious feet.

"When we were younger, something happened. It was the only way to keep her alive, and it worked." Aeyun took a moment to reconsider. "Or we thought it did. I'm still a bit – I don't know. But when I was able to tune evenly, and we were in such close proximity, it basically jumpstarted the process that started forever ago and – well, that's what you saw. My life was meant to be made hers."

Davah blinked at him. "Okay. First, wow. That's some kind of terror that's possible. Second, you meant to give up your life for the Thasian?"

The Thasian. It glared in Aeyun's mind.

"For Raeyu," he corrected, and Davah nodded, twisting his wrist to spur Aeyun on. "Raeyu is – she means a lot to me. She's the first person I met in the realms. She helped me, back then."

"Ah," Davah said, nodding again. "She does seem … soft." Aeyun hummed. Soft might not be the right word, but it suited the purpose of the conversation. "But what I don't really get is how you're still alive in the first place, and how your brother knew how stop it?"

"That's complicated," said Aeyun.

"I believe it."

"Davah," Aeyun said, taking a deep breath. His companion must have sensed something coming because he turned fully towards Aeyun, interest sparking across his gaze. "You remember how I said that I told Kaisa something dumb?" He got a nod. "Well, I told him that I'd Silenced Seraeyu."

Nothing. No reaction; maybe the slightest raise of a brow.

"And I wasn't lying, exactly."

"So, you … took away the mad Thasian's ability to tune?" Davah asked, slowly. Aeyun flattened his mouth in a line and offered a short affirmative nod. "And he got it back." Aeyun confirmed again. "What does that have to do with—" The pause was abrupt. Aeyun could see the dots connecting in Davah's head as his gaze widened steadily, his jaw dropping. He had severely underestimated Davah when he met him, Aeyun mused.

"*Fecking stars* – you can't tune! Except for that Vitality stuff, you can't tune anymore, and you couldn't tune with Essence until the Thasian became un-Untuned." Davah shook his head, somewhere between amazed and aghast. "You said it's like an exchange, two halves of the same function. Aeyun. Are you telling me that you gave up your ability to tune with Essence – the very fabric of the void itself – to take away his, too? That he can't tune right now?"

And Davah missed the mark slightly.

"Not quite," said Aeyun. He looked away, laughing nervously as he picked at the skin beside his thumbnail. "I didn't know what I did back then. I was only considering the end result. I'd unbalanced us." *Perfectly unbalanced, in equilibrium, together.* "Nothing is free. No tune is priceless, and no act, no exchange unpaid. I had called for Seraeyu to be unable to tune, and how the realms responded was by tearing us in half." He turned, and something about the concerned expression on Davah's face made unease swim in his stomach. "I didn't know," Aeyun repeated. "I didn't know, but how it was achieved was that realms unbalanced us. His call to Vitality resides in me now, and mine to Essence in him."

"Our mad Thasian has double the force of Essence as we speak?"

"Yes, but—" Aeyun bit his lip. "He's not mad."

"Sorry?"

"He's not mad. He's possessed." Aeyun took a moment to consider the statement in light of his most recent conversation with Seraeyu. "Was possessed? Still kind of is."

"Aeyun, friend." Davah was holding up his hands, as if it would help him process. "I'm a bit – something is lost in translation here."

Aeyun chewed on his abused lip once more before saying, "Seraeyu wasn't in control, when he'd done all those things."

"And how do you know that?" Davah's tone was disconcerting in the way that Aeyun couldn't tell what emotion lay behind it.

Maybe he shouldn't have disclosed so much. But here he was, so …

"I—"

"Have you been talking to him?"

That tone, Aeyun picked up on. That tone, Aeyun read as incensed, and the unease that coiled in his gut became a burning dread. No. No, maybe he really shouldn't have brought any of it up.

So, instead of his original intent, Aeyun said, "I saw her. The daemon that's possessing him. I've seen her over his shoulder, and I saw her when my brother banished my attunement with Essence." He paused. "Uruji doesn't know. None of them know; about any of it. Our unbalanced attunements, or about Seraeyu's possession."

Davah was quiet for too long. Aeyun felt the need to shout until Davah finally fixed him with a sharp look, asking, "Why'd you do it?"

It was the second time that Aeyun had been faced with that question in recent days, and guilt crashed upon him, just as it had before.

"I – maybe I shouldn't have. Raeyu was talking to me, and—"

"She asked you to do it?"

"What?" Aeyun asked, because Davah was giving him a look that bore into his very soulsong. "Yeah. Yeah, she didn't want Seraeyu to become a pawn of the Thasian Legacy."

The laugh that erupted from Davah's mouth was far from expected, a little cruel, and it had Aeyun flinching back. "Starry sea above," Davah wheezed. "What a fucking wreck of a family." Aeyun's face must have betrayed his confusion, because Davah elaborated. "She didn't want her brother to be a pawn, so she made him her own pawn." Aeyun furrowed his brow, and Davah waved his hands in the air again. "She didn't want him to play the game of oppression, so she oppressed him, and she used you, pawn-number-two, to do it."

"Davah," Aeyun admonished. "She was trying to protect him."

"I'd be very willing to bet that his life became even more difficult after that."

Aeyun couldn't deny that. It was something that he'd only allowed himself to think about more recently – something he'd been willing to admit to himself more recently – but many of the hardships that Seraeyu faced were due to the pressure placed upon him because he couldn't tune. And then there was the constant berating from Oagyu ...

"She hadn't meant for that to happen."

"Lots of people don't mean for lots of things to happen," Davah said with a shrug. "But lots of people also don't think about the bigger picture."

"I'm just as at fault here," Aeyun told him.

"Yeah," Davah said, looking Aeyun straight in the eye. "You are. How do you feel about that?"

Aeyun stared back at Davah's undaunted gaze. "Not great, to be honest."

"Good." Davah smiled bitingly at him, and Aeyun scoffed, half-amused at his brashness. "You *should* feel shitty about oppressing someone." Davah casually leant over and plucked out the book that Aeyun had stashed in his bag. "Then again, it's Seraeyu Thasian, so ..." He trailed as he flipped the volume open to a random page and began to leaf through it.

"You're very—" Aeyun's comment about how opposed to the Thasian Davah was cut short when a page was shoved in his face.

"Is this a stylistic choice, or is something missing here?"

The question regarded the blank gaps presented among the text, not just in the margins but amongst the lines, almost appearing as if something had been erased. Aeyun took the book from Davah's hands and turned a few more pages, noticing the same pattern of missing sections.

"No," said Aeyun. "No, that's weird."

"Why would a book about the animals of Ca'lorus be missing random information?" Davah asked.

Slowly, unwittingly, both of them turned to look back at The Veil.

"Hey," Aeyun said as he slammed the creatures compendium down on the table Uruji sat beside.

After their revelation, he and Davah hiked back to the a'teneum, eager to see if the most prolific reader of the group – other than Gama-of-Yun, who seemed about as with-it as a drunk mutt – had any further insight.

"Hello?" Uruji said, bouncing his gaze between the book and Aeyun, then to Davah behind him.

Da'garu was sat in the corner by the window, looking on curiously. A forest critter, a si'nac, was curled on her nap, offering a discontented chitter at the heightened activity. It settled again as Da'garu gave its fur a stroke, a huff escaping its snout before it rumbled a purr.

"Do all the books have these types of missing gaps?" Aeyun asked, opening to a middlemost page as an example. Uruji narrowed his eyes at the text, pursing his lips, then he looked back up and nodded.

"Uh-huh. I was going to ask you about that, eventually. Da'garu showed me, they're all like that."

"Look." Aeyun flipped a few pages. "There's information about what's in this forest – in the Ou'grobh – from the trees to the insects that crawl over them. But anytime there's a reference that seems like it's leading to something related beyond the Ou'grobh, it's just—" Aeyun tapped at a blank gap. Uruji looked up at him, wary.

"Well, yeah."

"What do you mean, *well, yeah*?"

"This area has obviously been sequestered. It's cordoned off by a giant barrier. There's more out there, and it's been wiped from these texts."

"Uruji." Aeyun closed his eyes and took a deep, calming breath as he crossed his arms. "I love you, but sometimes I hate you."

"Pardon?"

"When did you think it'd be a good time to chat about how you'd already determined that my homerealm is only a fraction of what it should be?" When he opened his eyes, Uruji was gazing back at him with the same doe eyes he had when he was only a wonder-struck child. Inwardly, Aeyun cursed at their power to make him instantly relinquish his anger.

"When you seemed more up to talking about it?"

"I'm up to talking about it," Aeyun said evenly. He sat himself down across from his brother, opening a few more of the books scattered on the table. Behind him, Davah settled against a bookshelf and, if Aeyun had been paying more attention, he would have caught the way Da'garu watched them as they interacted with natural, sibling ease.

It was in every book. The sections, words, and entire pages were absent in every single tome that Uruji passed over to him.

They spent hours spinning in circles, coming up with nothing to show

111

for it by the end. The only interesting new fact Aeyun gleaned was that apparently there were nocturnal arachnistalks crawling about that were invisible unless illuminated with just the right angle of light, so that would surely be a comforting fact for him to fall asleep to that evening.

Of course, it had only been a portion of the books in the building, but Aeyun suspected that all of them were the same. Information about the Ou'grobh, only so far as to not breach that which lay beyond. Not that it was un-useful. It just wasn't particularly useful for what he was searching for.

In sudden confession, Aeyun said, "There was a gate." It was only then that he realised that Raeyu had joined them, sat beside Da'garu by the window, the si'nac seeming to have vacated at some point. Davah was in the opposite corner, snug between two perpendicular shelves. "In Beldur."

"Oh, right," Davah chimed in, rubbing at his chin.

"It had Ca'lorus's writing on it."

"It did?" Davah asked, then his entire demeanour shifted. "Didn't you say—?"

The stilted reaction prompted baffled expressions to flood across those who hadn't been present at the submerged ruins.

"It did," Aeyun confirmed. The vision they saw … was the Yu-ta woman coming from Ca'lorus, then? Only he and Sakaeri actually witnessed the vision. They were the only two watching it play out, seeing *who*, what impressionistic heritage, had performed the act. The more Aeyun thought about it, the more the phantasmal figure plagued him.

"Okay, and?" It was Uruji who'd asked the question on the others' minds.

"Sakaeri and I saw something," Aeyun said, hesitant. How much should he disclose? "Like a memory, from when the gate was active. It was the moment the gate was destroyed. A woman just … well, destroyed it," Aeyun told them, feeling small.

Davah, however, decided that wasn't good enough. "Along with everyone around it. She came from here, you think?"

Aeyun really wanted to smack him.

"You saw a woman come from Ca'lorus, destroying a town on Mhedoon?" Raeyu asked, bewildered. Aeyun flit his focus to her.

Loose connections started threading in his mind. The companion to the fragmented soulsong that lingered in Raeyu's alicant, Seraeyu had said. *Did Raeyu not tell you? Or did she just not realise?*

What was it that Raeyu's stolen alicant held if Seraeyu's was so horribly daemonish?

He must have stared too long, because she softly called his name at his nonresponse.

"If there was once a gate that connected Mhedoon to Ca'lorus, then there must have been one here, somewhere. Maybe beyond The Veil." Aeyun knew he didn't address Raeyu's question, but he couldn't bring himself to without diving into other unknowns that he wasn't ready to get into, especially not in a room full of people. Raeyu eyed him searchingly, but Aeyun bit the inside of his cheek.

"Huh, so it's not a coincidence, is it?" said Davah. Under newfound attention, he fluttered his wrist in explanation. "The whole language thing. Ancient Mhedoonian tongue?" He grinned over at Aeyun. "I guess we *are* cousins, my favourite enigma."

Aeyun gave him a tired smile, then sobered. "That and, ah, before Lu-Ghan. On the island," Aeyun mentioned. Davah took a moment, but then his eyes widened, much like they had earlier in the day by The Veil. Aeyun was sure he put together the architectural similarities between the temple at Beldur and the one with the dead Sirin. *Stars*, even this a'teneum.

They'd not yet addressed the mask that lay peacefully beside Azura and the rest of the things they'd arrived with. The time never felt right. But Aeyun was starting to think he wouldn't have the luxury of time when it came down to it.

"Wait," Davah said, looking up, but he didn't continue.

"Right," Uruji spoke up, annoyed at the clear and purposeful lack of communication cycling throughout the room. "Whatever is going on, I hope you choose to share it at some point." He cleared his throat, settling his hands primly on the table. "If there's a gate – or what remains of one – beyond that barrier, and it seems there likely is, we still can't get to it as long as The Veil standing." He let it sink in for a moment. "It's very improbable that we will be able to break it down. We don't even know what it is, or why it was placed there. What if it's the only thing sustaining this area, the Ou'grobh? What if, out there, there's something that would collapse all of this? Is it worth that risk? Your entire birthrealm?" The question was aimed at Aeyun, and he didn't know what to say. "How'd you get to Raenaru the first time?"

"Uruji, maybe we shouldn't—"

Raeyu's soft interlude was halted by Da'garu gripping her arm. Da'garu looked intently at Aeyun, and it was then that he realised it mustn't have been explained to her in full, since Raeyu only knew as much as Aeyun had told her. And Da'garu wanted to know Aeyun's version. His recount of that fateful night.

Feeling stripped bare, Aeyun shifted back in his chair.

He'd also not yet explained to Raeyu that he believed his destination might have actually had to do with the compulsion to link to the alicant once imbedded in her arm. The companion to the one now carved into Seraeyu's chest. The one that had … answered Aeyun's call. Maybe it wasn't a Thasian who'd left the scar in that underground ravine, but *a'lud a'Ca'lorus*.

"It wouldn't be possible," Aeyun concluded. The anticipation in the room deflated like a balloon. "I can't attune to Essence."

"You opened a rift?" Uruji asked, purely out of curiosity.

"Not – I mean. Kind of. But, no," said Aeyun.

He wasn't entirely sure that he had much part in it at all, if he were honest. If the fragment from Raeyu's alicant was from Ca'lorus, and they somehow answered his plea, then they could have opened the rift, through Raeyu. And the look on Raeyu's face told him that she probably had no awareness of that, if it was the case.

"I don't understand," said Uruji.

Aeyun sighed, then his gaze met Da'garu's. She was still staring at him. Waiting.

"It was the night our parents were murdered," he said, and he couldn't bear to look anywhere else but at his estranged sister. The very one he'd abandoned that same night. "Mother had told us to run. I wanted to stay and help her after Father was felled, but she begged me to leave. When I'd gone to catch up with Da'garu, Mother was – she'd met her end. I was looking for you. I didn't know how far you'd got, but you were so small." Aeyun couldn't tear his gaze away, even when it clouded. Even when Da'garu's gained a glassy sheen. "I was searching, but I fell through a crag. I got stuck in an underground ravine and there was an Essence scar there. Next thing I knew, I was falling through the sky in Raenaru."

In the quiet that followed, Da'garu hooked her fingers on the high-collared shirt she wore, the one that funnelled up her neck. She tugged down and Aeyun could see the long-healed scar that slashed across her neck. Her free hand then shined in a radiant light, brought close to her neck, then it was snuffed out and she simply pointed at Aeyun with a saddened smile.

I'm only alive because you taught me how to heal when Mother said I was too young to learn; that I would hurt myself.

"Da'garu," Aeyun said, a hoarse quality to it. "I'm so glad," he told her, every bone, every muscle in his body trembling. "I'm so glad you're alive."

CHAPTER SIXTEEN

She'd never been so deep in the Tower before.

There was something rotten and weeping in these stoney depths. Sakaeri did not like the lingering unease that hung in the moss-slicked stairwell, the pungent stench of abandonment crawling up her nostrils. Seraeyu was ahead of her, every step looking like a death march. *What* was down here that plagued him so deeply?

Jaspen was not with them. He'd not been sought out, and Sakaeri didn't press Seraeyu about it. Whatever his agenda was, it was meant only for him and her. And that was okay. She could fill that role, a singular faction of safety, held only in her hands. Whatever pillar was needed that humid afternoon, Sakaeri could assemble it.

Seraeyu stepped on the lowermost landing, a quiet apprehension pulling his shoulders tight against the tendons of his neck. Sakaeri settled beside him, peering into the sweeping dark of the ancient cistern ahead. The door far, far above had been locked and chained, clearly cordoned off. Seraeyu, hand shaking as he slotted the key in place, a dogged sort of glint to his focused gaze, had popped the lock, silently indicating for her to follow him after he'd slipped in. And so she had.

He took a step, hesitated, then stilled.

"Seraeyu," she whispered, because this moment felt fragile. Breakable.

"The ore," he said. "Can you tune a brighter glow?"

Instead of answering, Sakaeri breathed in deeply, listening intently against striations across space that resonated with the glowing ore's hum. When she detected them, whistling around with a fuzzy floating quality, she called to them and urged brightening. A light to guide their path.

The cavernous walls woke with a corona of haloed light, flooding the shadows enough to permeate a long corridor. The old stone there glistened in mould-soaked perspiration, stagnated water slithering through risen walkways, algae congealed across its surface. It was empty, abandoned, an eerie wallowing quality to its vaulted heights. Somewhere above, a flapping of wings startled her, an umbral spectre of an animal darting from one spoked column to the next. *Winged wraithrats*, she thought.

"Sera, why are we down here?"

"To find the truth," he said.

Seraeyu finally strode on, leading them through the narrowing hall. There was a passageway that led off to the side, and he twisted around the corner of it, following its steep descent. Their steps echoed, mirroring that forlorn aura that bled into every corner of this strange underground. When they passed a cratered crevice, Seraeyu peered into it like it held answers. In the end it must not have, since he shook his head and traipsed ahead once more.

Their destination, it seemed, was an enclosed space where a plinth was positioned below an abused pillar, to its side a risen platform that led to wrought-iron gates. The closer they came to the whole of it, the more concerning details came to light. Like the inclusion of chains wrapped around that stained — was that blood? — pillar, hooked into its nicked exterior. The mucky colour washed down the side of it, collecting in darkened puddles of dried crust below.

Of all the things she expected to find, it was not an impromptu torture chamber.

Before her, Seraeyu gazed at the wicked compilation with a glazed disconnectedness. Slowly, with mechanical stiffness, he lifted his hand and turned his palm up, like he would find something there too. He did not, only the vibration of his own trembling fingers.

Seraeyu looked back at the pillar, then rubbed at his own wrist.

And wasn't that a smidge odd, if it was Seraeyu who'd probably done the torturing?

Oh *stars*. She hoped he didn't remember that, if it happened. And, with the evidence so clearly laid out before them, yes, it very likely did.

With a sharp inhale, Seraeyu turned away from the scene and made his way up the few steps it took to reach the platform with the gate, its curvature carved with strange symbols that looked both familiar and unsettlingly unknown.

Sakaeri studied the markings and their concentrations, slowly dawning on the realisation that they seemed like runes, but not the ones she knew. A calligraphy that she was not predisposed to. One that looked both rudimentary and intricate in a way her brain couldn't quite trace. It was when Seraeyu was stood directly below the arch of it that he looked truly a being of the endless starry sea, divined from the celestial aether, dressed in refined iridescent fusain hues. He looked over his shoulder at her, and she wondered what he would look like with star-spotted eyes. Instead, she came to know his expression which held apprehension buried below a determined armour.

Without uttering a word, she followed in his footsteps and gently intertwined one hand in his. She could be an anchor among invisible, volatile tides.

Seraeyu brushed his free hand across the uncanny markings, a drifting miasma spreading behind his palm, small sparks spreading across the traced expanses before dissipating like smoke. The iron gate creaked open, beckoning them to enter, and there was something within Sakaeri that very much did not wish to concede its call. Yet, she did, since Seraeyu pulled them through the threshold with care, like a fencat slinking through a darkened alley. But she would not let go.

Not now. Not again.

The path was dark, dimmer than the open halls of the cistern. It was cavernous, distant from the rest. As they trekked on, her eyes caught onto piles of torn-down boards, gaping voids leading to somewhere unknown.

The main strait was littered with shimmering ore, dampened among oppressive whispers in the air around them. There was a desolation that cried more ardently than before, and a stray thought pestered the back of her mind. These solemn extents carried that same liminality as burial chambers.

A bend presented ahead and Seraeyu slowed to a halt.

"Here," he said. "It started … here."

His hand slipped from Sakaeri's and her first reaction was to reach back out.

"Sera—"

"If we find them, I'm so sorry, Sakaeri."

Before she had a moment to parse that statement, Seraeyu turned the corner in a determined clip, a firm and directed cadence to his gait. But she would follow.

Sakaeri would follow.

It was only really the bend she had to navigate, since he'd stopped abruptly on the other side.

Far ahead was a chamber, water flowing down and filling sunken latrines that lined the room's edge. Before the streaming wall of water were two pillars, one intact with an amber crystal, the other crushed halfway down its length, jagged splinters of glasslike stone piercing the air. Lines pulled from the pillars, forming patterns upon the flattened area before them, the entire expanse of which was dusted with a generous layering of ash. But there were pieces that looked wrong, out of place. Cracked slivers of ivory and, two steps closer, she was halfway certain it was a mandible that she spotted poking from a particularly dense pile of soot.

Forgetting herself, Sakaeri staggered forward, encroaching upon that hideous truth. The tug of Seraeyu's fingers curled around her wrist drew her back, a heavy decision settled between them. Together, they walked on. As her foot landed between sooty ridges, something potent ballooned in the surrounding air. Distorted murmurs rose from corners she wasn't sure existed. It manifested broadly, a bit broken and weirdly dismantled, but present enough to see and comprehend.

Ghosting into place was a younger version of Jourae, enduring like she knew him to be, stood between those enigmatic pillars. His glitched image stared down at a young Yu-ta girl, knelt on the ground, as he ceremonially wrapped strips of rune-marked paper around his arms. Impressions of others flowed in and out of existence, reading as sages and other Thasian she had vague recollections of; all passed now, taken by time or sickness. Behind the girl stood a woman with an air of nobility, a grace curving off her shoulders, her own horns dressed in ethereal gems that surely would have jingled an enrapturing chime.

Paeyuni had always been stunning.

If that was Paeyuni, then before her must have been Raeyu, now offering her arm to Jourae, head bowed in dutiful assent. In the vision, the time-dusted phantom of Jourae plucked the crystal from the still-standing pillar, returning to young Raeyu who held herself steady with stonelike resolve. Like watching through shattered glass, the scene skipped and retracted, one moment Jourae standing, the next bending at his knees with daemonish tendrils of inky dark flickering around him. His eyes were blackened and split with opaline fissures, some indescribable aura awash with impressions of incandescent hues like smoke from his sharpened claws – because they *did* look longer, his fingers more knobbed and curled – and his horns looked ablaze with the same celestial flame. Those thin strips of paper flapped wildly, as if trying to escape his limbs. Their painted symbols sizzled as they burned under pressure, this nebulous power amplified.

To her horror, Sakaeri watched as Jourae's nail punctured skin, creasing down at Raeyu's elbow. A slinking poison crawled from the point of contact, melding across her shaking arm. Then, with almost callous precision, the alicant was pushed into place. All too soon, Raeyu was looking up, the expression on her face ill-suited to someone of such a young age.

She was not expecting it when a voice erupted around them, carried across the vision.

"You keep failing your side of this bargain."

It was not a voice she recognised, an odd lilt to the words, but its inflection sounded – of all things – Mhedoonian.

"You let—" and Sakaeri felt like she was drowning because it bled into her mind that it was her, him, them, yourself all at once, *"die."*

Jourae's image clipped and suddenly his thumb was on Raeyu's temple, the strips of paper now having burnt away, the glow emanating from him taking on a softer appearance. His eyes were instead more predominantly opaline with only a sprinkling of onyx specks. What she saw in that inscrutable godlike gaze was eternal damnation, heavy with regret.

The scene wound, like a clock twisting gratingly, and manifestations Sakaeri couldn't quite latch onto overlayed. All held in that same chamber. All dovetailed with phantasmal cries to be spared of this fate, or to be set free, or to finally reach absolution. Countless recollections of Yu-ta children, and some who were grown, kneeling obediently. Some with larger crowds, some with dwindled onlookers. Always with pacing sages, voiceless chants echoing in time with unheard chimes.

Then, terrifying and unwelcomed, came the stuttered visions of Seraeyu.

The manifested memory drifted past Sakaeri and the very tangible Seraeyu beside her, dragging a limp-limbed body of a Yu-ta Sakaeri didn't know. Seraeyu of present trailed his eyes behind the aether-etched nightmare, the ominous trail of crimson from a slashed neck causing him to pale entirely. The vision shifted and there was another body, another trail.

Sakaeri didn't know how to stop it, but she knew Seraeyu didn't have to watch it.

She grabbed his head and forced him to gaze at her. Away from the recollection of carnage.

"I am here," she said, because he looked so utterly alone. "And I am not going anywhere. And you, Sera, are not defined by the actions of others."

"Where is the distinction," Seraeyu whispered, grief glistening on his lashes. "Because it's *me* there, isn't it? And I'm not sure what I would do if I were trapped for millennia."

"You fool."

There was an awful premonition that rode on the statement's coattails. Sakaeri couldn't look. Instinctively, she knew who the words were aimed at. And she couldn't bear to see it. Not when it was Jourae, dragged and lifeless. Nothing brutish or strong. Just faded.

Seraeyu craned his neck despite his quick deterioration, tears trailing steadily now. His eyes widened. He turned a sickly shade of greyish green, his whole body shaking.

"Your love poisoned her as much as mine did him. You should have known it would kill her in the end. And yet you still played their game, like the mutt you were so clearly content to be – Thay-cee-en-ee. It must have terrified them, something so like us. The sages would never have allowed that child to live. Poor Ube, another victim in this retched game.

"I've not yet done my duty. Has beloved Ka'la'drius done his?"

Sakaeri wasn't sure she was entirely existing in reality just then, Seraeyu taking up the whole of her vision, his haunted expression forever burned into her memory.

"Ka'la'drius, is there truly no one who remembers now?"

She barely registered it when Seraeyu broke away to retrieve something, and she didn't dare look back as they silently left those forsaken depths. Just in case.

Sakaeri had enough of ghosts.

The gardens around the Tower weren't quite as diverse as those bordering Danu, but they were extensive, and that's what Sakaeri craved then. A space to disappear.

Seraeyu had retreated to his quarters after the whole affair; the reel of cruel intentions they witnessed. And it hadn't been the first time they spun in an enigmatic plane before her. She'd felt the same invasion of her senses in Beldur when that spectre of a Yu-ta emerged from the in-between to wreak havoc.

The scene had manifested then, similarly cold as the past hour had been. Those villagers were dissolved from existence, taken on what looked to be a whim, and Sakaeri hadn't wanted to witness it again. Aeyun had tried. She'd watched as he traced his steps, overtaken by panic and discovery, and she should have suspected then.

He wasn't so special after all.

It felt as though the more familiar she became with these nebulous concepts – Essence and Vitality – the more she could connect with them. Attune herself to them. Manipulate them. Notes, once overlooked and drowned in the greater chorus stood out to her now.

Was she *special?* Unique? Or just awakened?

The night critters chirped in synchronisation, humming a midsummer's ballad. While the Tower stood tall and imposing beside her, the fractured tree bark of weeping branches, tendrils swaying in the breeze, gave her the sense of calm she sought. It was always among the softened edges of nature that she felt the most at peace. Perhaps because it was so at odds with what normally filled her space.

A gentle glow haloed lobed leaves, beckoning her to sit beneath their shelter. As Sakaeri settled under the umbrella of sweeping amethystine foliage, she leant back with heavy eyelids and breathed deep, tasting the dusky perfume of unfurled lunarius. It was pleasant. A moment to pretend the realm wasn't opening its maw to swallow her whole.

"Sirin Yisuna."

A hushed call. But she dare not call it timid, considering who it came from.

"Sentinel Koali," Sakaeri responded, not opening her eyes.

It was quiet for too long. Enough time that Sakaeri cracked a half-hearted glare at the intruder of her most needed solace. There the Sentinel stood, visor flipped up and posture stiff. She looked an odd mix of constipated and apprehensive, and Sakaeri just didn't have it within her to compassionately navigate the woman's jilted attempt at conversation. Her soulsong was drained, stains of it having been left behind in the catacombs.

"Will you just say what you've come to say?" Sakaeri sneered, but it lacked its usual rough edge. "I'm not in the mood."

"I—" Koali began, then faltered. In a rushed movement, she sank to the ground and bent over herself, far enough that her forehead kissed the dirt below. "Forgive me."

After a few seconds lost in pure confusion – because Sakaeri did *not* expect this headstrong soldier to flatten herself to the ground – Sakaeri, very unsurely, said, "Sure."

"I did not know you were blessed. I have disrespected a chosen of the Yun, and I beg that the powers that watch us look past my indiscretions."

"Koali," said Sakaeri. "Stand up."

"I have committed a horrible offence to the all-knowing—"

"Stand up." It must have been stated low enough, deadly enough, that the Sentinel felt compelled to heed the order. Once Koali stood tall once more, hands immediately pulled to her chest in a sign of great respect, Sakaeri continued, "I am not blessed. Not by luck. Not by circumstance. Not by Yun. Never, *never,* bow to me like that again."

"But you wield their will! I did not mean to see, but I …"

"You came back," said Sakaeri. "To the arboretum." It was a nod that responded to her. "You shouldn't have seen that."

"I cannot unsee it," said Koali.

There was a whisper of leafy rustles between them and Sakaeri frowned. This was not at all how she wanted her night to go. She wanted immeasurable moments lost to nothingness. Just her and the silent, tender dark. Not Koali deeming her holy.

"Speak of it to no one," Sakaeri told her, folding her arms across her chest and leaning back once more. "Believe in your gods if you must. They have all but abandoned me."

"But you are …"

What? What was she? Who was she? Who did the realms cry out for her to be?

"Sit with me," she said. "Revel at the evening with me. We can blaspheme together."

She once thought Aeyun blessed. But it couldn't be trod both ways. If she could do the same, if her soulsong recognised those same strange unrealities, then he was not. Since she was not. And if things could not be explained by the divine influence of the Yun, well, what did that leave? Her imagination was paltry, but that revelation lifted to reveal what lay below. Unfathomable delirium, all of it. Melded to create whatever it was that wove existence. The fabric or framework or force.

Maybe it never was the Yun. Maybe it never was the alica. It just *was*.

Sakaeri just *is*.

"I do not understand," Koali said, and it sounded so very lost.

"We don't have to," Sakaeri said, thinking it as good an answer as any.

It wasn't unpleasant, not really, when Koali remained beside her, quiet in humble consideration of whatever lay beyond. Together they sat as the minutes ticked by, and Sakaeri allowed herself to slip into the fond embrace of stillness.

For a moment – just a few moments – life was nothing more than perfectly benign.

CHAPTER SEVENTEEN

"While your opinion is valued, you *must* accept the gravity of this situation," said Seraeyu.

He was as tense as Sakaeri had witnessed throughout this entire disastrous affair.

It's not that she had expected the meeting with the Councillors to go remarkably well, especially given that Seraeyu had by all accounts shunned them for the majority of the last year, but many of them did not seem willing to budge. They'd arrived in scattered intervals over the last two days, some with more pomp than others, hailing from all reaches of Raenaru.

"Forgive me, Praetor Thasian, but why *must* we when we have been victim to your rash actions over these last months?" The Jiryu Naju Councilman, Kagnu Joa, sneered, pointy nosed and adorned with the odd metallic styling of the regenerate corner of the realm he represented.

Jiryu Naju was once a dumping ground for schist and shale, the off cuttings of mining excursions held in that region. Once the mines were picked dry, the redundant miners had settled, little promise of a prosperous life in the capital, despite what the propaganda had said. They crafted their own metropolis of metal and mettle in equal measure. Resilient was a title given to Raenaru, however, it was probably the autonomous city-state of Jiryu Naju that had truly earned it.

"Your embargos have been detrimental, and yet you ask that we make room for those whom you have previously barred? With what excess, Praetor? Our own reserves have dwindled as a result of your fallacies."

"I am currently making arrangements to once again allow free movement, Councilman Joa."

"Would that not be counterintuitive to your carefully constructed barriers? All due respect, Praetor Thasian," said Kiloae Kaenuya, Councilwoman and representative of the monastic lands of Yunae, the hallowed domains of pilgrimage. Kiloae had the unenviable task of representing the isolated mountainous peaks of Hananae as well, since the silent monks there, the Naen, took their vows to heart. It was a wonder that the grey-robed mountain dweller behind Kiloae had graced the meeting with his presence in the first place. The solitary lifestyle the monks led ensured that a sighting was rare indeed.

Maybe Sakaeri should feel kindred, in a way, since she was Naen – nameless – on all her records too.

"The realms need to find solidarity in one another, now more than ever. If there is a looming threat, there must be bonds which can be relied on," Seraeyu explained. Sweat crawled down the back of his neck, and he looked very much like he would much rather stand and march right out of the meeting room.

"Have you not cultivated these already, Praetor? And very much outside of our influence?" said the weather-skinned Councilman Soujiya Prenuju of Kyu, the veritable anglers' haven beside the Great Sea Gate. The embargo and closing of borders would have held great negative impact across his region.

"I have called upon you for your insight now," Seraeyu grit out.

"It has escaped no one's notice that Councilwoman Jaguna Kaoruna is absent," Piya Praenao of Keou interjected with measured authority. The Councilman of Haebal's neighbouring seaside town always did have a gravitas. It was surely what got him elected in the first place; swift words and a commanding presence.

"Yes," said Seraeyu. Sakaeri suspected that Jaguna's horned skull was collecting dust with the other Yu-ta bones in the bowels of the catacombs. "Yes, I am aware. It seems Councilwoman Kaoruna is not available for duty at present."

Piya didn't miss a beat, saying, "How unfortunate."

Sakaeri would have offered Seraeyu a supportive gesture of some kind, but she was too preoccupied trying to ignore the persistent, penetrating stare of the Naen. His beady eyes bore into her, pinning her in place with uncanny singlemindedness.

"We must push past our own misgivings and consider what is best for Raenaru, for all the realms, as we decide what the future may look like." Seraeyu let out a huff of air that was disguised as a sigh, then he leant forward in that grand foliage-etched chair. "Orin and Raenaru have long held a strong alliance. It has served us well in the past, as I'm sure it will in the future. *If* we do not turn our back to their Majesty the Dracon's pleas now. If or when there comes a time when Raenaru must rely on Orin, would we not wish for the same good graces extended to us?

"The road ahead of us is shrouded in thickening shadows, and I believe it's best that we admit that we are not invulnerable. In large part due to the calamity that occurred in my own family, Raenaru has lost the guidance it has come to expect. I am a man who was never expected to take this role, yet here I sit. I am aware of my own shortcomings, and so I have called upon you, representatives of Raenaru, our realm as a whole, to rally with me and lead our people towards stability. We know of turmoil, and we do not need to add to it. Now is a time to *unite*, not bicker amongst ourselves."

"You speak of the realms as a whole," Kagnu said, his glare painting a stern expression. "And yet you already conspire with the Dracon to overthrow the Elders of Mhedoon. What is it, Praetor, that has you and the Dracon so intrigued with that already ravaged realm?"

Seraeyu was still. Then he leant back with eyes closed, humming discontent.

"Have you forgotten, Councillor Joa?" Seraeyu creased his gaze and directed it down his nose, piercing the glare Kagnu had settled upon him. "Mhedoon is wild. Beautiful, cerulean, and bursting with what feels to be ancient strands of alica. However, this enchanting realm is not just all fables and mystery. My grandfather, frail in his age – harmless – fell victim to Mhedoonian pirates. Merciless bandits who blissfully stole what remained of his life before the eyes of a child. With the events at Caiggagh, is it so farfetched to suspect that the culprit is Mhedoonian?"

"It's not Mhedoon, Councilman Joa. It is a radical, far too dangerous a sect of zealots for whom we search."

The stir of something rattled in the heavy air of the meeting space. Sakaeri flicked her questioning eyes at Seraeyu. How much of what he said constituted what he actually believed? He'd said that with far too much conviction, and she did remember a story about Oagyu's councilman father being felled at sea. What was his plan when it was laid bare?

The pressure shattered with Soujiya. "Regarding opening Raenaru's borders to Orin's Paladian refugees: I vote favourably."

"I vote favourably," Piya echoed.

After a muttered hymn of prayer, Kiloae said, "On behalf of Yunae and Hananae, our vote is in favour."

Kagnu stared unwaveringly at Seraeyu. "I do not vote in favour of this decision."

Seraeyu simply responded, "In place of the absent Jaguna, I vote favourably. The tally is five-to-one in favour of opening Raenaru's borders to Paladian refugees. With majority rule, this will be done. The meeting is now adjourned." He did not waste time, standing up as the last word escaped him. It was only Piya's call that had him pausing.

"Praetor Thasian! Can we expect to reconvene in the near future?"

"Yes," Seraeyu said, looking over his shoulder at his collected Council. "Until that time, please do find a moment to enjoy the upcoming festival. As ever in troubled times, however, continue to practice vigilance. It's during times of distraction that ne'er-do-wells strike. I will be sending platoons of Sentinels to all regions as a precaution. Please accept them graciously. They will very likely be away from their loved ones, so any kindness granted to them will surely be welcomed."

Several variations of *yes, Praetor* rang across the group. Sakaeri first chanced a glance back at Kagnu, who still looked surly and displeased, and then at the Naen. The monk, browless and with an inscrutable gaze, had not yet looked away from her. She slowed to a halt behind Seraeyu and instead stared back.

The oddest thing happened then. He smiled, the curve of it so pervasive that it creased the skin by his eyes, then nodded at her. Sakaeri nodded back, earning her a strange look from Kiloae, who turned briefly in the monk's direction.

"Yisuna." Seraeyu called.

She shook off the discomfort of something not quite right, deciding to turn and follow the realm's young arbiter.

She was alone on the roof, arms folded over the barrier's edge as she watched the sky paint a luminous, reverent orange. Seraeyu had gone to tell Jaspen the good news and arrange for communication to be sent to the Dracon. Sakaeri didn't feel the need to be there.

Haebal looked like it was on fire.

The rooftops reflected auburn in the sunset, and Sakaeri could almost see the flames grow, consuming. Haebal City, a place to call home. Haebal City, a place to flee. Haebal city, a place to protect. Haebal City, a place to burn.

To someone, those were all true.

To Sakaeri, Haebal City was just a place.

"Hey, Rae," she said. "It's been a while. I hope you're making it alright. I know those Thasian-nee boys can be a pain. One too smart for his own good, the other too dumb. Quite the combo." She sank further into her arms, chin resting atop them. "Have you seen some amazing things, where you are? A realm unknown. I still can't believe it.

"I think it might be better if you don't come back. I miss you, *stars* I really do, but I think it's better for everyone. So … I'll watch over him, okay? Sorry I have to stick you with the two terrors I'd promised Jourae I'd look after. You'll be happy, won't you? Finally unchained from duty? Will you and Aeyun eventually have little runts?"

A laugh escaped her, but it felt bitter. Unfinished.

"I'm trying, Rae. I'm really *fucking* trying."

It wasn't long enough before the rooftop door creaked open. Seraeyu settled beside her, two other presences sliding into empty spaces behind him. A Sentinel, a Draconguard, and a Praetor. What an odd crew they were.

"Stars above, it looks like it's burning," murmured Seraeyu. Sakaeri couldn't help but laugh at such a similar thought. "Soon, all those streets below will be glowing with lanterns. Soon music will play, food will be proffered, games will be won. It's not much, I know … but it's a start."

"Those sages will heavily influence the festival this year," she said.

Seraeyu made a glum sound. "Perhaps. Maybe that's okay. I only partook, never planned. Honestly wouldn't know where to start."

"Will you go this year?" Koali asked, her voice carrying softly on the breeze.

"I think I should," said Seraeyu.

"I'd love to see what this Festival of Hana is like in person," Jaspen admitted.

A smirk found its way to Sakaeri's face. Such a big-eyed, curious little critter, Jaspen.

"Sure," said Seraeyu.

It was a serene until Sakaeri interrupted with: "I think you're on Kagnu's list."

"No good, scummy Councillor! He dare judge your Praetorship when you look at the state of Jiryu Naju … the nerve of that man." Koali continued to mutter, something about *vermin* and *ungrateful leeches.*

"You know, it's strange." Seraeyu drummed his fingers across his cheek, chin in his palm, a shifted mirror of Sakaeri's pose. "I've heard rumours that there is a Kaisan Pit in Jiryu Naju. And now wouldn't that just be very odd if that was the case? Just what is the scheme, I wonder …"

"The monk, too."

"Hmm?" Seraeyu turned to Sakaeri questioningly.

"The monk. He smiled and nodded at me as we left."

Seraeyu considered her with scrutiny knitting his brow. "What monk, Sakaeri?"

Feeling entirely wrong-footed, she said, "the one behind Councilwoman Kaenuya."

"Ah," Seraeyu said, still with baffled observation. His attention was pulled towards the other two of the roof's inhabitant, then he gave her a morose curve of his lips, appearing to most a pleasant thing. "You'll have to tell me more about that later, this odd monk. For now, let's decide what's on the list for Jas's first time at the festival. Will I win him a prize? I've always been talented at drinking contests—"

"*Praetor Thasian!*" came Koali's aghast exclamation.

Sakaeri turned her back to the city to watch the banter unfold between the Draconguard, the Sentinel, and the Praetor. Seraeyu laughed heartily as he tried to convince Koali that a little debauchery was good for the soulsong. It settled warmly in her chest. Jaspen tried – and failed – to calm the teasing, giving a small chuckle of his own.

Sakaeri decided that some cheer was long overdue.

She watched Seraeyu slowly devolve into what could only be described as giddy amusement. Koali resorted to honest-to-stars covering her ears to not hear Seraeyu regale some of his more questionable experiences in a Bhu-Nan casino, Jaspen's face colouring at something particularly scandalous. Sakaeri smiled. For once, it felt genuine.

CHAPTER EIGHTEEN

Sakaeri pulled at her cowl. It wasn't somewhere she wanted to be recognised.

Draped in black cloth, it was easier to blend in, hobbling along with the rest of the Haebal's sinners seeking redemption, their shuffled footsteps casting long shadows in the glowing ambiance of ore-filled sconces, night above looming. The crowd flowed, funnelling towards their shared dedication and servitude.

Before her, the walls of the temple compound stretched high, sturdy doors having opened for only a brief glimpse into hallowed grounds. Heavy bells clanged, crying out across the rooftops that it was time for the monthly gathering; for blessings to be bestowed upon those devout enough to deliver themselves when called. Seeking direction from the stars.

"May the Yun embrace you," a Cleric by the door muttered, hands crossed over his chest in reverence for the godly beings he beseeched.

"And you," Sakaeri murmured in passing, slipping by as a father and child exchanged their own ceremony.

There were no weapons on her. Not here. Somehow it was always known when one carried implements of war. No weapons, no alicant. Only oneself in humble attire.

The inner gardens sprawled, full of weeping trees draped with stuttering chimes, serenading the grounds in harmony with the beckoning bells far above. It always made Sakaeri feel dizzy, the onslaught of sound and reverberation. The temple itself careened up in an elegant spiral, endless stairs leading to the uppermost spire. That, however, was not where the people gathered. Instead, they collected in the interior sanctum, in awe of the structure above their heads. But their eyes focused on the deep, ebony floor. They prayed in quiet mutters, confessing their misdeeds in hopes of forgiveness.

Among the masses, Sakaeri breeched the threshold, entering under a grand archway that was strung with fluted bells, trembling with the number of attendees passing below.

"Welcome, Children of Yun," the Grand Cleric at the head of the rounded sanctum called. He was long-bearded and dressed in folded robes, dyed in Raenaru's deep rouge, his knobby fingers gripped tightly around the shaft of a clergy staff. "We are glad to welcome you home once more, back under the watchful eye of our benevolent overseers. Find your place among their grace, there is room for one and all."

Sakaeri drifted towards a less populated section, near a striated column. An acolyte stood just to the other side of the pillar. Sakaeri did not waver, bending low and dropping to her knees, curling over herself.

"The Yun watch. They see your commitment to their tenants. Come, speak with them, and they will hear."

To the side, another Haebalian devotee murmured their penance, rocking anxiously with hushed whispers. Before her, a group of young siblings reprimanded one of their own for chattering too loudly. Until the oldest of them shushed the other two, his hands coming up to force their heads towards the floor.

"May the Yun extend their mercy upon our soulsongs," the Grand Cleric said, rattling his staff. "May they grant the purest wishes we hold dear. May they serenade us with hymns of the unknown so that we may understand. May they see us into a brighter era."

Sakaeri placed her hands flat on the floor and dipped down. The cold, glassy surface below kissed her forehead. She closed her eyes. "Has it always been a lie?" she whispered. "Do you watch at all?"

"The Yun are our light in the vast dark. They show us the way towards their divine provenance – peace and prosperity are provided by their guiding hand. They offer us insight from the Great Starry Sea, sung across the infinite symphony of creation and destruction."

"Did you ever guide your children?" Sakaeri asked, fingers tensing, scraping.

"By their glory, we understand our place. We, the Children of Yun, continue to pave the path towards paradise. We, the Children of Yun, live in their light, in awe of their omniscient power. We, the Children of Yun, uphold their celestial vision: a realm led under their absolute, all-seeing command."

"If it's a child's fable," Sakaeri breathed, sinking lower, "then why does so much of it ring true?"

"Open your hearts. The Yun hear you. They listen. They always listen."

" ... Are you listening, Aeyun?" The words barely slipped past her lips. "Do you hear me?" Around her, hushed prayers offered a quiet hum across the room, filled with hundreds of wishes and grovels. Words that reached out to be heard. To be answered. "Can you hear me?"

For a long breath, she listened only to the distant chimes and the mutters around her.

It was quiet in her patience. A deafening silence that held her captive. Slowly, she slipped her palms off the floor and unfurled, pulling back and placing her fists in her lap.

Okay, the affirmation swam across her mind. *Okay.*

Sakaeri stood silently, noticing the nearby acolyte's eyes following her as she rose. She navigated between those still knelt, speaking to the Yun.

I never needed them.

She wove through the last bowed devotees by the entry arch, stepping back towards the garden beyond. Shielding herself from the stare of bright pockets in the faraway sky.

I never needed anyone.

Her hand rose to clutch at her draped cloak, pulling it tight across her body.

"Child." A hand came to rest on her shoulder, pulling her to a gentle halt. "Are you alright?"

"I—" her words dropped out with a croaky noise.

"Sometimes," the man, shrouded and silhouetted in the lowlight, spoke, and Sakaeri had the faint realisation that it was the acolyte who had been near the pillar. "We find ourselves overwhelmed. This is okay, we are only mortal. Would you care to join me for a walk in the gardens? I find fresh air is quite rejuvenating." When Sakaeri didn't budge, the acolyte added, "I will walk. What path you tread is up to you."

The man – older than expected, for an acolyte, perhaps ten to twenty years Sakaeri's senior – proved his statement true, pacing forward in that calm fashion all the clergy moved.

For some reason, Sakaeri's feet decided to follow.

It was only a minute turn, but the acolyte checked behind him, then smiled serenely, his eyes crinkling at their corners. He pulled his arms behind him, one hand clasping his opposite wrist, and he walked as if he did so on air. As if he hadn't a care in the world.

Sakaeri couldn't fathom it. That pervasive sense of ease.

"Sing softly, child. We are only fleeting beings, made of love and starlight. The troubles of these realms are passing and temporary. Do not let them weigh too heavily upon your soulsong. You are valued. The entirety of the starry sea calls to you. Do you hear it?"

"No," Sakaeri found herself answering. "I do not."

"I do," the acolyte said. He paused beside a weeping tree, turning on his heel. "It sings a special melody, just for you."

"I ... appreciate your efforts," said Sakaeri. "But it's not necessary."

The acolyte watched her a moment, and Sakaeri noticed the smattering of freckles scattered across his nose and cheeks, illuminated in a stark strip of light painting across the garden, its glow escaping from a slit temple window. For the briefest moment, it almost seemed as if his eyes were an indiscernible hue, then they fixed on her, a bright peridot that shone all the more vibrantly in contrast to his snowy hair.

"No effort. Not really. You are a child of the Yun, and your part in this symphony is still being written. Do not lose heart. You are not alone on this journey." The acolyte stepped closer, and Sakaeri hesitated a step back. This, however, did not deter him from leaning in, grasping Sakaeri's hands between his own. "Though, I suspect you feel that you are."

"You're a strange Cleric," Sakaeri blurted for some inane reason.

"And you are no ordinary denizen," the acolyte said. He then dropped to a whisper. "I had honest intentions to lift your spirits, but I speak for a higher power." The sudden sharpness of the man's eyes had Sakaeri's hackles raising. "I suppose it's my turn. So ... " He placed his chin just beside Sakaeri's ear. "Ube's death was no mistake. And I would make haste now, unless you would like a Sirin on your tail."

What ... ?

What, what?

"I would go left – wait, no. Right, definitely right." With that, the acolyte pushed Sakaeri to the side softly. "May you live in the light of the glorious Yun," he said at full volume. "And may you go forth with confidence, Child of Yun. I will pray for you." His arm extended, gesturing to the right, a bright, befuddling smile upon his face.

Sakaeri stared, only for a second, then she twisted and walked on, following the path laid out for her. Between the brush and the foliage, it wasn't long before she felt the oppressive force that sung a tune culled in the style of a Sirin, manifesting in the opposite direction. When she chanced a look behind her, the acolyte was disappearing into a side entrance leading back inside the temple. A different figure in an acolyte's shroud stood in the distance, a sinking feeling crawling through her once she spotted them.

Sakaeri pushed the rest of the way towards the open gate, swivelling around it and escaping back into Danu. Formidable, consuming mists clouded her mind, filing into corners shut tight. The clergy. The damned clergy.

It was only a few streets over that Sakaeri let the acolyte's words sink in. *Ube's death was no mistake.*

What was it that the daemon's ghost had said in that cursed vision? Another victim in this retched game. That it would kill her in the end. That Jourae played their game. *Their game?*

Sakaeri could only barely see the steeple of the temple now, a speared obelisk above the roofline. The bell was quiet, sleeping peacefully until awoken once more.

Don't trust the clergy, these were words Sakaeri felt secure in.

But what of the acolyte?

The city felt different in the evening hours. Once alive and bright with bustling activity, instead its streets were so lonely it rang errant. There was a sickness that bled into its paved passages, professing a fear that swelled in the absence of the known. Some still stumbled from pubs, hiccupping as they mumbled their sorrows to the wind. Others skittered quickly indoors, eyes darting around, eager to vacate open vulnerability.

Haebal was no longer warm. A chill slithered in, following footsteps wherever they landed. Sakaeri found herself mourning fabrications that still existed in her memories.

Seraeyu would weep for these empty streets, when he saw them.

"Oi, you!"

Sakaeri almost didn't stop, but it was the glint of armour that gave her pause. She turned to peek discretely up at the Sentinel standing at the corner. He stared at her from behind his pointy helm, latched in concealment. When she didn't answer, he shifted a step, fist coming to rest on his hip.

"What are you up to?" he asked, threat masked with levity.

"Walking," she responded, feeling naked without her armaments. "Is that not permitted, Sentinel?"

"No need for wise-talk, just asking," he said. The space between felt increasingly more constricted, a tension rippling there. "It's important to pay attention these days."

"Your attentions are better spent elsewhere," Sakaeri told him. "I'm just after leaving the temple grounds."

The Sentinel hummed, and it sounded unconvinced. He didn't move, but neither did Sakaeri. She felt strangely as if she were in the wild, caught in the midst of a strained stand-off. She took care to adjust her ankles in a better angle to run when one of his feet fell forward with staunch purpose. Then he stopped again, his helmet boring a stare uncannily.

Just as his arm shifted towards the pommel at his hip, another Sentinel turned a corner, arriving evenly between them. They looked left, then right, and Sakaeri was confident that she would recognise this arrival's stature almost anywhere now.

"Sentinel," Sakaeri called, looking up towards the new arrival with stubborn confidence. "I hope you're having a pleasant evening."

Koali did not betray recognition, only nodding back procedurally. "As do I." Her hulking presence stood bulwark between rising threat. She seemed to have picked up on that. "Is there a problem here, Sentinel Agyuni?"

"Not at all, Captain Ujaen," the Sentinel said. "Only making friendly conversation. This one says she's returning from tonight's temple mass."

Despite the shield of ore before her face, Koali's burning stare penetrated right into Sakaeri's wilful gaze. Out of everyone in this city, she may in fact find that statement the most odd, considering her recent reticence for Sakaeri.

"And?" Koali asked. For a moment, Sakaeri thought it was directed towards her, but instead Koali turned, the vision of her back professing a trust Sakaeri was not yet sure she was deserving of. "What of it?"

"Mass is still in progress," Sentinel Agyuni spoke simply.

"We do not dictate others' acts of faith, Sentinel," said Koali. "And I do not tolerate the heckling of Raenaru's citizens."

It was quiet for a long moment, until Sentinel Agyuni spoke tightly, saying, "Understood, Captain." With careful consideration, he chose his path of departure, disappearing into the deadened night.

Koali had not yet turned when Sakaeri questioned, "You're not going to ask?"

"No," said Koali.

"I'm sure you'd like to."

"It is not my place."

"I can see why he's taken to you," said Sakaeri. Tension melted from her heels, and she crossed her arms, offering an easy smirk that the woman before her couldn't see. "You're quite loyal, aren't you?" Koali slowly looked over her shoulder, arms limp at her sides. "I'm still unclear why you're so taken with him, however."

"I serve hearth and home, as any good soldier does."

"No," Sakaeri told her. "No, that's not it."

The ore of lamps hung high above, dimming and brightening in waning intervals, cycling through natural pulls of innate energy. Around them, buildings towered, most of them gated and locked up as the shopping hours eluded the sweeping laneways of Cheyun. With just the two of them, the deafened thoroughfares felt rather peaceful and less desolate.

"I remember," Koali said, almost a whisper. "Newly recruited. Fresh on the assignment. I remember the day that I first stepped into that Tower. The same day Praetor Paeyuni left us." She twisted further then, more fully towards Sakaeri. "I never want to see that look on Seraeyu Thasian's face again. Because while I saw him shatter," there was a seed of quelled anger in her words, "others decided they saw something else entirely. I am nothing, not where the realms are concerned, but if I can be a safe place for one deserted child, I can enter the beyond knowing I've done at least one thing I'll never regret. One thing that I take pride in above all. I will never abandon that child."

Sakaeri watched Koali in a new light. It was warm, this one. She drew her feet together and pulled an arm towards herself, resting the edge of her palm perpendicular to her chest. With little hesitation, she reflected the movement with her opposite hand, undeterred when Koali began to raise a placating, embarrassed wave.

"Thank you," Sakaeri said, strong and steady. "For watching over him, for seeing him, when we failed to do so." Koali froze, her arm half lifted. "I only hope you let me stand beside you. That I can match your dedication."

"Do not jest," said Koali. "You are already there."

"I have many years to catch up on."

"I respectfully disagree."

"I didn't see him, Koali. Not truly." It felt shameful to admit. Another so close to her. Another quietly suffering, not so dissimilar to herself. And she'd elected to ignore it. Favour her attentions on her own misfortunes. Seraeyu was not the only she'd overlooked. "But I won't look away now. I will face any horror that comes to light at his side. He's been battling on his own long enough. No more."

"No more," Koali agreed.

"That little arsehole doesn't know how adored he is."

"Please watch your words, Sirin Yisuna!" Koali reprimanded in a harsh whisper as Sakaeri reached her side and they fell in step, heading back towards the Tower. "That is the Praetor you speak of."

Sakaeri laughed heartily, a grin pulling at her cheeks. She landed her fist once against Koali's arm in friendly camaraderie. "You suppose he's off bothering Jaspen right now?"

"I'd like to think so."

"Yeah," Sakaeri agreed, her chuckles tapering. "Yeah, me too."

"I'm loathe to admit it, but he seems rather reliable."

"For an Orinian dog," Sakaeri said, fully expecting another outburst from Koali.

Instead, what got was a soft: "For an Orinian dog."

Sakaeri's loud guffaw ripped across the street, bouncing jovially around suddenly less quiet corridors.

CHAPTER NINETEEN

"Sera," Sakaeri called.

He'd been hiding himself away more over the past few days, her probing knocks often on the receiving end of an apology and a quick excuse before the door was shoved back in her face. Locking her out once again. Today, however, was the festival, and Seraeyu needed to be present. And he needed to leave that stars-forsaken room.

Knock, knock, knock.

"Sera," she called again.

The egress cracked open with slow progress, the image of Seraeyu dressed in ceremonial robes and adorned with sparse regalia greeting her. Praetor Thasian was scheduled to appear today, and he was certainly dressed for the part. His expression, however, was grim.

"Sakaeri," he greeted. It came out flat.

"You look nice," she offered.

He fluttered his hand like it didn't matter. "I feel like I'm going to throw up."

The afternoon hours were already upon them, meaning that the festival would be in full swing soon. Just beyond those gates, Seraeyu would debut as not the son of a legacy, but the Legacy itself, once again treading familiar ground for the first time.

But Sakaeri would be there, too. Right beside him.

"Come on," she said. "It's showtime."

By the time they'd made it to the Tower entryway, weighty stares were already stiffening Seraeyu's movements. Even when Koali blocked one side, and Jaspen the other, Seraeyu's pace was stilted, chin forced high.

The Sentinels at the door offered Raenaruan signs of respect, which Seraeyu returned graciously. Sakaeri's attention flicked everywhere, looking for misnomers or strange auras. It was only the stray grouping of Draconguard in the corner who caught her interest. But their focus seemed to follow not Seraeyu but Jaspen, trailing after him as he strolled beside the Praetor.

Seraeyu's breath hitched when the heavy doors pulled open. He paused.

Sakaeri leant forward, her mask coming to rest beside his ear. She whispered, "We must continue, *Praetor*."

His hesitation only lasted a moment longer, then he was stepping into a courtyard aglow with lantern light; bulbous structures strung from weeping trees across the yard. To Sakaeri, they looked like soulsongs hanging in the air, gathered around ropey, sweeping amethystine leaves. Spirits dancing in preparation for twilight.

The sweet smell of popperlilies still floated on the breeze, but this evening the rich fragrance of lunarius unfurled beside it, the petals by the pond waking with the full moon that watched far above. It was the kind of evening that held aether in its grasp, the promise of possibilities teasing on a precipice.

"Haebal is waiting, Praetor," said Kaoli.

It had been a patient reminder, but Seraeyu locked up again.

"I know," he said, leagues away from his usual resolve.

"We are right beside you, Praetor," Jaspen said, his standard-issue armour claiming anything but.

"I know."

Sakaeri leant forward again. "You are not alone, Seraeyu."

"I know."

It was a sluggish procession to the gate, but no one pushed it. A fragile barrier was spread between the Tower doors and the courtyard gate, and each step fractured another layer of it. Soon, nothing would remain. Soon, Seraeyu would be beyond his cage.

Soon, Seraeyu would be exposed.

"Praetor," came the gruff greeting of a Sentinel at the gate. "We have patrols out in full force. Please enjoy your evening with confidence."

"You have my gratitude," said Seraeyu.

Sakaeri was sure he meant it too.

Finally, painstakingly, the heavy iron gates opened, the city eerily quiet behind them. Koali must have picked up on an odd tick of Sakaeri's body language.

"Stationed Sentinels have this area cordoned off."

Seraeyu stepped forward.

"Would there normally be a crowd here?" Jaspen asked.

Seraeyu stepped forward.

"In past years, yes. The city is passionate about its leadership."

Seraeyu stepped forward.

"Ah, I … see," Jaspen said, his helm's tilt giving away his glance at Seraeyu.

Seraeyu stopped.

"This is a bad idea," he said.

"You'll be fine, Sera," Sakaeri murmured, nudging him on again with a guiding hand pressed against his back. "You'll be just fine."

Seraeyu stepped forward.

"And you'll all be with me?" he asked.

Sakaeri's chest clenched a little. "Yes, Sera."

"Yes, Praetor," said Koali.

"Yes, Seraeyu Thasian," said Jaspen.

Seraeyu stepped forward.

"Okay." He took two more steps. "Okay."

It was near the bend at the end of the street where they encountered the first of the crowds. The juncture was overhung by a skywalk, decorated with festival lights and tassels. Masks were strapped to people's faces, their abundant likenesses making Sakaeri look like a commoner instead of a mercenary.

In the end, it was a child who noticed Seraeyu.

The point of a finger was followed by the lifting of excited voices, a clamour to press against the glass partition that built the wall of the skywalk. Sakaeri watched Seraeyu look up at them, eyes wide and foot shifted back, ready to bolt.

"You should wave, Praetor Thasian," Jaspen said quietly.

Mechanically, Seraeyu lifted his hand in the air, his sleeve collecting at his elbow. He offered a short jiggle of his fingers, then the din above them amplified. Sakaeri's eyes caught a few frowns amongst the smiles, and there was a hooded figure near the leftmost side whose aura was muted, contained in a way that had concern blossoming. She latched her glove onto Seraeyu's shoulder and urged him onwards.

He stumbled under her guidance, muttering, "The city is watching. The realm is watching." It didn't seem like a thought meant for his company.

They found refuge in a shaded alleyway, an overgrowth of vines shrouding its passageway in. Seraeyu fumbled a few steps ahead, then he pressed his hands to his cheeks and shook his head a little. With jilted inaccuracy, he started pulling the glittering threads of gems from his person, heaving in deep breaths as he did.

"This was a bad idea," Seraeyu said, yanking a delicate chain from his horns too roughly, a link snapping and strung beads clattering to the flagstones below. He watched them scatter, brow furrowed. "I can't play this role. I was never *meant* for it."

"Prae—" Koali began, but Sakaeri thrust her arm out to halt her words.

Instead, she treaded lightly to where Seraeyu stood, still pulling glided adornments from his body. Slowly, so as not to startle, she unclipped her mask and instead settled it upon Seraeyu's face. He remained frozen in place as she latched it behind his head, then she took his chin and angled his gaze towards her.

Sakaeri looked intently into those ore-shrouded eyes. "Tonight, you are Yisuna."

She fiddled with his hair to better disguise the distinction between his own horns and the mask's. In front of her, the expressionless mirror of Yisuna gazed back, silent.

He held out his hand, an offering of jewels and precious metals cradled within them.

"Take them," he said. "I don't want them."

"Okay, Sera."

"Sirin Yisuna," Koali said, subdued. "But who will you be?"

"Sakaeri," she told her. "I am Sakaeri."

"Sakaeri," Jaspen said, pulling her attention over. He lifted the faceplate of his helm, a smile hiding behind it. "A pleasure to finally meet you." His hand came up between them, outstretched in offering. She saw doubles of it in different iterations. But this time—

Sakaeri took his hand in her own and gave it a firm shake, a smile snaking across her face. "Sure, *Jas*. Nice to officially meet you, face-to-face."

"The full moon has done something to you all this evening," Koali said, flipping her own visor up with a put-on scowl. "All this sentimentality in the air."

"Don't pretend you aren't a fool for it," Seraeyu said, and Sakaeri wondered if she sounded muted in the same way when she spoke from behind the mask's barrier.

Koali offered a charmed grin. "I cannot claim otherwise, you have caught me."

Seraeyu stood a little taller, a little surer, as they stepped back into the main thoroughfares. The further they traversed, the livelier the streets became. His attention seemed to snag on every new fancy, from a particularly intricate festival display to a delicious ensemble of colourful fare. Sakaeri pulled up her cowl. At the very least, it would deter any less than wanted gawks at her features, should anyone recognise her.

The first opportunity that arose, she would adopt the persona of Hana. She'd be one of many among the crowd in the darkening hours. Both Hana and Yisuna. It wasn't her preference, though. Part of her wouldn't be able to shake the idea that she'd be fitting her tired feet into Aeyun's old shoes. Wasn't that a laugh?

They were well into the chattering, festival-enchanted crowds – Seraeyu trying to shove his hard-won stuffed rendition of a mythical pyrewing into Jaspen's arms – when a small gathering of Orinian Draconguard sidled up to their group. There were four total, one of whom wore gleaming armour embossed with strokes and patterns that professed his higher rank. In the ambient glow of orelight, shadows danced dazzlingly across their metalled shells. It was entrancing as it was ominous. Sakaeri wondered if victims of whole towns and villages once burnt to crisps by these same armoured silhouettes harboured the same fleeting thought before their lives were upended alongside their history.

Sakaeri stepped in towards Seraeyu and noticed that Koali mirrored the movement. Jaspen was still politely declining the fluff-bloated bird when his name was called.

"Commander Ephrite!" Jaspen blurted once he spotted the most impressive of the soldiers standing a head above the rest. He hinged into a stiff bow. "Glory be to Orin's Majesty."

"Glory be to Orin," the commander responded in a deep baritone. "And to Raenaru," he added, scanning across their hodgepodge ensemble, pausing at Seraeyu's masked features. "Please accept my apologies. I have business with Draconguard Verdanta."

Sakaeri didn't like that the man could still pick out Seraeyu in the crowd. But it was the blank casts of Orinian helms staring at them from beside Commander Ephrite that caused her skin to crawl. They remained vigilant at his shoulders, looking as though they dare not breathe until told to do so.

"Oh," said Jaspen, downtrodden.

Sakaeri inwardly gawked at how utterly uncouth he sounded, in the presence of his commander no less. Duty did not pardon anyone, despite whatever promises they'd made.

Seraeyu clung to his prize for a moment, then cocked his head in a way Sakaeri knew paired with a plastic smile. "Of course, Commander Ephrite." He turned to Jaspen. "Your realm calls. It's best you go."

Jaspen broke his bow to twist in Seraeyu's direction. "Right. Of course … Yisuna."

"I do hope you return him in one piece," Seraeyu jested, addressing Commander Ephrite once more. "Before you go, may I ask why I wasn't informed of your presence?"

"My arrival is premature. I am to accompany you in two days' time."

"Ah, yes," said Seraeyu. "The escort to Orin."

"Commander, if I may—"

"It's about Perodine and Jeta," Commander Ephrite cut in. It seemed that was enough to corral whatever protests Jaspen may have had bubbling up. "Come. Let's speak."

"Go on, then, Draconguard Verdanta," Seraeyu said, leaving little room for argument.

Festival patrons parted in wary appraisal as the Draconguard passed, but Sakaeri instead observed Seraeyu. He didn't move at first, just watching the small platoon fade into the crowd, then he clutched tightly at the pyrewing, bringing it close to his chest.

"The list of visitors we have that day is ever-growing," he murmured. "The Ministers will not be pleased with the divided attention."

"The Ministers should be pleased you're holding an audience at all," said Koali.

"Oh, don't be like that." Seraeyu passed Koali the pudgy bird, who stowed it with great care under the crook of her arm. "It's likely they've been waiting quite a few months for this."

"Yisuna," Sakaeri called, pulling him from the enveloping dark. "The playwrights have a stage in the Cheyun Square." She pointed towards the painted signage that announced the affair in garish explosions of colour. "It's about you, you know. *The Two-Fold Odyssey*."

"Well, it would certainly be a shame to miss a tale about *me*," said Seraeyu.

With one final glance behind them, the Draconguard long gone, the trio squeezed back into the celebrations. Jolly chords bounced from buskers and joyous laughter rung in their ears. Somehow, every note fell flatter than the one before.

"My blade shall be the one that binds our fate, felling all who stand against the will of Raenaru!" Hana on stage proclaimed proudly, his intricate and twisted blade held aloft for even the furthest audience member's eyes. He spun with a flourish and splayed his fingers wide, gesturing to the woman opposite him. She was dressed in luxurious fabrics and adorned with multi-spoked horns, looking far more wilderdeer than Yu-ta. "My saviour of the stars; the *ah-ka* of the ground we stand, the water we swim, and the song stirred in the depths of my soulsong – Yisuna! For you are the celestial heavens themselves, come to bless us with your grace and guidance!"

"My chosen Hana, you make this sacred claim, and so shall it be. My darling Hana, together we herald the new age of prosperity; a unity amongst Raenaru. So written it was in the stars that we would meet, so written it was in the stars that our legacy lives on. Raenaru is consecrated this day, made holy with our vow: together we weave destiny!"

The swell of orchestral music burst in time with the flares of show-fire and perfectly timed squalls. Sakaeri snickered, nudging Seraeyu's shoulder in amusement. The playwrights had gone all out on production, from costuming to the stage and props. They were all gilded in metallic sheens and sophisticated embellishments, really aiming to capture the illustrious retelling that was the tale of Herald Hana and Auspicious Yisuna.

A sniffle on the other side of Seraeyu had Sakaeri glancing over.

"Honestly," she deadpanned once she saw the watery troughs of Koali's eyes.

"It's magical, isn't it?" Koali spoke, garbled. "This story is so wonderful." She cleared her throat and flipped her visor down once her admiration was quelled. "Well! I think I'll just get us some refreshments, will I? Yes, yes, that's a good idea."

As she scuttled towards a drink stand, Seraeyu sighed beside Sakaeri.

"Sakaeri, I'm not ready."

"For what?"

"Whatever comes next."

"Whatever it is," she said, grabbing his hand. "I'm with you."

"I fear that may not be enough, love."

"Then I suppose we'll succumb together."

"I suppose we may."

"What's—"

The first blade stabbed into a wooden post.

Panic erupted instantaneously, pandemonium filtering in and slithering between empty spaces, the audience running for desperate escape. Sakaeri was cruelly separated from Seraeyu, knocked back by elbows and swinging arms. Steadying herself with a frustrated grunt, she centred her gravity against the mayhem so he could peer through the screams.

I hadn't felt their threat, dammit!

A now familiar voice cried out in pain. Sakaeri's head snapped to the side, her scanning search finding Koali. A dirk was painfully lodged into her shoulder, its pierce having sheared straight through her armour, and the nephrite sword she held dropped to the ground with a clanking wail, smothered by stomping footfalls around it.

Where is Seraeyu?

Sakaeri's heart thudded against her ribcage as she jumped to cling to a lamplight, holding herself above the ruckus to search over the manic sea of heads for Seraeyu. Too many similar masks among the masses. His crimson robes finally caught her attention as she found him skidding to a halt beside cowering stage actors. With sharpened urgency, he held out his hand and demanded the blade from the closest performer, his shielded gaze darting over his shoulder, a swift examination the chaos beyond.

Sakaeri dropped from her perch and dodged through the thinning commotion, shrieks circling around her as she ran. When she slid to a stop, the liberated blade's hilt was thrusted into her hands, the uneven quality of its temperance offering an unbalanced grip.

"I don't know how to use this properly," Seraeyu said by way of explanation.

"What about the dual-blade?"

"Yes, that one I do."

She pulled her Thasian-borrowed instrument from its sheath and passed it to him. Once in his hands, he cracked it open and deftly elongated a centre piece she didn't know had that mechanic, fitting them back together to form—

Oh. It was a dual-sided glaive. *Well then.*

It was just in time, too. Another dirk came hurtling through the air, Sakaeri's limp hold on the ceremonial blade becoming rock steady as she deflected its assault with a measured swing. The twang of metal hitting metal rung through the emptying courtyard, the thwarted weapon clattering down at the edge of the stage. Its etched wing glared up at her, mocking.

Sakaeri felt a presence beside her and glanced at Koali as she joined their small resistance, her off-hand pressed against her bloodied shoulder. Fortifying her stance, she pulled her palm off her wound and instead reached for a jewelled pommel at her waist.

"My left arm's no good with a sword," she grunted. "But I can make do with my alicant." Alongside her proclamation came the unfurling of a pyrewhip, its slither of flames licking the stones where its curl had settled.

"Good woman," said Sakaeri. "We stand together."

Seraeyu, however, seemed to have an agenda of his own. He stubbornly dropped off the stage to march into the courtyard.

"You call yourselves a righteous order," he snarled, the bark of it echoing off now nearly empty streets, even the actors having fled by then. "But you hide in the shadows like cowards!"

"Pot calling the kettle black, don't you think?" came a cackling reply.

"I don't claim bravado," said Seraeyu. Another dirk whistled across the scattered remains of kiosks and trinket stands, but Seraeyu warded it off with a calculated twist of his borrowed weapon. Sakaeri stilled her pursuit to be at his back, watching impressed as the shirked blade scraped across stone. "There's strength in knowing what you are."

"And what are you?" The call cooed from the darkest crevices. Sakaeri hated it. It reminded her too much of games played in her worst memories as a Sirin. "A deviant chimaera. Born to be put down."

"I am no chimaera!" Seraeyu shouted, but it sounded like two voices melding into one.

Flung blades split the space between them, this time aimed at Sakaeri and Koali. The Sentinel expertly flicked her wrist, her pyrewhip wresting a projectile away, while Sakaeri fended off two of her own with a harrowing clang of grating metal.

How many had surrounded them? Sakaeri tried to gauge the auras in the area, but an oppressive culling of energy shrouded her intuition. As she struggled to calm and focus her attunement, a suspicious ringing noise brought her attention back to Seraeyu.

Or rather, just past him.

A sage stood shadowed by the entryway to an alley, his hand rattling a staff. The chiming of bells grew in opposition to Seraeyu's flood of inky aether, its wisped energy pulsing in swirls around his feet. *He's losing it again,* Sakaeri acknowledged. When she tried to run to his aid, it was as if her legs were pushing through something thick and viscous, movement feeling like wading through heavy mud.

"I am *Sirin,*" said Seraeyu.

Sakaeri watched as something intangible split to overlay his image; an uncanny reflection of a woman loomed over him. A woman whom she recognised *from Beldur!*

"Seraeyu!" Sakaeri called, but it felt like her voice sank into oblivion, unravelled as soon as it drew from her throat. She looked beside her to see Koali resolutely trying to stomp her way through that invisible barricade.

"And my debt will be paid." Seraeyu lifted his hand that wasn't held steadfast to the elongated dual-sword, his fingertips sparking with blackened energy.

This was too close, too similar to that day almost a year back. When calamity first struck.

Bells chimed in unison now, loud and with startling clarity, sounding like they were coming from everywhere at once. Seraeyu cringed inwards and the dark miasma seeping from his form shrunk, quieted. With an irritated snarl, he shouted out and the bells' chimes faded, a forceful press of energy surging down upon Sakaeri's shoulders as Essence erupted across the square. It slunk up buildings and twisted into corners, dropping a shadowy blanket across the entire area. Its caustic grip drew in hidden Sirin – two of them – and several clergy folk like a whirlpool, their feet slipping across stone as if carried atop the sea of swirling obsidian.

Sakaeri grunted as she felt her knees smash against the ground. This *power.* It was on a different level. It was ... *godly.* Perhaps the crystal, perhaps that entity, was truly Yun.

"I will not be—"

It almost felt like time itself froze with Seraeyu's tied tongue.

Sakaeri struggled to look up, the fight making its way to her very soulsong.

With a sudden shift, she was standing, weightless as all that pressure lifted away. She was at first amazed at her own perseverance, then she caught eyes on Seraeyu's form. There among the aether stood not one but three entities. Seraeyu, in the middle and staggering to keep himself upright, was caught between two ethereal ghosts. To his right was the presumed daemon, a Yu-ta wraith with long hair and curled horns, her expression baffled as she gazed upon their third counterpart.

It shouldn't have been possible. But he often achieved the unthinkable, didn't he?

Aeyun, his phantasm white-eyed and severe, had one hand wrapped around the Yu-ta wraith's wrist, yanked back from Seraeyu's head. The other was holding firm upon Seraeyu's forearm, pulling at it with some strange urgency before guiding Seraeyu's hand to push the Yisuna mask to the side.

The Yu-ta wraith watched, silent as Aeyun leant down to Seraeyu's ear.

"Look at me." Sakaeri heard Seraeyu say. The small group of assailants who had been pulled to his feet seemed compelled to do so, their eyes adopting a milky sheen. "*Cah da'gum, da'ju cah.* You mistook someone for Seraeyu Thasian. You did not locate him this evening."

"I mistook someone for Seraeyu Thasian," several voices said in haunting unison, porcelain gazes all trained on Seraeyu's face. "He was not located this evening."

"*A'pan o.*" Seraeyu's voice had that strange dual quality again, Aeyun's bleeding through. But it *was* Seraeyu's when he stumbled back a step and groused, "Aeyun," the sound of it like a shout in the deafening quiet.

Sakaeri could swear she heard whispers of *sorry* and *soon*.

Aeyun's spectre looked up again, glaring at the Yu-ta wraith. Sakaeri breathed deep, centring herself, falling further into that aetherscape invading reality.

"Who are you?" Aeyun asked, and Sakaeri nearly jumped at the clarity of it.

"How peculiar you are, blood of Ka'la'drius."

"That's a Mhedoonian name. I'm not Mhedoonian," he said with a scowl. Seraeyu stumbled again, but Aeyun held him in place, Seraeyu contorting a little disjointedly.

"Are you not?" the Yu-ta wraith crooned. "Blood of Ka'la'drius ... blood of Ka'la'drius," she said, debating. "How have you come to be? A'gam said everyone was slaughtered, like the others."

" ... What did you say?"

"Aeyun, he said," the wraith continued, ignoring his query. Sakaeri wanted to call out, question something or stop something. But she felt stuck. An observer. "Not Aeyun. That's a Raenaruan name. So, who are you, blood of Ka'la'drius? *Where* are you?"

"Aeyun," Seraeyu rasped, trying to turn. "Now is *not* the time."

"What are you trying to hide, young Yu-ta?"

"You're misguided. A malformed whisper of the past," Seraeyu said, finally managing to twist, his eyes an odd dichotomy of uneven black and white, opaline streaks cracking through them.

The wraith turned a narrow gaze on him. "I am not misguided. I am exactly as I am meant to be."

"A killer and a *tyrant*," Seraeyu accused, grimacing as he teetered a bit. "How do you justify who you've slain? In the name of *what* justice!?"

The wraith said nothing, pensive, her image stuttering incorporeally.

"Who are the Sirin?" Aeyun asked. "What's their role in this?"

"The people or the Raenaruan bastardisation of them?" the wraith spat, vitriol returning.

"Aeyun, stop," said Seraeyu.

"The people?"

"Sírin. A great, powerful people. Robbed of their rightful lives and lands."

"Aeyun, *stop*."

"Then who are you?"

The wraith's grin spread wide. "Amanastré, strange blood of Ka'la'drius. Who are *you*?"

"Aeyun!" Sakaeri felt herself shout, the sound of it bursting like released tension. Finally, it managed to garner their attention. "Pull your head out of your arse and listen to Sera!" she called, begging her body to wade through the aether.

Seraeyu was gradually slinking further down, a crimson trail weeping from one eye, spiny black veins crawling up his neck. Likely *Amanastré*'s influence.

"Sakaeri," Aeyun said first when he noticed her, then, "Seraeyu!" He turned to support him, earning an indignant huff from the unsteady man.

"Well, aren't you full of surprises? Although," Amanastré considered Sakaeri for a moment as she battled onwards. "You would be the closest thing to Thay in existence."

"This doesn't need to happen," said Seraeyu. "We didn't ask for this." He forced himself up, straightening his back to look her in the eyes. "Neither did you."

"Reading while I've been banished?" Amanastré accused.

"It's cruel," was what Seraeyu replied with. "All of it."

"Sera, what are you talking about?" Aeyun asked.

While that bastard looked at odds about what to do, Sakaeri knew well. They needed to leave. Both of them needed to *go*. Seraeyu had to be freed of both their grasps, else he would crumble. He held himself tall, but he was splintering.

"Some things are better left buried, Aeyun."

Amanastré let loose a forceful laugh, then it was followed by tapering, malicious chuckles. "Seraeyu Thasian. I did not think you would be as wilfully ignorant as the rest."

"I'm not," said Seraeyu. "I know who and what I am. You keep calling yourself Sírin, so perhaps I'm not the one pretending. I also know that violence begets violence. I'm not interested in instigating more."

"Your very existence is violence, *Praetor*," Amanastré hissed.

"I didn't ask to be Praetor!" Seraeyu shouted.

"Sera—"

Sakaeri made it, reached them through the sticky aetherscape that tore the realm. As she pulled Seraeyu into her arms, she faced the man who stole her life – who had his own stolen before she met him – and said, "Learn restraint, Aeyun."

Seraeyu collapsed into her embrace and the hazy inversion of unreality faded alongside Aeyun and Amanastré's presences. Instead, the Haebalian square fell back into place, and Sakaeri sunk to the ground with her ward. The excess Essence and Vitality that had culminated within him was expelled through their leeched contact, and Sakaeri felt it filter through her, awakening all over again.

For a breath of nonsensical time, it was only Sakaeri and Seraeyu in nothingness; a moment that didn't exist, sat outside the praxis of place and belonging. Two sparks of light in the vast, endless sea.

Jaspen was the first to reach them, kneeling as they broke apart.

"Praetor," he said, concern written over his exposed features.

"Where's Koali?" Sakaeri thought to ask, finding it strange that she hadn't rushed over. Jaspen looked on the verge of a breaking point when he glanced over.

"I was terrified she had fallen victim, but everyone here is just … unconscious. What happened?"

"Let's go home," Seraeyu interjected, pushing himself off the ground shakily as he stared at the Yísuna mask before him, broken in half, one side entirely shattered. It must have dropped when Aeyun disappeared. "I'd like to go back to the Tower."

"Of course, Praetor. Let's – yes, let's go."

"Sakaeri," Seraeyu gazed up at her, looking like he'd been to the frozen void and back, his face partially smeared with browning scarlet. "Please see to it that Koali is returned safely. Round up any Sentinels and tell them the threat has been nullified. The populace must be reassured of their safety, so please relay my request that this is done."

At that moment, he was *Praetor*, leader of a city and a realm. A part of her wondered if he was even cognisant that he'd fallen so seamlessly into the role. Not wanting to be something was one thing. Not suited to something was entirely another.

"And the rest?"

Maybe she fell just as easily into the role of mercenary.

Seraeyu stared, a bit too disconcertingly dead-eyed. "Aeyun saw to that. Leave them. Deliver them back to their compound if you feel compelled to do so."

It wasn't the time. She had to remind herself of that. "Understood."

CHAPTER TWENTY

Aeyun gasped and stumbled back, becoming aware of his surroundings once more.

He was greeted by the glade around the a'teneum, morning's illuminated glare casting upon him, unforgiving. It refracted across that wide expanse of pastel sky. The calm of the grounds settled into his skin; – drifting breezes tickling wilderlilies, chitters of burrowbirds singing their waking serenades. It felt horribly malicious. Aeyun swathed in peaceful tidings, Seraeyu suffering turmoil.

"Why'd you have to do that, Sakaeri," Aeyun muttered, closing his eyes in frustration.

There was something Seraeyu knew, and Aeyun was so close. Just a little more and the picture would be clear. The wrought connection between Yu-ta and Ca'lorus and the Sirin and the Thasian. It was there – so surely there – and it felt like the key to ripping apart the barricade between fabrication and reality.

Ka'la'drius. Blood of Ka'la'drius. And A'gam.

Stars above, it had been *right there*, hadn't it? But if he was right, if it was true, wouldn't that mean something ludicrous? Unthinkable? No one was immortal.

Gods did not exist.

Yet one seemingly resided right under his nose, daft and forgetful, and another was snared around Seraeyu's heart. Seraeyu, who was contending with active threats; the damned sages in cahoots with Sirin to rid the realms of him. At least Sakaeri was there. At least they had one another, not entirely forsaken. He was glad.

"Aeyun," he heard behind him, soft and tentative. Concerned.

Every muscle in his body tensed. How much was witnessed? Slowly, fretfully, he about-faced towards his brother. It was as laughable as it was unfortunate that Da'garu stood beside him, wide-eyed and a fraction further back, partially shielded by Uruji's shoulder.

"Uruji," said Aeyun. *Dammit.*

"Aeyun, what in all the void?"

"I can … explain," he said, even if he wasn't entirely sure that rang true.

"Then start explaining," Uruji demanded. "Because I'm fairly certain I just saw a vestige of *Seraeyu Thasian* next to you. No," he shook his head, "not *next* to you. It was like he was an extension of you. Like what happened with Gama-of-Yun. And that's … things like that shouldn't be possible. It's *not* possible."

"It's complicated."

"You said you could explain."

"I can, I just …" Aeyun trailed. It felt pained, an idea dislodged. There was a sense of being caught-out, an act of betrayal. With this coming to light, however, there was something he wanted to know. Something he never had the right to before. "Did Father teach you do it?"

Uruji's brows furrowed, his expression adopting a familiar meditation. "Do what?"

"The rite?"

"You're asking *me* questions now?"

It wasn't often that Uruji got irate. It didn't suit him.

"Because those alicant – those daemonish Yun – are connected to this. There's a reason I was pulled to Raenaru, to the Thasian. I think it's … finally making sense, and I—" Aeyun paused and the words *extension of you* congealed viciously in his mind. He pulled his hands up and looked at his palms, as if they held the answer. They didn't, but there was a piece that slipped into place. *Blood of Ka'la'drius.* "I'm starting to make sense."

"I respectfully beg to differ," Uruji commented, clearly not willing to entertain ambiguity. "And you're not meant to know about those, Aeyun. Though, I'm not really surprised that you do." He glanced towards the a'teneum, where Raeyu was presumably still sleeping.

"Did he teach you the rite?"

Uruji was silent, considering. Beside him, Da'garu finally shifted to the side and began scoping the area around Aeyun, careful and hesitant. Intuitive, like something elusive lingered. He wasn't sure what she was looking for.

"It was all theory. I would have been at Seraeyu's if it had happened. It's not the kind of thing that can be practised, only done."

"Who are they?" Aeyun countered, distracted by Da'garu's cautious prodding at seemingly thin air.

"I don't really understand what you're asking," Uruji admitted.

"The entities in the alicant. Who are they?"

"There are no entities in the alicant."

"We're past the point of secrecy, Uruji!"

"I'm not lying! And that's a bit rich, considering you've not answered anything yet!"

"He didn't tell you? Or—" *did he not know?* That almost felt like an impossibility, as much as Raeyu not knowing felt extremely unlikely.

"They're just … they're just unstable alicant. It's an ancient art that we do; a meticulous, structured ceremony to ensure safe embedment," Uruji said, but it sounded off. Uncertain. "Aeyun, *why* did I just witness Seraeyu Thasian by your side?"

"Because he found that second alicant, Uruji," said Aeyun. "That second alicant, host to an *entity*, not just unstable power. And it overtook him; has done for the past year."

Horror pulled colour from Uruji's face. "What are you … saying? And that doesn't explain *this*."

"Blood of Ka'la'drius," Aeyun murmured, fruitlessly inspecting his palm once more. In his periphery, he saw Da'garu freeze. He turned to her. "But aren't we descendants of Ca'ille? Not Mhedoonian?" Da'garu was watching him with an inscrutable expression. Something, an insurmountable dread, welled with him as he shifted towards the a'tenteum, gaze lifted to the uppermost tower. "Who is Amanastré—" he swallowed, "—A'gam?"

The pulse that rendered was thunderous, a crack resounding and reflecting off all corners of The Veil. Almost instantaneous, Gama-of-Yun stood before him, rigid hand encircling his neck, fingers digging in and cutting off air. Aeyun stared down at him resolutely, even as he felt his feet lift from the grassy knoll.

"What have you done, foolish boy?" Gama-of-Yun spat, looking like someone else entirely. His placid smile was replaced with gritted teeth, his absent gaze instead steady and drowning, a depth of gruelling understanding reflected there. "How long has it *been*?"

Aeyun was just as suddenly dropped to the ground. He took a moment to steady himself while Uruji pushed defensively in front of him, glaring up at Gama-of-Yun. Da'garu, however, slowly stalked towards the risen *A'gam*, her attention flittering across the space around him.

Gama-of-Yun brought his hands to his head, his fingers threading into his hair, his expression fretful and tortured. "I remember," he said. "I *remember*." His limbs trembled, and he croaked out a mournful noise. "Oh, *stars above*, I remember." When he focused on Aeyun again, it almost felt as if he were looking through him. "It's time, then. It's this one. And it's you."

All was still for a moment. Gama-of-Yun seemed to take stock, his gaze darting around. Then he let out a shaky breath, pairing it with a huffy laugh.

"How awful. We'd hoped, and we were wrong."

"A'gam—" Aeyun ventured.

"Don't!" Gama-of-Yun blurted out, hitching a loud inhale. "That name is a curse. A'gam is a foul personage."

Aeyun couldn't find it in himself to care. "A'gam, who is Amanastré? Ka'la'drius?"

Gama-of-Yun gave him a long, hard stare. "What a horrid thing. This reckoning." He pushed the heels of his palms against his eyes. "Ca'ille, this isn't what you wanted."

"Ca'ille?" Aeyun asked.

Ca'ille. Ka'la'drius. Amanastré. A'gam.

Names invariably storied yet without history.

Gama-of-Yun unshielded himself and offered a wry smile, looking the slightest bit more like the hermit Aeyun recognised. "My dear cousin."

"*Cousin?*"

"Yes. And wife to Ka'la'drius." He paused, eyes casting from side to side, almost as if he were reading. "So, this is how it unfolded." Finally, his gaze fell to Da'garu, who stood to astray from them, most near Gama-of-Yun himself. She stared up unabashed, exploring the periphery of his form. "I have failed you," he said as he gave her head an endeared, gentle pet. "Both of you."

Aeyun found himself the centre of attention once more, the weight of it like sinking into the ground itself. He almost wished it were real; that the dirt would open an earthy maw and swallow him whole. Gama-of-Yun frowned deeply, a twitch squinting his eyes, as if he'd gleaned the wicked desire through simple observation.

"Peace or damnation now rests with Seraeyu Thasian," said Gama-of-Yun.

"Seraeyu Thasian," Uruji echoed quietly.

"Yes."

"How are you ... alive?" Aeyun asked. If Gama-of-Yun was Ca'ille's cousin, then he must be generations old. He should be bone dust. But there he stood, heart beating. Lungs breathing.

"Only through atrocity, A'vor." Gama-of-Yun shook his head, then he squinted once more, offering a soft hum. "But you've been right. The Yun are not gods. Nothing more than—" It was almost as if something struck him, his back going ramrod straight. With a strange, wooden quality, he looked over his shoulder towards the a'teneum's entryway. There stood Davah, his steps halting when he noticed the intense appraisal. The next words were whispered so quietly they almost went unheard. "Instruments of war."

Too sudden for the eye to witness, Gama-of-Yun warped across the glen, appearing before Davah, a loud crack in the wake of his shift. Just like the Bloodsong. Just like the Thasian.

"Oh, holy *frigid void*!" Davah shouted, shoving his body back against a stone column to create some distance. "What in all the starry sea—!"

"Davah," Gama-of-Yun said, deep and resonating. Davah fell silent.

Tension in the air swelled and Aeyun could see Davah's alarm rising with quick breaths, each one inflating his chest in shallow bursts. As the quiet elongated, discomfort grew. Aeyun's feet moved without him realising, carrying him across the grassy division. He was within a stone's throw when Gama-of-Yun started chuckling in that morbid, mirthless way again.

"Pre'ach'an was right," said Gama-of-Yun.

Davah's face paled and his eyes flickered to Aeyun, then past him to Uruji.

"It was true," Gama-of-Yun continued. "The legends. The crimes. The—"

"Shut up!" Davah shouted, tuning a hefty gale from the alicant lodged in his bracer. It did nothing to sway Gama-of-Yun's stalwart stance. Frazzled, Davah slid to the side and kicked backwards, putting more distance between himself and both Aeyun and Gama-of-Yun. "Don't say that, you *false god*. Don't just – don't just come out with that—!"

Gama-of-Yun fanned his arm to the side, gesturing to Aeyun and Da'garu in the distance. "Before you stand the descendants of Dread

Ka'la'drius – of Ladriuska-of-Yun."

"Ka'la'drius … *of Yun*," Davah murmured, awed.

"And you have already accompanied Ka'la'drius's chosen," said Gama-of-Yun.

Slowly, painstakingly, Davah's gaze caught Aeyun's. It was one of the first times that Aeyun had witnessed Davah wear horror, real horror, so raw. He couldn't figure out if it was for him or at him. When he took a step forward, Davah bumbled one back.

"Oh, *stars above*, friend, you – you're cursed. You're truly cursed."

"Ca'ille," Gama-of-Yun said, looking up to the pinnacle of The Veil, stretching his arm towards it. "Is this what you wanted?"

The familiar crack of the Thasian Bloodsong rang out, and in a flash Raeyu's form manifested before Gama-of-Yun. She pitched to the side, throwing her entire weight against him, tilting him off balance, knocking his arm down.

"Ka'la'drius is dead!" she shouted, digging her feet into the ground, her grim expression resolutely focused on Gama-of-Yun. "He's gone! It was going to end."

"Dear child," Gama-of-Yun said, gazing down at her listlessly. "How do you think he escaped torment? How did A'vor come to be on Raenaru?"

"*Protect my kin*," Raeyu whispered, her gaze adding to the number of eyes boring into Aeyun. "I understand, I'd guessed," she admitted, biting her lip. Then she looked up at Gama-of-Yun, a fierce set to her jaw. "But he's *dead*. Truly dead."

Gama-of-Yun gazed at her, the whole of it profound with sorrow.

"So are you, Raeyu Thay-cee-en."

"Do not reduce me to your antiquated terms!"

"Amanastré will destroy him," said Gama-of-Yun. Too soft. Too honest.

"*Oh starry sea*," Davah said, almost a whimper.

"Thay-cee-en-ee," Gama-of-Yun called out to Uruji, who now stood shoulder to shoulder with Aeyun. "Your kind have been manipulated."

"Stop," said Raeyu. It was dark. Dark, too dark. Not shining and warm and brilliant like the sun. Just cold; frost layering ice across water. "Your history is not our future."

"*Your* history!" Gama-of-Yun snapped, and it pulled any last inkling of good will from the atmosphere. "*Yours* and *mine*! This is not something you can pretend did not happen. It has already begun again, and with Ka'la'drius gone, Amanastré will be out for blood. Is … is …" he trailed, brows furrowing. His eyes were darting around again, consternation sweeping across his features. "Oh, Ca'ille," he lamented. "Is this the only way?"

Gama-of-Yun once again took stock of his surroundings, gaze lingering upon the towering structure of the a'teneum. A sigh escaped him, then he thrust his hand to the side, flexing his fingers. A strange zapping noise crackled to life, then a shimmering blade covered in runic symbols manifested, forming in what should have been air alone. Gama-of-Yun's grasp firmed around its hilt.

"I will knock down the pillars of this barrier," he said as he twisted and raised his claimed iridescent blade above his head, angled down one-handedly, its point an elegant line towards Raeyu. "But first I will fell you, Raeyu Thay-cee-en. And next your brother; legacies of the wretched Yun-Thay."

"You will try," Raeyu said ominously. She lowered her centre of gravity and pushed out her arm, lightning already beginning to crackle at her fingertips.

Amidst the surrounding protests, and before either of them could make a move, Da'garu slipped between. She faced Gama-of-Yun, an out-of-place smile on her face. Her hand reached towards Gama-of-Yun's cheek, and his sword-grip wavered slightly. Aeyun wasn't sure if the others felt it, but a wave of Vitality washed over the area, Da'garu's expression serene. Welcoming and forgiving. An opaline sheen flooded across her irises and everything slowed to a stop around them. No water falling, no animals skittering, no branches rustling. Just endless peace.

"*Just a little longer,*" Da'garu's voice reverberated around them. "*Okay?*"

"*My dear child,*" Gama-of-Yun's baritone rang out. "*This tale only has one of many awful ends.*"

"*Then let's try for the best one,*" Da'garu's light plea faded in fleeting wisps.

"*Then this is the choice you've made,*" Gama-of-Yun's voice echoed. A weight settled across them, then a sensation like being dragged through rapids. "*Good luck,*" the sentiment rang out like a death sentence, "*and may the Alkonos guide you.*"

Time warped and restarted with a blinding flash. When Aeyun's vision readjusted, they were no longer in the grotto housing the a'teneum. Azura was in his hands, his elbows crooked like he'd been expecting the ivory instrument to be deposited there. Around him the Ou'grobh shuddered, the same way trees did when a storm was on the horizon. Beside him, his precious people were collected, all of them faced the same direction he stared.

But there was nothing there. Only the endless maze of rustling foliage.

Something in him whispered, and the thought escaped: "I'll never find the a'teneum again."

"We have bigger problems than that," Davah said, gravely. When Aeyun looked over, he noticed the contemptuous glare Davah settled upon Raeyu, a bag slung over his back. "And you have some fessing up to do if you'd like to keep your other arm attached to your body."

Uruji glided in front of Raeyu, an ill-suited and menacing expression shadowing his features. "Threatens the apparent pirate."

"That actually makes a whole lot of sense," Aeyun muttered, then he stepped between them, Da'garu tiptoeing behind, if a bit closer to Uruji's side. "What we don't need right now is a fight. This forest is as dangerous as it is forgiving, and we need to make sure that we're on the right side of its favour. Da'garu," he turned to her, "is there anywhere we can go that isn't *there*?"

"Isn't where?" Davah's question went ignored.

Da'garu adopted a pensive look, then she raised her finger in triumph. She jutted out her elbow to start a linked chain – which Uruji responded to immediately, looping his arm with hers – and Aeyun felt like the realms were laughing at him when Davah and Raeyu kept watching one another like fencats at war. Aeyun forced himself in the middle, nudging Raeyu in Uruji's direction, then none-too-gently yanked Davah to stand at the end of the chain, hooking their elbows. Momentarily at a loss when he realised Raeyu had no arm for him to hold on to, he instead hesitantly wrapped a hand around her waist. She tensed, like she was expecting the exchange to start anew, but the connection remained docile.

"Lead the way, Da'garu," said Aeyun.

Not there turned out to be a cave in the cliffy edge of the wilderness. When aviary varietals chirped proudly as they dropped firewood kindling before Da'garu – a sure preparation for the night to come – Aeyun understood precisely what Uruji had referenced when he'd said that he thought Da'garu communed with animals somehow. Surely she must, if their self-satisfied trills that followed delivery meant anything.

Da'garu, however, made no show of it. She only smiled as they flapped away and added the new fodder to the growing pile in the centre of the shallow cave.

Davah was huddled in his own corner, rifling through whatever was in that bag he'd sported. Raeyu and Uruji were collected together, speaking lowly to one another. Aeyun leant on a wall on his own, distant and observing. He should have held his tongue.

Da'garu waved farewell to the last of their feathered deliverers, dropping the final stick upon the mismatch of wood. She looked expectantly – and somewhat excitedly – towards Uruji, who broke off his hushed conversation with Raeyu. Uruji, looking too weary for his age, smiled towards her kindly.

"Of course," he said, adjusting his gem-adorned bracelet. He delicately curled his hand so his fingers met, then he gazed intently at the small, unlit pyre and snapped with precision. The sticks burst to life in flame, casting a glow across the dirt-streaked stony walls. The warmth would be welcomed in the coming hours of chilled nighttime air.

No one moved from their perch, the only noise sounding when Uruji decided to retrace back towards Raeyu and settle on the soil beside her. Da'garu seemed at a loss, but finally she chanced a look towards Aeyun, sliding tentatively to sit by his feet. Feeling young again, like they'd just survived a trip to The Hold and were catching their breath before returning to overwrought parents, he sank down next to her.

"I heard you," said Aeyun. It was quiet, a moment meant only for them. "Your will can be heard through Vitality." Da'garu looked up at him with an expression he couldn't quite parse. "You're brave, you know. More than me, I think."

She gave a smirk then, giving him a self-satisfied nod.

Aeyun laughed lightly. "You've no humility, you know that?"

All it afforded him was a shrug. She turned to watch the fire, the reflection of it playing off her eyes. For a moment, just a second, he saw a tiny version of her, standing before a burning cabin. Before he could drown in that vision, he reached for Azura and pulled the bone aerofoil over, resting it ahead of them.

"I don't think I've had the chance to show you this yet." He smiled when she shook her head in the negative. "It's made of bone. Like Mother's old adornments. Her necklaces. But it's from the realms. Tenebrana, in particular." As he spoke, he watched Da'garu fall into the same fascination she did when he used to tell her stories about his daily adventures, enraptured with unyielding focus. It was pleasant, the feeling that crowded his chest. And he felt small next to her, but it was like returning home, hanging his coat and nudging off his boots, a pot of stew boiling on the stove in the kitchen. "It's full of acidic rain and swamps, this one. Not the best smelling place, but it has its charms. This is carved from an acid whale – a magnificent beast of wide waters, like nothing you've seen here. Oceans that span longer and so much wider than the Ou'grobh. A horizon that feels endless, and a sky that hangs above it all. No barriers. And this … this is Azura." Aeyun gently placed his hand upon the Ivory. "Azura got me through some tough battles. I'm sure they'd like to greet you."

The eager buzz that jolted through his hand was answer enough and he laughed, his eyes sparking with radiance. Da'garu, enthralled, looked to Azura, then him, then back to Azura. Slowly, cautious, she leant forward and hovered her fingers over the ages old bone.

"It's okay," Aeyun encouraged.

Da'garu closed her eyes a moment, then she opened them, and they reflected bright white. The gaze itself was haunting, and it was so rare that Aeyun got to see it for himself. She watched him for a moment, and he felt like she must've seen something there because her expression morphed into a tender grin. Slowly, she pressed her fingers against Azura's ivory, and Aeyun could recognise the soft resonance of remembrance pushing through its layers, sharing insight of younger years playing in swampy marshes, then adventurous excursions beyond, then practised hands that later worked nimbly with instruments to create the carved aerofoil before them. Suddenly, notions of his own movements on Quingan coastlines and within the Kaisan Pit flooded his perception.

Da'garu gasped and pulled back. For a moment, Aeyun was terrified he'd made yet another mistake as tears built in the corners of her eyes, the tune of his glowing eyes fading. Da'garu's remained radiant, indescribable colours filtering across them. Aeyun wasn't sure what he'd expected, but it wasn't for Da'garu to toss herself forward and wrap her limbs around Azura, clutching the ivory tightly.

Azura hummed across Vitality, the notes of it floating across him like a lullaby.

Da'garu uncoupled herself from Azura and snatched Aeyun's wrist, flattening his palm against the bone. Vitality rushed back at him in a wave, carrying impressions of *found me, saved me, heard me, loved me*. It took a beat before he realised these were from Azura.

Then, from Da'garu, a whisper of: *just like Mother*.

CHAPTER TWENTY-ONE

"Do you think they'll listen to her?" Sakaeri whispered.

"If they don't, they'll have me to answer to when I've returned. That should be motivation enough," said Seraeyu.

They were settled in their land-skimmer, the door latched, locking out the rest of the city and the realm beyond. The Thasian did not travel via hyperline anymore. It was instead always by armoured vehicle. This one just happened to have two Orinian Draconguard within it, opposite Seraeyu and Sakaeri. The land-skimmer in front of them hid a handful more, then the land-skimmer behind had a select few Raenaruan Sentinels brave enough to make the journey to their allied realm.

Koali had wanted to come, of course, but Seraeyu had instead given her temporary Praetorial authority in his stead, requesting that she *keep the peace* while he was away. The blubbering Sentinel had demanded that Sakaeri promise Seraeyu's safe return. This was then immediately followed with an apology for her uncouth behaviour and revision of her demand to a much-calmed request.

Sakaeri still hated that Koali held her in some odd, too-high regard after what she'd witnessed. It made her feel as if she were tricking her somehow, unwittingly playing a role that she'd never auditioned for. Unpleasant was the word for it.

Across from them, Jaspen sat pin straight, helm directed so unerringly forward that Sakaeri was sure he was staring at nothing but the curtained panels behind them. Beside him, Draconguard Commander Ephrite was considerably more relaxed, leant unworried against the curve of the craft where seat met siding. He was the only other occupant whose face was bare besides Seraeyu.

"I apologise again for the … eventful time you've had in Haebal," Seraeyu told the man. The hum of the vehicle filled the space around them as Commander Ephrite regarded him wearily.

"These are troubled times, Praetor," he said. "We know what to expect with troubled times."

"Regardless, Haebal and Raenaru are pleased to extend open arms to the displaced citizens of Paladi. The meeting held with the Council proved fruitful and both space and provisions will be accommodated in much of Raenaru's lands. We intend to keep families together, and extended relatives as near to one another as possible, if they must be allocated to another city or town."

"Kind of you, Praetor," Commander Ephrite said, enduringly passive as ever.

Sakaeri frowned behind her new Yisuna mask. This one was lifted from Koali's collection, graciously gifted to her once the initial shock of the festival's events had abated.

"Please feel welcome to speak freely, Commander Ephrite," Seraeyu said, plastering on that magazine smile again. "We are allied on this front, after all."

"With all due respect, Praetor Thasian, I'm happy to keep our acquaintance impersonal."

"Sure." Seraeyu's smile faltered. "Of course, that's entirely understandable."

An awkward lull elongated and heavied without sympathy, and Sakaeri desperately wished the journey ahead was significantly shorter than she knew it to be.

"Sera," she whispered again, as if it did any good against the surrounding silence. "Did you remember the stone?"

"Yes, yes. Thank you," Seraeyu mumbled quietly, a tad surly as he cast a dejected look out the window, warped with a layer of mirroring ore.

Before they departed, he and Koali had exchanged communication stones, just in case anything urgent arose in his absence. It had been a long time since the Praetor had so visibly left the city, much less the realm. There was every possibility that something could happen, especially after the disaster that was the Festival of Hana.

Sakaeri had perhaps enjoyed a little too thoroughly leaving their assailants in random places across the city, no doubt in a state of dire confusion when they came to and had little recollection of the conclusion of their evening. She wasn't entirely sure what it looked like when they reconvened, as she presumed they must have, but she did know that the citizens of Haebal were assured that the threat had passed and to please resume their daily activities.

Seraeyu had refused to talk about it. All she got out of him was: *Aeyun's an idiot.*

Not that she didn't agree. She very much did.

Jaspen cleared his throat. It was jarring enough that the land-skimmer's other three inhabitants glanced over, expecting something to follow. When it didn't, his stature somehow tightened even further. Commander Ephrite sighed, his bi-chromatic eyes closing briefly with a fortifying inhale.

"At ease, soldier. We've a long way to go and there's no sense in you losing a fight because of a muscle cramp."

"Understood, sir," Jaspen said, barely relaxing his shoulders. "Sorry, sir."

"Did you have the chance to burn a cigarette before we left?"

"No, sir."

"Right," Ephrite groused. "Praetor Thasian, would you mind if we let Draconguard Jaspen here pause for a smoke before the transfer to the sea-skimmer?"

Seraeyu blinked himself out of a stupor, a quizzical knit to his brow as he considered Commander Ephrite. "Of course not. He's welcome to break for a smoke whenever he likes."

"You needn't accommodate on my account, Praetor Thasian," Jaspen said, entirely and strictly formal. It had Seraeyu's brow creasing further.

"It's really no hassle," Seraeyu said, a little quieter.

Sakaeri belatedly realised something then. Orin, in this case, extended well beyond its borders and instead sat right beside Jaspen, masquerading as Commander Ephrite. Their smokeserpent would be dormant from this point onward, and something about that settled uncomfortably. The side of the sea-skimmer where she and Seraeyu sat suddenly felt smaller, more confining. She uncrossed her legs and instead leant forward, elbows resting atop her thighs, fingers touching to meet and steeple. There was no reason for her to let what space they had go to waste.

Commander Ephrite eyed her for a moment. Whatever he was looking for, he either didn't find it or decided it wasn't worth the effort. Instead, he tilted back and rested his eyes, mouth pressed firmly in a line as he explored whatever inner dialogue was happening in his mind. At his side, Jaspen finally relaxed, his grip upon his glaive slackening. His Draconguard helm inched ever so slightly to the side, and Sakaeri felt far too *looked at*. In turn, she settled her gaze on his gaudy faceplate, hoping she was winning whatever this odd staring match was that they'd entered.

"It's all the bloody same," Seraeyu muttered beside her.

"Sorry, what was that, Praetor?" Commander Ephrite asked, barely cracking open an eye.

"Nothing at all, Commander!" Seraeyu said chirpily, then he slumped against the window. He continued with a gloomy, "Nothing at all."

Sakaeri stood to the side next to Commander Ephrite while Jaspen smoked a hastily rolled cigarette and Seraeyu pestered him relentlessly, seemingly aiming to get some sort of rise out of him now that he'd become petrified in the shadow of his superior.

"The Praetor reminds me more of himself now," said Commander Ephrite. "A bit more like how he was before the tragedy. It must've been harrowing, being placed in a position like that while still grieving."

Sakaeri considered the commander for a moment, his gaze still locked ahead, then she watched as Seraeyu flippantly made a go at stealing the cigarette from Jaspen's mouth, which the Draconguard anxiously avoided with a calculated tilt of his chin. "He's a different type of strength than Praetor Oagyu."

"I didn't say otherwise."

"Do not underestimate him."

"I never said I did."

"Seraeyu Thasian is very much the linchpin of our realms."

"Perhaps that's true."

"Is it in good faith that your Dracon invites us to Orin?"

"Do not forget that Orin is propositioning Raenaru for assistance."

"I'm sure you know the same as I do that nothing is ever one-dimensional."

"Is it in good faith that your Praetor offers his assistance?"

"Yes," Sakaeri said, turning to look up at the commander. "It is."

Commander Ephrite glanced down, then he gave a contemplative hum.

"You should know," Sakaeri began, "I watch everything."

"I've no doubt," said Commander Ephrite. He brushed off some invisible dirt, then marched ahead, nodding briefly to the segregated packs of Draconguard and Raenaruan Sentinels who'd taken reprieve with them by the pier. As he came to stand beside Jaspen, clapping a hand on his shoulder, Sakaeri took the quiet moment to gaze across the bay to Keou.

It was the same as she'd first witnessed upon her return; glossed over with daily activity, hiding a mould of quiet despair beneath. Would its lapped quays brighten soon, she wondered. How many days until stability bled back into normal routine? Something had shifted, and it felt irreversible. Irrevocable. Raenaru, Haebal, the Thasian. None of them were infallible. With that revelation came reflection, an admission that times change.

Nothing was permanent.

Sakaeri's gaze trailed back to Seraeyu, feeling unsettled to find his own attention fixed upon where she stood lonesome on the sloped cliff face. He tilted his head in a gentle gesture. *Are you okay?* it said. And how funny it was that he cared to find out. As a courtesy, she nodded curtly.

I'm okay, she conveyed. And, surprisingly, a part of her believed it.

The wake brought them closer to the Great Sea Gate, trepidation trailing behind their arrival. Beside her, again in their confined corner, Seraeyu took a deep breath, his fingers lacing together atop his lap. Sakaeri mirrored the motion, her own nerves firing with anticipation.

They were upon the in-between. That vast aetherscape that hooked their lives into an enigmatic web. Sakaeri didn't know what they would find there now that their eyes were open to it. And she wasn't sure she wanted to look at it, whatever it was.

"Praetor Thasian," said Jaspen. The entire platoon, uncomfortably wedged into sea-skimmer, turned their attention to him, but his focus remained on Seraeyu. "We will soon be floating in Orin's seas."

"Yes. Thank you, Draconguard Verdanta," Seraeyu said quietly.

"All will be well, Praetor," Jaspen told him, but it sounded like the cusp of a deeper sentiment. "Trust in your company."

Seraeyu hesitated a moment, then slowly his fingers parted unwoven and his hand instead grasped Sakaeri's, breaking her own lacing to instead rest their intertwined hold in the middle. Not a word escaped him, but his palm tensed in her hand.

Sakaeri wondered what happened when they'd transferred from Lu-Ghan to Raenaru all that time ago. What had Seraeyu endured among the endless expanses, alone?

She did her best to ignore the faceless shells of Draconguard, but the bi-chromatic stare of one Commander Ephrite had her itching. He stood and passed by, his gaze lingering on the pair of them a moment before he bellied up to the transponder to negotiate with the on-duty gatekeeper. Everything stretched like static, their conversation fading to the background, until Commander Ephrite tossed a look over his shoulder.

"If you wouldn't mind, Praetor Thasian, officiating this gate jump?"

"Of course," Seraeyu called back, a twitch flinching down his arm. "I will do so."

He stood, their fingers parting, and Sakaeri's palm felt cold. When he reached the transponder, there was a stuttered response, presumably from *the Praetor's* sudden appearance, and Seraeyu's body language adopted that familiar reporter-ready pomp. He gave his authorisation and laughed pleasantly at whatever the gatekeeper said. When he turned back, his movement was stiff, feet intently and purposefully placed down in a straight line.

They'd reached the centre of the Great Sea Gate. Seraeyu stood before her, and the first cry of aethereal attunement reverberated across those megalithic rings, deafening in its roar.

Both Sakaeri and Seraeyu recoiled, power rolling across them in waves. Spheres of water floated up beyond the panels of the sea-skimmer, responding to the rending of reality. The space around them felt vacuous, consuming. Eerie as it was strange and hungry.

Sakaeri wasn't prepared for *this*. Was this what one heard when they listened to the vastness of the void? When they heeded its call? Is this what Aeyun waited for each time they jumped? It felt like being ripped from the fabric of what made them, and that it was screaming in response.

"Seraeyu," she whispered, reaching, then her comprehension of what lay before her imploded, leaving only impressions in its stead. There among the primordial plane of endless black, eruptions of energy bursting in the distance, stood not just Seraeyu, but Amanastré.

Amanastré was floating, as if drifting amongst the starry sea. Her arms were wrapped over her torso, like her body had been prepared for a funeral pyre, and her long silvery hair fanned out behind her, two regal horns erupting from the crown of her head, curling and spoked in ways that looked too primal to be distinctly Yu-ta. A serpentine suit stuck to her like a second skin, looking as if it belonged to martial ranks too confident in their own abilities, and a long scar lashed across her face, marring features that would have otherwise been considered beautiful.

This woman looked like a god. This woman looked like a Yun.

According to Amanastré, however, she was Sírin.

What exactly was Sírin?

"Sakaeri," Seraeyu called, and Sakaeri was compelled to look away from the frozen being cradled in the nothingness before her.

"What is she?"

"A vestige of the past. Something that no longer belongs but is unwilling to leave."

"A spirit?" Sakaeri sidled up to Seraeyu, the two of them peering at the dormant, daemonish presence.

"Close. A fragment of a soulsong."

"Sera," she said. A look beside her revealed Seraeyu's temperament having gone pensive. Silent. "I don't like that a fragment of something's – some*one*'s – soulsong was preserved in an alicant to be called upon by the Thasian. It seems—"

"Cruel? Heartless? Cold? Callous?" Seraeyu listed, his expression still stony. "It was. It is. Our legacy … *the Legacy* is a dirty one. But the weight of it is … suffocating."

"Sera—"

"What choice do you make," he asked, finally turning towards her, "when you have the power to dismantle the realms themselves?"

"Seraeyu," she said just as Orin lurched into place around them, her call vocalised amongst the sea-skimmer's creaking metal interior. She was still sat on the hard bench, her arm extended. When he finally grabbed her hand again, she said, "whatever feels right."

Seraeyu stilled, watching her as if he half expected her to say something incriminating.

"Trust your judgement. I do."

"You're too kind, Yisuna," is what he decided to respond with, taking his seat beside her.

Sakaeri's eyes drifted across the hull to where Jaspen's helmet watched on. She had to wonder, too, where would he stand when the crux of whatever this movement was met its climax. To her, it seemed her statement rang true: Seraeyu Thasian was the linchpin of the realms. Whether he pulled apart that hinge, that was up to him.

If he chose to upend it – herald a new damnation – with whatever lay at the core of this so-called Legacy, she would burn the realms to ashes beside him, ushering whatever would rise in its place. If Seraeyu Thasian – son of loving Paeyuni, brother of steadfast Raeyu, ward of clever Uruji, aethereal link to Aeyun – decided the realms should bend an ear to this dissonant history, bear witness to whatever it might mean, she would ensure he stood tall as he professed their newfound fate.

Seraeyu Thasian wasn't the monster the realms wanted him to be.

But Sakaeri could be, if Seraeyu's reality called for it.

CHAPTER TWENTY-TWO

"Welcome, Praetor Thasian," the Dracon greeted as they arrived at the grand entry hall of the Spire, seat of power within the great realm of Orin. Its glistening halls were nestled among the very centre of Mercur's gouged city depths. The Dracon, of course, was fabulously adorned, as she always seemed to be, a generous draping of fabrics twisting around her form as she made to stand from her throne, a leftover from a bygone era.

Seraeyu unlatched his respirator mask, trusting in the air that Rosalyn Rhodan deigned to breathe so easily. Sakaeri dislodged her own, a bulkier contortion to accommodate her Yisuna mask, and dutifully took Seraeyu's discarded one in hand, decidedly not relinquishing it to one of the few Raenaruan Sentinels in their diplomatic envoy.

"We are honoured to receive you here in Mercur," the Dracon went on to say, and Sakaeri spotted a few well-placed Eyes around the room. Did Seraeyu know this would be a broadcasted event? Even if he hadn't been made aware beforehand, he caught on quickly, his gaze scanning over the cross-pupil stiffs strategically placed across the hall.

"A generous reception, Dracon Rhodan," Seraeyu said, purposefully stopping a few paces ahead of where he should, if he were aiming to accommodate the Dracon. It resulted in a bout of awkward silence before the Dracon quietly cleared her throat, plastered on a smile, and took a few distinguished steps down to level with the newly arrived Praetor. Seraeyu smiled back, the corners of it curling smugly. "The honour is all mine."

"This is a momentous occasion, my dearest friend," the Dracon said, chuckling as if they were indeed old friends. Seraeyu played his role, gently reaching towards Rosalyn's wrist so that he could clasp her elegant hand between his own, leaning forward cordially.

"Something written in the stars, my darling Dracon."

"I couldn't agree more," she said, carefully removing herself from his grasp when it was appropriate to do so. "Come, we shall chat over some tea, Praetor Thasian."

It was customary, Sakaeri knew, but she still didn't like watching Seraeyu walk off on his own with the Dracon. That drawing room, however, was only meant for the elite. Along with the Sentinels from her homerealm, she drew her ankles together and slammed her hand perpendicular across her heart, watching Raenaru's most powerful disappear beyond a heavy metallic door. Across the hall, the resident Draconguard slowly rose from their knee, bending back to height as their Dracon left the premises.

She cast her eyes over the crowd of them, but it was difficult to parse Jaspen from their ranks at a distance. Commander Ephrite had seemingly slipped into the masses as well. Else, he'd left the room entirely.

"My brother had gone to one of these before," a Sentinel behind her whispered. Sakaeri turned minutely to observe as he spoke to his conversation partner, a somewhat stout Sentinel beside him. "He was pissed that *I* got to go this time."

"Oh yeah? Why's that?"

"Haven't you heard? Political functions on Orin follow the old tenants. You know, wine and dine? The ball later will have a fountain of wine. A fountain, Onyi."

"So? We'll be geared up and can't go boozing anyway."

"No, Onyi. No. See, that's considered rude. The whole envoy is meant to partake. It's considered rude and untrusting otherwise. So, get ready to booze and schmooze. In the name of the Praetor, of course."

"Of course."

Sakaeri turned on her heel, the respirator masks in her hand clacking with the movement. The two Sentinels jerked and straightened to attention, slamming their hands over their chests in a show of Raenaruan respect, as if she herself were the Praetor.

She'd be lying if she said she didn't revel in that. Just a little bit.

"I'll be watching you two," she said, sure it was the first exchange she'd ever had with either soldier. They nodded and gave stilted affirmations while she tried to smother a snicker. A tap on her shoulder had her turning again.

"Sirin Yisuna," Jaspen asked, his address a welcome familiarity among opulent tapestries. "A word?"

She nodded and let him lead on. They navigated the hall, passing groups of Sentinels and Draconguard, twisting between granite, filigreed pillars until they came to a nondescript doorway. It appeared a service entrance. Maybe it was. She followed him still, traipsing down dark corridors until they reached yet another door – one which released with the hiss of a hermetic seal. Once it slid open, he extended his arm to shepherd her in.

What she found was something between a balcony and a sun terrace. Not as if there were sun to be seen on Orin. Much less in the depths of Mercur. Its glassy panels framed the darkened city expanses, lit in flashes of florescent ore that flooded its shaded crevices. A city forever in darkness, Mercur.

"What's this?" Sakaeri asked as Jaspen slipped in behind her.

He shuffled around the edge once the door clicked shut with another hiss, seating himself on the ground in a far corner, indicating for her to join him with a small tick of his head. It occurred to her that she held no hesitancy to do so, that Jaspen's aura was pestered, but that it was open and welcoming towards her. Trusting. She decided to run with that.

"Smoking room," Jaspen said, pointing towards a purification machine attached above the door and on the far side of the room. He then went about flipping up his faceplate and fetching a pack of smokes stowed in the pouched sewed to his belt. There was a comfortable quiet as she settled next to him, denying his offer for her join in. "They're around the place," he indicated with his free hand, snapping his opposite fingers to procure a small flame, lighting the stray sprigs of tobacco that curled from his cigarette. "I'm not the only Orinian who took up the habit as a comfort far from our smoggy homerealm."

"Surely not," Sakaeri agreed, pushing her mask up and to the side. "What's this nonsense about partaking in a ball?" She knew it was tradition, but did *this* particular occasion call for it? An agreement to move displaced refugees to Raenaruan soil?

"It's a celebration," Jaspen muttered, blowing smoke out of the corner of his mouth. "Folks would like to celebrate."

"You don't seem particularly celebratory," she noted. He really didn't. In fact, he seemed rather sullen. As if to verify that, Jaspen let his head fall back as he let loose a groan.

"I want to be, but … " he scanned the still empty room, eyes darting to the door for a moment, then he pulled his hand to his mouth as if to grab the cigarette. "My sisters oppose the occupation—" oh, so he was calling it that now, "—and the Commander is concerned they've joined the Resistance. He thinks he has intel confirming it."

"Ah," Sakaeri said as he pulled away his cigarette away to exhale. "That's complicated then."

"Succinct as always, Sirin Yisuna."

"Don't get smart with me, Verdanta."

"I've done it. Secured their route. But they're nowhere to be found to tread it." Jaspen sighed, flakes of ashen debris drifting in the gentle breeze procured by the purifier. "Mother and Father are beside themselves."

"That's pretty rough."

"Yeah," he said, chuckling morosely. "Yeah, it is."

"And you?"

"Hm?"

"Where do you stand?"

"With my *family*, Sakaeri."

"Sounds like that's pretty unsteady ground at current."

He just stared at her for a moment, then hung his head and took a long drag. "*Shite*."

"If it makes you feel any better," Sakaeri said, leaning back against the glass. "Mine are all kinds of fucked up. Pretty sure not everyone agrees, too. Some of them died for whatever it was they believed in." *Poor Ube, another victim in this wretched game.* It was a line that had been haunting her since she'd heard it echoing in cavernous catacombs, her run-in with the strange acolyte only fuelling the fire beneath it. "I'm finding out new bits every day that make me question things I was never meant to question. If I'm honest with you, I'm damn terrified of the answers."

"You're brave, though," he murmured.

"I keep telling myself that."

"Yeah, me too."

"I think you are."

"I'm flattered, Sakaeri." It sounded like it should have been sarcastic, but not a single note of it was. Jaspen was sincere down to his bones. Sakaeri appreciated that.

She chose not to answer and instead settled in. Beside her was a person slowly taking up a more dedicated part of her brain, in a section labelled things like *important* and *trustworthy*, and he needed to stew in silence for a while. And he obviously wanted company while he did. That was easy. That she could provide.

"That little Orinian *witch*," Seraeyu spat as he stomped into his room.

Sakaeri sat on the ridiculously large, round bed in the centre of the lavish space, where she'd perched herself for the last two hours as she'd awaited Seraeyu's return. Jaspen had eventually decided he'd wallowed enough, then offered her a hand up and didn't even bother telling her where her dedicated quarters were. Instead, he simply told her where Seraeyu would be directed, likely which room would be his, then made his leave.

"What'd she do?"

"Oh, you're here," Seraeyu acknowledged her, then scowled. "Good, now I can complain to you. Can you *believe* that she first gave me cold tea, then she talked my ear off about nonsense – literal nonsense, I don't *care* what colour is in stars-damned season specifically in Mercur's West End – and then she shirked me off on her ladies-in-waiting, saying that she was sure we'd like to catch up. That was *one time*—"

"Scandalous, Sera."

"Yes, it was. Which is precisely why I cannot relive that particular evening as *Praetor*. So I spent the last hour politely trying to deny a little rendezvous and slip away. Starry sea. And now I have to get ready for an event taking place in—" he glanced towards the clock on the wall, "—a half-hour, for the love of—"

Seraeyu paused, ceasing his incensed pacing to glare at her.

"Why aren't you ready?"

"What do you mean?" She looked down at her Sirin attire. "I am ready."

"Dear, blessed Sakaeri," he said, scanning her form. "You are not."

"What's that supposed to mean?"

"You see, love," Seraeyu sat down beside her. Something in her told her to narrow her gaze. "I need you to look your absolute finest. You'll be interested to know, despite what dearest departed father Rhodan believed and the wool the populace of Orin so avidly pulls over their eyes, our very own Rosalyn Rhodan has very particular preferences indeed, and they do not fit with Orin's rather conservative culture."

"Are you trying to whore me out, Sera?"

"I simply need you to catch her eye so that it's not focused on me. I need to be able to chat freely, else I won't get *any* information."

"And I couldn't get this information for you?"

"Starry sea, no. You know how the aristocracy is, Sakaeri. Too full of people who love the sound of their own voice, only willing to listen to another if they think it'll benefit them. And who's more influential than the Praetor?"

"On Orin? The Dracon."

"Will you just … " Seraeyu sighed, exasperated. "Please?"

"It's rude to ask this of me, you know."

"Since when was I known for being considerate?"

"Sera," Sakaeri said, taking her turn to sigh. "Oftentimes, you're too considerate for your own good."

"Hm. Agree to disagree. Now, we have—" he glanced at the clock again, "—twenty-five minutes to look ravishing."

Sakaeri was not used to gowns.

They rarely played a role in her life, maybe once on a Sirin mission. In fact, huh … that's how she could approach this. A Sirin mission. Given by the Praetor. It was, wasn't it?

She watched her reflection as she twisted to one side, then the other. The luxurious fabric of the dress shifted with her, a deep violet to pay homage to Orin's colouring. Her waist was slimmer than she thought it to be, but maybe that was just the bodice of the gown. Perhaps that why all the models in Cheyun looked like that, as if chiselled from stone moulds. The laced sleeves did wonders to cover the scars on her arms, including the burn mark welding warped metal to her bicep.

Seraeyu had gazed sadly at that for a while, coming over to gently rest his forehead against her temple. She'd allowed herself to lean into it, accepting his willingness to shoulder her pain alongside her, a warm blossom of affection drifting into parts of her soulsong she thought empty.

In thanks to Orin's rather traditional practices, her dress did a fine job of covering the hardened skin that Aeyun had left when he'd removed Kaisa's claim. Before her, she stared at a face painted in makeups she never wore, mulberry lips the colour of her usual mask, her mutated, catlike eyes staring in stark contrast against her regal appearance.

Despite herself, her mind pulled a question from depths she'd meant to lock away.

If I'd ever been seen as Jourae's daughter, would this have been my reflection?

Seraeyu dropped the war fan in her hand. "Yes, yes, you're stunning. But you are every day, don't become vain on me now."

"You're calling *me* vain?" she asked, gesturing to his ensemble of very bold Raenaruan ruby, wrapped around him like an advertisement.

"Beauty knows no bounds."

"I'm pretty sure you're meant to say that to someone else, not yourself."

"Eh," he shrugged, then reached out a ring-adorned hand. "Let's make an entrance. I used to be quite good at it."

"Behave, Sera."

"It's like you know me too well."

The function was in full swing when they arrived, music floating over the crowd like a melodic entreat to release inhibitions and live for the moment. Sakaeri was so far out of her element it was laughable. Beside her, Seraeyu was smiling and waving at those they passed, offering pleasantries to every other person.

It again rose from unlocked depths: would she have done this, in another life?

"Ah, wine," Seraeyu said, pulling her along with him. She grimaced before she remembered that she was without her Yisuna mask, carefully schooling her features instead. "Lovely, lovely wine," Seraeyu muttered, sounding a little anxious himself as he grabbed two goblets of mauve liquid, shoving one towards her. His gaze darted to the side, then he laughed nervously. "Good luck!"

And that was how Sakaeri found herself standing in a gown, staring bug-eyed at a goblet of wine, alone in a room full of noble society as the Dracon approached her.

What in the *starry void* was she meant to do now?

"Are you part of the Praetor's envoy?" was the first thing that slipped from Rosalyn's mouth, painted red. "I do not recognise you."

Really? Sakaeri thought. *You don't?*

She supposed the last time she saw her face, Sakaeri was in a considerably less able state, likely covered in blood and bruises and who knows what else. And that was just the reminder she needed to remember how ugly the Dracon could be beneath that carefully crafted, accentuated exterior.

Sakaeri smiled in a way she thought was likely demure, dipping a polite nod.

"Yes, I look after Praetor Thasian, serving my realm," she said, adopting a silken tone, very much enjoying shaking the Dracon. "As any good soldier would do."

"Forgive me if I say you do not appear the battle-hardened soldier."

"I forgive you," said Sakaeri.

"Oh, well, yes," Rosalyn said, colour rising beneath her layers of makeup. "I suppose that's quite gracious of you."

"I am many things," Sakaeri told her, purposefully trailing her gaze down, "most admired Dracon."

"I ... see," Rosalyn eyed her, only to jump when a Draconguard came up to whisper in her ear. "Understood, thank you for informing me," she told the footman. "Please do excuse me. It seems the duty of Dracon is never far." Rosalyn smiled in what seemed true remorse, then spun on her heel and followed the Draconguard wherever he was intent on leading her.

"Sorry, Sera," Sakaeri mumbled under her breath. She really couldn't be bothered to chase the king of Orin. If she found her again, that was up to the Dracon.

She eyed the drink in her hand and tentatively took a sip. It was sweet. Syrupy as it caked her tongue. Not at all to her taste.

Well, Sakaeri was a creature of clandestine affairs. Perhaps it was time to explore that. With that in mind, her placed her discarded goblet on the next available table and wove through the crowds, seemingly growing as the minutes passed. Seraeyu had well and truly disappeared somewhere. Hopefully getting information. Or at least having fun.

She slipped out a side door and revelled the moment that the door shut behind her, drowning out the heightened volume of celebrations. Dark corridors were calling her name, and she slunk across them with ease, feeling more at home among the shadows. It was well into her wandering that whispering voices caught her attention, rising from hidden crevices on the far end of a long, shaded hallway.

Generally, she wouldn't have thought much of it. But there was something in the inflection that gave her pause. It was a distinct accent. Lilted and matching with images of wide oceans and blue horizons.

"Their target is in sight," someone said softly. "It's almost time."

Fuck. Someone once said there was no rest for the wicked. They were right.

She needed to get to Seraeyu. Now.

Careful to not give away her location, Sakaeri retraced silent hallways, bursting back into the main reception hall just in time for chaos.

The resistance had arrived, geared and masked, dropping from the ceiling and crashing through windows, letting poisoned Mercur air seep into the pristine Spire. Sakaeri needed to find Seraeyu. She hiked up her skirt and slipped her Yisuna mask from her thigh, strapping it around her head, throwing her contort of respiration contraption over it. Seraeyu had his own. Surely he would have taken care of it by now. But still …

But still.

"Sakaeri!" Jaspen found her first, suited up and out of breath. "I think he's up by the throne."

No sooner had he said it did she start in that direction, only realising a moment later that he wasn't beside her. "What are you doing?" she called back.

"The Dracon," he said, looking conflicted.

Sakaeri stalled. "Dammit." She didn't have time for this. She turned away and sprinted towards the top of the room. Sure enough, Seraeyu's form appeared before her, respirator mask secured in place. She tuned a gale to propel herself the rest of the way, skidding to a halt just beyond him, gazing at his back now.

"Sakae—"

A figure emerged from the flooding smog, a blade held in their grasp, aimed with precision to press against Seraeyu's neck. Their body with lithe, smoke from the poisoned external air twisting around them, obscuring the turmoil of their backdrop. A braided plaiting of hair slipped off a slender shoulder, swinging as the knife's sharp edge wrestled against Seraeyu's attempts to push away.

"Your sins have piled high, Praetor," a familiar voice said.

Sakaeri had the *worst* luck.

"Tell me something I don't know," Seraeyu jested back. The idiot. "I can't die just yet though."

Sakaeri wasn't sure what Seraeyu imagined his retaliation to be, but she knew she couldn't give him the chance.

"Sera!" she called, watching as he tensed in response. "Not this one."

Seraeyu cursed as the blade held against his neck pressed closer.

"What game is this?" the assailant asked.

"What happened to you," Sakaeri asked, "Saoiri?"

"How do you know—"

"Have they seen your face?" Seraeyu broke in, his hand coming up to wrap around Saoiri's wrist. The one that steadied the blade.

"What?"

"The Draconguard. Have they seen your face?"

When she didn't answer right away, Sakaeri gave a harsh whisper of: "Saoiri!"

"No, I – no, what?"

Seraeyu's hand filled with crackling Essence, zapping Saoiri's slender wrist, causing her to release her blade in surprise. Seraeyu dropped his arm to catch the hilt – colour Sakaeri impressed – and then shoved Saoiri in Sakaeri's direction.

"I'll leave this to you," said Seraeyu.

Sakaeri caught Saoiri in her arms and locked her there. "Sera, don't be rash."

"I've got a smokeserpent to find," he said with a wink, saluting before he disappeared into the hazy chasm of battle.

CHAPTER TWENTY-THREE

"Let go of me!" Saoiri spat, trying – and failing – to wrest her arm from Sakaeri's grip.

"I don't think I will," said Sakaeri. She continued to pull them away from the fray, disarming any attempts to sabotage her efforts. Saoiri wiggled like an eel on a hook, however, and it proved difficult to subdue. "Will you stop resisting?"

"Will I – will I stop resisting?" Saoiri asked, ironically becoming more pliant as the question escaped her. "Are you kidding? Will I stop resisting?"

"Were you always dramatic?" Sakaeri pondered the days they'd spent in each other's company. "Maybe it was just that Aeyun and Davah were worse."

"Aeyun and Davah?"

"Are you going to repeat everything I say?"

" … Sakaeri!?" The burst of recognition was louder than Sakaeri was comfortable with, so she none-too-gently elbowed Saoiri in the ribs. "You – you traitor! Is this where you'd gone? Ran off to *the Praetor* and betrayed your family?"

"Always labelled a traitor," Sakaeri mumbled, yanking the pair of them through a hissing door, finding reprieve in a smoking room. The same Jaspen had led her to earlier that night. She wasn't even aware she'd been aiming for it, but it was as good a place as any to stow away. "There's a lot you don't know, Saoiri. But no, actually. I had the lucky break of becoming one of Kaisa's Pit playthings."

Saoiri stumbled as Sakaeri pushed her away, far from the door she guarded. Now in full view, Saoiri's features came to light, mostly obscured by the ventilated mask wrapped over her chin. But dark circles shined below her goggles. Her weary gaze settled upon Sakaeri's far-too polished form.

"What are you doing here, Saoiri?"

"What are *you* doing here, Sakaeri?"

"I'm doing what I can. They're alright, as far as I know."

Saoiri continued to watch her blankly, then she straightened up and folded her arms over her chest. Her tactical clothes had her looking older somehow. More serious. It seemed strange, when Sakaeri's memories dressed her in softer fabrics. A milder demeanour.

"I don't see why I should tell you anything," said Saoiri.

Sakaeri sighed. "He won't hurt you, you know. Seraeyu."

"It's not about me. It's about the countless others who've endured this tyranny reigned by the Praetor and the Dracon. It's continued for too long. Someone has to stop it."

"Since when is that *someone* you?"

"It doesn't have to be. It could be anyone."

"Like Davah? Did his ideals finally bleed their way into your brain?"

"No. My priorities aligned when I witnessed Draconguard murdering elderly in broad daylight."

It wasn't beyond the realm of possibilities. Sakaeri knew things like this *could* have been taking place. Those with power tended to abuse it. But to have a first-hand account ... if Seraeyu knew how dirty the Draconguard were playing their occupation, he may have held off on offering entrance to Paladian refugees, instead leveraging his provision of space to finagle the culling of Orinian influence among Mhedoon. And he'd only just convinced the Council that this was necessary as well. Sakaeri was sick of these games.

"What a horrid reality," said Sakaeri. "You have my sympathy."

"I never asked for it." Then suddenly, "Where's the alicant I gave you?"

"Shit!" Seraeyu crowed as he burst into the room with Jaspen in tow, nearly bowling over Sakaeri in the process. "Shit, shit, shit, shit, *fuck*!"

Jaspen was splashed with blood, the splatter of it glistening upon his onyx-coloured armour. His glaive was held white-knuckled in his hand, the sharp edge of it dripping with the same horrific red. His faceplate was cracked, its missing sliver exposing a cornered expression. Like an animal pinned by its predator.

Beside him, Seraeyu was victim to a whipped line of deep red. Just enough to profess his place as a bystander to tragedy.

"What happened?" Sakaeri asked, just as Saoiri slipped a stray dagger from behind her back, tensing for attack.

Jaspen was quicker, hurling down his glaive. The blade stopped just short of where Sakaeri had skid to a halt before Saoiri, its weighted swing held shakily in place by Seraeyu's steadying hand. Jaspen was breathing heavily, gaze darting between the three of them. Sakaeri wondered if, in that moment, they looked like friend or foe.

"Stand down, Verdanta," Seraeyu said quietly.

Sakaeri nudged Saoiri back a step behind her. To her relief, Saoiri complied without complaint, allowing them to both retreat from death's caress under Jaspen's glaive.

"Praetor, Seraeyu, I ... " Jaspen said in a voice that sounded barely his own, his grip trembling enough that Seraeyu was able to whisk away the wavering weapon, instead pulling it down, held docile.

"I'll protect you, Jas. This won't come for you."

"What happened?" Sakaeri asked again.

"I killed a Draconguard," Jaspen whispered. It felt like the air around them washed out like wet paint against the admission, only distant noises of commotion echoing down lofty Spire halls. "I've betrayed my realmsmen."

"Will they not wonder why the Praetor didn't just Bloodsong his way from disaster?" Sakaeri asked, her iron grip dragging Saoiri along beside her while Seraeyu mirrored the same with Jaspen on his opposite side.

"Not helping, Sakaeri."

"No, really, what if word gets around that you *didn't* do anything? Don't we already have enough eyes watching, scrutinising? Some might think you weakened. Others might think you ... *you*."

"I did not want this," Seraeyu grumbled. "I never wanted this." They rounded a corner and were left with two directions. One back towards the fray, the other towards escape. "Are you suggesting I go in there and make a scene? Don't we have enough to contend with?"

They stagnated, and Sakaeri sighed. "Saoiri," she began, "if you ever once trusted me, I beg you do it again now. I will tell you anything you want to know once we've made it to safety, but right now I need you to not try to kill me. Or Sera. Or Jaspen."

Saoiri stared at her.

"Okay?" Sakaeri asked, impatient. It was *not* the time for dalliance.

Saoiri nodded.

"Jaspen, you know what happens now. What could happen now. We need you with us – *with us* – because I cannot drag all three of you out of here. I only have two hands," Sakaeri told him. He nodded absently, then tensed up and turned to Seraeyu.

"You can't, Praetor Thasian! If it goes wrong—"

"Then I have everyone I need on hand," said Seraeyu.

"Sera," Sakaeri urged him.

"Jas, stay here with, um – Saoiri? – and we'll return before you know it. I'll put an end to this, and we'll return to Raenaru. Together, yes?"

"Don't ... " Sakaeri looked at the two of them. "Don't kill one another, alright? We've all seen enough corpses." Then her and Seraeyu took off running.

When they re-entered the hall, the haze had risen high, and the remains of skirmishes could be seen. Clashes of blades still rang in the distance, and gusts of air swirled noxious fumes across the expanse. Flames remained unseen, unbidden for fear of igniting flammable smog that threatened to eviscerate them all.

"Okay," Seraeyu murmured beside her.

He held out his hands, taking a deep breath. Sparks of black started at his fingertips, then warped striations of it pulsed below his feet. He steadied his stance and breathed out, the centre of the room feeling like it dropped out with it. Sakaeri watched as plumes of smoggy air flattened as if crushed, revealing several felled from all sides; Raenaruan, Orinian, and members of the Resistance. The occupants left standing were slammed against walls and pillars, divided unevenly between creed and rank. Strangely enough, the Dracon stood by the far door, an Eye watching the scene play out by her side. Another game. Another play.

Now it was Seraeyu's move.

Sakaeri leant down and whispered to him, "The realms are watching."

"This ends now," Seraeyu called out, the sound of it registering oddly among the rising tides of Essence. "This battle is done. Let the dead profess our profound failures this day. This fight has no winners. Only people left grieving." He adjusted his hands, spreading his fingers as if to persuade the level of pressure. "We must do better. Our borders are open. Seek me for an audience. I will listen. But know: I do not negotiate with those who instigate reckless violence." Sakaeri was fairly certain Seraeyu was staring directly at the Dracon. "I will not tolerate ploys of fear or threats against my people. If we must talk, it will be civilised. If you seek justice, act in favour of what is just."

"You sound like a hypocrite," Sakaeri warned him quietly.

Seraeyu cursed under his breath. "Else we will lose all that truly matters. We are *all* denizens of the realms. When will the day come that we live that truth?"

Seraeyu's control on Essence waned as his eyes began to colour black, so he relinquished his tune and once-pinned soldiers found their footing, eyeing one another distrustfully.

The smoke hadn't risen high enough by the time the Dracon ordered, "Kill them."

In awed dread, Sakaeri stood by Seraeyu's side as Orinian Draconguard twisted and lodged their glaives into the bodies of resistance fighters. Those left standing scrambled for a quick escape, leaping back through shattered windows, and the Raenaruan Sentinels scattered between cracked columns stood at attention, awaiting Seraeyu's command.

"We ... " Seraeyu trailed, watching the empty space between as haze covered garish remains, the murky air obscuring the gaze of the Eye across the hall. "We have overstayed. Raenaru's envoy will return tonight. I will do so separately," he told his Sentinels. He laced his fingers with Sakaeri's and, much quieter, said, "I am fading. Let's go."

She didn't need to be told twice.

When they returned to where they'd left their tagalongs, she halfway expected for one or neither of them to remain. Yet they did, even if they did so in tense silence.

"Before we're stopped," said Sakaeri, "let's get far from view, then find our way back to Raenaru."

"Sakaeri," Seraeyu huffed beside her, pressing a hand to his chest. "It's all I can do to keep the daemon at bay. Forgive me."

Inky spindles crawled up his neck. They didn't have time. They never had *time*.

Sakaeri grasped both his wrists and looked him in the eye.

"Let me share your burden," she said. Power coursed through her, escaping off her skin in little pinprick shocks, her vision becoming radiant and consuming. It felt as though the aether whispered to her, telling her of secrets unknown, until it fizzled into nonexistence and finally those poisoned tendrils shrunk back beneath Seraeyu's collar.

"What in all the realms? You are ... like Aeyun," Saoiri marvelled.

"She is most assuredly not," Seraeyu rasped, his throat again ravaged by Essence. "He's rather like her, though."

"Aeyun?" Jaspen muttered, still bleary-eyed in shock. "You know this … Aeyun?"

"Not the time," Sakaeri said, "nor the place."

Noises of gathering movement sounded in the distance. They needed to go.

It was a back-alley hotel, rife with mould and broken ventilators and critters that held residence in places like these. Sakaeri had been assured that the air was pure enough to breathe in their room. She decided to believe it for the sake of brevity and convenience.

"Where are they?" Saoiri asked, positioning herself as far from the group as possible, huddled in her own personal corner. "What'd you do to them?"

"I did nothing, you wraithrat," Sakaeri said, seating herself on a rickety chair positioned near an equally ratty desk. "Where'd you go, anyway? It was only Davah and Aeyun who infiltrated the Kaisan Pit."

"The Kaisan Pit?" Jaspen asked distantly, momentarily distracted from Seraeyu's attempts to dislodge his bloodied armour.

"Don't worry about that," Seraeyu hushed him, but Jaspen's piercing blue gaze continued to direct towards Saoiri.

"They infiltrated a Kaisan Pit?" Saoiri asked, sounding rather aghast. Sakaeri didn't blame her. It was as ridiculous as it sounded.

"Have you heard rumblings of a Bone Soldier?"

"That was Davah?"

"That was *Aeyun.*"

"I thought he wouldn't do that again after Caiggagh," Saoiri mumbled.

"So Caiggagh actually was him." Sakaeri sighed. Of course it was.

"Caiggagh?" Jaspen's voice drifted over, sounding on the cusp of desperation.

"Don't worry about that," Seraeyu said again, managing to pull a section of plate mail off. He held it aloft in delicate appraisal before grimacing at the crimson staining, setting it aside.

"You said Kaisa got you. They came to rescue you?"

"That, and to get stolen ore. I guess Kaisa took it all in Caiggagh, huh?"

"That had been Kaisa?"

Seraeyu paused after yanking another piece of armour off Jaspen, who sat much like a raggedy doll, braced against the sooty wall. "Did literally *none* of you talk to one another? And who are you, anyway?"

"You're Seraeyu Thasian," Saoiri stated, as if it were truly sinking in. "You're Seraeyu Thasian? He's Seraeyu Thasian?" She directed the last question towards Sakaeri, exasperation seeping in.

"Ill-mannered little fella, isn't he?" Sakaeri snickered.

Seraeyu made a sound of protest. "I resent that!"

"I'm Saoiri Pre'ach'an. And *you* killed Aeyun's father."

Bitterness swelled, divisive. Sakaeri watched as Jaspen's gaze shifted from Saoiri back to Seraeyu, his brow heavy with concerned confusion. She wasn't entirely sure what he found there, but it had his eyes widening and his hand lifting, an intimacy to the movement that felt out of place in their dirty corner or Mercur. Seraeyu twisted away from him, fingers curling into the removed metal shell he held.

"That I did," he said quietly.

"You admit it," said Saoiri.

"You didn't, Sera," Sakaeri interjected, stifled in the now ruptured atmosphere. "That wasn't *you*."

"Pre'ach'an, you said?" Seraeyu asked, bypassing Sakaeri's statement.

"Yes."

"What an unfortunate coincidence."

"You're a pirate?" Jaspen asked, still worriedly glancing towards Seraeyu.

"No," said Saoiri.

"She's a smuggler," Sakaeri filled in, her gaze similarly glued against Seraeyu's profile. He was pensive, a shadow pulling across his expression, an absence in his eyes.

"Was a smuggler," Saoiri corrected.

"Is there a difference?" Jaspen dared to add.

"There's a difference," the other three said in mistaken unison.

"What did she mean that *wasn't you*?" Saoiri asked.

She'd yet to remove herself from her corner. Seraeyu had finally slumped back down beside Jaspen, slowly working at another latch of armour until Jaspen softly pushed his hand away and went about undoing it himself.

"Do you trust this woman, Sakaeri?" Seraeyu asked tiredly. She mustn't have responded soon enough. "Did Aeyun?"

"I think he did," Sakaeri considered aloud, ignoring the odd look Saoiri cast her way. "He told her he would build a gate. To somewhere *else*."

"Build a ... gate?"

Seraeyu huffed a small laugh at poor Jaspen's expense. He offered two light pats against what remained of his shoulder guard before yanking it off him. "You're just learning all sorts of new things today, aren't you Jas?"

"Do not – do not speak to me like I'm a child, Seraeyu Thasian," Jaspen admonished. Seraeyu looked back at him, first a little surprised, then sheepish.

"Sorry. Sorry, you're right." Seraeyu cleared his throat before directing his gaze steadily towards Saoiri. "Alright, Saoiri Pre'ach'an. If you must know, I am host to a daemon. A fragment of a soulsong wronged long, long before our time. It was my own rash stupidity which led to its wrangled control of my agency. I was, most unfortunately, very much unaware of myself when I'd taken Jourae Thasian-nee's life. His, and any others whom I have the displeasure of unremembering."

"Was Jourae Thasian-nee's son's name not Uruji?" Jaspen asked quietly.

"It is," Saoiri said, scrutinising Seraeyu's form. "Uruji. And also Aeyun. And his daughter is named Sakaeri."

"I forgot I told you that," Sakaeri admitted, splintered ice washing into her stomach. "And just what have you relayed to your friends within this Resistance?"

"You are from the second house of Thasian?" Jaspen murmured in awe.

"Not that," Saoiri said, kicking off the wall to sit on the edge of a creaky bed. "None of that. I was still holding out hope that they … "

"They're alive, Saoiri. They made it there," said Sakaeri.

"Then why have they not come back?"

"They don't seem to know how," Seraeyu supplied.

"It might be better if they stayed there," said Sakaeri.

Seraeyu nodded sagely. "Yes, it might be better if they stayed there."

"So you can continue to reign terror?" Saoiri asked, the soft lines of her face pulling into something harsher..

"So that *they* do not fall prey to the same fate. Aeyun is too single-minded to think practically about anything. And I don't know what choices he would make, if pushed."

"In what sense?" Sakaeri asked. Seraeyu had been frustratingly tight-lipped about their connection, and she was devastatingly curious about it. And its ramifications.

Seraeyu gave her an exhausted look. "You want to have this conversation here? Now?"

"I'd like to have this conversation *somewhere, sometime*. Why not? We're already in deep, aren't we?"

"What do you *think* I mean, Sakaeri? You know how he is, searching for great purpose."

Sakaeri wanted to believe she knew what he meant, but was he even aware of Aeyun's connection with Raeyu? His tethered fate?

"How much do you know about those two, Sera?"

"I'm not sure what you're referring to."

"Then I'm not sure I'm sure what *you're* referring to."

"Stars above, you two do the *exact* same thing you and Aeyun used to do," Saoiri complained, impatiently resting her chin in her palm. "You truly are just all one big, fecked-up family, aren't you?"

"What do you know that you're not telling me, Sakaeri?" As Seraeyu stood, he ignored Saoiri's trailing gaze and Jaspen's quiet appraisal. He walked to glower down at Sakaeri, arms folded crossly. "If it's something important, I should know."

"You want to condemn me for keeping secrets? Amanastré, Sera?"

"What did you say?" Saoiri's entire body language changed, almost like a string had pulled her spine straight. "Amanastré?"

"What's it to you?" Sakaeri bounced back, curious.

"She's a legend," Saoiri began unsurely. Her curiosity won out as she continued, "An evil Yun who tore the realms asunder. They say she's why we're divided. Amanastré heralded an apocalypse, bringing with her the power of the maelstrom. Changing the realms' fates forever. It was a tale passed from pirate to pirate. In older text, I think she was described as something else."

"Sírin?" It flew from Sakaeri's mouth without prompting.

"No," Saoiri gave her a weird look. "It was Yun-something. Yun … Yun-Tay?"

"Yun-Thay," Seraeyu said, sombre. "It was Yun-Thay." He covered his face and groaned, a manic sort of laugh creeping through. "Yun-Thay, Yun-Tay, Yu-ta. What difference does it make?"

"Yu-ta?" Saoiri repeated, drawing back.

"And what did you pirates have to say about Ka'la'drius?"

"That he made a deal with a daemon, an evil Yun who … " The pause was deafening. "Brought about the end of an era. Driving the Yun from their home with an endless tempest."

"And what do they say of the Thasian and Thasian-nee?"

"That you are monstrosities," Saoiri whispered. "Warped chimaeras that rose from the ashes of warfare, the daemon's deal providing your Bloodsong in exchange for continued reign."

"It is baffling," Seraeyu said, shaking his head with a depreciating smile, "how very right and very wrong those tales are. And yet they are still told all the same."

"What did she mean when she said I am the closest thing to Thay? She looks a distant relation, not really Yu-ta." Perhaps it was foolish to ask with their company, but Sakaeri spent the majority of her life in the shadows. In this instance, she wanted illumination.

Seraeyu sighed. "Because, in a way, you *are* the closest thing to Thay. And she is also Thay. As much as she is Sírin. Yet it's only one of those she seems to accept."

"Thay, as in: Thasian?" Jaspen ventured softly, still sat on the ground, but his blood-tarnished armour was well out of sight now. He almost looked like an entirely different person without that shell, only wrapped in breathable, standard-issue undergarb instead.

"You are ever perceptive, Jas," Seraeyu said over his shoulder, spoken with an undercurrent of warmth that felt at odds with these cold revelations.

"And *I'm* the closest thing to Thay? Not—"

Her instincts were kicking in. Something akin to wait, watch, listen.

This was important. No trifling thing. It was ground shaking.

What choice do you make, Seraeyu had asked, *when you have the power to dismantle the realms themselves?*

Thay-cee-en-ee the daemon's ghost had admonished Jourae's corpse.

Blood of Ka'la'drius, she had referred to Aeyun, perturbed as she was frustrated by it.

Then what in the starry void was *Sírin*? And what in the endless aether was *Thay-cee-en*? And *Thay-cee-en-ee*? If those pirate tales rang true at all, and Amanastré was said to have ripped the realms asunder ... what if, perhaps, it was only one realm, torn from the rest? And Amanastré hated Yu-ta. Hated the Thasian. Was forever seeking Ka'la'drius. *Beloved* Ka'la'drius, she'd said. *Blood of Ka'la'drius*, she'd called Aeyun. Ka'la'drius, who's said to have made a deal with a daemonish Yun, who traitorously drove the Yun from their home, ravaging it in an endless tempest. That the Thasian were warped chimaeras – the same term the sages used – having risen from the ashes of warfare.

"We are—" *Yun* did not quite escape before Saoiri interjected.

"What is the Alkonos?"

"Where'd you hear that term?" Sakaeri asked abruptly. It had only been in forbidden manuscripts that she'd come across it. Hidden among a wealth of lingo that studious, and very dead, astrologists peppered throughout their dusty files.

"There is nothing good that can come from this," Seraeyu warned, looking pale as he shakily leant against a moistened wall. "We are asking for war."

"You're in one, if you haven't noticed," Saoiri bit back. "It's going on, right under your nose. It's not just oppressed Mhedoonians you need to worry about, *Praetor*, but the rest of the realms you all so easily overlook. If it's peace you seek, now that your mind has pulled itself from the nether of the daemon you claim controlled you, you're in for a long journey.

"This past, whatever truth or lie remains hidden within it, may well turn tides in some form of favour, but the ocean is moving, and it is vast. You cannot stop a wave from crashing just as surely as you cannot stop a storm from raging above turbulent waters. I don't think any of us will see a peaceful end to this – whatever it may be..

"With all your knowledge – with all your *hubris* – what will you fight for, Praetor?"

"Freedom," Seraeyu said, frowning. "I will endlessly strive for a freer, fairer realms."

"I believed in a fair future once," said Saoiri. "But that belief died with Elder Emagh."

CHAPTER TWENTY-FOUR

"Too much has happened today," Sakaeri heard Seraeyu whisper in their darkened room.

It was not to her whom he spoke. It sounded distant, huddled in a corner unseen. She kept her eyes closed. Saoiri's soft snores told her rest had been achieved for their resident Mhedoonian, somehow. She'd looked tired enough. Had likely been operating on sheer force of will this whole time.

"There is much about the realms that yet eludes me, Seraeyu Thasian."

"You insist on tacking on 'Thasian' every time, Jas?"

There was a stretch of quiet before Jaspen whispered, "If I'm honest, I'm no longer sure what I'm calling you when I say that name."

"Then simply stick with Seraeyu?"

"It's much too familiar."

"Then what shall you call me?"

" ... I suppose Seraeyu is most fitting."

"There we go. How are you, Jaspen?"

There was a hitched breath, then a solemn sigh. "I'd not expected to see her there. I couldn't sit idle while she was cut down. I did not mean to ... but I will never regret saving her life. No matter who was struck down. Saving Jeta is worth a thousand – worth endless – Draconguard, if it means she is safe."

"That's a dangerous oath to take, Jas."

Sakaeri had assumed Jaspen had felled a fellow guardsman in favour of saving Seraeyu. Perhaps this was not the case.

"For my sisters, my family, I would forsake all."

Ah. So his sisters *had* joined the Resistance then. That must have been difficult to contend with. For all the time she knew him, his relations seemed constantly on his mind. This must have felt like being ripped down the middle. She understood it. Just a little.

"I will keep that in mind," said Seraeyu. "How's that wound?"

"Not as bad as the eyes that will haunt me during my next sleep." There was a brief shuffle, then, "What are you doing, Seraeyu?"

"There was a song," Seraeyu said, sounding further away. "My mother used to sing it to me when I was upset. Would you like to hear it?"

It was silent for a long moment until Jaspen offered a lumpy *sure I would*. She didn't need to see his face. She knew what it likely displayed as: splotchy with red.

Seraeyu's soft humming filled the musty room, unfurling tenderly amongst the desolate dark. She caught gentle words and woven phrases here and there – pleasant evocations of meadows where one's sorrows would disappear, and moonlight that smiled down, offering a warm embrace – and she could almost imagine Paeyuni singing the same to her children. Furnishing their dreams with soothing visions of blissful harmony. Kindness that outshined everything beyond.

It was a lovely thing, Sakaeri mused, to lull one to slumber.

Sakaeri rolled on her side and swallowed a yawn before it broke free. Ebbing an eye open, she saw that Saoiri was already awake, curled up tightly against a rotten headboard, gaze piercing intently against something on the floor to her left. Following her narrowed focus, Sakaeri caught sight of Seraeyu and Jaspen. Seraeyu's cheek rested tranquilly on Jaspen's shoulder while the Draconguard's head was propped crookedly against the wall, a position sure to leave him with a crick in his neck.

"Oh, that's precious," said Sakaeri.

It had Saoiri jumping, her back slamming into the wood behind her. Seraeyu surged up from sleep, looking for all the realms like he couldn't quite manage to open his eyes the whole way. A hand was held out in front of him, presumably placating the non-existent daylight.

"I'm up," he said. "I'm awake."

Jaspen made a pained noise and rolled his neck.

Sakaeri felt vindicated in her prediction.

"*You're* Seraeyu Thasian," Saoiri murmured distantly, as if she still hadn't quite managed to reconcile that.

"The one and only," Seraeyu muttered back, rubbing at his eyes. "Ugh, even my eyes feel like they're covered in a layer of mould. But I do not trust that excuse for a shower in the corner."

"Best not," Jaspen conceded. "I don't think these alleyways' pipes have been purged for a while." He nodded to himself. "I would advise against the water here as well. Only drink the pre-bottled imports on the left side of the aquifer."

"Okay, back to Raenaru we go," Seraeyu decided, standing up with a stretch. He gave Saoiri a sidelong look. "Are we booking for four?"

"Just like that?" Saoiri asked.

It wasn't that Sakaeri blamed her. She really couldn't. Seraeyu had a strange sort of compulsion about him, his underwhelmed attitude a little jarring when compared to the numerous other facets that caught the attention of the realms.

"If you want," he said.

"And if I chose to leave? Right now? You wouldn't strike me down?"

"I've no desire for senseless violence. Aeyun might haunt me more than he already does, and if you leave it would simply mean another pair of watchful eyes looking after this one's sisters." He pointed indistinctly towards Jaspen.

"Your sisters are part of the Resistance?" Saoiri asked blandly. "And you don't mind?" She aimed at Seraeyu.

"I have been trying to pull back Orinian occupation for a while, actually," Seraeyu said grimly. "It has hit several complications and might be even more difficult now."

"You're not placing the blame solely on us. We are liberating ourselves from under *your thumb*, which you've yet to lift. And Aeyun haunts you?"

"Hmm," Seraeyu eyed her for a moment. "In a sense."

"You ask a lot of questions," Sakaeri commented, flicking a speck of grime off her Yisuna mask.

"I really think you don't ask enough," Saoiri countered.

"I ask just enough to get the picture. Turns out my intuition is spot-on. Godly, one might say." Sakaeri aimed the last bit purposefully towards Seraeyu, who hummed again and narrowed his eyes at her.

"Space for four," Saoiri determined. "Aeyun was looking for answers. Surely you all have some more hidden away."

"You'd be a shite Sirin," said Sakaeri.

"Good thing I'm a smuggler, not a Sirin."

"I thought you said you weren't a smuggler?" Jaspen asked, gazing forlornly at his pile of Draconguard armour in the corner.

"I'm sorry, who are you again?"

"Jaspen Verdanta," he told her, as if by automatic recount. Then he turned his head and gave her a wry smile. "I'm still not quite sure how you're all acquainted."

"Jeta and Perodine's brother," Saoiri acknowledged after a moment. He looked as if he ached to inquire about them, but he kept his mouth shut. "I met Sakaeri when she'd bought something from me, then again when … "

"When I was contacted by Aeyun," Sakaeri finished for her, aiming to tread lightly.

"And Aeyun Thasian-nee—" Jaspen began, only to be interrupted.

"Krunan," Sakaeri corrected, then pursed her lips. "Allegedly."

"Sakaeri," Seraeyu reprimanded.

"Aeyun Krunan ties you all together?"

"I suppose he does. Don't tell him that," said Sakaeri.

"He was taken in by Jourae-nee," Seraeyu supplied helpfully, "back when we were children. He'd taken up smithing; anything Thasian-nee brand you own was likely crafted by his hand. He and my sister were … quite close. Never far apart. Until he left, that is, and presumably decided to take up a life of ore smuggling?"

"It threw me, too. Did you know he was *selling* his wares?" Sakaeri grinned mischievously when Seraeyu reacted precisely as predicted, clutching at the ring chained around his neck rather than Mhedoonian pearls.

"He was *not!*"

"He was so. Let's tell Uruji if we get the chance."

"To withstand one of his thou-shalt-not-compete lectures? No. No thank you."

"He was searching for something," Saoiri said, looking very much like she wanted to crawl out of her own skin as she watched them. "The, um, ore."

"Right. Which ore?"

"Gate alicant," Saoiri hesitantly told Seraeyu.

"Which was stolen and is now with … "

"Kaisa," Sakaeri finished for him. "Who knows how to use *runes*, starry sea."

"That vile Pitmaster knows of ancient Runic Arts?" Jaspen asked.

"He knows how to use runes?" Seraeyu asked. There was a lapse where he stared into the distance, then dread dripped across his features, creasing them with tension.

"He draws them to command subordination," said Sakaeri. Absently, she rubbed where Aeyun had erased her own subjugating mark.

"Like … a … descant?" Seraeyu spoke slowly. "I *knew* he looked at me strangely! Sakaeri, he hasn't even *tried* to see me yet. Aeyun warned me against him. I think he was right. I need … I need to talk to Aeyun. I need to … " his thought tapered off as he started pacing.

"He was oddly focused on him, you know," said Sakaeri. Seraeyu paused his next step with prolonged anxiety. "Kaisa was weirdly obsessed with Aeyun."

"Who is … who is this stars-damned *Kaisa*? I need to talk to Aeyun."

Seraeyu, much to everyone's surprise, took a deep breath, then opened his eyes to reflect sinking obsidian, pale iridescent spots populating the dark. And it didn't sound at all mortal when he spoke next.

"Cah, A'Vor a'lud a'Ca'lorus da'Ca'ille n da'Ka'la'drius."

"What's he doing?" Saoiri was the first to ask in the resounding silence.

Seraeyu had collapsed onto the floor, Sakaeri only just catching him before he smacked his head on the ground. It was odd, more than odd, whatever this was.

"Talking to … Aeyun?" She wasn't entirely sure. She'd seen Aeyun manifest beside him, but this was different, like Seraeyu was taken somewhere else completely.

"He can do that?"

"This would happen, on occasion," Jaspen said, settled upon the edge of an abandoned bed. "Back before, when that daemon manipulated him. Only then he would collapse and regain himself. This is … not quite the same."

"Are they amongst the aether?" Sakaeri thought back to fleeting moments held in endless expanses, full of nothing but darkness and bursts of energy. "Communing in the in-between?"

"Is that possible?" Saoiri asked, watching Seraeyu's still form as if expecting him to jolt awake. He did not. He just lay still and cradled in

Sakaeri's arms.

"It really shouldn't be," said Sakaeri. "Not like this."

"Had they always held this connection?" Saoiri asked.

"If they had, I don't think they were aware of it."

"What is it that connects them?" Jaspen asked. He considered the resting form of Raenaru's tireless leader. Sakaeri wondered what he truly saw when he looked at him.

"I don't think that's my answer to give," she said. "And I don't think I fully understand it anyway."

With little in the way of warning, Seraeyu's eyes flew open, dotted, as if belonging to the Great Starry Sea itself. He took one look at Sakaeri, then plucked her arms away and shuffled intently to the side.

"What, Sera—"

"We have a problem," said Seraeyu. It held a strange, layered quality. "A few problems, actually."

Sakaeri *knew* that overlay.

"Aeyun," she stated.

"Aeyun?" Saoiri perked up, her eyebrows drawn in confusion.

Seraeyu – or Aeyun, rather – glanced at her and gave an awkward wave. "I'm sure Davah would say hello if he could, but he's probably having a quiet meltdown right now." Then he double-took. "Wait, Saoiri?"

"Where's Sera?" Sakaeri asked.

"Um. Right, that. Probably with the others. So that the *other one* wouldn't be."

"Other – *the daemon*? She awoke?"

"We've really … meddled in something bigger than ourselves," Aeyun-as-Seraeyu muttered, his mannerisms looking odd in Seraeyu's body, his palms pressed flat together, fingers' edges pushing against Seraeyu's lips. "Sakaeri, there isn't a solution here. I think there's a distinct possibility we're being hunted by the last remaining Yun. The barrier above Ca'lorus is cracking, maybe dissolving. I can't return to Raenaru the way I came since I was called to Rae's alicant and it's – well, you know – and there don't *seem* to be any gates here. And I really hope this guy is trustworthy, because—"

"He's fine," Sakaeri gestured lazily towards Jaspen. The displaced Draconguard was looking pallid from crown to collarbone, his eyes tracking frantically between them.

"—Please stay away from Kaisa. He's planning something. The Pyromancer mentioned the Stimfal? Stay away from him until we can figure this out, together—"

"Together? You're actually trying to come back?"

"Did you miss the part where I said we may be actively hunted by the last remaining Yun?"

"She's usually dormant."

"Not – no, not her. Gama. Gama-of-Yun. This ageless sage on Ca'lorus."

"Not Ka'la'drius?"

"Ka'la'drius is dead. Sera is *very* forthcoming with you, isn't he?"

"I like him better than you," she informed him, crossing one leg over the other to bounce her foot, glaring at him.

"Sakaeri. I don't know how to return and right now, as we speak, Raeyu is probably figuring out that Seraeyu is aware of himself again."

"You didn't tell her? You cheeky, stars-damned bastard! Of course she'd want to know that – oh, I don't know – her brother isn't the puppet of a vengeful daemon?" Sakaeri *really* wanted to wring his neck. "Okay. Alright. How did Uruji get to Ca'lorus?"

Aeyun-as-Seraeyu heaved in a centring breath. "He was thinking of reuniting with me, and the alicant in his dagger – the dagger! You threw my dagger!"

"I won't apologise for it."

"No, no. It was similar in make to Uruji's. There might be a chance it has the same alicant. Did it ever return to you?"

"No, but that tune could have been broken once my glove was stolen. Or it's currently hurtling towards Kaisa, I don't know."

"You'd said it wouldn't return if it was stopped by someone or some*thing*, right?"

"Right."

"Well, let's hope that some*thing* prevented it from leaving Ca'lorus." Blood pooled and dripped from one of Seraeyu's eyes. Sakaeri fought the urge to rub it away, and Jaspen tensed and leant forward. In preparation for *what*, Sakaeri wasn't sure. "Right, it's time. We'll come back soon, I promise."

"Aeyun," Sakaeri called, feeling the thrum of attunement fading from Seraeyu's form. "You should know: the Bloodsong, or its alicant, I guess, looks like a seed."

"It looks like a—" Aeyun-as-Seraeyu's look of bafflement dropped away as his eyes faded back into their natural amber-brown. "Bastard," Seraeyu said, no overlay. "I had to sit and pretend beside my very one-armed sister, an apparently very alive Uruji, one hollow-eyed mini-Aeyun with a penchant for pets, and one far too perceptive Mhedoonian. Davah, was it?" He swiped at the drying trail on his face. "Lovely … But it *was* nice to actually see Raeyu."

"Seraeyu?" Jaspen tested, like the name itself fought to claw from his throat.

"Yes?" Seraeyu turned to Jaspen. "Was he cruel? He can be a right arse without meaning to."

"No, he was just manic. Gama-of-Yun, Sera?" Sakaeri asked.

"Yes, he's meant to be dead. But then again, so were the rest of them."

"Are you an actual Yun?" Saoiri burst out. "Are you an *actual* god?" She had her arms wrapped around herself, a frightful expression in place. As if the schema she categorised the realms was cracking, fading. Maybe it was.

Seraeyu answered with a mulish: "I really think that depends on your definition."

CHAPTER TWENTY-FIVE

Davah did not like his chances. The odds were forever twisting towards unsightly depths of disaster, and he wasn't keen to tip them further.

He'd wanted to know, initially, if the tales rang true. If his mentor only spun them out of spite, or if there were grains of fact among them. *Pre'ach'an was right*, the false god had said. And what a terrifying statement that was. If it was to be believed – and all evidence certainly pointed that direction – then the woman sitting across from him was the daughter of daemons. And the man he'd travelled with was the product of a long, foul curse, placed upon his lineage from the very daemons Raeyu Thasian hailed from. Horrible arbiters of violence.

"Pirate, pass that bowl here," Uruji demanded, frowning. He held out his hand expectantly for the collection of nuts at Davah's side.

I cannot believe that I've managed to wrap myself in this void-damned mess.

Davah said nothing but grabbed and held out the container. It was snatched from his grip with little ceremony, then deposited beside Raeyu, who offered him a flat-mouthed grimace.

Stars, this is such stinking shite.

He sighed and cast his eyes across the remainder of their camp, spotting Da'garu playing with some big wolfish thing that had been following them since the day prior. They would have remained in the cave, but it had collapsed. Just as The Veil seemed ripe to, if left unattended. But how did one attend to a giant pastel, jelly dome that cracked with jolts of lightning? Davah certainly didn't know. And neither did Aeyun.

Truly, he was happy for the guy that he'd seemingly done a pretty solid job at reconnecting with his estranged sister; their moment over Azura must have rekindled something abandoned between them, and that's great. But it didn't solve anything. And the Thasian and Thasian-nee brood were a tight-lipped bunch, so Davah got to watch as they all obstinately held their tongues.

Then again, when Davah was asked about Pre'ach'an, he just deferred the question to Raeyu, who never seemed inspired to share those histories with the others. Whatever version she harboured. Davah wasn't dumb. He knew the old pirate tales were likely lacking in absolute accuracy. But hadn't even the false god proclaimed them true?

"Aeyun," Davah said standing up. "Isn't it time we—"

Aeyun yanked him over, his eyes fading black into white and populating with bright spots. "Davah, they can't know—"

And all too suddenly Aeyun stood there with a vacant, cosmic stare, his joints collapsing. Davah dove forward to hold him upright. And dammit, dammit, *fuck*, dammit! Selfish bastard! This was so far beyond unfair to task Davah with this – about what he very much presumed to be about

Seraeyu Thasian, of all the people in the realms – and yet here he stood. Supporting his damned favourite enigma so that his stars-doomed scheme didn't immediately blow up in his face. What a reckless man. Davah was a reckless man, but Aeyun was a *reckless* man.

Thankfully the others seemed occupied enough that they must've thought Davah and Aeyun were just having some weird, intense conversation. It wasn't so far out of the norm, he figured. So as long as it didn't last too long, it wouldn't draw suspicion.

When a full three minutes passed, Davah grew impatient. And their resident Yu-ta folks were starting to toss odd looks their direction. *Stars, why am I doing this?*

"Ah, ha, ha, I suppose, friend!" Davah said loudly just to fill the awkwardness, hoping to sway attentions away. "You want me to carry you? Strange request, but okay!"

Because how in the void else am I going to move you?

"Is … everything okay?" Uruji asked, genuine worry overwriting whatever ire he held for Davah.

"Yep!" Davah chirped, turning so that he could pull Aeyun onto his back. "All fine!"

"Aeyun," Uruji called instead. *Clever bastard.*

"He's fine, sure, he just—"

"—Fucking kidding!?" Aeyun shouted, stumbling back before steadying himself. Which he did by grasping at Davah's neck, nearly choking him.

"Stars above, friend, what are you—?" Davah threw his hands off and twisted to face Aeyun, only then it registered that something felt off. Sounded off. Looked off. His eyes still reflected the heavens. "Aeyun?" He tested quietly.

"Yes, that's me. Aeyun," very clearly Not-Aeyun said.

"Right," Davah deadpanned. "Better not turn around and be caught-out, *Aeyun*."

"Aeyun?" Uruji called again, concern bleeding through.

"Uruji-nee?" Not-Aeyun asked softly.

"Yeah, buddy. Placate him quick," Davah whispered.

"He's alive?" Not-Aeyun murmured back, but it didn't seem directed towards Davah. His face pulled into an expression Aeyun rarely wore, something betraying youthful hope, and it made the contrast all the more sharp.

"Hurry the fuck up," Davah warned. *I hate this. I really, really hate this, Aeyun.*

"What?" Not-Aeyun called, actually doing a pretty good impression of Aeyun's intonation. Behind him, Uruji hesitated, still looking unsure as to if he should stand up.

"Are you … okay?"

"I'm fine," Not-Aeyun replied with confidence, almost ruining it when he added a relieved, "Uruji."

"Are you sure, Aeyun?" Raeyu asked, and Davah watched as Aeyun's entire body locked up, eyes widening. It was that moment that it fully sank it that he was standing not in front of Aeyun, but Seraeyu Thasian.

"Yes, Rae," Not-Aeyun managed to say.

"You said you wanted to talk?" Davah offered, feeling himself shutter against this imposter version of his friend. His comrade. His co-*liberator*.

"Yeah," Not-Aeyun said, glum.

They walked a few paces further, settling just far enough where they could sit and whispers wouldn't carry. Davah dropped down with folded arms, glaring at the drooping man before him. Aeyun's body practised a much more ginger descent than Davah had ever witnessed from its true owner. It would be funny, actually, if Davah wasn't wishing for quick release from the situation during every waking moment of the entire encounter.

"Seraeyu Thasian," he stated.

"Who are you?" Not-Aeyun asked, wary.

"Davah. Aeyun hasn't mentioned me? How cold of him."

"Aeyun hasn't mentioned much of anything."

"Hm, yeah. You Thasian and Thasian-nee seem to all share that trait."

"I don't know what you know." Not-Aeyun squinted, looking strange with his star-dotted eyes. Like he was accessing him with heavenly judgement. And wasn't that a laugh?

"Can't say I'm entirely sure what you know, either. But I'm going to guess that you *are* Seraeyu Thasian and not the daemon controlling him."

"No, I am not Amanastré." Not-Aeyun frowned, then sighed. "Aeyun said you're having problems with A'gam?"

"Aeyun said? Just casually? That we were having issues with Gama-of-Yun? Like a playground feud?"

"Well, it's not exactly like we have loads of time when we speak with one another!" Not-Aeyun hissed and ... what?

"As in, multiple times? You're in regular communication?"

At that, Not-Aeyun screwed up Aeyun's face in annoyance. "You know, this is his own fault. *I* told Sakaeri on the first opportunity. He's got to get over his paranoia. Sometimes you can't get by carrying it on your own."

"Weirdly wise for a prick like you," Davah said, ignoring the offended huff it awarded him. "The Sirin is with you?"

"Sakaeri, you mean? Yeah, she's here. Oh, so is your friend in the Resistance."

Davah's mind blanked. His friend in the Resistance? The Resistance had dissolved and gone underground. Had the occupation instigated a resurgence? He wasn't sure he knew anyone in it anymore. "Who's that?"

Before Not-Aeyun could answer, a speeding ball of fur trampled by, kicking up dirt and grass, pulling his attention elsewhere. Onto Da'garu.

"Tell me I'm going daft but ... does that woman look like Aeyun?"

Da'garu chased after the wolfish beast, a giddy smile on her face, then she suddenly stopped and turned to stare at Not-Aeyun. Her eyes washed white and Davah felt strange inklings of something just beyond the surface, as he always did when either Aeyun or Da'garu practised their attunement with Vitality. Some filtered notion of recognition shot across the knoll, pegged squarely against Not-Aeyun, who stared back, eyes once again wide.

"Well, it would make sense, wouldn't it?" Davah asked, leaving Not-Aeyun to parse the rest.

"She spoke to him at his parents' graves."

"Wait, what?" There were at least two things in that sentence that stood out.

"Listen. You've got to get Aeyun's Essence back from me. Somehow. Then, whatever you do, don't let him return. Amanastré will have it out for him, and this place, and she *will* find a way if it's within arms' reach. I think I can trust Sakaeri to finish the job, so he needs to get—"

"Kid," Davah interjected. "This place is already falling apart thanks to the false god. And Aeyun can't take that back. He'll die."

"What? Why would he die?"

"Because he already gave up his life for your damned manipulative sister, and the fact that he doesn't have his Essence to hand over on a silver platter is the only thing keeping him alive. Your family is *starsdamned* fecking wreck."

One bloody tear slipped from his eye, carving a path down his cheek. "What?" And then, just as reckless as Aeyun, Not-Aeyun looked over his shoulder towards Uruji and Raeyu. "—seed?"

"Hello, my favourite enigma," Davah sing-songed, grinning tightly. "I just had the loveliest conversation."

"Davah. Davah, don't be angry," Aeyun turned back, looking at him almost impishly.

"Funny, the things you learn through just *one* conversation."

"Davah, I saw Saoiri," Aeyun said, an obvious misdirect.

One that worked far too well, given that Not-Aeyun mentioned being with his friend in the Resistance. So … "What in the frigid void is Saoiri doing in the Resistance?"

"Huh? She was just with Sakaeri and the others."

"Really? Because your pen pal said she was in the stars-forsaken Resistance!"

"Hey!" Uruji called, a few strides away. "*What* is going on?"

"Nothing!" They both shouted at the same time, agitated.

"Get you're shit together, friend. Figure out your priorities. Right now, mine is getting back to Saoiri. One thing I will never forgive myself for is if I let her become *me* without even trying to stop it. Saoiri doesn't need that. She doesn't need that."

"Davah, what did Pre'ach'an's stories say?"

Fuck it. I'm not a Thasian or Thasian-nee. Why should I hold on to this?

"That the realms would be ripped asunder by the cursed children of Ka'la'drius. The betrayer who was tricked by a daemon into massacring a people and destroying a realm. A once great pirate who took a poisoned deal to ascend to godhood, only to become a daemon himself. That

Amanastré, a warlord, a Yun of judgement, brought about the Era of Thasian. Tell me, because I'd be willing to bet, the woman on Beldur had horns, right? A Yu-ta?"

Aeyun didn't answer, just stared.

"It's said Amanastré's second reckoning spells the end of the realms." Davah turned to Raeyu, who'd encroached upon them alongside Uruji. She frowned back at him, conflicted. "How much of that fits your narrative, I wonder."

"All the pirates tell these tales?" Raeyu asked evenly.

"Why, so you can plan their demise? Pre'ach'an's wasn't enough?"

"They were just soldiers who defected. This legend glorifies it into something it's not. And it places an immovable target on Sera's back."

"You're delusional if you think it's not already there."

"Soldiers who defected?" Aeyun asked. Raeyu didn't look at him.

"It was in the text I was made to read. The army of legend. The Yun."

"So you knew there were no gods, yet you let the clergy continue." Davah scoffed.

"It was the way of things."

"This is why I never liked you sycophants."

"Hey!" Uruji interjected. "As much as this is something we should aim to settle, what is that?"

Everyone turned towards where Da'garu was stood near the edge of the forest clearing, shifting shadows just beyond the treeline, and something in Davah's veins crawled in icy dread. The warped figures drifted closer menacingly, and Davah felt the primal notion to run take root in his very soulsong.

"We've been here too long," Aeyun said, calling towards Da'garu and asking her to return to them, slowly. Her wolfish companion was nowhere to be found. "Take my arm," he said to no one in particular.

"What is that, friend?"

"The restless," Aeyun said, staring unblinkingly, his irises growing brighter. "And the consequence of a duty I never inherited."

CHAPTER TWENTY-SIX

Sakaeri felt more herself, cloaked in a dark shroud. They'd meandered back towards better-connected districts, stopping by a physician on the way to dose up on antimicrobials. The likelihood was that they'd all been exposed. No harm in being overly cautious.

Jaspen needed them for certain, his clammy skin professing his overexposure the day prior. Poor lad probably felt like he was swimming. Between sickness and shock, he'd surely need a few days' rest once they'd returned.

It was still odd, seeing him without a clanking layer of gleaming onyx. He'd packed it up in a lumpy rucksack without a word, puzzling it in place with strange, apathetic precision. Perhaps a few days would turn into a week.

"They probably think I'm dead," Saoiri whispered harshly. To one or all of them, Sakaeri wasn't sure. "Or that you or the Dracon has taken me hostage. That's not what you're doing, is it? Taking me hostage?"

"Are your hands bound?" Sakaeri asked.

"That's not the only thing that makes someone prisoner."

"Look, ah," Seraeyu paused a moment, then snapped his fingers in self-satisfied success, "Saoiri. We've been over this. You come, you're welcome to help our efforts to dissuade the realms from imminent tragedy. You leave, we'll trust you do so with the best intentions, that you will remain loyal to your missing companions, and that you'll keep an eye on Jaspen's familial relations, agreed?"

"You masquerade precocious so well, you know," Saoiri told him, edging away from a bubbled, globby secretion seeping down from corroded metal above. She patted at her head, then gave a sigh of relief once they'd dipped past the gooey threat.

"It's in the how-to-be-a politician manual."

"And you're not at all how I imagined," she added.

Seraeyu shrugged, readjusting his cowl to keep his heritage disguised. "I've found that most people are not as they first appear."

When they made it to the Elavatum – a grandiose building that hosted a multitude of elevators that led to the surface – Jaspen stepped before the group with a grim expression, the tug of his frown still visible despite his newly adopted dual-respirator mask.

"Let me handle our passage." His gaze lingered on Seraeyu, then it fell to Saoiri. "Our crew is odd enough. The fewer questions are asked, the better."

"Would they not just let me through?" Seraeyu asked.

"I am ... not sure," Jaspen admitted. "And I'm not keen to test it."

"Would you not be on a list, given your sisters' affiliations?" Saoiri asked. Not an unreasonable question. Sakaeri had wondered the same.

"I … could be. If I'm taken, it will give you all the chance to run."

The sentiment sat heavy between them.

"No," Seraeyu said suddenly. "I refuse. No." He shoved past Jaspen and stalked up to the ticket master. Sakaeri watched him as he went. If she stopped him – if *any* of them stopped him – it would be cause for a bigger scene. And four people acting cagey in a corner was suspect enough. At least his presence as Praetor would make such suspicious behaviour make more sense, his aim obvious; keep anonymity among the masses.

"He is frustrating," Jaspen commented, posture pulled tight.

"He is who he is," Sakaeri said, narrowing her gaze when the ticket master responded to Seraeyu in a fidgety, nervous reaction.

"And he's on the way back," Saoiri added, her statement ringing true as Seraeyu turned around with four plastic cards fanned between his fingers. He twitched them victoriously, grin apparent with the way his skin creased beneath his eyes.

"Turns out all you need is a bit of persuasion," Seraeyu said upon his return, parsing out a card to each of them.

"And the threat of the Praetor's smiting retribution," Saoiri muttered.

"Hey now, none of that," said Seraeyu.

"*Was* there none of that?" Sakaeri bade, but Seraeyu just gave a noncommittal hum.

They scanned their passes and slipped into a chromium-plated elevator, watching Mercur's depths elongate below them. As they ascended, a serenade of ivory keys played. Sakaeri couldn't decide if it relaxed her or put her more on edge.

"These are meant to be good for transport to the Great Sea Gate as well. Though, I imagine not many sea-skimmers will be headed towards Raenaru," said Seraeyu.

"A pilot will take us direct in a private transport if we pay him under the table," Jaspen said, then sighed. Sakaeri wondered how pitted his conscience felt under all the regulations he continued to break. The poor soldier was dying inside, she was sure.

"Resourceful as always, Jas!" Seraeyu responded chirpily.

"Okay, but … if I tell you that it can't be someone in particular, it cannot be them. Alright?" Saoiri shifted uncomfortably. "It's just … it wouldn't be good. If I was seen cavorting with you."

"I'd rather not know," Jaspen said, looking up towards the elevator's ceiling. "I don't want to know who your contact is. Don't tell me."

"Yeah, sure," said Saoiri.

"Right, isn't your face somewhat … known?" Sakaeri asked, squinting at the former smuggler. "I seem to remember you and Davah having caught the eye of Madame Reaper."

"Right," Saoiri said, a completely unsatisfactory non-answer.

"What was Aeyun doing with you two?" Seraeyu cocked his head sideways, brow quirked. "He wasn't a poster child for lawful citizen, but to go from respectable metalsmith to ore-smuggler. How had you met?"

"He was looking for ore," Saoiri provided flatly. "So were we."

"He did just kind of up and left, didn't he? It was very strange."

Sakaeri debated it a moment, then said, "I think he had to." The uncomfortable weight of curious stares fell upon her. "He was to be hunted."

"By whom?" Seraeyu asked, the question well and truly bewildered.

"Well," Sakaeri began, looking instead towards the city far below. "By me."

"What?" Saoiri was the first to ask, the word erupting in gut reaction. "*What?*"

"I wasn't going to," Sakaeri mumbled, feeling cornered. "I was just tasked with it."

"Wait," said Seraeyu. "As a Sirin?" The question received a brief nod. "So it came from the clergy?"

"No, it came from Oagyu." Sakaeri specifically avoided looking at their stragglers, instead staring solely down at Seraeyu.

Oddly enough, Seraeyu shook his head. "No, Sakaeri. My father took counsel from the Clerics. They whispered in his ear since the day Mother died, and he'd listened intently to every word they fed him."

"The clergy wanted Aeyun dead?" She asked, then considered another task that had been thrust upon her. "The clergy wanted *Kaisa* dead?"

"Oh, this—" Seraeyu closed his eyes and wagged his finger, "—this means nothing good." He pinched the bridge of his nose, huffing out a heavy sigh. "You know, there's something that's been bothering me. Quite a lot, actually. Perhaps it's time we visit Uruji-nee's mother, no?"

Kllunna Faratina. Rarely spoken of, and even more seldom seen.

Sakaeri had observed a woman in Jourae's company. Always in the opposite corner of him. She was said to be a gifted Oracle, a position only granted to those blessed with the insight of the Yun, locked away in the deepest bowels of monastic compounds. She originally hailed from Tenebrana but was raised and reared in the mountains of Yunae.

Her presence in Haebal was fleeting. Three years at most.

Even so, Sakaeri remembered her well. Tall and beautiful and silent. Absent.

Young, teetering on legs that didn't have near enough meat on their bones, Sakaeri had peered into a life she'd not yet realised was stolen from her. Hidden in the alleyways that no one bothered to look into, her wide eyes trailed after the elegantly robed Kllunna, watching as she took delicate steps behind Jourae. Always too far behind.

It often appeared a procession. A mourning line, tugged forward by Jourae's focused footfalls, always assured and fixedly in a loop towards the Thasian Tower.

Sakaeri watched as Kllunna's belly swelled, then as it flattened once more, but her arms remained empty. The infant – because it never looked like *her* baby – was instead carried and coddled by housemaids from the

Tower. Then by Jourae, who smiled down at Uruji like he was the sun incarnate. And, as Sakaeri watched, her young mind was boggled, because Uruji's inquisitive eyes swivelled, occasionally catching her own hidden in darkened shadows, and she held no disdain for the newest Thasian-nee. And it wasn't that Kllunna did, not really, it was more that she seemed to feel nothing, entirely apathetic.

It wasn't long until Kllunna's presence disappeared from Raenaru entirely. It had been a hushed departure, and the realms were less concerned with the Thasian-nee than they were the Thasian themselves, so any infiltrative reports were few and quickly discarded. What Sakaeri saw instead was the extra care Jourae offered his son, who was always in his arms. Attached to his leg, his hand, sat atop his shoulders, little fingers wrapped around the curved horns of his father's head.

Sakaeri, as much as Seraeyu, knew where Kllunna ended up.

She had not gone back to the clergy, her penultimate duty satisfied with her bearing of a Thasian-nee child. An exit clause, that's what it was. She had taken spoils offered to her from the Thasian estate, then swept herself away to Lu-Ghan, never turning an eye towards either Tenebrana or Raenaru. Sakaeri had encountered her only a few times as a Sirin. With the way the woman lived, she'd be surprised if she remembered she had a son at all.

When Sakaeri had sliced the neck of a pepperstim mogul, his product having bled too deeply into Raenaru's underground, a powdered narcotic dusting the hands of aristocrats with too much time on their hands, she'd seen Kllunna's draped form watching dazedly from a lush chaise in the corner, sat beside another few addicts who may as well have been on a different plane of existence. Kllunna drifted through Bhu-Nan as if in an endless dream, as far as Sakaeri could tell. Composed on the outside, lost to herself behind closed doors.

"Why now?" Sakaeri asked Seraeyu, who was now clasping a hand around the ring draped from his neck.

"She was an Oracle, Sakaeri. And more than that, Uruji has been gone for some time now. There are no Thasian-nee. Would the clergy have not sought her out by now?"

"You haven't seen her, Sera. Oracle or not, Kllunna is no longer whatever woman she was when locked up and barricaded behind the Clerics' walls."

Seraeyu seemed to just ignore that statement altogether. He plucked a communication stone from his bag and etched atop it. "Koali will not be happy to hear of our detour, but I trust she will keep things in order in my absence."

It wasn't the first message sent to the Sentinel, plenty of placating ones having been delivered after the chaos that was the Spire's ball. At one point, Sakaeri thought the stone would crumble to dust with how often it rattled.

"Then, we are not headed to Raenaru?" Saoiri asked, beating the ding of their elevator's arrival by mere seconds.

"No," Seraeyu said, strapping his respirator mask around his head, gazing at the endless haze that sat in Orin's atmosphere behind the glassy atrium that greeted them. Beyond a sweeping platform of slate tiling, clear partitions barricaded the oily laps of Orin's ocean, sea-skimmers bobbing in the far distance off long piers. "We're going to Bhu-Nan."

CHAPTER TWENTY-SEVEN

"Do I want to know why you know where to go for this?" Sakaeri asked, wary as she watched Seraeyu navigate Bhu-Nan backstreets like he'd trekked them by memory alone. Given, these were backstreets of the wealthiest corner of the city, yet backstreets all the same.

"No," Seraeyu said simply.

"I feel like I do remember some incriminating coverage of some of your exploits here," said Saoiri. She seemed unsure of whom to follow, swapping her proximity to each of them in disorganised intervals. For the moment, she was beside Sakaeri.

"I'm sure I don't know what you're talking about," Seraeyu said, quick in a way that communicated, *yes*, he very much did know what she referred to.

"No need to dreg up the past," Jaspen muttered beside him, earning himself a brief but appreciative glance from the Praetor.

"Too bad I feel we're about to do just that," Sakaeri noted, since surely they'd be connecting with an old contact of Seraeyu's. She wasn't sure she wanted to know everything he may have experimented with, and she wasn't sure it was a great idea for Seraeyu to be traipsing this ground at all.

Seraeyu paused in front of a nondescript door, snug beneath the stairs of a building towering above, its lights snuffed to offer a shadowed corner for the crowd of them to huddle. He paused for a short internal debate, tugging his hood closer to his face, then he stepped up and knocked in a rhythmic pattern. The same Sakaeri had knocked to get into the pepperstim den many years prior. *Wonderful.*

It took more than a minute for someone to crack the metal hinges. The open gap revealed a stern face and a grim appraisal; an otherwise rather bland-looking man, dressed in a black suit and a loosened tie. "If my eyes don't deceive me, I'm pretty sure it's Seraeyu Thasian gracing my doorstep."

"Your eyes don't deceive you," Seraeyu said flatly.

The man in the doorway gave a haughty sniff, staring down his nose at the Praetor, then he scanned across the group of them. Barefaced and dressed in dark cloaks, they probably looked liked anyone else who may stumble up to his abode. No-name, wealthy brats with too much time on their hands. "Wouldn't have expected a visit from you now."

"I need to ask you something," Seraeyu said, his darting eyes giving away quelled anxiety. Anyone could pass them out here. *Anyone.*

"Oh, yeah?" the man asked, yet to move. In purposeful barricade, his arm came up to rest above his head in the doorjamb, his body leaning towards it.

"Come on, Fhen. Let us in," Seraeyu demanded, equal parts desperate and impatient.

Fhen squinted, frowned, then sighed and stepped aside. He fanned out his arm to indicate their approved entry. "Thought you were a delivery," he said as they entered a dim-lit sitting area. It looked lived in, plenty of seating and a few stray blankets. "Reserves have gone a bit dry. *You* might be to blame for that, actually."

"You'd really be better off dropping the habit, Fhen," Seraeyu told him, sinking into a deep-set cushion. "I've told you that."

"You've said differently before."

"I'm done with that."

Fhen eyed him for a moment, then cast another gaze across his companions, all of whom had settled themselves uncomfortably around the room. Sakaeri had opted to lean on a wall, just close enough to the door in case this *Fhen* decided he didn't want to talk.

"Why are you here, Sera?" Fhen asked. Whether he noticed or chose to ignore the bristle of Jaspen's hackles, Sakaeri wasn't sure.

"I told you: I need to ask you something."

"And?"

"Kllunna Faratina."

"You need Kllunna? Why?"

Sakaeri wasn't sure how to feel about this Fhen character being on a first-name basis with Kllunna, or what it might mean. And she didn't really want to investigate it. Yet, the thought teased in her brain: *did Seraeyu have repeated run-ins with Uruji's mother?* And *could he have been there when I was on the job?*

"Have you heard from her?" Seraeyu asked, not letting up.

"You're not taking her into custody or anything, are you?"

"No," said Seraeyu.

Fhen stared him down for a bout, then sighed, jerking his head towards the hall. "She's upstairs with a few others. You might not find her good company right now." Seraeyu just gazed back, stony. "Fine, sure. I'll get her. Then you talk, then you leave. You're a bad taste these days, Sera."

"Sure," Seraeyu said shortly.

Sakaeri watched Fhen leave. As he did, he glanced up at her with an inscrutable look, but didn't say anything. Left to their own devices for the time being, Saoiri started inspecting the room – looking for what, Sakaeri wasn't sure – and Jaspen still stood stiffly in place, appearing as if he could desperately use a cigarette.

Seraeyu must have noticed the same, since he said, "Light up, if you want. Wouldn't make a difference in here. Might even help, the smoke."

Hesitantly, Jaspen fished out a stick and snapped a fire to life from his finger. He took his first drag and almost visibly melted with his exhale. Seraeyu stood up and walked over, plucking the cigarette from Jaspen's mouth. He stole a long drag, staring up at Jaspen intently, then slotted it back in place. Jaspen raised a shivering hand to steady the rolled tobacco.

Interesting, was all Sakaeri had time to think before the door pulled open and Kllunna stumbled in, her fingers dragging along the doorframe. Sakaeri, being the closest, grasped onto the woman's elbow and steered her towards a cushion, depositing her gently and stepping away just as quickly.

Kllunna laughed, a slow, melodic thing, then she leant back and gazed forward.

"Uruji?" she called out, looking towards Seraeyu.

" ... No," said Seraeyu. He pulled down his hood and crossed the room, kneeling before Kllunna and taking her hand between his own. "Seraeyu. Sera."

"Oh," she said. "Right ... Sera."

"How are you, Kllunna?" Seraeyu asked, enunciating his words. She gazed back. A giggle bubbled from her throat, her other hand petting across Seraeyu's. She didn't answer, just smiled. Seraeyu frowned. "Do you know where you are?"

"Fhen Jan-Bhan's," Kllunna crooned, smiling wider in euphoria.

"Do you know who I am?"

"Paeyuni's son, Se—era," she said, drawing out the first vowel of his name.

"Right. And—"

"Paeyuni, your boy looks like you," Kllunna gazed beyond Seraeyu's shoulder.

Sakaeri glanced curiously where her gaze had affixed but she only found a deep teal wall. She turned back to the pair of them by the edge of the sofa. Seraeyu was looking down. Collecting himself. *Why are we letting him do this? Why am I letting him do this?*

Then, *this was his choice. It's not mine to make.*

And finally, *but this is Uruji's mother.*

"Kllunna, Paeyuni isn't here," Sakaeri found herself saying. It drew their eyes her way, and something felt pinning in the depths of Kllunna's attention.

"No, Sakaeri. She is *everywhere*," Kllunna said with a wide smile.

Sakaeri felt her heart jolt. There was no reason for Kllunna to know her name.

"Ube, too. There is so much of Ube's song in you," Kllunna stood, languid and swaying, her hand drifting from Seraeyu's. "I was never Ube. I would never be Ube. But I did what she asked, didn't I?" Sakaeri's muscles tensed as Kllunna got closer, long hair sliding off her shoulder. "Hid you. Said you died. Took her place. She saw it through my eyes. Saw why. Understood why. Why I walked away. You—" her fingers stretched, aiming towards Sakaeri's forehead, and there was an energy that formed there, reality warping in the space between. "Why—" Kllunna's voice continued, distorted, and a thread of something tugged in the air between them, unfurling into a vision of a cold room, a mother on a table, a baby just born, the babe wailing in Kllunna's arms, others stood in a half-circle around. A dagger in a hand, a begging cry, a door shutting, and a body left behind. "Understood—" Kllunna's voice floated by again, and Sakaeri got a glimpse of something. A forge, sat in dark expanses, someone hammering at the anvil. Then came scenes of Seraeyu's death. Again and again. And again. A gorge in his chest, bloodied and pooling, then his eyes opening wide, body knitting together, and by then only he and Sakaeri stood in the void.

"Why," he said, sounding like thousands of voices at once. "Why." Again, several voices reflected. But then there was a broken, quiet, "Why?" that didn't sound at all like Seraeyu, but Aeyun, and the Seraeyu before her clawed at his chest, heaving in panic.

"Why?" she found herself repeating, its vibrations rippling off in the dark.

Hammering continued in the distance. Slow and rhythmic. Hands reached to grasp her own, drawing them up, and suddenly she had her fingers gripped around a hilt, its blade buried into a chest. She looked up, terror welling, and met Davah's gaze.

"This is why," he said, and the hammering got louder. "Why you—"

"Cannot kill him," a small voice said, a whisper slipping in and out of existence, and Sakaeri looked down to see a little girl, her ghostly hand gripping Davah's. "You cannot kill him," she said again, and it was like all the static dropped, only her voice remaining, her bodiless form shining brightly in the smoky chasm. "You *must* understand."

Sakaeri strained against the pressure that washed over her, the swirling derision of push and pull.

"And *you* must find him," the girl said.

"Why?" Sakaeri found herself asking again, then everything fell away, and she found herself back in a dim-lit den, Kllunna in front of her. Seraeyu had tugged away Kllunna's wrist, and Jaspen had her shoulder yanked back. In the background, Saoiri was a half-step away from reaching out behind Kllunna's back. "Who?" she asked, voice level, but mind vast distances away.

Kllunna laughed, carefree and diluted. "He who hammers fate. It's not – it's not, you know … it's not your command of alkonos. It's that you can *see*. You can … walk it."

"Alkonos?" Seraeyu asked, yet to release her wrist.

"Who hammers fate?" Sakaeri asked, undeterred.

"I don't know," Kllunna giggled, swaying. "He just sits. And *clang, clang, clang* …"

"Alkonos?" Seraeyu asked more forcefully.

"It speaks to me," Kllunna whispered, closing her eyes as she leant his way. "I listen. I've always listened. At times it is cruel, but it doesn't know."

"And what of Uruji? What is his role in all this?" Sakaeri's callous tone was not lost on her nor the surrounding group. But she was tired of these games. "Your son. What is his role?"

"Uruji is destined. Same as the rest of you." Kllunna wasn't smiling now. She stood limply, wresting her arm from Seraeyu and tipping out of Jaspen's grasp.

"Destined? Fate? What nonsense. If that vision was indeed the past, all you did was leave a woman begging for her life, carrying her child away as a dagger claimed her death."

That revelation staled the room.

"Let's ask what we came here for," said Sakaeri. "Has the clergy come for you? Have they contacted you? Contracted you?"

"They ask nothing of me," Kllunna muttered, stumbling back towards a chair and dropping into it. "I tell them nothing. That thread has been cut. I am their Oracle no more."

"Then we're done here," Sakaeri decided, turning to leave. She made it as far as the small sunken courtyard outside before – her very last expectation – Saoiri caught up with her.

"What did you see?"

Unsure how to put it to words, she called out the one thing that might mean something to Saoiri: "Your precious Davah."

The hotel room was quiet. It wasn't quite as humid and dingy as the one in Mercur, but it was nothing extravagant like when Sakaeri had last been in Bhu-Nan with Saoiri, both Aeyun and Davah in their cohort. The building still towered to dizzying heights, a glass window offering a picture of evening normalcy that felt grating behind Sakaeri's retinas. There was nothing that inspired complacency anymore. As she stared through the panel, the streets far below blurred with the vibrancy of a thousand lives Sakaeri would never know.

The lights were off. No one bothered to turn them on, so each of their shadows melded with the floor, leaving no lingering impressions behind them. Seraeyu was sat in a chair, his head rested on the wing, his eyes cast not towards the city skyline but beyond it, somewhere in the liminality of memory and experience. Jaspen was quietly fussing with a kettle in the kitchenette, carefully plucking out bags of dried tea, mugs, and a spoon. Saoiri sidled up to Sakaeri, long braid swaying, her fingers folded behind her back.

"My mother had the gift," she said, the words soft like an admission. Sakaeri didn't look over. Didn't flinch. Didn't react. Just listened. "She was meant to be protected by the Elders. When a child shows an affinity for miracles, they are sheltered; kept hidden. It's one thing for a person to be blessed – cursed – with the Sight. It's another for them to be Mhedoonian.

"The clergy came as missionaries. They always do, trying to weasel their way into our shrines and tombs. One of them figured out that you don't get people to talk by telling them what they should believe in but rather listening to what they have to say. Making them feel secure, lured into a false friendship. Someone gave up my mother's name, having been drawn to the claims of this acolyte."

Sakaeri watched a light swap from purple to blue, then to a glittering green. It barely looked like a city at all, a kaleidoscope of churning colours.

"One of the Elders had a son. He'd rejected the idea of playing the good subject. He didn't like the rules that bound his hands, stamped out his ideas. He'd left before he was of age, making a name for himself that sowed fear year after year. But when his mother, staunch in her belief of the old ways, unwilling to budge from structure, reached out to him on a stone that hadn't rattled for several years, he sailed back. He retrieved my mother in the dead of night, bringing her out to sea. It wasn't her fault she got sick. She got to hold her child for a few years, anyway. And Davah told me stories of her from the time I wasn't afforded. He made her sound like a right scoundrel. Maybe she was. Maybe he idolised her that way.

"I was on that vessel the day it sank. Davah made sure I didn't go down with it. I never saw my father again, his grave lost in the depths of the sea." Saoiri took a weighted, shaky breath in, full of turmoil and acceptance in one twisted swallow, and Sakaeri felt her sharp stare settle on her profile. "Davah said, only once, that my mother told him never to dance too near the clergy. That, if he did, he would forfeit his freedom. That, if he did, the realms would suffer for it."

"Who is Davah, really?" Sakaeri heard herself ask.

"He'd tell you he's no one. Just a man with far too much luck on his side." Saoiri gave up on getting Sakaeri's attention away from the visage of Bhu-Nan, so she instead joined her appraisal. "I always thought it was strange that he was at the right place at the right time. Like some intangible string pulled him along. But when my grandmother met him, with all the wisdom expected of an esteemed Elder, she told him, very clearly: you attract malignancy as much as you do blessings of old; keep your hands steady, Da'bhe."

"As obscure as any ingratiated to faith," said Sakaeri.

"Elder Emagh said Davah and I would encounter destiny. Something great and awful; something worth setting out for. She said she could feel it in the air the day we left. I think there's a reason Davah's not here." Saoiri looked over her shoulder, gaze cold, pinned right on Seraeyu. "I don't think you're important at all. I think you're just a poisoned weed."

"Perhaps," Seraeyu responded, blinking slow, as if bored. "I met this Davah, if only briefly. He seemed a man as much as I. Just a man." He paused to think a moment, then continued, "Though, I supposed I may have met you both far before now. When your father slit my grandfather's throat and drenched me in cold realities on open seas."

Sakaeri shifted her weight and twisted, eyeing Raenaru's Praetor wearily. Oh, how she wished he wouldn't put his foot in his mouth. It would make her duty far easier. Saoiri, however, did not seem to be in a fighting mood, only frowning back at him.

"Did you know that Pre'ach'an seemed to have expected him that day? That my grandfather purposefully set out, offering his helmsman specific coordinates? In fact, he did not ready weapons at your father's approach. He only waited in patience as the vessel neared. He'd died with a hand extended, fingers stretched towards a truce, I suspect."

Saoiri's breath seemed caught at Seraeyu's words, but she didn't respond, only tracked Jaspen as he offered a brewed cup of tea to Seraeyu, keeping one in hand for himself.

"I don't think we have the luxury of holding generational grudges. You know as much as I do that something catastrophic is on the horizon, and—" Seraeyu paused to look into his cup, as if it held clarity within its steaming surface, "—and I'm afraid everyone may have a part to play. God, ghost, or otherwise. I've learnt something I wish I realised a long time ago: it's not skills or talents or affinities that matter, it's what you chose to do and what you're capable of, in a moral sense. It's whether you choose the best of what may be many evils, and if you at least try to accomplish good. It might be unfair to say I want that wholeheartedly. That my efforts are always for some altruistic end. But I can promise you one thing: I do not want the worst of it to be all there is. I want to believe it can be better."

Jaspen was watching Seraeyu with his mug still and forgotten in his grasp, his focus unshakable. Sakaeri understood his fascination. She knew the man before her as a child, brattish and lonely and begging for attention. She watched him transform in the worst of ways, losing himself to futile efforts to attract love and compassion, as well as to strange substances filtering through his veins, too often caught by scrying Eyes. Just recently she watched as he gained and lost it all in one go, and now he sat with words on his tongue that sounded sensible and prudent yet remained elusive and unheard by most.

"What do you *really* want, Seraeyu Thasian?" Saoiri asked.

"The impossible," Seraeyu said, smile wry and bitter. "I am tired of tyrants and those who elevate them. Yet I want a resolution without further bloodshed. I want my own freedom, a silly notion. Childish. It's not something I can expect, not really. Our realms are built on opposition, and I cannot expect to offer my hand without a blade ready to sheer my head from my neck. And why should I? To someone else, I am everything that should be dead and buried. In some ways, they're correct. Mine is a legacy of awful misdeeds and manipulations. So, perhaps, my wish to release generational grudges is a selfish one."

Saoiri stagnated, then her shoulder twitched, just a small jerk. Slowly, and very purposefully, she slipped her dagger from the holster snug on her thigh, the sound of its blade clattering to the floor harsh and loud in the quiet of the hotel room. She held her hands up in a sign of non-aggression, stepping forward with intention until she stood directly in front of Seraeyu.

Sakaeri almost wanted to laugh when Saoiri extended her hand to him. Another one. Another one who saw Seraeyu's vision. Another one who was willing to bet on him.

Seraeyu sat idle at first, then handed his tea back to Jaspen, who took it without question, looking like he was witnessing something worthy of record. Perhaps he was. It wasn't all that surprising to Sakaeri when

Seraeyu grasped her hand in kind, but it did curl confusion in her mind when Seraeyu slid forward to remove himself from the chair, forcing Saoiri back a half-step. He knelt to the floor, drifting his other hand to cradle her tentative agreement in both his palms, his head angled down, neck vulnerable. "I hope I achieve something to deserve whatever it is you offer here."

Sakaeri saw the very moment Saoiri truly came to internalise what Sakaeri was loath to admit in her early days as a Sirin. It was never about fighting one man; one ruler or villain. The goal didn't stop with the disappearing of Seraeyu Thasian. The aims of those who wanted *better* instead rested in the dismantling of corrupt agendas and oppressive regimes, all in the hopes they wouldn't rise again. But they always did. So it was for the interludes of peace they strove. Those precious moments that were all too fleeting, forgotten when the next period of strife erupted, often in a violent collision.

The question that remained now was: can Seraeyu Thasian herald this passing, wistful dream into reality?

Saoiri tightened her grip and pulled up, urging Seraeyu to his feet. "We are equals," she said. "In the future coming."

"We are equals already, Saoiri Pre'ach'an."

CHAPTER TWENTY-EIGHT

KAISA
DO-NOT-RETURN

Sakaeri stared as the last letter burnt and its etch evaporated from the communication stone in Seraeyu's palm. "That feral sewerfish has finally decided to rear his ugly mug?"

"Will Koali be alright, you think?" Seraeyu asked, carving an affirmative into the smoothed rock. "I hate to think what Kaisa might do, should he turn impatient."

"Listen to the Sentinel. She means to protect you," said Sakaeri.

"Funny, his timing." Seraeyu sighed maudlinly as he pocketed the stone, then he brushed his hands down his clothes – likely desperately unwashed for his tastes, given he'd been in them for two days too long.

"Where to then, *Praetor*?" Saoiri asked from beside the window, perched and peering at the avenue below, its corridor dappled with morning light. The title had been drawled, but it lacked bite, unlike the way it had been spat one city prior.

"Well," Seraeyu considered, closing his eyes and tilting his head in thought. "We are on Lu-Ghan. Kaisa is not. Aeyun, I've been told, is out a score of precious alicant. Perhaps we should rectify that."

"You – you cannot be serious, Seraeyu Tha—Seraeyu." Jaspen's fingers twitched. Sakaeri was sure he was already craving a vice to stave off his anxieties. "You want to go to that *vile* Pit? Now?"

Seraeyu smirked broadly at Jaspen, nodding his head only once. "You see, dear Jas, Kaisa is a slippery fish – sewerfish, says Sakaeri – and right now, right this moment, I know where he is. Which means I know where he's not. If there was ever a time to infiltrate, it's when we can be most assured that he will not be present, and thus ..."

"Now," Sakaeri said flatly. "How beautifully idiotic and rash of you."

"I'll have you know that it's a better plan than whatever foolish nonsense Aeyun came up with. I'll bet he just went barging in without reservation, thinking he could brute force his way through. See, I think we can manage clandestine. I've snuck in and out of all sorts of wicked places."

"None we need to know," Jaspen said to quickly, already patting his pockets.

"He actually came in disguised, you know. Him and Davah. Fought a few rounds before he managed to encounter me," Sakaeri told him. She wasn't keen to go back.

"*Fought a few rounds* – see? Brute force," Seraeyu reasoned.

"It's not that I'm disagreeing," Saoiri began, re-plaiting the ends of her hair, "but this isn't some trip into a wine cellar for a particularly tempting vintage. This is a monstrous colosseum with a rather high count of Kaisa's flunkies within it."

"Were you not an ore-smuggler? Now a member of the Resistance? Surely this wouldn't be daunting to *you*," Seraeyu said, peering up through his eyelashes at her, hands fisted on his hips, challenging.

Saoiri frowned at him and poked one finger on his forehead, forcing him back with measured pressure. Sakaeri was halfway certain that was the first time she'd voluntarily touched Seraeyu, except for the handshake shared between them the evening prior.

"I have a sense of preservation, believe it or not," she said, snarky.

Seraeyu shrugged. "Well, suit yourself. It was nice to meet you, Saoiri Pre'ach'an."

Seraeyu began making all the preparations one might before departure – checking his pockets, ensuring his clothes were in order, then finally grabbing the small satchel he'd kept on his person. Sakaeri glanced at Saoiri's obstinate expression once before striding towards the door, opening it and waiting for Seraeyu's exit and Jaspen's stilted chase behind him.

Sakaeri had only managed a foot in the threshold before Saoiri called out a sudden, "Wait!" A stream of frustrated utterances followed under the former ore-smuggler's breath. "*Fine*, you boorish eejit."

"Excellent!" Seraeyu said jovially.

Saoiri had etched a communication stone – and Sakaeri *still* wondered how wide that net she'd established was cast – and soon they found themselves outside a derelict-looking warehouse that formed vague recollections of awkward run-ins and ore-lit tunnels. Outside a rusted door, Saoiri carved a symbol on the stone one final time before stashing it back out of sight.

Seraeyu was donned in a hooded cloak, like the rest of them, but he'd once again adopted Sakaeri's Yisuna mask. It didn't stop Jaspen and Sakaeri from hulking over his shoulders. This was the longest Seraeyu had been in the open for quite some time, and Sakaeri was starting to feel like the slightest trip could break a nation. Seraeyu indeed walked a fragile path.

Despite its appearance, the door did not creak when it opened, its hinges oiled for quiet entry. A stern face, creased with wrinkles from a perpetual frown, greeted them. The man's sharp gaze tracked down, his wide frame a barrier all its own.

"Little Doon," he groused, arms folded. "What needs sowing?"

"Tides have changed, Pen. I need something from the Madame."

The looming giant of a man stared, emotion agnostic, then he clicked his tongue, jutting his chin as he said, "Who's your posse? Don't seem too keen to show their faces, them."

Sakaeri couldn't claim to have expected it when Saoiri calmly stated, "Praetor Thasian, his sell sword, and an Orinian Draconguard."

Pen's eyes widened, his muscles tensed, then he burst out laughing, like it'd been punched from his gut. "Stars, little Doon. Is that what you consider a good joke?" He scoffed, continuing, "Fine, you and your little resistance fighters can go on ahead. You know the way."

Saoiri nodded, not looking back to make sure the rest of them were following, marching inside when Pen allowed them entry.

Sakaeri did not appreciate her gambit, but it got them a step further, so she continued undeterred, grimacing at the drab warehouse interior, curving around a stack of crates she remembered hiding a latch in the floor, just behind their wooden bodies. There was no Reaper's Hand by the entryway, and Sakaeri had to wonder just where the rest of them might be. Instead, their small group was able to slip into the tunnel below with no interruption, soon surrounded by dank stone walls and strings of lit ore.

The last time Sakaeri had seen this, she'd been poisoned. Best not to dwell on that. Not now. Not when they needed a favour.

"This is a horribly bleak surrounding to call home," Seraeyu commented idly.

Saoiri seemed to ignore him in favour of a particular door that Sakaeri recalled bitterly. She wondered how often Saoiri came here now that she was with the Resistance. And how trustworthy an alliance between the Resistance and the Reaping Hands was. As far as Sakaeri was concerned, she wouldn't afford the Madame a modicum of benefit. It was business, so what business did the Resistance offer, exactly?

"Well," the Madame smiled serpentine behind the Reaper's Hand that opened the door to the lush, sconce-lined office. "Isn't this a pleasant surprise. The Doon child has returned."

Sakaeri flicked off her hood and glared, blessed retribution running through her head even if her hands came to rest idle by her side.

"Lovely to see you alive, doll. Did you enjoy your excursion?" Madame Reaper leered, settling herself into her tufted chair. "Nothing personal, I'm sure you know."

"We want to make a deal with you," Saoiri told her, side-stepping the grunt and placing herself in front of the mahogany desk. "It's a fair one."

The Madame quirked her brow, tapping her fingers against her gaudy bronze hand clip. "Go on. But first, might I—" her eyes darted to her hooded attendant, "—would you leave us for now, Gau? I would so appreciate if you fetched me that favourite drink of mine, the one with mint? You know it." She fluttered her fingers with a smile that may have been charming on someone else. The man did as asked, lumbering out and clicking the door shut behind him. "Now, who else graces my presence today?"

"That's part of the deal," Saoiri told her, leaning against the desk and fishing an alicant from her bag to twiddle between her fingers. "We reveal an identity you'll be quite interested to know in exchange for the whereabouts of the Lu-Ghan Kaisan Pit, as well as any exploits it may have."

"You would make me an enemy of Kaisa?"

"You believe that he would assume you gave him up?" Saoiri paused her fiddling and gazed down at Madame Reaper. "Will you take the gamble? You first, you know."

"It's hardly a secret. You can get there through his recruitment teams any day."

"Competition isn't on the table."

"Is this indeed resistance work, Saoiri of Kilrona?" Madame Reaper considered Saoiri for a long moment, then cast her scrutinising gaze across the group of them, flickering her attention mainly between Seraeyu's masked form and the looming shadow of a hooded Jaspen beside him. "Or is this perhaps something *else*. It's odd that a Sirin would be in your employ."

"A free enticement: this is well beyond the Resistance."

The Madame hummed, then smiled with all the smarmy fervour someone in her line of work could muster. "You've intrigued me. It's in the wraith-trodden lands. Where the ancient powers coalesce, so they say. Where the bones of monsters are said to lie, and alica wells deep in forgotten stratum. That is to say: go to the consecrated plains at the edge of the Fan-Bhan region; you'll find it in the holy rock stacks. Funny, isn't it?"

Saoiri showed little reaction, except her staunch attention. "And exploits?"

"You expect me to know—"

"He comes and goes enough," Saoiri cut her off.

The Madame gave her a furtive glare, then she said, "He is a prideful man. A visionary, deceptively or not. Not every Kaisan wishes him their guide, however, their guide he will remain until some better alternative presents themselves a viable option. It's an apathetic realms we live in. Not much shines brighter than a sharpened blade pointed towards the future. And, what else have you to show me?"

"What if—" Seraeyu began, taking a step forward. Sakaeri forced herself steady. Let him do what he did best: *talk*. "What if, I shine that barest bit brighter, *Madame*?" He stood before the garish furnishings, and Saoiri slipped to the side, allowing him centre stage. "What if I shape the definition of something more enticing? What if I provide an avenue that Kaisa, in all his haughty ostentation, cannot? What if *I* am the hand that, as you may favour it, reaps the rewards of the future to come?"

Sakaeri saw the moment the Madame laid eyes on his face, the colour draining from her own. It was, perhaps, the first of the few interactions she'd had with the woman where she looked not only surprised but quite possibly astonished at just who entered her vision.

"Praetor Thasian," Madame Reaper muttered, just a wisp in the wind.

"Chaos is coming, Madame," Seraeyu told her, and Sakaeri could hear his put-on grin. "You'd best choose your alliances wisely."

"You say this as if you declare war," Madame Reaper said, everything about her presence icy and equally frozen.

Seraeyu considered her quietly a moment, then said, "I needn't declare anything. You know as well as I do that a silent war has already begun."

"And here you, inherited leader of all Raenaru, stand with a member of the Resistance, daughter of the sea-buried Dread Pre'ach'an." Madame Reaper's steely eyes dragged from Seraeyu to Saoiri, then to Sakaeri before they landed on Jaspen. "As well as a Sirin who ought to be dead, and whomever this mysterious fellow might be. Indeed, you paint an intriguing picture." The Madame blinked slow, pursing her lips, then she smirked at Seraeyu and drummed her long, aubergine nails against her cheek. "From the looks of it, Praetor darling, you hold alliances with everyone and no one. With whom do I speak? The fearsome heir of the Thasian, the holder of the ages-old Legacy, or with the second son, Seraeyu Thasian? I have not forgotten the boy you were mere months ago. Have you truly changed so much?"

"You ask as if I can't be both," Seraeyu said, flat and steady.

Sakaeri watched as his hands clasped behind his back, woven fingers hidden from Madame Reaper's gaze. She flicked her focus back over his shoulder, waiting for the Madame to say something she might regret. Something that might sow her fate, as it were.

"We all have many masks, Seraeyu Thasian. I only wonder who's left barefaced beneath them. A tyrant or a king? A martyr or a prophet? A fool or a hero?"

"Are those not all one and the same?"

Madame Reaper huffed an entertained laugh, dropping her chin into her palm, eyelashes drooping as she watched Seraeyu. "So a king must be a tyrant? A prophet a martyr, and a hero a fool?"

"Often that's the case, yes."

"Then might you fit that schema?"

"I'm no king. The Council exists for a reason, and I mean to see that realised. I've not died, and I don't speak of a greater being who guides me – I will leave those summations to the Clerics. I've been fooled one too many times to consider myself gullible now, and hero is a title awarded by the public who witnesses a great feat, it's not something I can claim myself. I am simply a man who holds his own beliefs. They've taken me here. So this is what you see: nothing more than what stands before you."

"Would you like to know what I see, Seraeyu Thasian?" The Madame curled her lips, her jewellery jingling as she offered a tilted, wolfish smile. "I see a blade. Whether it's radiant or with a fine edge, well … that's up to you, isn't it?"

CHAPTER TWENTY-NINE

"It's not that I don't trust your judgement—"

"But you don't."

"—I just fail to see the logic in sharing your intention to seek out that wretched Kaisa's lair, when she's clearly in cahoots with the fanged smokeserpent."

Seraeyu paused beside Sakaeri, his eyes squeezing shut like he was wrangling patience all the way from his toes. Rain spat down from the sky far above, washing the atmosphere with a sluggish and dreary grey, rising steam diffusing the glow of signs and long verticals of light, spearing up to greater heights. Most of Bhu-Nan's city-dwellers rushed for cover under bridges and awnings, but some embraced the sombre drenching from the heavens, lumbering towards whatever destination might be calling their name. Then there were the folks who had nowhere else to be, the ones in gateways and under meagre substitutes for shelter. It was an image Sakaeri herself recognised from her youth.

"It was a quick and easy way to get an answer, and I'm afraid time is not on our side," said Seraeyu. Ahead of him, Jaspen flicked a soggy cigarette from his fingers – a profound failure in the damp surrounds – and he offered a glare over his shoulder that looked as if he may very literally be biting his tongue. At that, Sakaeri raised a brow.

"The rail line can get us to the edge of the region. Even if we left right this moment, Seraeyu, word could surely get to Kaisa by then," said Saoiri. "The quickest route might take two days. It's a big risk."

"But *we* are here, and *he* is there. Suppose he did turn tail immediately, wouldn't that still leave us at least a day ahead of him?" Seraeyu asked, brushing past both the stagnant Jaspen and Saoiri to tread on ahead. Sakaeri was pretty sure she heard something under his words. Some sense of panic. A seeded worry that was twisting its thorny roots into his system. "If not now, when? He – I think he—" Seraeyu sighed, then whispered over his shoulder. "I think he *knows*. If he does, he hardly sees me as a threat, and rather a much more useful tool. I'm very much done playing others' games, thank you. It's time to play my own."

The roar picked up as the sky's pelting got heavier, soaking through their hoods, darkening their shoulders. The starts of a low, rushing flood rose across the streets, carrying debris and harried shouts with it. A powder-ore tube cracked at its bottom beside Sakaeri, its glowing dust syphoning out and draining, leaving that corner a little darker than before.

"Tell us what you want to do," Sakaeri called above the rapturous din.

"I need to know," Seraeyu called back, trudging against the roughening flow.

"Know what?" It was Jaspen who shouted out this time, taking one heavy step behind the Praetor. Sakaeri thrust her hand back and wrapped it around the most waifish of their crew, pulling Saoiri along with their stride.

"If he figured it out!" Seraeyu's voice was beginning to drown under the torrent.

"Figured what out?" Sakaeri yelled, squinting against her blurred vision.

Seraeyu stopped and turned, and he could only barely be heard behind Yisuna's mask, "Alkonos."

"What is this alkonos?" Saoiri asked where they'd sheltered in an elevated alcove. A sudden river rushed beside its entrance. They aimed to wait it out. It never lasted too long.

Seraeyu breathed in deep and gently rubbed water off the Yisuna mask in his hand, watching as stray drops hurtled to the ground. "I found a tome. It was locked away in the catacombs, behind a runic lock of some kind. A glyph, as I now know it. It was a Cleric's manuscript. An account of the far ancient past. It spoke of a greater purpose; a duty to carry the burdens of continued prosperity. But I read it for what it was: putrid, twisted recounts.

"It held several testimonies. The tale of the Yun-Thay, a mortal weapon bred for militant order, perfectly engineered to bleed resources dry with the greatest efficiency, all in the name of the Yun. It is no – it is no *wonder*. No miracle. There is alica, the threads of elemental force, and there is alkonos, the metaphysical that binds it. A spectrum of power; creation to destruction and back again. And then, there is the Alkonos, the great wide – it may well be the Great Starry Sea itself, I don't know. And I have been holding on to this – this *nonsense*—"

"The Yun?" Saoiri cut in, and it was only then how entranced Sakaeri realised she'd been. The researchers were *right*. A boundless, endless sea they all resided, full of wild energies and lights and life. How spectacular it all was. How blasphemous it all was.

"The Yun," Seraeyu repeated, then his gaze found Sakaeri's. "If you had the power ..." he trailed, and she was reminded of his words *to dismantle the realms themselves.*

"I trust you," she told him.

Seraeyu licked his lips, made a distressed sort of noise, then asked, "What is a god, really? Perhaps the Yun were, to some. A peoples, or maybe an organisation that sailed the Great Starry Sea, conquering, as far as I can surmise. The Thay were property, for lack of a better word, of the Yun. Reared in facilities of powers I don't understand, mechanics that sound fiction, brought into being by fusing some embryo of Sírin makeup. And the Sírin ... There were notes. A journal belonging to Ka'la'drius, a Mhedoonian man. Raeyu had it shoved behind books in her room. He'd joined the Yun voluntarily, some regime of strict training. Learnt about things he wasn't meant to know through his partner, who's now wrapped a piece of herself around my soulsong. A Yun-Thay, the *purest* of the Thay, a mix of the subjugated Sírin and those of Ca'loran descent; another realm colonised – lost. Or thought to be."

"A realm thought lost?" Saoiri whispered. The air around them felt condensed, weighted with this very moment. This one conversation.

Seraeyu nodded. "I presume it's what you're thinking."

"But *I* am the closest to Thay?" Sakaeri asked unbidden. She hadn't meant to, not really, but Seraeyu's wry smile eased her towards the answer.

"I said the Yun colonised that realm, yes? Often this comes with the problem that, soon, not everyone fits. Ideals, space, commodities, resources. Mhedoon was, at some point, not inhabited by Mhedoonians. At least not until Ca'lorans were cast off to what was written to then be frozen wastes. No idea what Mhedoon play resident to before Ca'loran undesirables were exiled to it."

"You're telling me that I'm ... Ca'loran?" Saoiri asked, sceptical.

Seraeyu turned to her with a frown. "Are you? Some ancestry, maybe. But is that what dictates you?" He took a sharp inhale, lifting his hands, curling his fingers inwards, nails sharp, but not near enough the talons Amanastré boasted. "These are Sírin, if we speak of ancestral heritage." His palm brushed over one of his cured horns, gripping it as he said, "As are these. So, am I Sírin? Am I Yu-ta? Am I a man of Raenaru? Am I indeed a Yun; will I demand worship? Or am I Thay-cee-en, a demarcation of my lost experiment label, a bred and designed mutation towards whatever machine of war they wanted to create?" He looked up, staring right at Saoiri as he asked, "Will you too call me a chimaera?"

"This ... doesn't make sense. If the Yun were this ceaseless organisation of militia, then where are they now? How does an entity that strong just disappear?" Saoiri's question rang a brief silence between them, and Sakaeri didn't want to consider her non-answer too long. She knew of those who hated the Yu-ta. Feared them. She didn't think Saoiri was one, but doubt expanded in the wake of quiet.

"A coup, and a rebellion. Led by two soldiers who were meant to suffer for eternity as aethereal batteries. Gifted to the Thay-cee-en who gave them up, rewarded with a lasting Legacy for it. The Yun were decimated. And whoever they may have been, they may well live among us, their children's children's children, on Quinga. Raenaru. Lu-Ghan. They were stamped out, so isn't interesting that there is one cult claiming the benevolence of the Yun? Snatching children when they're said to be *gifted*? Who founded the clergy but a god themselves, unable to relinquish their chokehold on power? I don't know what secrets they keep in their compounds, but I imagine they're even more enlightening than what I've scraped from what's really a fan letter and classroom notes."

Sakaeri watched as Seraeyu smiled wide, almost serene.

"And that is what I know. That's why she hated them, the Yu-ta.

Descendents of the Thay-cee-en and Thay-cee-en-ee who followed them; those who gave her and Ka'la'drius up. Who cratered their operation from the inside out. A manifestation of anguish and anger. Who claimed to resonate with me, ha! What a lovely, horrible thing to say to a person."

"I am not a follower of the Yun faith," Jaspen said quietly, tentatively. "If what you say is true, this would cause uproar. The very hierarchy that is the foundation for many, whether they revere or hate Yu-ta, the Yun, the idea that there is or is not ascendant beings, watchful and omniscient. That it is forces of alica, and perhaps this alkonos, that apathetically weave what we know to be life ... and it's – what of the great beasts? Those that embodied alica, those that were said to be hunted for game and greed and riches?"

Seraeyu stilled, contemplative. Then, with uneasy regard, he said, "There was a passage. In this Ka'la'drius's journal. A field mission. The Yun favoured potent alicant, which often came with dangers. They'd been deployed on Orin, which he claimed was beyond renown in its beauty, and they plundered a mountain rife with rich ore veins ... taking down the beast which guarded it. He wrote that it was like murdering the mountain itself, a creature of that kind of wonder. I – there may have been—"

"The Yun doomed us." Jaspen cursed under his breath, trying to pluck his pack of cigarettes from his soggy pocket. "What glory do we have left? A broken realm with an environment inhospitable, our resources butchered like a pufferpig. Our own gods slain by marauding imposters. And still we claim that glory be to Orin, and glory be to Orin's—" Jaspen cut off, his hands twitching with failed efforts to light his cigarette, eyes wide and unwittingly meeting Sakaeri's own.

"Majesty," she finished for him.

"Orin's majesty," Jaspen whispered back, looking one word away from frustrated tears.

"Even if, once upon some forgotten time, Orinian folk fought for their realm and not their Majesty, the Dracon, they take up arms for her whim today," Saoiri reminded. "We don't live in this awful past, however true or false it is. We live *today*. When Mhedoon sits oppressed. Where Orin crumbles more daily, pushing further into Raenaru through *your* good graces, *Praetor*. Tenebrana still wallows, forgotten, and both Lu-Ghan and Quinga are desperate to cling onto their sovereignty. There are problems we face here, now, without the distraction of the past!"

"You're a foolish child," Sakaeri sneered at her, taking a moment to wring a section of her cloak. "If you think nothing just said would affect the wars waged in sequestered corners, you do not understand the realms and their follies. Those who vie for power will use any fodder afforded to them, and this – all this – is a catastrophe on a silver platter. Imagine telling a populace that the gods they worship are false, cruel invaders who sought their realms resources alone. You've seen one example already. Imagine confirming the fears of those Yu-ta xenophobes, that our heritage is mottled in experimentation. People believe Raenaru untouchable since the

Thasian are blessed with divine power, but—"

"But I am just a man," Seraeyu cut in. "And I don't want our next era soaked in bloodshed. And not *our* as in Raenaru, but the realms. If this Kaisa understands alkonos, the history or the practice, he could usher in a new age of Yun under a different name – do you see it? He may not sail the stars, but he has a wide web, many followers, and is himself a tactician who, I would assume, keeps a close cohort of equally ambitious individuals. And, lest we forget, Sakaeri herself confirmed that the clergy wanted Kaisa dead. If my assumptions are correct, and their fanatic faith is based on the insidious ideas of whatever Yun evangelised enough to gain a following, then they would fear Kaisa for only one reason."

"That Kaisa might crush the Yun faith altogether, through some means," said Sakaeri.

"The Stimfal, then?" Jaspen asked.

Seraeyu cocked his head, confused, so Sakaeri added, "When Aeyun paid a visit, he'd said someone from the Pit mentioned the name. I've not heard of it, but I can only imagine it has something to go with stim itself."

"There is something," Saoiri began, hesitant, "that I've overheard in my time in the Resistance. Some folks had participated in his games for some coin. They said the prize was some position in his ranks. I think it was that; the Stimfal. And … it's, well, it's quite obvious … but Kaisa is his title. The Kaisan Pits have been around longer than him. No one knows who Kaisa actually is – the fact that we *do*, at least in terms of his appearance, is uncommon. But we don't know who Kaisa is, not really. He, like Seraeyu, is not a monolith, but a man with a past. If he knows so much … how?"

Seraeyu squinted up at the sky beyond towering structures, rain falling lighter now, traversable. "And how much? Settled then, are we? Let's go."

CHAPTER THIRTY

"Cah eh'ju, a'garu ca'ju," Davah repeated the Ca'loran mantra, muttered under his breath. Aeyun's murmurs echoed his own, and he spared his herald of disaster a look of disdain.

They'd not yet been able to shake the restless spirits from following them, their lingering gloom drawn to their group like bugs to a fire. When Aeyun had said it was a task neglected, he hadn't anticipated learning that Aeyun's mother was a soothsayer, shunned by Holden Folk. Nor had he expected both Da'garu and Aeyun to start stringing up shards of animal bone around their campsites. It was like watching someone turn in a circle, only to emerge like they were upside down and backwards. A'vor da'Ca'ille had burst forth from his own grave, and he looked the part with ivory accoutrements strung and wrapped around his limbs like ceremonial garb. Davah considered his own new bracelet of wiseowl bones; Aeyun said their remnant of soulsong warded against malevolent wraiths. Davah wasn't so sure.

As always, Aeyun propped up Azura in the near middle of the camp. Its pearly, striated face stood guard against a world unseen, just beyond the radiance of Vitality.

"They're anxious." Aeyun looked up at the cracking sky above them, its pastels burning grey and ashen on their fault lines. "Maybe they feel something on the horizon."

"Yeah, friend, the same thing the rest of us do; dread," said Davah. He circled the camp one more time, repeating his learnt verbal command to dispel soulsongs in limbo, guiding them back to the vast beyond. Trailing him, Da'garu's eyes dimmed from their glowing white sheen as she nodded. The job was done for the moment.

"We have to find that dagger. There has to be a way," Aeyun muttered, conducting his new ritual of tossing flaxen petals into the fire, yet another ward he'd procured.

"Remind me what that does?" Davah asked.

Aeyun looked over and blandly offered, "Scares off the arachnistalks. They don't like the sweet smell of it."

"I think there just wasn't any space in that brain of yours to care for ore, huh? Now I understand. Herbs, bones, and smithing. That's what Aeyun is made of."

"The way the forest moves," Uruji began, standing from where he'd been rifling through his knapsack, pulling out a bound journal of notes he'd been jotting from the a'teneum's collection of tomes. "It should be near impossible to find one, isolated dagger, if it's here to be found at all. But if you can identify something I can pull on, maybe I can guide us. I've tracked trails in worse conditions following hollow resonances."

When the shadows appeared, Uruji prioritised his goals on the spot. Whatever ire he held for Davah, or even for Aeyun, was tossed aside in favour of practical planning. Davah could appreciate that, even if Uruji's sudden business-like regard left him feeling like he was walking with two left feet, the oldest of their group yet likely not the wisest. Even so, Davah didn't need wisdom; he'd survived on cunning this long.

"Stories to tell, little brother?" Davah asked jovially, nudging a branch dangling clacking bone just a smidge to the right.

"Don't call me that," Uruji said calmly, then ignored him as if he were a needy child and proceeded to talk to the perceived adult Davah just arrived next to: Aeyun. "Was it like my own? Can you remember? Any distinct features it held?"

Aeyun tossed one last petal into the fire and watched the flames curl in a daze, entranced. "Maybe. It had a nephrite blade. I don't think that nephrite can be found here. Not in The Hold, and likely nowhere in the Ou'grove." Aeyun turned towards Da'garu curiously, who was solemnly gazing past the edges of their site. She must have felt his appraisal, her chin twisting over her shoulder. "Da'garu, have you come across a stone that holds solid strands of a sort of purple-black on its face? It would be glassy in appearance and smooth to the touch. You've not, have you?"

Da'garu contemplated a moment. As she sieved through memories, Davah listened to the rustles of the shifting forest and wished it was the Great Starry Sea above him, not some ripping, imitation watercolour. He missed the brisk air of the open ocean, or even the muggy refrain of a city in the sweltering heat. Instead, his nostrils filled with an unfamiliar sharp scent of muddy stagnation, only shifted when the breeze deigned to shuffle the smell of damp and dusk. There was no freedom here, and Davah longed to revive the feeling.

Da'garu's conclusion came with the shake of her head and a tiny, frowned pout. On observation alone, her mannerisms were far removed from Aeyun's. Time and place had structured them, and Davah found it a wonder that Da'garu retained a strange whimsy at all, given the truths of her background.

"Nephrite, then," Aeyun told Uruji, who nodded in affirmative. "You have any?"

"I do," Raeyu spoke up, turning her attentions towards their gathered group, pulling it from where she'd been counting their rations. "In my bag. That glove – you know it."

Uruji blinked a few times, startled, then asked, "You carry that with you?"

"It's a reminder," Raeyu said, then turned her back to them once more, dividing and re-dividing groups of nuts and berries.

"What's the glove?" Davah asked, curiosity getting the better of him.

"It's from that day. Worn when we first came here," Uruji supplied, fishing through Raeyu's belongings to retrieve the elusive article.

"Nephrite – a training glove?" Aeyun asked, then he muttered to

Davah, "It's armoured but agile, good for emulating a gauntlet without the bulky restriction."

Uruji gave a small *ah-ha!* of success, pulling out the dark-threaded glove, its top indeed shielded with a frame of nephrite boning. "Alright. Let me try tuning. We may get lucky yet." The silence that followed was pierced with cries of stirring critters well into the wood. Davah began to feel as if the whole labyrinth of trees watched them, peeling back layers to peer at their efforts in amusement. When Uruji suddenly opened his eyes and smiled, the curve of it looking like it would suit Aeyun all too well, it didn't surprise Davah when he said, "I felt something."

"It keeps moving!" Uruji groaned frustratedly.

"No, we're moving," Aeyun rebuked, just as flustered.

They'd been trying to triangulate the precise location of the missing dagger for two far too long days now, and Davah wasn't finding the brothers' banter cute anymore.

"I'm telling you, Aeyun, the dagger is moving," Uruji said through gritted teeth. Aeyun shifted Azura on his back and gave Uruji a deadpan look. "It is! I'm trying to do what you instructed: breathe with the forest, sense its flow. Its flow is not moving the same direction as the dagger. The dagger is *moving*."

"You sure you're not just confused, small-god?" Davah asked idly, squinting into the brush ahead of them. The flow of the forest, what bollocks. It was like being sucked into an undertow, carried by the water's whim. Davah could get general notions of *this way* or *that way*, but it was never a cardinal direction, instead a shove or a push, his body feeling the incline before his feet landed.

"No, I'm not confused. The resonance of the nephrite is very clear, piercing through, and it's almost like the forest is twisting in concentric rings. Not entirely uniform, really, but one leap one direction should compensate a jog in the opposite one. But it's not."

"If it's moving," Aeyun said, looking like he swallowed bitter swill, "*if* you're right – that means it's moving."

"Stellar observation, Aeyun," Uruji said dully.

Aeyun groaned under his breath and continued, "No, I mean, it's moving because someone is moving it. Someone has it, and someone is moving around the Ou'grove. And that's—"

Da'garu suddenly bolted to the front of their group and slammed a finger over her mouth to incite their silence. She then raised both hands and dropped them lower, implying they should get closer to the forest floor. Davah had long learnt to trust local advice when given in urgency, so he obliged her command, watching as Raeyu, Uruji, and Aeyun all followed suit. Da'garu crouched and led them towards a small canopy made by a fallen tree crashed into its brethren, offering just enough shelter to shield from whatever threat encroached.

The air changed direction and blew rancid, Davah's nose crinkling in response. He shifted and accidentally nudged Raeyu, who glanced at him unappreciatively, but otherwise ignored him.

Shrew, Davah thought.

A rustling grew and blurry figures filtered into view between the trunks of trees, their auras seeping a sickly aether that seemed to pull and bend the surrounding light. Each edge of their limbs warped uncannily, and Davah's throat caught; these phantoms bled unease, their drifting forms sowing dread and strange tidings.

Da'garu watched them slip across sprigs of flora, short stalks fluttering in their wake, her eyes tracking them like a fencat watching someone circumnavigate their territory. Aeyun was leant up beside her, his gaze tracking the same direction. At least until he glanced at Davah once, then twice, with confusion. Davah raised his eyebrows back at him, then turned forward once more on instinct, forcing a shout down when a warbling, pulsing absence of light sat where a face should have been, only a hairsbreadth from his own.

The Ca'lorans of their crew tensed, their attention snapping to the mournful spirit that peered with a curious, tilting head at Davah. Despite this one's departure from the pack, the other figures slunk on, filtering in and out of sight in the distance. This one, however, continued to leer, and Davah's skin crawled when a notion of being witnessed crept down his spine. The spirit bristled, its odd shape growing and spiking, almost as if spooked.

Davah tried to keep all his blood in his head. He couldn't pass out and very well fall into this thing. This thing that Aeyun implied was a wandering shadow of a forlorn soulsong. This thing not yet dissipating and re-joining the Grand Symphony that played eternal. Which was a bit sad, wasn't it? In that moment, the puffing, formless being before him took on a wistful hue, and Davah frowned. It was only right that one hoped to find peace one day, right? Whomever or whatever this was, it was yet to be graced with it, and Davah hadn't realised he'd extended his palm until the phantom creature jerked to seemingly peer down at it.

Eejit, he reprimanded himself, but didn't withdraw his hand. The spirit stilled, its edges smoothing. It tentatively swerved to the right, then to the left, then it extended its own touch. On contact, loneliness carried through, and Davah felt shame and a stretching denial wash over him. Long, so long, trudging through ruins, red and blazing, then grey and smouldering. Long, so long, going in circles, can't be found, long, so long. It was green, but it was grey. Colour was gone, nothing remained. A great everything of nothing.

"*A'garu, ca—*" his mouth was whispering, but the spirit quivered and he paused, "*. . . ju.*"

"*Juuu,*" the being hissed, and it should have sounded menacing. Somehow, in the walls of Davah's consciousness, it blended into something horribly tender and sombre.

"Don't you want to?" he asked quietly, forgetting himself, his company, and the learnt fact that he shouldn't be entertaining the strange phantom.

"*Juuu*," the spirit hissed again. "*Caaa*."

"*A'ca*," said Davah. "Yeah, I – I exist. I'm here."

"*Caaa*," the phantom groaned, the sound of it bending unnaturally.

"Not here," he told it. "Up there; out there. It's time, isn't it? To return to the beyond? *A'garu, ca ju* – yeah?" Davah clenched his fingers around something incorporeal, but desperately real in his palm. It should, shouldn't it? This wandering shadow surely wanted rest, didn't it? "*Cah* – go, aren't you tired?"

"*Neee*." Its spectral body fizzled with defiance. "*A'nammm, ca'aaa*."

"*Nam?*" Davah asked confusedly, then said, "So, no? You want to wander more? Not done yet?"

"*A'nammm, ne cahhh*."

"Yeah, okay," Davah told the flickering form retreating from him. "Do as you like, then. Maybe find me when you're ready, I guess."

"*Juuu*."

"Yep. Me. Now go on, you'll lose your friends."

"*Cahhh*," the spirit hissed, waning out of view, drifting back.

"Yep, my strange friend. Bye now," Davah jiggled the fingers of his now achingly cold hand. "See you around."

It didn't take much longer for the wispy shadow to slide into the gaps between trees, shifting out of eyesight entirely. The heart lodged in his throat dropped and Davah inhaled deeply, shaking out his arm, turning to the group – who all stared at him like *he* was the spirit.

"What?" he asked.

"What in the world were you talking to?" Uruji asked when he'd got a brief and squeaked affirmation from Aeyun that it was safe to speak.

Davah blinked. "What do you mean?"

"You were talking to the wind, pirate. Or so it looked," Raeyu admitted, turning her attention to Aeyun at the end of her statement. Aeyun spared her a quick glance, his face an unnatural pallid, stark against the green background of the Ou'grove.

"No, I wasn't," Davah answered lamely, following it with an apprehensive, "right?"

"What did you see?" Aeyun asked, swallowing thickly.

"Some phantom, I don't know. Same as you, yeah?"

"Yeah, but … those shadows aren't typically seen by someone not attuned to Vitality," Aeyun told him, slowly lifting himself from the ground. "And they don't *talk*."

Davah cocked his head and hummed. "I mean, have you ever tried? It wasn't ready to go, it said so."

"Yeah," Aeyun said, sounding like it should have been a *no*. "It did. I've never seen that. Those lingerers are usually horribly aggressive. Why do you think we send them at every campsite perimeter?"

"Because it's your forgotten duty, and you're just doing it? Did you ever consider they might be a part of the Grand Symphony as well? In their own way?" Davah didn't miss the way Da'garu's gaze grew wide and glassy and inspired. She almost looked like a young Saoiri when he'd tell her stories about her mother's antics. "What's it lingering for anyway? If this is all it has left, maybe it'll figure it out before the final send-off. Wouldn't you want that chance?"

"Davah, you don't get it. Best-case scenario, they leech off people, feeding off their energy while following them. It's terribly unnerving for the host; like they're constantly exhausted. Worst case, a group of them prey on a vulnerable victim, making them lose their wits entirely, their soulsong becoming so twisted it's unrecognisable." Aeyun rubbed his hand from his nose to chin, heaving a heavy sigh. "And you just had a nice little *chat* with the thing."

"I don't know what to tell you, friend," Davah told him. Truly, he didn't. "I just remembered back at the temple and those Sirin who lingered there. Probably a shock for them, right? This thing, it touched me, and I felt … I don't know. Something dire. Maybe saw where it died. Steely ruins on fire."

"Steel?" Aeyun asked. "Ruins of steel on Ca'lorus?"

Huh, yeah, didn't consider that, Davah thought. Ca'lorus was either trees or the mismatch of stone and vines in The Hold. No predominant steel anywhere.

It was Uruji who spoke what they were all presumably thinking:

"Did you see a vision from beyond the Ou'grove?"

CHAPTER THIRTY-ONE

The bloodbarley danced in dusk time breeze, winding through an undulating landscape of deep ruby. Around them, the air was light and powdery, the heat and thickness of the dry lands beyond the mountains. It was the time of day where pyreflies came out to play, a seldom stray light flickering across darkening horizons. Sakaeri dusted her fingers across the tops of the fluffed stalks, looking over her shoulder towards the solitary freight stop in the distance.

They had been able to bribe a distributor, climbing into a big empty car, barrelling towards the middle of nowhere. It hadn't escaped notice, either, the sparseness of the enclosure. Sakaeri wondered if he would have taken less to transport them, if he was hard-up for business. This year's yield was a disappointment, she heard.

Seraeyu had traipsed ahead, stomping with his knees high, his borrowed Yisuna mask slung around his neck in the absence of a crowd. Sakaeri watched him, his silhouette framed by the greying sky and held in a sea of gentle scarlet. He peered into the distance, studying the ridge of cresting peaks, then he turned back to the rest of them, the breeze twisting ever so slightly with him.

In that one, solitary moment, she watched him with eyes focused on future visions of what may be hope and a silly desire for something *better*. His choices, she realised, were now his own, and she was curious what he would do with them.

The glow of pyreflies reflected across his dark, amber-brown eyes, and his expression held the weight of a thousand questions, all of which pulled at a different, bare-thread string. No longer was he the child following the back of his towering sister, nor was he a neglected son begging for attention. Seraeyu was a man who had come into his own, forced into decisions that no one should have to make. Even so, he stood with grace befitting his disposition, passionate and moulded by a realms too conniving for his soft heart. And she was proud, she acknowledged, to know him, even if the vast majority of those who spoke his name never truly would. It was stranger still when a lengthening distance partitioned Raeyu and Seraeyu in her mind.

Through younger eyes, Sakaeri viewed him as a nuisance. Now he was nothing but light, despite the dark that sparked this whole ordeal. Brutally, her mind asked, *is Raeyu truly the shining sun I painted her to be*?

"Sakaeri," Seraeyu called, Jaspen and Saoiri joining him ahead, they too gazing back at her. The three of them considered her with nothing snide, nothing disgusted or fearful, only a docile and fragile trust, forged in the most unlikely of scenarios. "Aren't you coming along?"

Sakaeri breathed in the scent of wheaten landscapes, the evening's serenity softening the stony wall inside of her chest. "Always," she told him.

It was nighttime when they reached the base of the mountains guarding the transition from the consecrated plains to the holy rock stacks and the desert they sat within. With the daytime temperatures cooled in the evening's embrace, it was safer to travel without fear of sweating their wits right through their pores. Instead, Jaspen led the pack with a sustained flame burning above his palm, their group squeezing into the narrows of a pass.

Distant howls harmonised with the crunches of dirt and rock below their feet, and the occasional brush of some variety of animal running across the foothills had Sakaeri's eyes darting around them, searching for menacing or suspect auras. Aether flowed in balance, however, nothing spiking or sporadic. The only discordant resonance remained Seraeyu, who seemed to absorb greater energy than he output. It made her wonder precisely how Essence functioned in parallel to other forces. If that energy grew within him, mustn't it be expelled in some way? Surely it was unhealthy to skew towards all that destructive power. Was it tearing him apart from the inside, too?

It was around another bend that the reflection of a firepit flashed across the clay-striped walls of the pass, the echoes of an impromptu campground bouncing off their faces.

Seraeyu re-secured his mask, and Jaspen and Sakaeri matched stride to lead, hands on the hilts of their respective weapons. Jaspen's temperament changed, structured to the point of fabricated, a false sense of ease emanating from his form. Sakaeri allowed him to take point as they twisted around the curve of a rocky ledge, a modest site coming into view.

A pair of caravans were parked in the innermost edge of a flat alcove, a fire kindled between them with five individuals huddled around it. They were dressed in practical wandering attire, but each had at least one less-than-practical alicant accessory on their person, professing their status of relative success.

Merchants, Sakaeri concluded, studying their packed cargo. Scavengers of the holy desert, selling their rare finds for significant profit.

"Well, hello, folks," one of them said with a wave and a beckoning smile. He was the tallest among them, slim and lanky, his dark hair tied loosely at the nape of his neck. "Funny to see a group of wanderers out this far and this late. Can us humble sort help you any? Lastminute wares for … wherever you're headed?"

"A generous offer," Jaspen said, walking forward with practised pacing. Sakaeri could practically see his soldier training ingrained in each step. Never a blind spot open. "We're only passing through. Any trouble ahead?"

"No, no. Not much of anything hides in the sands and tundra. Legend has it that any with impurity of heart burn under the sun's harsh glare." The merchant paused to think, grinning. "Though, I guess that might leave room for the impure to wander under the cover of night."

"I came across a tunneller once," the woman nearest the fire contributed, puffing a few rings of smoke from a long pipe. "Damn near lost my nerve to ever go back." She sighed, crossing one lithe leg over the other. "Yet here I am with this guild again."

"Can't forget about the bones," a petite man groused, oiling the blade of his sword without glancing up. "Not sure I want to know what monstrosity that belonged to."

"Well, thank you," Jaspen said, aiming to bypass them, hesitating to allow Seraeyu time to walk on his side furthest from the merchants.

The petite man flickered his sharp eyes up, his sword-caring efforts halted. Sakaeri watched as his aura stitched tight, his own modified eyes latching onto hers. Unlike hers irises, however, his displayed horizontal pupils, their furrows a harsh mix of purple and red, stark against dusty skin. "Hold on, now," he told them.

Sakaeri narrowed her focus to him, sifting through memories and trying to figure out if she knew this man. It wasn't common for people to experiment with their eyes outside of undergoing the procedure to become an Eye. The next foremost profession was when one became a Sirin. And this man was not someone she recognised from the ranks.

When it felt like he should have said something more, he only stared at her, his gaze just as peeling at her own. Finally, he gruffly asked, "You've got business out there?"

Sakaeri schooled her face. He considered her *something*, but it wasn't Sirin, was it?

"Yes," she decided.

"Don't recommend it," he continued, frowning. There was a hitch of hesitation, then he broke their stare and went back to his blade. "Foul stuff, all that."

"Len," the overly freckled woman beside his admonished, "stop sticking your rotten nose where it doesn't belong. They want trouble, they can find it. Long as it doesn't kill our profits, it's their funeral."

The man, Len, grunted but didn't look up again.

Sakaeri sensed Jaspen bristling before she even turned to him, so as a matter of placation she pounded a heavy fist on his sternum and said, "We'll be off, then; our funeral is waiting."

The last of their mercantile group, a greasy faced man who'd maybe had one malted drink too many, stifled a laugh at that, raising a hand in farewell. "Not sure what a Yu-ta is doing all the way out here anyway," he muttered.

Sakaeri felt every muscle in her body tense. She was yet to look fully away from the man with the mutated eyes, who hadn't bothered to look back up, but she saw the remaining three beyond him shift their direction, curiosity baited.

Had it been her or Seraeyu the man referred to?

"It is strange, isn't it?" the freckled woman said, leaning forward where she sat on a protruding rock. The drunkard beside her cackled something frothy, a dribble escaping the corner of his mouth when he took another hefty swig.

"Thought we didn't stick our noses where they don't belong," Len murmured, his cleaning cloth squeaking across metal.

"We're just passing through," Jaspen reiterated.

"Won't be bothering you further," Saoiri added, pushing Seraeyu ahead of her with a clipped laugh.

Sakaeri stood by her assessment that Saoiri would be a shite Sirin.

"We've no interest in trouble," Sakaeri assured the merchants, who now regarded her with wary appraisal. "Though, I have no problem causing a little while slipping by."

"Not interested in a fight, girl," Len said, finally looking back up. "If you're looking for what I think you are, we saw Jjenka and his crew headed eastbound. Like I said, wouldn't recommend it."

"Just curious," the woman with the long pipe said, holding the carved flute languidly, "the little fellow there in the nice cloak and the mask. Raenaruan, isn't it? Some spirit they revere?"

"You wouldn't be interested in selling the mask, would you?" the lanky man asked, tilting with an intrigued peer at Seraeyu, half-hidden behind Jaspen's shoulder.

"No," Seraeyu said simply.

"Shame. That's a shame." The woman toked out a few more smoky circles. "Would fetch a nice price in the right networks, that one."

"If you're done," Saoiri said impatiently.

"Your funeral," the freckled woman repeated, waving them off and losing interest.

"Word of advice," Len called, "retribution never served anyone well. The mask stands out, but your face does too."

And, finally, Sakaeri realised. This man knew her as the Widowmaker. She narrowed her gaze, asking, "East, you said?"

"East," he confirmed, yet again ignoring her for his favoured sword.

"Oh, wow," Saoiri murmured beyond the mountain pass.

The arid tundra mixed clay and sand, the holy stacks finally in view, the cradle they sat within stretching far beyond what the eye could witness. The sky above was not only obsidian but woven with trails of stars and rivers of colour not visible from the dense cities across the realms. The scenery was like a painting, contrived from the mind rather than built from nature and the disasters that carved it. And Sakaeri felt something here. Something ancient and thrumming; perhaps it was why the holy stacks were claimed holy.

The chill had set in, and the group of them walked closer now. Sakaeri relied on Saoiri's small magnavaid to point them east, and they trekked under a sea of glittering heavens, the ground they walked cold and silent.

"It's not fair to you all," Seraeyu told them, breaking the peace. "To drag you with me. Thank you for being a part of this, whatever it is. I won't forget it."

"He was right, that Len," Sakaeri admitted, scanning the desert ahead. "My reappearance will not go unnoticed, and your mask does stand out. It was two masked men who made a mockery of the Pit ... Idiots, the both of them."

"And Seraeyu Thasian will have less impact?" Seraeyu asked.

"If Seraeyu Thasian keeps his cowl up, yes."

"This is ... a much larger scale, but maybe we can do a one-two-three – um, four job, like how Davah, Aeyun, and I used to," Saoiri suggested, huddling her shoulders inwards for warmth. "One to watch, one to distract, and one to sneak in. Another for muscle, maybe?"

"What did Aeyun do?" Seraeyu asked.

"Watched."

"So Davah distracted?" Sakaeri snickered.

"Why do you figure that?" Saoiri turned to her, one eyebrow raised.

Sakaeri gave her a long look.

"Yeah, alright, he's a talker, he is. I snuck in, usually."

"So," Seraeyu interjected, "what? Who's who?"

"Well, really, you have to sneak in, don't you? Your feral form of aether may come in handy, or something. And you have to remain unseen anyway. And Sakaeri's eyes are best suited to watching, aren't they? That leaves muscle and a distraction. I ... don't really qualify for one of those." Saoiri gave a depreciating laugh, holding up her arm in example.

"What will you do?" Jaspen asked without humour. Sakaeri figured he didn't like the idea of anyone being placed in that role.

"Kaisa knows me, my face anyway, but his Kaisan may not. And, really, my main affiliation is Davah and Mhedoon for him. Maybe Pre'ach'an, if he bothered to learn that much." Saoiri stretched, then dropped her arm down, gazing purposefully away from the group of them. "Arguably, as part of the Resistance, I have a vested interest in gaining allies. It's not the worst angle."

"You'll guard me then, Jas?" Seraeyu smirked over at him, holding the Yisuna mask in his hand now, removed but not fully torn from his face.

All too seriously, Jaspen nodded and said, "With my life."

Seraeyu blinked once, then he looked down and his smile turned achingly gentle. "With anything but that, Jaspen."

A wave of something intangible pulsed through Sakaeri's body and she snapped her head away from them. In the far distance, in a cluster of holy stacks, flares of aether visible to her eyes whipped and then dissolved out of existence. It would burst forth like a rising balloon, then shatter and reform itself in a stream of constant energy at work.

"What is it?" Saoiri asked, having noticed Sakaeri's distracted gaze.
Sakaeri sneered at the ebbing aura ahead. "I found it."

CHAPTER THIRTY-TWO

One, two, three, stop.

Four, five, six, go. Good.

Sakaeri tracked Seraeyu and Jaspen as they disappeared into a mess of a crowd. Too many of them when there weren't matches going, too few for any sort of event. They looked like a strange mix of folks as well, many of them nervous. Sakaeri recognised that look. Flighty and jittery, some instead excited and antsy.

New recruits, they must have been.

The main hall was as over-the-top as everything else. Gilded in gold, tiled mosaics of battle scenes splashed across the ceiling. Sakaeri, balanced on metallic beams, wondered if she looked like a combatant herself from this far elevated. Some character in a story never told. Around her, above her head, people shouted with weapons brandished and elemental forces of alica swirling around them. It was a gaudy depiction of glory that never manifested the same in an actual fight.

No, when it came down to it, there was only adrenaline and the desire to keep living. Anyone who said they lived for battle had a screw loose. In those moments where Sakaeri *had* to fight, she never relished in it. There was one thought that played: *I have to.* For payment, to live, to finish this job. Then she would quash the guilt a move on, at least until she was alone, staring into the distance and wondering if she really *had to* after all.

Echoes bounced up from below, shoes shuffling on slabs of marble, and Sakaeri focused back on her duty: be the eyes. Watch their backs.

Saoiri had sweet-talked the Kaisan at the front, allowing the rest of them to sneak by – no thanks to Jaspen's almost-trip that nearly had him slamming into the back of booth – and she'd filtered into the same crowd, near them but at a distance. Good. This was going okay for now. Kaisa had been too confident, and his Kaisan too incompetent.

A bulky man with a stilted gait made a round far below where Sakaeri had perched herself. His finger pointed out at a wispy fellow in some form of pitiful intimidation. Sakaeri grimaced. She definitely didn't miss the Kaisan.

Seraeyu's hooded figure was drifting towards a hallway, and Sakaeri glanced to check her own entry point. There was a large gap for airflow, easy manoeuvring for her. Still going well.

Saoiri was chatting with a recruit, smiling in a friendly way. It was strange, Sakaeri considered, that she looked remarkably like Davah had when he'd first met Sakaeri. Saoiri had been paying attention, it seemed, and she chose to emulate him to *deceive*. It made sense, really, but it said nothing complimentary about Davah.

Thoughts of Klluna's imposed vision surfaced again. A shadow in the stars, the clangs of a hammer to an anvil, the girl who held Davah's hand. Had it been Saoiri's spirit, clinging to the man she knew, asking her to stay her blade? But who was it that needed protecting, because it had been Seraeyu who crumbled, but Davah's chest who took her dagger.

This alkonos was a funny business, and Sakaeri didn't know how to parse it. She could *walk* the Alkonos, Klluna had said. Was that her skill, walking a plane unreal, navigating a field unseen? Is that what it meant to be Yun-Thay? Or was it simply Sakaeri?

Seraeyu slipped into the hallway, Jaspen close behind him, and Sakaeri watched as no one took notice. A tad unorganised, weren't they?

Saoiri kept up her conversation, drawing the attention of a few others around her.

This was still going well.

Sakaeri snuck over the beam, tracking to the gap in the upper wall to remain above Seraeyu and Jaspen. There was a steep drop on the other side, the grandiose architecture fading into something more clinical and practical beyond its initial facia. Sakaeri checked behind her once, the recruits and their surly Kaisan command still none-the-wiser, and she kicked off the ledge, dropping down and tuning a quick gale to soften her silent landing.

Jaspen spared a look behind him, his mouth set in a firm line, and Sakaeri nodded at him in affirmation to continue on, letting her pace lag behind the pair of them. Seraeyu hadn't even turned at all, focused on his progress into the bowels of the Kaisan Pit.

They needed to get to higher ground. Kaisa's personal effects would be stashed away in his office, locked behind some barrier, Sakaeri was sure.

The quiet patter of feet indicated Saoiri's delayed arrival, joining them in the empty hall. It didn't take long for a stairwell to be located. It was still going smoothly, but there was something that ate at the ends of Sakaeri's nerves.

This was easy. And it shouldn't be easy.

By the time they'd trekked half the length of the Pit, climbing several stories higher, managing to elude the very few Kaisan roaming, Sakaeri's veins felt like they were on fire. One discretely exchanged glance with Jaspen, who still walked carefully several steps ahead, told her that he was having similar thoughts.

As if in response to their anticipation, a sharp, static noise crested in the silence and a once-still mini holocaster buzzed to life, particle ore dancing in its glassy panes. At this size, imaging was more nebulous, but it formed all the same, and Sakaeri's heart dropped as the blurry likeness of Jjenka appeared on the face of it.

"Oh, you *must* be stupid," Jjenka's voice rattled, his crooked smile the clearest visualisation. "You thought you could waltz in here undetected? You thought we wouldn't *know*?" Jjenka tutted and Sakaeri tore her attention from the holocaster, checking on Seraeyu, Jaspen, and Saoiri. Seraeyu hadn't stopped, so Sakaeri pinned her anxiety to the acrid hollowness in her stomach and continued forth. "We're coming for you, Bone Soldier."

That halted all progress.

They didn't speak, didn't dare, but when Seraeyu finally did peer over his shoulder, Sakaeri saw the same question in his gaze: Aeyun was here? Now?

A patter of quick feet sounded from the stairwell to Sakaeri's left. She slipped out a dagger, flattening herself to the door's edge, blade held aloft. And she almost stabbed the target, too. If it hadn't been Wen who looked at her with big, rounded eyes and surprise in her expression.

"Sa—Sakaeri," Wen sputtered, attention flitting from the sharp edge of the dagger to Sakaeri's dilated, hunt-ready eyes. "I hoped I'd never see you again."

Sakaeri didn't lower her weapon, but also didn't move to finish the deed. Instead, she simply stated, "Wen." Jjenka's obnoxious laughter sounded from the holocaster down the hall. His jeers continued, promising the Bone Soldier's doomed.

"What are you doing?" Jaspen hissed, his hand outstretched and ready to tune. His gaze was focused, steely, and Sakaeri wondered if, in that moment, he even had a second thought about the possibility of burning Wen to nothing but cinders.

Wen's eyes tracked from Sakaeri to Jaspen, to Seraeyu hidden behind him and Saoiri further still. Then she focused back to Sakaeri's blade. "Let me help you."

"Really?" Sakaeri asked flatly. "That easy?"

"Him, that soldier Jjenka's screaming about – he has a chance, doesn't he? It's unnatural, what he can do, but it might be enough to put an end to this horrible plan."

"What horrible plan?" Sakaeri pressed, shifting the dagger, forcing Wen's attention.

"What are you after? I'll help and I'll tell you what I know."

"Why would you do that?" Sakaeri sneered.

"Kaisa made it out like he was the only one, the only way. But that Bone Soldier can do the same thing. And – and maybe you can, too," said Wen.

Sakaeri dared to ask, "Do what?"

"Speak to the spirits of the aether. Descant."

"I don't—"

"Will you make a decision, Sakaeri?" Seraeyu asked impatiently, his head popping around Jaspen's shoulder, his hand wrapped around the man's lifted wrist to placate him.

"Pra—Praetor – why are you--?"

"You want to help, Wen?" Sakaeri asked.

Wen looked at her with utmost confusion, a foreign realm's leader just on the periphery of her vision, then her gaze darted to the side at the sound of footfalls on the lower stairwell. She whispered, "Come with me."

"Whatever you're seeking, it'll be in his vault. I'm sure he has wards of some sort, his office is littered with runes," Wen said, ushering them down a long hallway lined with windows, all facing the interior of the massive Pit. "But I imagine you have a way around that, Praetor Thasian?"

"Perhaps," Seraeyu said coyly.

"I can understand a change of heart, but why turn on Kaisa now?" Jaspen asked, suspicious. He stood at Wen's opposite side, filling the space that Sakaeri couldn't occupy. Saoiri still held the backmost flank, head swivelling over her shoulder enough it surely made her neck sore. Their arrangement almost had it looking as if Seraeyu led the front.

"The Stimfal. It's awful, what he's doing. I – he was testing it, teasing the possibility when he did what he'd done to Sakaeri. But now … this isn't better than the life any of us sought to escape. This is ambition gone too far. Hundreds of gullible soulsongs, all puppets of Kaisa's making."

"The Stimfal … are made mindless? He's recruiting an army of mindless grunts?" Sakaeri asked, disgust seeping in. What a horrible thought, and an even worse reminder of her own trouble here.

"Not even. He's creating fodder. It's only a small few who get to claim themselves officers of the Stimfal, and they aren't thralls. He gifts them these strange eyes. Implants them so they don't need to go through the procedure themselves. I don't know where they came from."

Sakaeri wanted to vomit. "I do."

"And what does Kaisa want to do with this army? It's strange that a syndicate head of his renown would aim for higher glory than what he already has. It's a terrible and comfortable life he lives, isn't it?" Jaspen asked.

"I don't know, but it's always seemed like Kaisa had something else in his sights. The Pits were only an avenue there. The way he spoke, it was like a grander scheme was always the goal. Like the Pits were child's play."

"Why are you here at all?" Seraeyu asked. Sakaeri was sure he already knew.

"There aren't many options for people like me, Praetor," said Wen.

It was the same reason Sakaeri became a Sirin. Why Jaspen became a Draconguard.

"I wish that weren't the case," Seraeyu told her. Wen didn't respond.

Something had been bothering Sakaeri since they'd vacated the stairwell. "You said I descant. I don't."

Wen gave her an odd look. "Then how else did you speak with Goeth?"

"What do you mean? The old codger is chatty as all the void!"

"Goeth was never there, Sakaeri," said Wen. "He's been gone for a long time."

"An Orinian prisoner?" Jaspen asked. "What had he done to anger Kaisa?"

"Goeth was Kaisa's uncle. They had a falling out. Kaisa had him imprisoned. I barely knew him. He died the first week I arrived."

Sakaeri blinked, asking, "And how long ago was that?"

"Maybe a decade?" said Wen.

"I spoke with a ghost?" Sakaeri wondered aloud.

Seraeyu hummed, considering, and said, "Then you know how it feels."

Focusing on the finer point that they all seemed to have missed, Jaspen muttered, "Kaisa is Orinian?"

The conversation trailed as they came upon an ornate doorway, and Sakaeri was struck by the fact that it looked remarkably similar to the gateway in the catacombs beneath the Thasian Tower. But there were no metal bars here, only thick slabs of iron framed by a runed band of archway.

"Sera?" Sakaeri questioned as Seraeyu reached out a hand to touch the archway, a casting of inky miasma following his tracing fingers. Latches clicked open and hinges squeaked as the metal egress invited them in. Seraeyu wasted little time, Jaspen striding in behind him, but Sakaeri was stopped short by Wen.

"I'm sorry," she told her, dropping her chin. "I really am. It doesn't make up for it, but I wish I'd done something. It was cowardly of me to stand by. I could have done something."

Sakaeri studied her. Chestnut eyes and raven hair, just as she knew her, but somehow more tired and sporting a few new scars that hadn't been there before. Sakaeri jostled her shoulder and led her into the office at her side, saying, "You're doing something now, aren't you?"

CHAPTER THIRTY-THREE

"You really are idiots, *fuck* that's just too funny," Jjenka said when they entered, standing with his arms folded in front of a desk laden with crystalline ore. The broadcasting Eye blinked, his crossed irises shuddering in that telltale way that indicated the end of a transmission. "Like I wouldn't be *here*." Jjenka indicated to the rest of the lavish office, its curtains blocking out the scenery of the Pit below. "Like I wouldn't realise. Where is he?"

Sakaeri wanted many things in that moment. She wanted to be done with this mission. She wanted them to be somewhere else. She wanted Jjenka to shut up. She also wanted to know where Aeyun was. And, perhaps most of all, she wanted to rip the eyes out of Jjenka's skull. Because those weren't his eyes. They were from her sister in arms, Hylian, and there couldn't be a realm where he was allowed to keep them cradled by his rotten brain.

Jjenka peered through spiked pupils, his irises now a haunting silver. He'd already appeared a predator before, his natural eyes a stark and exacting blue, but now he looked like precisely what he was intended to be: a manufactured weapon. Sakaeri knew what Hylian's eyes were attuned to as well. They were quick, seeing weak points in movements and anticipating the most effective action.

Jaspen didn't wait. He barrelled on ahead, glaive at the ready. With a shout and a splintering crash, Kaisa's desk was split down the middle, crystalline shards shattering down and a paperweight in the shape of a pyrebreath cracking on impact against the floor. Jjenka laughed loudly as he darted backwards, his companion Eye stoic and side-stepping the debris.

"Kaisa's wards don't lie. He's here, that shitbag who mopped up on the Pit. Where?" Jjenka asked, sneering mockingly as Jaspen lifted his weapon from the shimmering rubble.

"You will move out of our way," Jaspen demanded, once again readying his sharpened blade. "This will not end as you desire."

"*This will not end as you desire*," Jjenka mocked, hands dancing side to side. "Who're you to threaten me, eh? What's this, huh?" He evaluated Jaspen with quick scrutiny. "A standard-issue Draconguard weapon? Speaking in that proper little tone? You're not fooling anyone, you shitty Orinian knight."

"We won't ask again," Sakaeri told him, taking two long steps to match Jaspen's advance. "Move or die."

Jjenka pulled two curved blades, one for each hand, from over his shoulder, twisting them with a flourish before curling down with a wolfish grin. "Let's go, then."

Sakaeri didn't waste more words of warning. She shoved Seraeyu back, who stumbled into Saoiri. With a quick twist of her wrist, she pulled out her war fan, hooking her finger into the loop at the end to spin it wide, each blade clicking into place. "Jas!" she shouted, and he braced in a guarded stance as Jjenka leapt at them, a manic chortle following the Kaisan as he went.

Jjenka slunk down like a fencat, curling back up to swipe out at Sakaeri, who kicked out a heavy boot to deflect his blade. "You know," Jjenka mocked with a cackle, "these eyes must make you angry."

Sakaeri sidestepped Jaspen's slamming glaive. It crashed into the tile below, cracking it, and both Jjenka and Sakaeri slid backwards. She didn't give Jjenka the satisfaction of an answer, instead flitting her attention to the Eye who stood on the sideline, a hand held before him to tune if need be. And, Sakaeri figured, she could render both *need* and *be*.

She tossed out a fist, fire bursting to life beyond it. The force of it slammed forth, the Eye side-stepping as the explosive flames cratered the dressed window behind him, shattering the glass. The drapes pulled and wrapped around the edges of the newly created hole, fabric tearing on jagged shards.

"Tut, tut," Jjenka called out, narrowly avoiding a gale from Jaspen that would have knocked him off his feet. "I'll have to add that to your debts, Widowmaker!" He laughed as he wove between Jaspen's efforts, divided by alicant and his held weapon.

The Eye by the wall was ready to retaliate, but Wen stepped between them. Sakaeri watched as she withdrew the stiletto blade from its sheath at her waist. Her stance didn't falter, and her feet planted solid as she told the Eye, "I'm done with this shitty death hole."

"Fool," the Eye said, just as lifeless as his gaze was.

"Let go, *now!*" Seraeyu's voice drew her attention. He was struggling against Saoiri's stubborn hold.

Saoiri pulled at his arm, snarling, "You *want* to be made mincemeat, *Praetor?*"

"Just stay there," Sakaeri crowed at Seraeyu, who glared something terrible in response.

"Awe," Jjenka cooed condescendingly. "The Thasian shitstain has *friends!*" Another loud cackle trailed behind him as he skidded on his knees towards Jaspen, crossing his blades and barely missing clipping Jaspen's ankles. On recovery, he managed pry the powdery green alicant from Jaspen's wrist, tossing it out the broken window with a grin.

Sakaeri clicked loose a blade from her war fan, its trajectory just shy of Jjenka's ear.

"*Bitch*," Jjenka spat, twisting back to height, scowling at her.

"I'm your opponent," Jaspen boomed, his glaive swinging down again, lodging into a stray shelf on the wall. "*Shitstain*," he hissed Jjenka's term back at him.

Sakaeri tossed another blade, jumping to the side to get a better angle.

Jjenka was too quick, perceptive of the attacks coming at him. Sakaeri must have not been the only one to notice, since she saw a creeping, inky miasma slinking towards Jjenka's feet. *Seraeyu Thasian*, Sakaeri thought, *crafty bastard*.

To ensure his plan, Sakaeri tossed two more blades, one at each side of Jjenka to force him into one lane of movement. He scoffed in annoyance, moving backwards, then stilling. The vindication Sakaeri felt when his eyes widened was beautifully petty, a smile curling on her lips despite herself. Jaspen had glanced down at the floor once, noting the curling cull of inky aether around Jjenka's feet, then he shoved out his glaive and buried it into the junction of the Kaisan's shoulder.

Jjenka cried out with a snarl, shouting to his Eye companion, *"Get over here!"*

Sakaeri spun on her heel and launched herself at the Eye. Wen had him at the tip of her blade, but Sakaeri shoved past that and ripped what remained of her war fan in an upward arc from the Eye's hip to his sternum.

The Eye looked down at his stomach, torn and disembowelled, then he stumbled back and fell halfway out the broken glass window, murky entrails trailing with him. Sakaeri tuned a gale to force him the rest of the way through it, trying to ignore the vengeful wet slink of his innards following his plummet.

When she turned back to the scene, Jjenka was backed in a corner, Jaspen's glaive still pierced brutally into his shoulder. Seraeyu had Essence dripping from his hands, slithering in waves across the floor to wrap around Jjenka's ankles.

It could have even worked out, Sakaeri would like to think, if Kaisa himself hadn't stepped through those barricaded doors in the back of the office. It startled Saoiri enough that she jumped back and nearly bowled into Wen, who steadied as she watched Kaisa's entry with naked terror.

"Oh, my. Oh, surely *not!*" Kaisa laughed, and Sakaeri barely caught the diminishing flashes behind him as the heavy door latched shut, a series of runic markings igniting and hissing before snuffing to blackened etches once more. "This is quite the scene."

"We're too late," Saoiri called in haste, snatching one of Wen's wrists and dragging her towards where Sakaeri waited, a scrape of crimson beneath her battle trodden feet.

"With this kind of crowd," Kaisa said, leering from his raised vantage on the steps, "you'd think you all *know* something."

"We can talk, Kaisa," Seraeyu said, but his eyes were already bleeding red. Fainting or Amanastré, neither was a good option.

"Stay where you are," Jaspen spat behind gritted teeth, forcing the glaive's point deeper into the junction of Jjenka's shoulder and chest.

"Fuck, alright, you shitty soldier. *Fuck, stop!"*

"I have nothing to gain from you, Seraeyu Thasian," said Kaisa. He took one leisurely step down, not even deigning to assess the damage to his office, just smiling spitefully ahead. "Not when I stand to gain everything without you."

Kaisa's aura was wrong. It was too flat. Too dull. But there were sparks of something not breaking out from within its wrangled aetheral pulse, but overtop it. Like sutures or stitches, sowed shut to keep power concentrated and hidden. It wasn't something Sakaeri was familiar with, and it wasn't something she liked seeing. It also wasn't something she wanted to test her luck with.

"Run, Sera," Sakaeri said before the thought even congealed. Seraeyu spared her one quick glance, then she said it again, with a bit more force, "Run."

He didn't hesitate this time.

Seraeyu spun with a shout of, "Jas!" A command to follow.

By some nebulous force, Kaisa had pulled his office doors closed with an extended hand, but Sakaeri grabbed Seraeyu's arm and syphoned his amassed energies, bursting right back through the barrier. Kaisa's laugh would have sounded entertained if Sakaeri didn't know better. But she did. And Kaisa held little patience for things that disobeyed.

A quick check over her shoulder revealed Jjenka wobblingly holding his bloodied shoulder, grimacing at their retreat. Kaisa was not giving chase, and that … that was almost worse.

"We need a quick out," Sakaeri barked at Wen.

Wen took two more heavy sprints forward, attention flitting first left then right, then she said, "Steal a land-skimmer." As if that were a simple feat to do. "They're on the ground level, in the cavern-bay."

"We're about as far from there as we could be," said Saoiri.

"We make due," Jaspen decided for them.

"Sakaeri," Seraeyu said, and it almost felt like the realm washed white, their pace slowing and sounds echoing. "She is shouting, angry. She's … she says she's been fooled."

"We've no time for a god's lament," Sakaeri murmured back, then the realm fell back into place, and they continued down the long white hall.

She should have figured they'd do something stupid like hop the rail in the stairwell. On the way down, flights zipping by with gaining momentum, Saoiri's scream echoed the loudest. Sakaeri only hoped they had strong enough tuners with the right ore on hand. Otherwise, they'd meet a quick and awful end to an already awful plan.

CHAPTER THIRTY-FOUR

"Do you even know how to drive this thing?" Saoiri said in vexation over her shoulder, fingers digging into the edge of her seat.

"Sit the fuck down," Sakaeri spat back at her, eyes darting across the blinking console. All manner of widgets and accoutrements jeered, a wheel jutting into the space directly opposite her. *No.* No, she didn't know how to drive it.

"It's that yellow button to start it up, with that switch on the far right," Wen provided helpfully, peering out the back window of the modified land-skimmer alongside Seraeyu, who flapped his hand behind him in a silent order for Sakaeri to move. "I think."

"*Fuck*," Sakaeri growled, reaching for the recommended controls. Jaspen was sat in the seat beside her, looking warily down at the pedals beneath his feet.

He grimaced as he asked, "Why is it built like this?"

"Kaisa has trust issues," Wen said, then, "ah, you really ought to move, Sakaeri!"

"Get the damn craft going!" Seraeyu ordered, twisting his upper half backwards.

"You fucking try it!" Sakaeri shouted back but *got the damn craft going* anyway. It revved to life with a vengeance, its engine a roar in the echoed hanger, the angry purr of it greeting the Kaisan who came funnelling out of the stairwell. "Now, Jas!"

With the press of Jaspen's foot, they first zoomed backwards, a rare curse escaping his mouth in a clipped exclamation, then they were shooting forward. Right toward a heavy metal door. *Damn it all and the whole of the shitty starry sea!*

"Door!" Saoiri squeaked. The closer they got, Kaisan shrank in the distance behind them. She continued shrilly with, "Door! Door, door!"

"I *fucking see it*, thanks!" Sakaeri hissed, jerking away from Saoiri's pestering.

"Adamantine," Jaspen said as he braced himself against his seat.

Oh. *Oh*, that's right! "Yes, Jaspen!" Sakaeri cackled giddily, yanking at her necklace. "You brilliant, smokey serpent!" She didn't look over to see if he appreciated the comment or not, instead clasping the adamantine pendant in one palm as she held out the other one, Saoiri lurching forward to keep the wheel steady.

Open, she told it. *Open. Rip. Tear apart. Let us through.*

The scream of curling metal wailed across the cavern, a sharp edge of light peeling in from where the doors yielded Sakaeri's demand. But those doors were at least a few stories tall. They weren't just bars on a window, and Sakaeri felt it physically canting against her body, one tune grating against another. She needed more. She needed force.

Sakaeri grit out, "Get Sera," to Saoiri.

"Oh starry sea, how are you doing—"

"Get Sera!" Sakaeri demanded with more urgency. Saoiri hesitated, then darted out of sight as Jaspen stretched awkwardly to steer. Soon, Seraeyu was beside her. "Can you—"

"Yes," Seraeyu said before she finished, his fingers curling over her shoulders, a pungent zap of energy settling into her bones with them.

With an electric inhale, Sakaeri felt like the realms were hers to play with. Like the very fabric of them would bend to her will, and like all she had to do was ask. Her vision tunnelled, and it was only her, Seraeyu, and the looming, gargantuan doors ahead of them, creasing and crunching and tearing apart.

All was silent, consuming. A scream without sound, a force without mass.

Crumble, she told the barrier.

Violently, as if smashed from a height, the doors shrunk in on themselves, flinging off their hinges and sending shrapnel scattering. They tore through debris, and Sakaeri finally breathed. Seraeyu's fingers slipped away, and Sakaeri stared ahead, inhaling and exhaling harshly through her nose with her hands dropping back to the wheel Jaspen had leant over to steer in her stead.

They were out, and the dessert spanned before them, dust kicking up behind their speeding land-skimmer. They would live, at least for one more day.

It was only Sakaeri and Saoiri who had wind-attuned alicant, so they took charge of shifting sands and dirt enough behind them to cover their stolen land-skimmer tracks. The sun was setting, the nighttime chill creeping in again. No one had come. Not yet.

Sakaeri dusted her hands, now covered in a thin layer of brown grit, and took a moment to consider her former companion. Saoiri tuned with air like she tuned with water. Her arms moved in fluid arcs, smooth even when she twisted her wrists to unfurl a small cyclone. Her braids still looked childish, and her build was still girlish, though she was probably a similar age to Seraeyu.

Saoiri swung her arm out once more with a grunt, then she levered her foot and kicked out, the tread of her boots shovelling little granules with it. She folded her arms and tilted her head toward the darkening sky, stars only just starting to wink through in the distance.

Sakaeri had every intention of leaving her to it, whatever it was she was working through. But then Saoiri spoke up.

"It's a little strange, isn't it?" Saoiri asked.

Sakaeri didn't respond, only paused her retreat.

"A fabled mercenary. A knight from an oppressive regime. A faulty child of a legacy. An unimpressive daughter of a pirate legend. And now a casteless ex-Kaisan." Saoiri looked over her shoulder. Sakaeri couldn't quite make out her expression, half hidden by the swell of bone and cartilage. "And this wasn't fate?"

"No."

"If it's not, why the in the frigid void am I *here*?" Saoiri asked, turning away again.

"And I would know?"

"No," said Saoiri. "I guess not." Then, "I miss him."

"Aeyun?"

Saoiri laughed bitterly. "Yes, but no. Davah."

"Ah."

"Am I bothering you?"

"No," Sakaeri answered honestly. She wasn't bothered. Nor was she interested. But she could stay, if it meant Saoiri wouldn't sulk for the rest of the evening. When Saoiri didn't continue, Sakaeri did instead. "I miss him, but don't tell him I said so."

"Davah?"

It was Sakaeri's turn to laugh, but hers was light with humour. "No. Davah had a knack for annoying me. Aeyun."

"Really?" Saoiri asked, looking over her shoulder again as Sakaeri came to stand next to her.

Sakaeri nodded. "Yeah. Him. Uruji. Raeyu. They were all I knew."

Saoiri hummed, the now bright stars pulling her attention once more. "It's hard to imagine, you all. Young, innocent once. What did that even look like?"

Sakaeri considered it, folding her own arms to mirror Saoiri. She squinted at the most luminous star to the left. "Innocent? Hardly. It was never simple. Not really. But …" An unwitting smile pulled one corner of her mouth, quirking just a bit higher. "It was fun, sometimes. Eventually. I didn't really come from comfort. One day, Raeyu Thasian passed a little Yu-ta girl, all bones and nearly dust. Just shivering in an alley. I'd tried to steal her bracelet. I barely had the fucking strength to grab it." Sakaeri scoffed. "I didn't even let go when she looked down, her big golden eyes wide and surprised. I was gone for her then, I think. Dug my own tragic grave at first meeting. Pathetic … but worth it. She took my hand, dirty and scabbed and scummy, and dragged me back to the Tower. Just like that. Always collecting strays, Raeyu." Sakaeri smiled, and it rested as an harsh, biting thing across her face. "I think she may have known from the beginning. That Jourae sired me. That Ube was my mother. I think she knew so many horrible things she never said. And now … maybe I didn't know her at all."

Saoiri let a few beats pass before saying, "People aren't perfect."

"Oh, I know."

"I used to idolise Davah," Saoiri admitted. Somewhere in the distance, a creature skittered, then it was quiet again. "A silver tongue through and through. He was young still, but he looked like a giant to me. And my father respected him, like actually respected him. Probably because he'd tricked him. Sold *Pre'ach'an* a counterfeit, apparently. And got away with it until they crossed paths again. He was a good deckhand. A good navigator. Could catch his own fish, rig up a sail in no time flat. To me, he was like a hero, the perfect pirate. I used to follow him around like a chicklet, always calling his name. I don't know how he kept his patience with me." Saoiri laughed and it dragged, weighted with memories. "But he did. *Hey little fish, come look at this,* he'd goad me. *Oi, i'sil'ke, let me tell you this funny story about your mam,* he'd call me up to the lookout, all animated. Grinning. He made her sound amazing. Unstoppable … But there's something else to Davah." Saoiri's eyes darted to the side once, like she wasn't sure she should be saying anything at all, then she looked down, scuffing her toe. "I have no idea what life was for him before Pre'ach'an. I was really little, but I remember when he finally joined the crew, it was in the dead of night. Only one fire burning on deck, and the lads dragging him on, all covered in blood. He didn't talk for a week. I just sat and stared at him for half of it. Maybe he just figured I wouldn't go away and gave in.

"It was Davah who saved me. He'll say it was the other way around, but he was the one who got me off the ship in time. Who swam to shore with me on his back." Saoiri's lip trembled then, only shortly. "But he was always the giant. *Saoiri, think about your actions. Saoiri, don't even try it. Saoiri, don't you worry about me. I'm always grand, you know that. I've got too much to do for this to be it for me, have a little faith, huh?*

"But he never told me what it was. What he has to do." Saoiri turned. It was quiet, her stare crawling into Sakaeri like a crashing wave. "But Elder Emagh said destiny awaited, and you saw him in your vision from the Oracle. What does the Great Starry Sea want with Davah?"

"I have a question for you."

"Huh?"

"I have a question for you," Sakaeri repeated calmly. She'd recognised something. Something that she'd seen in both her hits and hirers. "I've made a lot of my choices for two reasons: to live, or to make sure what I love lives. Aeyun makes a whole lot of reckless choices in some mislead wish to be a martyr. Sera, I think, holds a lot of guilt, and a loathing that pushes him towards what he thinks is better. Jaspen told me himself that everything he does is for his family, however far that extends. I'm still figuring out Wen, and honestly she might be figuring it out too. But what about you? Davah? What drives you?"

Saoiri twisted her toe further into the sandy ground.

"I can guess. You *want* purpose, I think. Once through your father's dream, then through your Elders'. Maybe now with the Resistance—" Sakaeri raised a subtle finger when Saoiri opened her mouth to protest. "I'm not saying you don't believe in what it is your fighting for, just that you sought it out all the same. But your friend, Davah. I think there's something so deep set in his soulsong that it's bled into his heart and brain. He held his cards close, *I'm just an ore-smuggler, don't mind me*. But then he spoke with a conviction like it poisoned his every thought. Davah believes in something so viscerally, I think it's led his whole life. I don't know what it means, but I think Davah saw something in Aeyun when you both met him. A chance to peer behind the veil. To what end … I guess we'll find out."

"You don't trust him."

"*Stars*, no," Sakaeri said with a chuckle. She smirked then. "But I didn't use to trust anyone. I guess I've gone soft."

"Sakaeri," said Saoiri. Sakaeri lulled a lazy gaze her way. "He's not a bad man, I swear. Really, I swear it."

Sakaeri smiled at Saoiri, a pearl that hadn't yet cracked under pressure. It didn't matter so much if he was *bad*. What really mattered is if he was *dangerous*.

And if Sakaeri really thought about it, yeah. Sure, he had all the markings.

In their earliest encounter, Davah had been wary of her Yu-ta heritage. *I'm just sticking around to find out*, he'd told Aeyun. *To see*. He never had been particularly fond of the Thasian, though admittedly many weren't. *Don't cause trouble*, he'd told Sakaeri, *we've had enough of it*. Which we?

"I have another question for you, Saoiri."

Saoiri looked at her with trepidation. The Holy Stacks shivered between chilly dust motes, and the air had turned crisp in the seep of night, the lights above not enough to warm it.

"Was Davah a Yu-ta hunter?"

"*What?*"

CHAPTER THIRTY-FIVE

Davah remembered hacking violent fits of water as he rose to the surface, a girl too small for the history of her name clutched close to his body. Around him were the remains of wreckage, bobbing in broken bits of metal and planking. His crewmates, or parts of them, undulated dully with the faux-placidity of the open water. Davah held Saoiri tighter, hoisting her further up his shoulder. It had gone wrong. Everything had gone wrong.

"We've been had!" I'da'agh, first mate to Pre'ach'an, had hollered, just before everything went to the wretched void.

In that moment, Davah hadn't run to his assigned harpoon-cannon. He hadn't, because he knew that his captain's daughter was tucked behind a sail, trying to spy on her father's dealings. And what a scene she must've witnessed.

The first assault came in the form of blasted fire, projected from extended hands of the Thasian fleet. It rocked their vessel, Davah stumbling over his feet. A crewmate passed him by, shoulder clipping shoulder, and feet thumped along splintering decking. He knew this was the end. It was bound to happen in this kind of life.

He passed another harpoon-cannon that remained unmanned.

Davah knew a battle lost, a captain gone.

"Davah!" a young voice had cried out, jerked in time with the whipping of her body around the second of the smaller masts. Davah braced his hand on the rail, just a short distance down from where a projectile battered through it not a moment later. The leaden ball cratered a section of grating and fell through to the lower deck, a pained scream following its plummet. Davah snapped his attention back to Saoiri as her fingers scrabbled to keep hold of the hammered pole, her face splotchy and eyes watering as she screamed another panicked, *"Davah!"*

Davah planted one boot down, balancing his centre, then he dropped lower and made a run for it. The leeward side bowed deep in the wake of alica onslaught, the backlash of competing forces and the meeting of wind and fire. The surrounding air sizzled, heated and charged, and Davah's treads slipped on the now waterlogged deck, the metal creating a slick sheeting. Shouts and frantic yells mixed in his eardrums, but he instead focused on snatching loose, flapping rigging.

There was a distant, *"What are you doing, lad!?"* but Davah ignored it.

The vessel was tipping, Mhedoon's ocean threatening to swallow it whole, but he steadied his grip on roughened rope, palms burning as he pulled against it to pace a path towards Saoiri, who still clung with shaking effort to the mast she's tethered herself to.

"Hold on, Saoiri," he'd called out to her. *"Don't go giving up now, alright!"*

"Davah!" Saoiri had cried out, the sound of it scratchy. *"I'm scared!"*

"*That water doesn't want your soulsong today*," Davah had shouted, straining against the weight of gravity and forces of tuned air pulling him towards their assailants and a suffocating death under unforgiving tides. "*And these feckers behind us won't get it either.*"

"*No mercy!*" Some officer on the Thasian vessel had crowed. "*Damned Doon pirates!*"

"*Not a chance.*" Davah had used his grip on the rigging and the friction of his boots to haul himself the rest of the way to Saoiri, another crewmate sliding past him and joining several others in the ocean below, wheezing a final breath through a perforated stomach. Davah caught Saoiri's wrist just as it slipped from the pole, grunting against the strain it placed on his hold to the rope, now carrying his own weight plus hers. "*I've got you,*" he'd said to one or both of them, he wasn't sure.

The vessel gave a great shudder, and a terrible ripping noise cut through the sounds of the fray. Davah yanked Saoiri to his hip as best he could, solidifying his white-knuckled hold, and he chanced a look at the wreckage as the flailing rigging swung. Soot wafted against flame, manifested gales carrying embers higher, and cannon fodder still blasted holes into the vessel he'd called home for years. His nostrils stung against the smouldering heat, nothing but smoke on the wind, and the sounds of death and destruction were starting to set in with the chilling thaw of the adrenaline that created a hardened shell against emergency. As he mentally recounted the ore set in his profiteered jewellery, his vision caught on a lone boy in the middle of the Thasian vessel's deck, blood spattered across his shoes and trousers, horned head on full display, unlike the soldiers who rushed around him, or those who lined the edge of the monstrous boat. He was staring at his hand, which he had outstretched as if to tune.

"*Bloody Yu-ta scum.*" Davah spit, curling himself protectively around Saoiri's quivering limbs. "*I'll ask my pal the ocean to keep us safe, okay? Trust me, little seasnail?*"

"*I trust you,*" Saoiri had whispered, tucking herself into his side.

Davah remembered thinking, *I fucking wish I did, too,* as he let go of the rope, calling on a tune to form a film around them as they broke the surface of water.

Now sat in a grove with a soon-to-be-abandoned camp in a strange realm that shouldn't exist, Davah fished out the long-dormant communication stone that shared a pair in Saoiri's possession. *The Resistance,* he thought. *Who the fuck told you to get involved in that? Batty old Emagh can't be a proponent, surely.*

He was ripped from his ruminating when Uruji gasped and said, "Oh! I think I've got it!"

It was strange this time, when they formed a chain to traverse the Ou'grove. Davah had paid a little more attention when they skipped through trees, aiming to feel the flow of life around him and to slip with it rather than against it. When they syphoned through, he almost felt like he could sense the brush of every tree, every blade of grass. Like a whisper in his mind before it was washed down a river of green.

Vitality, Aeyun had called it. Life. Creation.

Below the ground, fungus fed on decaying matter. In distant shadows, wraiths of forgotten soulsongs milled, aimless. Death, too. Vitality felt like a misnomer.

His feet tripped on their return to steady ground, and it wasn't dissimilar to slipping over a waterlogged deck.

"Hey," Aeyun said as he dislodged his hand from around Davah's elbow. "You alright?"

Davah blinked once, and it felt like a hazy sheen faded with it. He forced a smile and turned to Aeyun, saying, "Yeah, friend. Don't you worry about me."

"You sure?" Aeyun pushed.

Davah turned a step, offering Aeyun a hushed stare. Green eyes bore into his own, like they read between lines Davah didn't even know he'd written. There wasn't time for this. "Yes, Aeyun. Let's get a move on, yeah?"

"What *is* that?" Raeyu's breathless question drew their attention. She was pressed up against a tree trunk, her arm wrapped around it so she could peer beyond. Her posture was locked up, defensive but curious, and it didn't take Davah long to figure out why.

Before them, past the break of trees, was a meadow of wilderflowers, interspersed with a species of flora that consisted strange, iridescent stalks that curled at their ends. It wasn't that which captured Raeyu's attention, though. It wasn't that, nor was it the vein of alica that splintered through the rock-face to the left. It was the bird that pecked at it.

The creature was tall with strong legs, talons curled into the dirt as it hammered its ridged beak once against the glittering fissure of alica in the stone. Its long body shook with impact, its fluffed feathers rippling, teal brushing against a shifting refrain of pearlescent hue, three long plumes of similar colour draped across the meadow behind it, their ends fanned white, almost looking like petals.

It went to slam its beak into the ledge once more, then it suddenly shifted and its milky, pupilless eyes centred onto their position. On top of the milkiness was a marbling of sparkling flow, as if the creature's eyes themselves were alight with alica.

"It's seen us," Uruji informed them, lowly and slowly, as if some of them might be too daft to pick up on that. Davah decided to ignore it.

"Is *this* what's been resonating with you?" Aeyun asked his brother, who scrunched his nose and gave one terse nod.

"Why would a beast have the dagger?" Raeyu murmured back, slinking a smidge closer to the tree. *Coward*, Davah thought.

The bird trilled, cautious and quiet, not yet moving. Just staring.

The breeze shifted and Davah picked up on the smell of rotting.

"What is it?"

Davah jerked back in surprise, drawing a sidelong glance from Uruji.

What was that? he thought.

"Is something wrong?"

It wasn't long before Davah connected that the disembodied voice likely came from Da'garu, who had shuffled forward, a hand extended, placating.

"I can help."

The bird trilled again, a little louder, taking a staggered step back. Da'garu stopped.

"Da'garu," Aeyun whispered, looking torn between following her forward or yanking her back. "What are you doing?"

Davah suspected that Aeyun knew exactly what she was doing. Just like, somehow, Davah could *hear* what she was doing.

Da'garu ignored them. *"Are you hurt?"* She breached the meadow, careful to step between flowers. *"I can help you."* The creature made a squawked noise, its wings spreading wide and flapping, the length of them longer than Davah expected. It was when it did this that he spotted something lodged in the tender meat of its side, otherwise hidden under its wing. *"I can help you,"* Da'garu conveyed again, coming to stand before the creature.

"Aeyun," Raeyu said quietly.

Aeyun was four steps behind Da'garu, within close distance so he could yank her back if need be. Uruji, almost at his side, looked tense enough to vibrate out of his skin.

Da'garu coaxed the strange aviary beast docile, her one hand placed gently on its beak while the other conjured a tune against its puncture wound. As she grasped the dagger's handle, Davah felt a shift. It was like dropping pressure too quickly or standing up with a head rush. His reality flickered, as if a glitching holocaster screen, and it suddenly felt like the realms and that beyond them were full, so much greater than before, the feedback toward his soulsong overwhelming and hazy, crushing.

'Davah,' a voice said, and this time it was different from the light and airy interpretation of Da'garu's call through Vitality. This one was soft, wise yet young.

Pressure built in his head, and Davah struggled to look away from the warped vision of Da'garu serenely tuning with a bird that shouldn't be there. The surrounding trees looked green and mossy, but also full of rivers of light, flowing and branching. It was almost like looking at two scenes at once, one he understood, and another he couldn't quite grasp, just beyond comprehension. Shadows flickered like he was zipping through a tunnel on the hyperline, and his stomach shivered as if he were falling. Beyond the periphery, a vast nothingness loomed, bursts of light flashing to life and dying just as quickly.

'Davah,' the call sounded once more, and he turned towards its source; his discarded knapsack, sat on top of dirt but also a strange field of the incomprehensible. Beside it there was the form of someone small, young. Just a child. The girl, indistinct with undefined features, seemed to smile in

demure relief, her long hair swaying as blurry hands pressed over her heart, her dress fluttering as she raised her heels. '*You hear me!*'

There was an odd twist above her head. Like a sharp halo or – or horns. Davah pressed a palm against his temple and took a staggered step forward. It felt like wading through mud.

'*Please listen – there is still time!*'

Time? What about time?

What was Davah doing?

'*Oh, no. It's too much. Davah, I beg you listen.*' She reached out a tiny hand, awaiting his return grasp. '*If you hear me, I will not lead you astray. Do not give in. I can help you.*'

Davah's head felt leaden, and his eyes were flooded with too much stimulation, nothing making sense. He closed them, feeling like he was floating at sea, and focused on one point of origin. It sounded with clarity:

'*Let me help, please.*'

"Davah?" Aeyun's voice broke in, and it felt like a breath of air rushing into oxygen-deprived lungs.

Davah twisted around, nearly tripping over his feet. He struggled to open his eyes, fearful of the realm he'd be presented with. But it was plain. Expected. Forests and flowers and branches. Nothing streaming, only light filtering through from the ripped pastel sky.

"Was it a restless? Did one call to you?" Aeyun asked, squinting at him. The scene behind him was a relatively celebratory one, Da'garu petting the feathery side of the odd creature they'd happened upon, and Uruji and Raeyu watching her in awe. Davah was nearly in front of his dropped bag now. "You really shouldn't have encouraged that other one."

"These restless," Davah said, and his throat hurt. Like it was raw, scraped with aether. "What had you said they were again?"

Aeyun frowned. "Lingerers. Parasitic fragments of soulsongs yet to pass."

"What do they want?"

Aeyun's frown deepened. "I don't know. But it's dangerous for them to linger, they're meant to move on to the Great Starry Sea. You remember the mantra, right?"

"Yes," Davah muttered. The pain in his temple throbbed. "I remember the mantra." He paused briefly before his next question. "And they always have that strange, wispy body? Like dark, fizzing smoke? Never anything else?"

Aeyun gave him an odd look then. "Body? No, it's like dark smoke, yeah, but there's no body. Why? What did you see?"

Davah was pretty sure what he just saw wasn't one of those phantom shadows. Not when reality warped with it. He was also pretty sure that Aeyun was, quite possibly, unaware that those *lingerers* formed a shape at all. He wondered if Da'garu, if their parents who showed them these rituals knew. If it was, by a strange happenstance of fate, only Davah who, by no real fault of his own, was made aware of it.

"Smoke," Davah said, looking right into Aeyun's eyes and daring him to question it.

Suddenly there was a huge gust of wind and petals fluttered into the air, scattering in a barrage of colours. With a loud warble, the beastly bird flared its broad wings, the press of air below them flattening the emerald blades of grass. It rose with a heavy drag, staring down at Da'garu with its haunting eyes for a long moment, then it was shooting upward with unnatural force, soon soaring high above the forest's canopy, its three long plumes trailing after it. And Davah, eyes narrowed and gazed honed, could swear the thing warped through the cracking barrier above. *That* shouldn't be possible, should it?

"It – that creature tuned, didn't it?" Raeyu asked as she, Uruji, and Da'garu came to join them. "I didn't imagine that?"

Da'garu smiled widely at her, and Uruji floundered for a moment, a croaky sort of noise escaping him, then he shook his head. He must have decided it wasn't the thing to focus on, because he cleared his throat and held out the dagger, its nephrite blade still smeared with the beast's strangely gluey blood, and said, "So, we have it now."

They all stared at the weapon, then one moment bled into another.

Uruji cleared his throat again. "Now what, Brother?"

"It's …" Aeyun almost looked like he was going to reach for it, then his hand skirted back. He sighed. "So, you arrived here thanks to Father's other dagger. Tuning with it and finding its resonation. Thinking of me – my soulsong – that could have done it. May have. But Father had said to think of somewhere safe, hadn't he? Away from where you were, where the active danger was?" Uruji nodded, sceptical. "I think we can assume the gate alicant in its pommel may have come from here or already had a connection to here. It could even … be the reason my home was originally built where it was, where you ended up. Something there, maybe."

Uruji's brow drew down, and he asked quietly, "Those ruins were your home?"

"I think I understand," said Raeyu. Her golden eyes glistened as she offered Aeyun a smile that looked just a little sad, as if a dream once had slipped through it, a silent release rather than a fretful wail. "It wasn't fate. Not really."

"No," Aeyun agreed with the same remorseful tone. "Not really."

"Understand … ?" Uruji prompted.

Aeyun shared one last long, lingering look with Raeyu, then he brought his hand up to rub the back of his head with a puffy sigh. "So, when I happened across that mark on the ground, deep in that cavern, I probably didn't know it at the time, but I was reaching out. Something within me held the right note, because it reached the last lingering fragment of my and Da'garu's ancestor, the one who cause that scar to form on the ground I stood." He paused, and Davah wondered if it was genuinely difficult to reconcile, or if Aeyun was being overwrought, as he tended on occasion. "Ka'la'drius, husband to Ca'ille."

Raeyu smiled again, and this time bitterness broke through the initial sombre. An acceptance stitched behind her lips, caught between her heart and her teeth.

"The same soulsong who resided in Raeyu's Bloodsong." Aeyun paused again, before murmuring, chin down, "Which is a seed that no longer houses his fragment."

"A seed?" Davah spoke without really meaning to. *Well, I've started now.* "That thing you got from the Madame?"

Aeyun glanced up at him, then he dug in the pouch at his side and pulled out his winnings from Madame Reaper. Raeyu's breath hitched at the sight of it. "Yeah."

"What are you doing with one of those?" Raeyu said in a rushed whisper, attention darting from Aeyun's face to the small amber mass and back again.

"It's not at all that strange here," Aeyun explained, rubbing his thumb over the smoothed surface as an inky vine curled out and wrapped around his thumb. Da'garu wiggled her index finger at it as if it were a baby. "And no one is in it. It's not really used for that kind of thing. At least not here. Not now."

"Okay," Uruji said, eyes closed like he held all his patience behind them.

"So," Aeyun continued quickly, clearly tipped off that a brotherly dynamic Davah wasn't familiar with was about to play out if he didn't. "When I called, Ka'la'drius's soulsong fragment answered and pulled me to it; to Raeyu."

"So, it's as Gama-of-Yun said. His will was satisfied, and he could finally return to the Grand Symphony in the stars," Raeyu said, inhaling deep as she angled her head towards the canopy. "*Protect my kin*, that's what he'd begged of me when we'd merged. I didn't know what it meant then. I'd guessed, only a little while ago."

"Once their will is satisfied, they move on? For good?" Aeyun asked.

"When their last wish is satisfied, they no longer have a will to tether them. Before you ask, I never knew Amanastré's."

"Then we have a chance," Aeyun decided, a new wind of determination behind his words. "Uruji," he called, and his brother's eyes snapped open, his pensive concentration breaking. "I'm saying all this because I think there's a way with you, and with that dagger. It's ... something that should have been said a long time ago. And not by me. Not Raeyu. But her."

Raeyu tore her focus from above, blinking once at Aeyun. Then realisation seemed to have set in. "Oh, Aeyun. Are you sure? Now?"

Rather than answer, Aeyun bit his lip, clenched his fist around the seed, its vines receding into his palm, and he said, "I'm quite clearly not Ube's child." Uruji nodded, and Davah could see the cog already starting to turn behind those sharp eyes of his. "But she did bear a child with our father, with Jourae. Older than us. Not lost at all, actually."

"Sakaeri," Uruji said, and it was hard to identify which emotion fuelled it with the way his expression shuttered.

"Yes," Aeyun confirmed. "And she's the one who shares your blood. And she's the one who last tuned with that dagger. The traces of it should still linger." Aeyun looked at Uruji, and Uruji looked at Aeyun. If there was a secondary conversation being had, Davah couldn't quite pick up on it, but he *could* tell that Raeyu and Da'garu sensed the same tension. It was the lies, Davah suspected, more than the admittance itself.

"I'll do it," Uruji said, gaze locked with Aeyun's for a beat longer before he looked down at the gluey-bloodied dagger, his fingers curling tightly around it. "I'll get us home."

CHAPTER THIRTY-SIX

"Here?" Sakaeri asked Seraeyu sceptically.

He'd claimed to sense something on the fringes, back towards the mountain pass. The land-skimmer made for quick travel, and for that everyone was grateful. Sakaeri was loath to admit that the closer they got to the towering strata, the more she sensed *something*, and that it was strangely familiar. When they reached a crack in the mountainside, they'd stashed the land-skimmer in an alcove, trekking through the shadowed narrow. On its opposite side, a long, weathered-stone bridge greeted them, motes of dislodged sand curling over its edges. Long unused torches sat with crumbling alicant ore, and a whistling gorge below looked to drop to the very core of the realm.

"Oh, I don't want to cross that," Wen commented, hand a visor over her eyes.

"Nothing to worry about then," Seraeyu told her.

Sakaeri finished Seraeyu's statement with, "You won't." She pointed to the ground below their feet, bulked with rock and perched over a short drop. Seraeyu gave her an flat look.

"So you knew."

"I got notes of it in the pass."

"And this tune you've been channelling … is Essence?" Saoiri asked, daring to peer over the edge. Jaspen yanked her wrist back when she stumbled over a stray piece of gravel.

"I mean … it's like a trace of, ah—" Seraeyu first darted a look at Sakaeri, then towards Jaspen, then back at Sakaeri. "Of myself?"

"Yeah." Sakaeri grimaced. "Yeah, I thought that's what it was."

"Sorry, explain to us common folk, will you?" Saoiri sneered, then offered a stilted word of thanks to the rogue Orinian Draconguard who'd pulled her from the ledge.

"Jjenka thought the Bone Soldier was at the Pit," Sakaeri told them, wincing at the silent regard Wen gave her. This was a lot for someone who hadn't a clue of elsewheres and broken histories. "He wasn't. We were. Sera was."

"What's that got to do with anything?" Saoiri asked.

"Nevermind that," said Seraeyu. "Jas, can you drop me down there?"

Jaspen looked where Seraeyu was pointing directly over their cliffy edge. He shuffled around Saoiri and Wen, side-stepping Sakaeri with a weirdly commiserative look, and looked over. "Down *there*, Seraeyu?"

Sakaeri understood his hesitation. It was at least a two-storey drop.

"Buck up *ore-smuggler*," Sakaeri told Saoiri, clapping her on the back. "You have the other air-based alicant. Let's—"

Saoiri had quickly loosed her bracer. She pinched it delicately between two fingers, holding it out to Wen.

"Are you kidding?" Wen asked, aghast. "I don't even know what your plan is."

"Easy," Seraeyu provided with a sharp smile. "We go down."

"Come on, Wen, darling." Sakaeri extended her hand and paired it with a mocking grin. "Entertain the wishes of the girl who got away."

"I was *glad* you got away," said Wen. She was flicking her attention between the bracer now sat in her palm and Sakaeri's still offered hand, which fluttered with the shrug of her shoulder. Wen bit her lip and squinted up at the dawning sky, then a sharp exhale left her nose. "*Fine.* Alright, fine."

"I knew you liked me," Sakaeri said, snatching Wen's wrist and pulling her to the cusp of the rocky ledge.

She'd walked backward on her way, looking at the strange collection of change-makers gaining distance with her footfalls, and she had to laugh to herself. Saoiri looked ready to puke, still too soft for the realities that scraped at her. Jaspen barely paid her any mind, and that was either a blossomed trust or a growing obsession elsewhere. Which brought her to Seraeyu, who wore a smile that didn't quite filter into his eyes.

Learning truths was a bitch.

"Hey," Sakaeri said to Wen, quieter this time. She let go of her wrist, continuing with, "I never said thanks, so ..." Sakaeri fanned out her arms, back to the ledge, then she smirked and tipped back.

Above her, as wind rushed past her ears, Wen popped over the rocky face and called, "You still didn't!"

Sakaeri braced her palms behind her and forced out a softening gale to make a smooth landing, flicking her hair as she looked up with a finger-wiggling wave. Wen put a fist on her hip, narrowed her gaze, then she made like she was stepping once, shooting down in a sheer drop until the last moment, where she gently met shoe to clay.

"Impressive," Sakaeri admitted.

Wen dusted off her shirt with a light chuckle. "Trouble," is all she said.

"Hey!" Saoiri called from up above, waving an arm broadly. "Still up here!"

"You don't have to be!" Sakaeri shouted back.

It was Jaspen who ended up going next, and Saoiri who ended up jumping last. When they were all on solid ground again, Seraeyu paced for a moment before he wandered to a crevice and let out a disgruntled noise. Sakaeri sidled up to him and crossed her arms.

"Really?"

"Mhmm."

"Alright, then," she said, and it prompted their journey into the dank cavern below.

"Wow," Saoiri said as she twisted around a spongy growth. Before them, lit in the bioluminescent glow, was a ratty, rusted sea-skimmer, its topmost hatch lodged in a spore-encrusted fungus. "Tell me you see that."

"What in all the stars," Seraeyu muttered, veering around in the shallow water, its slosh announcing his change in trajectory. "*He* did this?"

"How?" Sakaeri wondered aloud.

Saoiri seemed to have caught on. "Aeyun pulled a craft through a rift? Did he actually build a gate?"

"Obviously not, or they wouldn't be stuck on Ca'lorus." Seraeyu responded, and it was oddly stripped bare. Distracted. He closed his eyes for a moment, stepped once, then shifted minutely to the side. "Where'd you come from," he whispered. Sakaeri felt strangely like a voyeur. "You pulled on threads where? What chord rung out, Aeyun?"

Sakaeri considered the scene before her as Seraeyu sussed the wreckage with a feeling only he could follow. Traces ebbed at Sakaeri's consciousness, but nothing called to her. Still, she wondered. It was something that hadn't been tried. If she could ground Seraeyu by taking in and extrapolating his excess Essence, could she instead be a conduit for him? The aim of his tune?

"Sera," Sakaeri called out to him. She lifted her elbow for him to grab. "Maybe I can see it, if you will it."

Seraeyu gave her a hesitant look, and she wondered if it had anything to do with the same reason she felt like she was intruding. He didn't say anything, just wandered to her and quietly clasped his fingers around the crook of her elbow. It wasn't a quick process, almost like a tide washing in. First there was a buzz that permeated the background, then she began to feel the pull of something different. Familiar but far, torn and mirrored like a reflection. Seraeyu but not. Aeyun but not.

Remnants of moments curled into being, sounds and echoes and a guiding presence just on the other side of real. As Sakaeri gazed before her, fissures slithered where they shouldn't, and she began to see the tears in time and space. A discordant refrain of Aeyun's prior presence, and the reverberation of his and Seraeyu's constant cyclical dance of aethereal push and pull between planes of nonsensical making. This call, this lingering tune, originated somewhere familiar.

"I see it," Sakaeri said, and it felt like it dripped into the far reaches of the Great Starry Sea. "I can lead us."

"Your eyes are … " Wen's voice flowed in and out of her mind.

Sakaeri distantly acknowledged what they were. Yun. Heavenly. Those of the gods. She felt like one. Always felt like one, in these moments. "I can take us."

"Okay," Seraeyu said beside her. It felt safe. Trusting. Lifting. Predetermined.

"Take us," the Thay-cee-en ordered the Thay-cee-en-ee, and so it would be.

Sakaeri came into being with a breathless inhale. It sank into her lungs with a chill as she scanned the vast dark in front of her. She was met with a deep plane of nonsensical direction, bursts of energy expanding and collapsing all at once and not at all.

Time, it seemed, held little agency here.

There was no smell, only the idea that there *should* be. There was no taste of the unknown, no distinction between the nerves under her skin. There was sound, though. Elongated and swirling, a deafening vacuum of drowned pressure. It made her feel as though she was underwater. Her eyes, however, stung at the sight of nothingness.

Endless, effortless nothingness. Except for the glimmer of *something* that gave her direction. Pulsing and beckoning, sat somewhere in the cradle of space and time.

Sakaeri was in the in-between. The aether, or the Alkonos, as she'd come to learn.

Perhaps the void. The Great Starry Sea itself. It looked like it, anyway.

She stretched out an arm and brushed her fingers through the threads of space before her, a wispy blackness trailing them. *That I can* see, she recalled the words spoken by Kllunna. *Walk it.* Maybe the Oracle was right. But Sakaeri had more to worry about than herself, so she turned in a direction she thought might be behind.

Sakaeri was a mercenary. She was a woman of weapons, so she saw little difference in this task compared to others. Do what you know, someone had once told her. So she had, taking a blade and slicing it through the air, dragging fragments of reality with its sharp edge.

Seraeyu was the first to follow. He gingerly stepped through the tear, toeing onto the vast nothingness. When his feet planted firm, Sakaeri reached out.

"Trust me," she told him.

Seraeyu gazed at her with blackened eyes. She wondered what he saw. Shadows and mazes, if his words held credence. Even so, he told her firmly, "I always do."

Their fingers intertwined, and Sakaeri felt the passing of knowledge; vision and sight.

Seraeyu's eyes pricked with white, their spherical manifestations bleeding like watercolour to streak opaline. "Well," he said sardonically, "look at that." His opposite hand stretched behind him, and soon Jaspen, Saoiri, and Wen formed a chain behind him.

Only they weren't complete. It was strange to have someone in full view but to only visualise their impression. A blurry, undefined silhouette that moved in clipped segments.

"Only the blink of an eye," Sakaeri whispered to herself, watching as the tear she'd made stitched together, oozing black to an inky plane, unbroken.

Seraeyu observed their companions' shifting shadows. "They won't remember."

"No," Sakaeri acknowledged. "They won't, will they?" She shifted her stance and instead re-focused on the glimmer of destination among the sinking deep. "I know where to go. I can sense it."

One step felt like a thousand, felt like falling backwards. But Sakaeri knew her finish line. Up or down, left or right, it was all an avenue towards that one beacon. Seraeyu held steady as she trekked on, even as pressure grew and they dipped into something unnatural, unreal. Flashes of colour whirled by, one moment there, gone the next.

Sakaeri wondered, if only fleetingly, just what the fabric was she sifted through.

It could have been a minute or days. There was a notion in her mind that she should be tired, but she felt calm. Placid. And soon that call of destination warped in front of her. Translucent fragments of place and space; land and sea and sky.

They'd arrived.

"Sera," she said, and it tore up her throat like knives.

She glanced behind her and there he still stood, a trail of three impressions behind him. But there was another to his side, and one more extending in reflection from the soles of his feet. Amanastré was pacing the length of their line, tracing their edges with her long fingers. Her horns still curled regally, and her hair floated broadly in the ebb of the void. She said nothing, only watched, impatient. Sakaeri's attention went unnoticed.

Below Seraeyu, under his feet like a mirage in water, Aeyun's likeness spoke animatedly to someone unseen. It was like watching through a rain-muted window, silent at a distance. Seraeyu wavered, weary, his eyes heavy and half-lidded. This Alkonos, it seemed, favoured Sakaeri for one reason or another.

When she turned again, ready to free them from the aetheral hold, an aborted gasp escaped her as she saw the image of an acolyte. The very same as the one who'd taken her to the gardens of the temple. He stood with his eyes closed, holding a stance Sakaeri was unfamiliar with, his middle and forefingers pressed as pinnacles against his forehead, forming an oblong shape between them.

"*You are not alone, child,*" his voice echoed, mouth still. "*Be ready.*"

With the awful feeling of matter rending, Sakaeri was falling forward, phasing through the acolyte's shrouded image, through the clouded, storm-brewed sky, all the way down to a rocky outcrop lapped by angry ocean waves. Several thumps followed her collapse, and she pulled herself from all fours, her grasp on Seraeyu having broken on descent.

The smell of moss and seaweed. The cry of gulls swooping over water. The bite of wind washing over the shore. The sharp grit of stone mixed with the tickle of sparse grass.

A laugh bubbled from her chest, scraping at her already raw throat. She dropped and rolled on her back, staring up at Raenaru's sky. Back at the foothills of the Sirin Nest.

"Of course it's here," she accused the rolling thunder.

Or maybe Aeyun's shadow left in the Alkonos.

"Of everywhere, *here*."

CHAPTER THIRTY-SEVEN

Sakaeri passed the wind-worn statues that hadn't haunted her steps for many a day now. Their faceless presentations still glared through forgotten ages. She didn't feel welcome here. Hadn't since Kaisa had left it a graveyard of a battleground.

Birds still chittered and the air still carried the scent of mountain leaves. It was nostalgic, but the tumultuous sky above did nothing to help her anxious reprisal of a past left behind. In her mind's eye, she remembered filing into the courtyard behind a girl twice her age and ahead of a boy a couple years younger. The girl died the next year, and the boy a few after that. It wasn't an easy life they'd taken on. But everyone who arrived through these dirt-trodden paths, crushing weeds with poorly placed steps, was used to skewed odds.

Now, however, no one was left to espouse expectations.

The Sirin were dead. Whatever had risen in place of the shadowy order was a poor reflection of what Sakaeri had known it to be. Pawns of the clergy. Maybe that was their true form.

It wasn't Sakaeri's.

"Sakaeri," Seraeyu whispered, walking a few steps ahead. He took in the broken columns, the building patched together from ruins, and the shrine that dove off the edge of the mountain. He knew what this was. "I've never been here," is what he decided to say.

The rain had been drizzling lightly until now, but it heavied with another growl of storm above. "I'd be surprised if you had been," she told him.

"This is where the Sirin are reared?" Jaspen asked.

Sakaeri watched as his hand traced a delicate pattern in the stone of a column. Its top was crushed into the ground beside it. She looked past him to the mounds that looked fresher dug than anything else in the ghost of a training ground. A garden between classes.

"It's where the Sirin died," said Sakaeri.

Which of you buried them?

Wen was quiet, taking in her surroundings. Just as warily, she peered up at the sky, a hand shielding her eyes. The rain steadily painted her in a dripping cloak. Her brow twitched and her eyes narrowed. Sakaeri wondered what crossed her mind.

"You know," Saoiri said, folding her arms as she traipsed on, "that symbol." Sakaeri followed the point of her finger to the celestial carving at the pinnacle of the shrine's archway. It looked just as the one on the fortified walls of the clergy's had, a sun with spindles. A light for one to forever seek. "It's sort of like that one from before." Saoiri turned, rain whipping with the ends of her braids. "Did you know that?"

"Yeah," said Sakaeri. "Yes, I noticed that, too."

"Mean anything to you?"

"I'm thinking it might."

In Sakaeri's periphery, Seraeyu's head snapped to the side like he heard something. The torrent still raged, chilling to the bone from this altitude, but Seraeyu just pushed hair from his face and trudged across the muddying field. The corners of his eyes faded black, leaving the remaining window of his iris looking more golden than amber-brown.

He meandered a few steps, then a small, disbelieving laugh left him as he gazed into the thundering bellows above. "Small miracles. You're unbelievable," he whispered.

A sudden crack ripped the atmosphere asunder, the noise of it rupturing in a way that could be mistaken for a distant bolt of lightning. It came with the flashing of nonsensical colour, and the appearance of one clean rift in the centre of the yard, a mid-distance between Sakaeri and Seraeyu.

Uruji appeared in transposed materialisation, like the realm was piecing him together in time with the drop of his foot. He was looking down, a dagger in hand, its nephrite blade sparking with the residual resonance of aether, Essence and Vitality crackling equally. The hand that held it looks singed, like it had suffered the brunt of force for too long. He steadied himself, looked up, and Sakaeri felt something choking seize her chest.

He first caught sight of Seraeyu, a strange emotion crossing his star-dotted eyes, which were losing their Yun-fabled veneer with each passing second. Then Uruji drew his gaze to Sakaeri. His grip on the dagger tightened and Sakaeri could swear it split her down the middle. But he held it idle, look lingering for only a second more before he pulled his other arm from the tear. With it, as if a resolution foretold, came *her*.

Raeyu Thasian.

Raeyu Thasian stumbled forth, bright, golden gaze widening with a gasp.

Raeyu Thasian stood before her, tugging the rest of Aeyun from the rift behind her, his arm having been looped around her. Raeyu Thasian was back in Sakaeri's sights, but she didn't even look at Sakaeri, attention hooked on Seraeyu, her hand leaving Uruji's and body leaving Aeyun's hold. A noise curled from Raeyu's throat, something thankful and desperate, and her palm came to cover her mouth.

Movement snagged Sakaeri's focus. She saw Davah slipping out of the tear before it stitched shut in a seam of iridescent light. He dropped Aeyun's wrist and strode across the courtyard, eyes catching on Sakaeri's just once before he looked past her.

"Dav—"

"What are you doing here!?" Davah called over thunder, the subject of his question, Saoiri, shrinking back against it. "*What* are you doing here!"

Saoiri froze, one foot ratcheted behind. Her hair and shoulders were drenched, making her look smaller than normal.

Davah reached her and slammed his hands down on her shoulders. Sakaeri could only see their profiles now, blurred as rain pelted down. Davah squeezed then shook her once, too gently. Too fretfully. "What are you doing *here?*" he asked again, quiet and suggesting privacy.

Sakaeri let them have it. She had other arrivals to divert to.

Raeyu was upon Seraeyu now, struggling to say his name, tears cresting down her cheeks. *Pretty even when she cries*, Sakaeri thought mournfully. Three steps back from the elder Thasian sibling, Aeyun stood.

Sakaeri could see the oddness of his aura, fluctuating and blindingly radiant, but quelled as if he willed it so. He was dressed in strings of chipped and mismatched bone, looking like he belonged at a heretical ceremony rather than the Sirin grounds, but his obnoxious ivory aerofoil missing from his back. Even so, he seemed a villain from fables she remembered hearing in her youth; cautionary tales of a peoples with the power to dictate the songs of the dead, those with the unholy ability to manipulate the cycle of time and recall. He looked to be a daemon, a herald of what the clergy abhorred.

She took a moment, tracking the exchanged between Seraeyu and the man who held the other half of his soulsong captive.

What must it be like, that type of strange truth, she wondered. What does one say, do?

"She knows," is the first thing Aeyun said, resident of the known realms once more.

Seraeyu composed himself, as he had many times before. Faced with something he had to tackle. Another hurdle, another act he had to pull off. Seraeyu set his jaw, burying regret behind it, then he hoarsely mumbled, "*Bastard.*" Just as quickly, his gaze left Aeyun's and his arms were wrapping around Raeyu, who melted into him with relief, her fingers pressing against the back of Seraeyu's head, pushing him to her shoulder.

"Sera," Raeyu sobbed. "Sera, I'm so sorry. I'm so sorry."

Sakaeri smiled wryly. They needed this. Two guiding stars of an empire reuniting. It was as it should be, and Raeyu would again herald their small, strange cohort towards a brighter day. Seraeyu deserved to be relieved of that burden. He'd carried it for too long. At least, together, they could anchor in something sturdier.

Sakaeri's gaze lingered where Raeyu's arm stopped abruptly. Her sleeve was tied off, as it would be for the remainder of her days. Sakaeri could be the sword that arm would have held. She would dedicate her life to it. She already had.

"Sakaeri," Aeyun's voice reached her before she noticed him by her side. He'd come to her then. She eyed him solemnly. He carried himself differently, tension in every joint. "Sakaeri, where is he now? What has he been doing? We have to be ready. Sera will have to be ready for him when he comes. We've got to figure out what he's doing—"

"Who?"

"Kaisa."

"He's figuring out how to hunt Seraeyu," Jaspen said, coming to stand beside Sakaeri. She looked up at him. His aura was much easier to read, irritated with sharp jolts, forcefully managed with an even temper.

Aeyun considered him briefly. Revelation must have sparked, because he nodded and said, "*Ah*, you're that guy."

"From when you possessed him, yes," Jaspen said steadily. He sounded strict, just as one would expect from an Orinian Dracongard, but Sakaeri watched him a second longer. The subtle downward curl of his lip said more than what Jaspen would have liked.

"Are you all gods among us?" Wen interjected from where she leant on a wall, shielded under an overhang from the rain they all subjected themselves to.

"You fancy me a god?" Sakaeri threw back at her with a smirk.

Wen didn't respond, instead tucking a lock behind her ear with a frown.

"Sakaeri," Aeyun said again, reeling her attention once more. "We've got to prepare. And Seraeyu has to be ready for it."

"How?" she asked blandly. "*How*, Aeyun? Because we just ran with our tails between our legs. He's already far beyond us crippling him from the start. We need *allies* now. Armies and signed treaties. We are already at war, it's just that no one's outright said it yet." Sakaeri gave a bitter chuckle. *The little smuggler was right.* "Welcome back, by the way. You big idiot."

Aeyun blinked at her, his mouth opening once before closing again. He nodded slowly, a wry pull tilting his lips up at their corners. "Thanks, Sakaeri."

Sakaeri hummed an acknowledgement at him.

"Sakaeri." Uruji stepped up beside Aeyun, considering the dagger in his hand contemplatively before sheathing it behind him. He stood straight with all the drilled poshness one raised in aristocracy would. Just as proper, he said, "It's good to see you."

"Sure," she told him. He flinched. Her brow dropped. "You too."

"May I ask about how things are; Haebal? And, respectfully, who these people are?" Uruji asked patiently, determinedly watching her and not their bystanders.

Ah, Sakaeri thought. *Yes, I suppose he would be curious.*

"Well. Haebal is still standing. For now. And we have one Dracongard turned smokeserpent—"

"I'd appreciate if you refrained from calling me that."

"—and one runaway Kaisan—"

"I agree with the Orinian turncoat; don't call me that."

"—and you've already met one of the Dread's crew. She's yet another."

They turned to witness Saoiri wiping at her face, red with anger and embarrassment. Harsh, low words were whispered between herself and Davah, who stood close as he loomed over her, one hand up with a tune to shield them both from the rain. All at once, Saoiri's eyes widened and Sakaeri felt an outburst coming before it happened.

"Well, she's *dead*! So it doesn't matter now, does it!" she shouted at

Davah, who abruptly snapped his jaw shut. Saoiri shoved past Davah and bypassed the Thasian on her way into the shrine.

Davah dropped his tune and instead lowered his head into his awaiting hand. "Well, *fuck*. Dammit," he muttered, just loud enough that it carried.

"I need a smoke. If you don't mind …" Jaspen told them, or likely Sakaeri alone. He cast one last wary look at Aeyun, nodded respectfully at Uruji, then patted down his pockets as he headed in the opposite direction. Sakaeri couldn't gauge if he glanced at Seraeyu and the quiet reunion the siblings shared under soft tones and whispered confidences. If she had to guess, she'd say he did. And, looking at those two, Sakaeri would guess they barely knew Saoiri had passed them only moments ago. Whatever conversation they held, it had Seraeyu's expression guarded, Raeyu's hidden by her angle.

Sakaeri swallowed a lump in her throat, pushing it down alongside her pride, and she called out, "Raeyu." The elder Thasian turned then, looking to have been in the middle of a thought. She smiled widely, shakily, at Sakaeri.

"Sakaeri," Raeyu breathed, eyes shining in that way they always did, pulling Sakaeri in without fail. "I'm so glad you're safe!"

It felt like one of many endings. One she'd reckoned with a few times throughout her life. A disappointment flared, but Sakaeri brushed it away, offering a smile of her own.

She hadn't even noticed me yet. Smiling. But vacant, distant.

"Of course, I am." Sakaeri walked towards them, and Seraeyu watched her arrival with a seriousness she'd grown far too used to on his face. "Let's all catch up on the back terrace? It has a veranda. No sense in us getting more soaked than we already are."

"Oh," Raeyu said kindly, as always. Amicable to everyone. Sakaeri wasn't an exception. Only occasionally. And not for a long time now. "Yes, let's do that. That – that sounds like a good idea." She paused a moment, then looked over at Davah, a smile that looked a little sharper than before gracing her features. "You don't need to come along, if that suits you better."

"Oh, har har, *princess*," Davah spat towards her. "Hurry along. I'll be right behind you." He narrowed his eyes at her return glare and *what? What the fuck was that?* Sakaeri wondered. It must have shown on her face, because Davah was passing her saying, "Don't get your knickers in a twist. It's fine. We're *fine*, aren't we, Aeyun?" The question was so saccharine sweet it made her grimace.

Aeyun mirrored the look. "Tone it down, Davah. It's not the time."

Davah waved him off. "Yeah, yeah alright. Whatever you say, my enigma."

"I'll leave you all to it," Wen commented as Sakaeri chased Aeyun's steps. She nodded her chin towards the rest of them, all filtering into the shelter of the shrine. "It seems like your lot have plenty to work through. Catch me up later? Without all the noise?"

Sakaeri let the request sit with her a beat. Then, with light amusement that belonged in better days, she said, "Yeah. I'll be sure to do that."

In the many futures that unravelled from that moment, and the several that followed before and after it, there were too many featuring circumstances that blistered from the wake of decisions made. In a number of them, Wen was run through with a callous sword, bleeding out under a crying sky, a curse on her tongue. Several hundred more saw her beheaded, and a quiet bunch had her spotted by someone other than Kaisa and Jjenka, or the Eye that dutifully trailed them. Another Kaisan who said they'd search the ground. Someone who pulled her to combat, where, in the smallest slivers of possible realities, she prevailed in a precious few.

In all of those threads, however, the symphony always hit a crescendo on the terrace. And balance would be had, with harmony arriving without bias and with stoic apathy.

Sakaeri would always bear witness; it always hitched on one choice.

– THE CRESCENDO –

THE ORINIAN KNIGHT

Jaspen was halfway through his cigarette when he heard the commotion; an explosion and the rattle of clattering stone. There may have been many at odds in this one strange temple, but he did not think that it would end in blows, not ones so fuelled by alica or alkonos that they shattered the resident architecture.

No, there was something in the air, lingering with the pungent torrent.

It could have been that pirate, or that Aeyun fellow himself. Trouble seemed to circle him, the spirits of alica seeking some untold vengeance, perhaps. He hadn't seemed all that special to Jaspen. He arrived a man, and he spoke as a child. Seraeyu claimed that he was the crux of it all; Jaspen for the life of him couldn't see why. A hapless sort, unaware of anything beyond his own skin and bones. Consideration only for his own endeavours.

He'd not investigated Mhedoon as his companion Davah did. He'd not asked Sakaeri or Seraeyu about Raenaru or Haebal as Uruji did. He'd only asked, single-mindedly, if Seraeyu was *ready*. As if it rested on Seraeyu's shoulders alone, a burden Aeyun could help execute, but not dissect. So Jaspen didn't understand why Aeyun sparked such intrigue.

There was a connection between him and Seraeyu, their brief exchanges making that more obvious still, and it had something to do with Seraeyu's returned sense. The dots, however, had not yet aligned. What had this Aeyun done to manifest such a situation?

The realms were restless. If nothing else, Jaspen understood Orin, and he knew the function of the Dracon. She would move soon. Seraeyu would have to be back in his seat as Praetor, or the Dracon would seek a means to an end to satisfy her goal, which Jaspen very much hoped aligned with what she claimed, providing for her subjects.

The night of the ball bothered him. The Draconguard were no bumbling laggards. Commander Ephrite had spoken to him a mere few days prior to inform him of his sisters' allegiances.

Had it been planned?

Had sacrifices been intended?

It was treason to think so. But then Jaspen was already a traitor, wasn't he?

Another shattering crash sounded, and two was too many. He flicked the stub aside and hefted his glaive over his shoulder. He was in the breezeway, lined with chipped reflections of a past unfamiliar to him, and the first encounter he had was with the woman who now held alliance with his sisters in the Resistance.

Whatever it was that Saoiri was about to say was lost when they heard an anguished scream. No more questions; they were running.

– *THE CRESCENDO* –

THE DAUGHTER OF DREAD

Everything was going wrong. Saoiri had trusted that Davah would support her and always – *always* – be on the side of Mhedoon. The Orinians had leashed them like mutts, commanded by a Dracon who cavorted with Kaisa.

Kaisa, who was raising an army of mindless, witless soldiers with little else to turn to. There were surely glory seekers among them. There always were. But there were so many who were probably escaped Mhedoons, or stateless Orinians even. It was a callous reality, and Saoiri was no longer blind to it.

The Alkonos, and alkonos and alica themselves, could wait. Their lives and those of thousands – millions – others were on the line with this brutal, quiet war already waged.

Saoiri pressed the heels of her palms to her temples and sank into the stony alcove she'd found refuge in.

Why had Davah reprimanded her?

She remembered him, even when she was young and on a pirate vessel, staring at her father's shadow. *Freedom or death*, he'd say. *Never let anyone tell you your own opinions.*

But when he'd arrived from a tear, ripped into the endless beyond, he looked different. He *sounded* different.

He looked like a man Elder Emagh would have wanted to speak with. Whether to cleanse him or learn his ways, Saoiri wasn't yet sure.

Davah was wrapped in bone, little shards of ivory twisted around his limbs in muted reflection of Aeyun's own strange adornments, and his eyes shined like the moon on a cloudless night. Just like Aeyun. Except, unlike Aeyun, Davah looked like he found something profound.

Aeyun, Saoiri thought, looked lost. Had he always?

She was no longer dazzled by his words, nor enamoured with the way he fiddled with his bracelets or bracers or rings or necklaces. All implements he made but never used.

In the face of war and strife of Saoiri's own, Aeyun was no longer a beacon. She'd realised that it had been a fleeting obsession; a young fascination. When she saw him again, there was a rush of warmth and a desire to get to know him in the here and now, but he'd seemed to barely share the sentiment. And that – well, that had stung. But Saoiri found she hadn't been affected by it nearly as much as she would have assumed a year ago.

It had hurt worse when Davah told her what-for about joining the Resistance.

But – *freedom or death*, he'd said. *Never let anyone tell you your own opinions.*

A crash sounded, then a second one followed not long after. Saoiri took a moment to peer through the pane-less window's frame. The sky rolled with thunder, and she tasted death on her tongue. Something was woven into fate this day, and Saoiri was no longer childish enough to think she could evade it.

When she'd forced herself up, wiping once at her eyes, she'd nearly slammed right into Jaspen's shoulder as he rushed down the hall. *A smokeserpent*, he'd called himself. A traitor, he'd claimed. She wasn't so sure.

Before she had a chance to say anything at all, a scream sowed terror in her soulsong.

That was either Sakaeri or Raeyu, and neither was a good option.

– THE CRESCENDO –

THE LOST PRODIGY

"You are alive?" Kaisa observed with a chuckle.

Uruji could sense the immense power roiling from his frame. It was an unregulated mix of the spectrum of alkonos, but the fluctuations crashed like waves. This Kaisa was indeed a force to be reckoned based on that alone. The erratic structuring made more sense when Uruji saw the man's arms as he spread them wide in glee, a painful scratch of runes carved up the sides of them, not dissimilar to the symbols painted on ceremonial ribbons his father had shown him.

Kaisa, Uruji was immediately sure, knew far too much.

An Eye walked alongside a presumed Kaisan behind the unwelcomed Pitmaster, and Uruji stood patient. There were many of them here, too many, standing at this precipice, and he couldn't let his emotions rule his actions like with his father's demise.

He had to be calm. He had to stay *calm*.

He needed to use his mind. It should be simple. There was always something, wasn't there? At least one course of action. Deduce how they might navigate this, and what this man might want. How Uruji might deny him it. He just needed *time*.

"Our dear Praetor here said you were gone," Kaisa said, leering at Seraeyu at the edge of the courtyard, Aeyun by his side. "But Raenaru's benevolent ruler has been missing for a week. And it is ever so nice to see you, too, lovely Raeyu Thasian."

Uruji didn't tear his eyes from Kaisa and his posse. Not yet. The Eye's pupils didn't shiver, so what was Kaisa waiting for? What was the show he wanted broadcasted? To what end?

Uruji didn't think the Stimfal sounded all that different from the Yun, and there was plenty of trouble in that.

A blast of punched fire slammed into the wall behind Kaisa, Sakaeri's spread hand retracting and shaking out excess energy. "Don't you dare lay a finger on her. Not here," she growled, taking one slow and calculated step. "Not anywhere."

"Oh, my lost jewel, don't be so harsh to your old master, hm?" Kaisa said, clasping his ringed hands together and tilting his head imploringly. "You must be angry to see me here, I know. I know, love, I know. Yet here I am, so I'm afraid you'll have to accept that."

"I don't have to accept anything involving you."

Just as Sakaeri was about to pass Uruji and become first in line between Kaisa and their small reunion, Uruji reached out a hand and pulled her back. Her gaze landed on him, and she watched him in that odd way she had since he'd returned. Like she didn't quite know how to react to his mere presence. It was beguiling as it was frustrating. It was as if she somehow knew their linked lineage had been revealed behind her back.

"Don't," he said. "Don't."

"Fuck, you must just love the thrill of battle, huh, Sa-kae-ri? Miss the Pit?" the Kaisan – not the Eye, but mutated irises all the same – jeered, and Sakaeri tensed in Uruji's grip.

"Worthless scum, walking this temple—!"

"What do you want, Kaisa?" It was Raeyu this time.

"I just want to shake things up a little," Kaisa said, then he wrapped his fingers around his neck, a rune on its left side igniting with his touch. The next words he spoke resonated as a descant. "I want Amanastré to make herself known."

Something crumbled under force, and all at once, the realm felt murky in shades of milky white and inky obsidian.

– THE CRESCENDO –

THE FOOL PIRATE

Davah still held the Sirin mask in his hand when the realm went blinding and dark at once. While the Raenaruans argued their purpose, he'd slipped over to a solitary corner, rifling through his knapsack for answers. When his vision evened after the sudden rend at Kaisa's demand, there was a great roar of reality on either side of him, a narrow path of placid calm ahead. At its end, there was a woman – no. There was a god.

What else could she be? Tall and skin like a pearl, horns spoked and curling like a wilderdeer, silvery hair long and flowing, a suit that shifted like scales.

She was of the stars. She was a god. She was—

"Oh, child," the woman spoke, whispers of energy and light fading and repopulating around her. A god called to him, beckoned him. "I sense your conviction. I can taste your justice. Come. You and I harmonise across generations. We sing one another's song, and we are meant to be as one."

Davah found himself standing, stumbling, through this mess of nothing and everything. It forced itself against his skull, yearning and crying out, caressing his steps as he progressed onwards. It was only a niggling tickle that held him back, not yet at her side.

"You know," Davah said, and it felt as if it floated away from his lips, reducing to echoes, then soundless. "I always hoped there was something. I always wanted there to be something."

He stumbled another two steps, and the scrape on his fingers pulled taut, like a string fastened with a stubborn knot.

The vastness around them warbled, a reality bending and unbending, and Davah felt woozy. "But there are no gods."

"Only a fool would believe me a god," the being said, smiling and stretching out her hand. "Do you think me a deity?"

"Maybe," Davah said, and his foot landed sturdier. "I don't know what that means anymore."

"You seek to right wrongs, child of Mhedoon. I can help you."

"I know what I seek."

"I offer you my power, my kindred one. Will you take it?"

"I know what I need."

It was in the midst of another step that the incessant inch returned, and Davah twisted to look at his hand, which he only now realised was held behind him. Two of his fingers were tugged by something small. Something formless and iridescent. If he really focused, he could see a figure form from the connection, skin and muscle and bone melding to become a little hand. A little hand, a little arm, and a little body to match.

The face of a child pieced together, and she stared up at him with big, haunting eyes. Silvery hair, and small horns. She pulled for attention again, for his focus, and Davah felt caught in an undertow. The girl's mouth moved to form words, but Davah couldn't quite hear them. Couldn't quite listen to them.

"Only a fool forgets their aim," the god called, and Davah felt himself drifting.

There she stood, the embodiment of the heavens, and she watched Davah with unbroken determination, like he himself could bring to fruition everything he sought. Everything *they* sought.

A distant ring bounded in the back of his mind. His name, only a quiet call from a saddened, soft voice, like a rainbow over water, or a seashell on a shore. Innocent, precious moments, unsullied by the weights of horrid shadows. But the tone spoke to something wise. Something learnt. Something ancient.

"Davah," the god before him called, reeling his focus to hone on her once again. "Together, we will reap justice," she said, and he realised he stood in front of her now. "You know the next step."

He did. He could feel it so viscerally that his surroundings condensed and spiralled wildly. This was it. This was the moment. This was the moment everything was set free.

This was the end.

It was only after his outstretched hand, doused in feral black energy that sparked with jolts of electric white, plunged into the god's chest, clutching onto something welded to her ribcage, did he look up into her wicked, satisfied grin.

'*I will stay with you,*' came the quavering voice of the child, but Davah couldn't tear his eyes from his god – his false belief – as Amanastré's features became another's. '*This is an unfair fate. I will be here, if you will it, until the end.*'

The compression of aether lifted and behind it stood Seraeyu Thasian, shocked and bleeding from the gaping hole in his chest. The Bloodsong, thorns latched to skin, was held in Davah's crimson-drenched hand.

– THE CRESCENDO –

THE HEIR TO A LEGACY

Raeyu screamed. The realm had been ripped asunder at Kaisa's forced descant, then everything pieced back together and Seraeyu was dying. She spiralled for one unbelieving moment, taking in the image of Seraeyu's gaping chest. Davah stood before him, the culprit with a bloodied alicant in his hand.

"Seraeyu!" she called again, her voice breaking between the syllables.

Fuck Kaisa. *Fuck* duty and circumstance and the damned tainted Bloodsong. The Thasian were nothing. It was all for nothing. If her brother – her baby brother – died it was all worthless. Nothing mattered. Nothing, nothing but—

"Sera!" she cried out again.

This couldn't be right. Not him. It was never meant to be *him*.

As she ran towards him, a million things played through her memories:

"Rae, why can't I come with you?"

She'd wanted him to but couldn't say yes.

"Rae, why can't I do what you do?"

She'd wanted to say that he could, but that he shouldn't. That was why. It's why she didn't let him. She wanted him to live without the burden she carried. The ugly truth of it all.

"Rae, why does he hate me? Why can't I be good enough?"

He was. He was always good enough, exactly as he was. Oagyu just never saw it. That wasn't Seraeyu's fault.

It wasn't Seraeyu – it wasn't him – this can't be him—!

"No," she said when she reached him, her remaining arm first pushing Davah away before her hand pressed on Seraeyu's sternum. Seraeyu's familiar amber eyes, so similar to her own, looked at her in some great and unfathomable understanding that should never have had to be there. "No. No, you're fine. You're alright. You'll be fine, Sera. I'll fix this. N-no. It can't—"

"Rae," Seraeyu whispered wetly, the words slick with the red that dripped from his lips. "Bind his ... Essence ... somewhere else."

Raeyu looked at him as static curled around the task given.

Seraeyu gazed at her, unyielding, "Ae ... yun."

Too soon, his body was sagging into her, and she breathed in quick inhales. It was a balance. A give and take. That's what it was. That's what it always was.

Wasn't Raeyu living a life stolen but unpaid? Hadn't Aeyun promised the Alkonos its due many years back? But he'd stayed. His soulsong incomplete, and not his to give. And it hadn't been for a long time, had it?

Seraeyu wasn't able to tune for a reason, she knew that but never dug. Now, the question bubbled to the surface, and the answer dried with clarity.

Aeyun couldn't tune. Seraeyu couldn't tune. Yet they could both manipulate different ends of the alkonostic spectrum.

Raeyu's blood ran cold, her body becoming clammy as she opened herself to her surroundings; Aeyun on the floor, rapidly losing himself as participant to a deal long left unsatisfied, a strange exchange of energy pulling from Seraeyu and syphoning through Aeyun to Raeyu. Despite Uruji's best efforts, it didn't quell the flow.

Raeyu was killing Aeyun.

Raeyu was killing Aeyun because Seraeyu was dying.

Raeyu breathed in deeply, clutching Seraeyu's limp body to her, tears cresting down her cheeks. So this was it then. One last callous act. In the name of love, she would.

– *THE CRESCENDO* –

THE FATED BLACKSMITH

Aeyun felt the moment Seraeyu was set to die.

The miasma faded, and the realm became real once more. Derision was in the air, and he knew something horrible had come to pass. In his mind's eye, he'd seen this moment play out in a thousand ways at once, all occurring in the same instance. At the same time, he watched as every next second flipped, minute changes to every one of them.

So this is what it was to harmonise with the Alkonos. Clairvoyance. Omniscience.

Seraeyu was dying. And it was Davah who'd sentenced him to it.

Time segmented and Aeyun saw Raeyu turn in slow motion, a scream on her lips. Uruji was just behind her, forgoing his focus on Kaisa – who looked remarkably delighted, pleased that his plan had succeeded – to rush towards Aeyun. Their movements flickered.

Aeyun felt Essence rush in and leave him almost as suddenly. But in those moments between, he saw everything.

In his vision, Davah stood with a trembling grasp on the Bloodsong, a seed with a broken spirit. It was something he'd seen before. He knew he had.

There's no way to know, Gama-of-Yun had said, *and the knowledge of this will skew unfavourably. If you want any chance at something better, you must forget A'vor.*

And so he had. For a while.

It was impossible to ignore the Alkonos's endless wells of knowledge now, spread in nonsensical waves and patterns and sounds and notions. And that meant that Aeyun was close to it. That meant Aeyun was dying.

"Bind his … Essence … somewhere else," Seraeyu was demanding, even as he himself was losing a battle against the quiet edges of the void. "Ae … yun."

Even now, he was asking on behalf of another. Even now, at the cusp of a silent eternity. Aeyun knew Seraeyu's soulsong. He knew it so well now that he felt foolish for not recognising it before. Memories that hadn't yet formed washed over and through and around him. So many choices, so many pasts and futures, all at once everything and nothing at all.

He knew what Raeyu decided. He knew, and it broke his heart all the same.

To love and to not be chosen in return – it was a sting without ease, and it was cruel to know Sakaeri wouldn't feel vindicated that Raeyu didn't favour either of them.

The only reason Sakaeri hadn't moved – the only reason she'd stayed her blade and not sought retribution against Seraeyu's killer – is because she listened to the Alkonos once before. But there was no way of Aeyun having known that. Aeyun shouldn't know what Sakaeri saw. But he did. He knew. He felt it; anticipated it and remembered it.

This was the end. And he knew what Raeyu decided.

– THE CRESCENDO –

THE LINCHPIN OF THE REALMS

"I love you," Raeyu whispered into his ear, her limbs shaking. "I love you so much, Sera. I want you to know, I never meant to hurt you. I love you."

Seraeyu felt numb. They were kind words, but there was a chill to his bones that didn't let him consider them fully. Instead, he only wanted to take away what it was that made her weep. "I ... know."

Each word felt like a monumental effort. Nothing felt put the right way around anymore, and Seraeyu wondered if he should be lamenting a life lost. Davah's face had been the start of his shock, all pale and horrified as it was, but that had since faded as he realised what was to come.

There was always the chance for this kind of end. He'd known it might happen.

The familiar weave around his soulsong left him like a tune on the breeze; soft and peaceful and pliant. Seraeyu was letting this go freely. It was Aeyun's to take, and now someone else's to house.

There was more Seraeyu wanted. More he wanted to do. To see. To change.

But there wasn't time now. Maybe there never had been.

It felt like she needed to know, so he told Raeyu, "I love you."

And then it was silent.

... And then sound came back in a rush of pain and colour and vibrancy that felt like too much too fast.

Seraeyu gasped and coughed, his lungs hollow and aching, his eyes watering, his blood rushing. It was too much, too real and tangible. He rolled to the side, on the slabs of the terrace now, and Raeyu lay unmoving, faced away from him.

But she – that wasn't right.

Aeyun, draped over Uruji's lap, drooped motionless. Lifeless.

But Seraeyu was alive.

"*No*," he told the radiance in the lingering aether. "*You made a promise.*"

THE SAINTLY SIRIN

Sakaeri watched as she lost three people she cared about in succession.

The first to leave her was Seraeyu. He'd slumped onto his sister's shoulder, who fumbled and collapsed under his weight, and then the magnetic force that had led her through these past months was no more. He was gone just as easily as one of her marks was, and the realms were without Seraeyu Thasian.

The next to leave her was Aeyun. Aeyun of Krunan. Aeyun Thasiannee. A'vor of Ca'ille's descent. The man who fell from the stars and changed all their lives with his increasingly turbulent choices. Choices that she would never again get to berate him about. Choices that led to him disappearing with little more than one last glance her direction.

The last to leave her was Raeyu. Hadn't even Sakaeri said that Raeyu would give up the realms for Seraeyu? That she loved him so dearly, more than life itself. When the observation made long ago, before such implications mattered, came to manifest with a whispered descant and Raeyu's sobs as she held her brother close, it ripped another hole in Sakaeri's already patchwork heart. As Raeyu fell to the ground, a sad smile that claimed acceptance went with her, and Sakaeri could do nothing but watch her first love, forever doomed, as she rejoined the Grand Symphony.

Sakaeri had been telling herself she could handle the worst.

She couldn't.

The first emotion that filled her was rage. Burning and desperate for something to repent for the atrocity before her. Davah still stood, bloodied and wide-eyed, staring at the three bodies lined on the ground. But Sakaeri couldn't – she couldn't – because something out there in the great beyond told her she *couldn't*.

That's what it was, wasn't it? Her dagger plunged into *his* chest, never Aeyun or Seraeyu's.

Repentance she couldn't claim.

She turned, ready to exact her fury on Kaisa and his men, and witnessed the exact moment that Jaspen sliced the Eye's head from his neck, a nightmarish spray of gore to follow. It was too late. Whatever had been seen had surely been shown, but the Eye's red hair smeared alongside his blood, and his body thumped down heavy on stone.

"Oh *shit*," Jjenka said, skittering to the side as Saoiri lashed out with a burst of righteous flame, a blade in her opposite hand.

Sakaeri stared at Kaisa, but Kaisa looked past her in confusion, his mouth twisted and his brow drawn. When Sakaeri followed his gaze, she saw Seraeyu. Seraeyu, with eyes reflecting the Great Starry Sea itself, as he rose on wobbly, unstable footing. Once standing, he spoke in a tongue that carried little sense to Sakaeri, energy unfurling around him, and she wasn't quite quick enough when Kaisa frustratedly bellowed, "Why won't you stay dead!" as he brushed his hand across his arm, extending a pulsing wave of uncanny force that pushed Seraeyu stumbling back.

"I made a promise," Seraeyu said, voice rasping as he tripped once towards the edge.

Sakaeri stared in awe as her vision widened. As she comprehended the layered decree that Seraeyu's mouth had uttered, but another force had dictated. Kaisa grew impatient.

With one flick, Seraeyu was sent over the edge. But now – never again – there was no ledge that Sakaeri wouldn't follow. So she braced herself and sprinted forward, diving off the broken terrace to catch him. Her precious family, who she would never again let go.

Momentum allowed her to slam into Seraeyu's falling form, her arms wrapping around him as they dived headfirst down a valley of blurred reception. "I'm with you," she told him.

To the bitter end and further still.

ACKNOWLEDGEMENTS

I have been humbled by kind words offered by those who resonated with this story. To everyone who has encouraged me to keep writing, keep telling this tale: thank you. To Sapro, who has yet again provided a beautiful cover for this series: thank you. As always, I would like to thank you, dear reader, as you continue to be a part of this adventure.

I've said it once, and I'll say it again:

This story comes to life with you.

If you enjoyed this story and would like to support independent publishing, please consider leaving a review of this title on your preferred retail or review outlet.

The Symphonic Masquerade

Prequel Novella - **How Strange the Son**
Book One - **Where the Silence Sings**
Book Two - **Why Dead Gods Weep**

Omnibus Hardback - **Where the Silence Sings**
(*Included* - **How Strange the Son**)

Omnibus Paperback - **Where the Silence Sings**
(*Included* - **How Strange the Son**)

If you would like to read more about
The Symphonic Masquerade series, including an
online pronunciation guide, visit:

www.emeryblaine.wordpress.com

More by Wild Door Publishing can be found at:

www.wilddoorpublishing.com

See you next time!